Eddie regarded th⸻ ⸻ ⸻ he gunfire stopped. "Definitely don't think we want to go in there." The pitch of the helicopter's engine changed, suggesting that it was circling the building.

Looking for more targets.

"That doesn't leave us with many options," Nina replied. There was another, single door in the corridor wall on their side of the chasm, but reaching it would require going back down the dangerous slope before hopping onto the stub of a beam at what had been floor level. She retrieved the case. "Keep hold of my hand until I can jump across."

"For Christ's sake, just leave the case, will you?" He frowned. "Wait, what's in it? It's those fucking statues, isn't it!"

"Yeah, and after everything I've been through to get them I'm not letting go of them now."

"After all the trouble they've caused, the world'll be well rid of them," he countered. "Give 'em here."

"*No*, Eddie," Nina insisted, clutching the handle more tightly. "I don't have time to explain right now, but they're a part of something big—something *amazing*. I have to find out what it is."

He shook his head. "No, you—"

"You asked me to trust you a minute ago," she cut in firmly. "Well, trust *me*. Please, Eddie. It's very important."

"All bloody right," he said after a moment. "I won't smash 'em, I promise. Now get moving, will you? If that chopper comes back—"

"I'm moving, I'm moving," she protested, extending her free hand to him and starting down the slope. He held on to her, leaning forward as far as he dared. She neared the broken beam and took a deep breath, swinging the case in her hand. "Okay, and a-one, a-two, and a-*three*!"

By Andy McDermott

The Hunt for Atlantis
The Tomb of Hercules
The Secret of Excalibur
The Covenant of Genesis
The Pyramid of Doom
The Sacred Vault
Empire of Gold
Return to Atlantis

Return
TO
Atlantis

Return
TO
Atlantis

Andy McDermott

BANTAM BOOKS
NEW YORK

A Bantam Books Mass Market Original

Copyright © 2012 by Andy McDermott

Published in the United States by Bantam Books, an imprint of The Random House Publishing Group, a division of Random House, Inc., New York.

BANTAM BOOKS and the rooster colophon are registered trademarks of Random House, Inc.

Originally published in the United Kingdom as *Temple of the Gods* by Headline Publishing Group, a Hachette U.K. company.

ISBN 978-0-553-59366-2
eISBN 978-0-345-53575-7

Cover design: adapted from Blacksheep Design by Carlos Beltrán
Cover photographs: © Funkystock (temple), © Alexis Rosenfeld (research submarine)

Printed in the United States of America

www.bantamdell.com

9 8 7 6 5 4 3 2 1

Bantam mass market edition: September 2012

For my family and friends

Return
TO
Atlantis

PROLOGUE

The ocean had no name, nor did the gnarled land rising from it. There was no one to name them. In time there would be, after the scarred primordial world had completed another four billion orbits of its sun, but for now it was utterly barren. The planet could not even truly be said to be dead; it had never seen life.

Yet.

Had people from that far future somehow been able to stand on the nameless obsidian sands, they would have seen a world very different from the one they knew, countless volcanoes spewing smoke and ash into the sky. This was a landscape in flux, growing literally by the day as the planet's molten core forced itself outward through the cracks in its crust.

The hypothetical observers would have found their glimpses of the heavens through the black clouds just as unfamiliar as the world beneath them. Above was an almost constant fireworks display of bright lines searing across the sky. Meteors: lumps of rock and rubble too small to survive the transition from the vacuum of space, atmospheric friction incinerating the building blocks of the still-youthful solar system miles above the ground.

But the larger an incoming meteor, the greater its chances of surviving the fall.

Among the fleeting streaks of fire was something brighter. Not a line, but a shimmering point of light, seemingly unmoving. In fact, it was traveling at over ten miles per second. Its stillness was an optical illusion—it was heading straight for the black beach like a bullet fired from the stars.

The light flared. The rock was surrounded by a searing shock wave of plasma as it plowed deeper into the atmosphere, its outer layers fragmenting and shedding in its wake. But it was large enough to guarantee that no matter how much mass was burned away, it would hit the ground. An impact and explosion powerful enough to obliterate everything within a radius of tens of miles should have been inevitable.

Until something extraordinary happened.

The meteor flared again, only this time the flash was an electric blue, not a fiery red. More flashes followed, but not from the plunging rock. They came from the sky around it, great bolts of lightning lancing to the ground. The observers, had they existed, would have noticed a distinct pattern to these bolts, as if they were being channeled along the lines of some natural force.

And the rock began to slow.

This was more than the braking effect of the atmosphere. The meteor was losing speed in almost direct proportion to the growing intensity of the lightning flashes. It was as though the world below were trying to cushion its fall . . . or push it away.

But it was too late for that. Even as the electrical blizzard raged around it, the meteor continued its descent. Slowing, still slowing, but not enough—

It hit the beach at several times the speed of sound, unleashing the same energy as a small nuclear bomb. A blinding flash lit the volcanic landscape, an expanding wall of fire racing out from the point of impact. Tens of thousands of tons of pulverized bedrock were blasted skyward. But even though it was now only a small fraction of the size it had been minutes earlier, the new arrival from the infinite depths of space, glowing red hot at the bottom of the newly created crater, was still over a hundred feet across.

Then the ocean found it.

Water gushed over the crater's lip, the sea greedily surging in to claim the new space. The churning wave front crashed against the meteorite—and another explosion shook the beach, outer layers of burning rock shattering in a swelling cloud of steam as they were suddenly cooled.

Gradually, stillness returned. The lightning died down, dark clouds rolling in to repair the tear in their blanket. Before long, the only movement was the eternal slosh of the waves.

What remained of the meteorite at the bottom of the new lagoon was now even smaller, only the heart of the traveler remaining intact. But for the first time in unknown ages, that core of strange, purple stone was exposed to something other than compressed rock or the harsh emptiness of space. *Water*, working its way into every exposed crack to find whatever was within.

It took time, six whole days, before anything happened. Even then, the time-traveling observers would have needed a microscope to see it, and still been profoundly unimpressed. A tiny bubble, the product of chemical processes at work within the ragged rock, broke free and rose to the water's surface, to be instantly lost among the foaming waves. It was not the most inspiring beginning.

But it *was* a beginning.

Life had arrived on Planet Earth.

ONE

Zimbabwe

Four Billion Years Later

The heat and stench were as inescapable as the cell itself. The thick stone and clay walls of the former pioneer fort trapped warmth like a kiln, and the small, stoutly barred window providing the only ventilation opened out almost directly onto the row of latrines at one side of the prison's central courtyard.

Fort Helena. Hell on earth for those unfortunates imprisoned within by the country's despotic regime.

A bearded man sat statue-like in one dirty corner of the gloomy cell; his stillness partly because of the cloying heat, and partly because each movement brought pain. He had been delivered to the prison a day earlier, and as a welcoming gift given a beating by a group of guards before being taken to a dark room where a grinning man had provided him with a hands-on demonstration of some of the numerous instruments of torture at his disposal. Just a sample, he had been promised. A full show would soon follow.

Someone else was in the torture chamber now, screams echoing through the passages. The guards had made a point of dragging the victim past the bearded man's cell so that he would hear the desperate pleas for mercy. Another sample, a demonstration. *You're next.*

A new sound, this from outside. A rising mechanical thrum—an approaching helicopter.

The man stirred, painfully levering himself upright and going to the little window. He ignored the foul smell from the latrines, narrowing his eyes against the harsh daylight as he watched uniformed men hurry into the courtyard to form an honor guard. Behind them came the prison's governor, a squat, toad-faced man in small gold-rimmed glasses. From his look of apprehension, it was clear that the new arrival was important.

The prisoner tensed. He knew who was aboard the helicopter.

Someone with very good reasons to hate him.

Dust and grit swirled as the helicopter descended. It was an elderly aircraft, a French-built Alouette III light utility chopper converted to what was known as "G-Car" specification by the addition of a pair of machine guns. A veteran of the civil war that led to Rhodesia's becoming Zimbabwe in 1980 . . . now being used as VIP transport for a man who fought in that war as a youth, gaining a nickname that he retained with pride to this day.

Gamba Boodu. "The Butcher."

A guard opened the cabin door and Boodu stepped out, head high as if daring the still-whirling rotor blades above him to strike. Despite the baking temperatures, he wore a long black greatcoat over an immaculately fitted suit, the coat's hem flapping in the downdraft as he strode across the courtyard to the governor. Sunlight glinted off gold: a large ring on the middle finger of his right hand, inset with a sparkling emerald. That same hand held an object that he swung like a walking stick, its end stabbing into the ground with each step.

A machete, its handle decorated with lines of gold.

The bearded man remembered the weapon well. Some years earlier, he had wrested it from the militia leader and used it against him. The result was a deep, V-shaped line of pink against the Zimbabwean's dark skin, the scar the aftermath of a blow that had hacked clean through flesh to leave a bloody hole in his cheek like a second mouth.

He smiled, very faintly. The injury was only a fraction of what a murderer and sadist like Boodu deserved, but among his many unpleasant characteristics was vanity: Every look in the mirror would provide some punishment.

The smile disappeared as, formalities quickly over, Boodu and the governor marched into the prison buildings. They would soon come to the cell. The man returned to his filthy corner.

Footsteps over the screams. The wooden cover of the peephole slid back; then came the clatter and rasp of a key in the lock. The heavy door swung open. A guard entered first, pistol aimed at the still figure, who responded with nothing more than a fractional raising of his eyes. Next came the governor, broad mouth curled into a smirk, and finally Boodu himself. The machete's tip clinked down on the stone floor.

"What a pleasant surprise," said Boodu, his deep voice filled with gloating satisfaction. "Eddie Chase."

The balding Englishman lifted his head. "Ay up," he said in a broad Yorkshire accent. "How's the face?"

The line of the scar shifted as Boodu's expression tightened. "It has healed."

"So who'd you use as your plastic surgeon? Dr. Frankenstein?"

The governor angrily clicked his fingers, and the guard booted Eddie hard in the side. He was about to deliver another blow when Boodu stopped him. "Leave him for me," the Zimbabwean rumbled. He ground the machete's point over the floor, the sound as unpleasant as nails on a blackboard. "I'm going to have some fun with him."

Eddie clutched his aching ribs. "You're throwing us a big party with cakes and jelly?"

"The only thing that will be thrown is your corpse,

into a pit," said Boodu. He rasped the blade over the flagstones again. "You caused me a lot of pain, Chase—professional and personal. Getting those criminals across the border made me look very bad in front of the president. It took me a long time to get back into his favor."

"Leaving the country 'cause you don't want to have your family raped and murdered doesn't make you a criminal."

Boodu snorted sarcastically. "If you oppose the president, you are a criminal. And my country has far too many of these criminals—this prison is full of them. They must be dealt with. Firmly." He paused to listen to a shriek from the torture chamber. "Like your friend Strutter. A dog of war, spreading sedition, arranging for mercenaries to work for criminals. Mercenaries like you, Chase."

"Not anymore, mate. I had a career change."

"Yes, I heard. We do still get the international news here in Zimbabwe, even if it is filled with lies about our country. You married an American, no? I'm very sorry." He laughed. "But I also heard that you got into some trouble, hey? You are wanted for murdering an Interpol officer! I was almost tempted to turn you over to them. But then"—he turned his face to display his mangled cheek to the prisoner—"I remembered that you gave me this."

"My pleasure," Eddie said with a sardonic grin.

"It will soon be *my* pleasure." Boodu advanced, tapping the machete on the floor. He nodded to the guard. "Hold him."

Eddie was kicked again, harder than before. While the Yorkshireman gasped for breath, the guard hauled him up and shoved him against the wall.

"Here," said Boodu, mouth somewhere between a smile and a snarl. He brought up the blade and sliced through one of Eddie's dirty, ragged sleeves—and the skin beneath. Dark blood blossomed on the fabric.

Eddie choked back a growl of pain. "You fucking cockwipe!"

"When I was told you had been arrested, I had it sharpened. Just for you."

"Hope you had it sterilized too," said Eddie as the guard released him. "Wouldn't want to catch anything." He examined the cut. Boodu had been right about the machete's sharpness; the African's sweep had only been light, but still enough to open up a stinging gash in his arm.

Boodu laughed again. "I'm disappointed in you, Chase. You knew you were a dead man if you ever came back to Zimbabwe—so I congratulate you on your bravery, at least—but you were a fool to be so open about it. We were watching all of Strutter's contacts. Did you really think we had forgotten you?" He gestured at Eddie's face. "A beard! That was your disguise? Very stupid. You must have spent too long in America, with all the comforts of marriage—you forgot how the world really works."

"I didn't forget," said Eddie. Boodu was about to say something else when a prison official appeared at the door and indicated that he wished to speak to the governor. The two men exchanged muttered words, eyeing Eddie suspiciously, before the militia leader went over to join in the sotto voce discussion.

Before long, Boodu let out a sharp "Ha!" and, swinging the machete almost nonchalantly, turned back to Eddie. "Where is it, Chase?"

"Where's what?" Eddie replied, face a portrait of innocence.

"You have a radio transmitter. My pilot picked it up and then used the prison's own receiver to triangulate its position. This cell."

The governor was already defensive. "We searched him when he was brought here."

"Not well enough," said Boodu, his look suggesting there would be repercussions for the oversight. "So that's why you were so open about coming here to rescue Strutter. You thought a homing beacon would help your friends rescue *you* if you got into trouble." He shook his head. "Not from here, Chase. Not from Fort Helena. Now, where is it? Or will I have to cut you apart to find it?" He raised the machete again.

With a defeated look, Eddie unfastened his trousers. "Don't get all excited, lads," he said as he reached into the back of his underwear and, straining in discomfort, extracted a small tubular object from where the sun didn't shine. "Ow! Christ, you've no idea how uncomfy that was. Made my eyes water."

Boodu was about to take it from Eddie when he noticed the unsavory coating on its metal surface and instructed the guard to hold it instead. With an expression of great distaste, the man held it up for his superiors to examine. It was around three inches long and a little over an inch in diameter, one end rounded off. A red LED blinked at the other, flat end, a tiny switch beside it. "Does the switch turn it off?" Boodu asked Eddie. The Englishman nodded.

Boodu gestured to the guard, who clicked the switch with a thumbnail. The LED went dark. Chuckling, he regarded Eddie again. "You shouldn't have set it to transmit on a military frequency, Chase. A stupid mistake."

"Oh, I dunno," said Eddie. A sudden confidence in his voice was accompanied by distant sounds from outside, a series of flat thuds. Boodu stiffened, realizing that the situation had somehow changed. "It wasn't to tell my mates I was here." A broad smile exposed the gap between his front teeth. "It was to tell 'em *you* were here."

He dropped and shielded his head—

A rising high-pitched whine told Boodu what was happening—but too late to do anything about it as mortar shells struck the prison.

A hole exploded in the corridor's ceiling, shrapnel ripping into the head and back of the prison official. The governor was also hit, the blast flinging him into the cell. Both Boodu and the guard were thrown off their feet as more detonations tore through the building.

Eddie lifted his head as the first round of shelling ceased. As planned, the bombs had been fired to impact in a pattern around his cell as soon as the beacon was switched off. Risky, but he'd had confidence in his collaborators' aim. The mortars were just over the top of a small ridge almost a mile from the fort, set up and sighted on his position by surreptitious use of a laser rangefinder during the early hours of the morning. So far, they were on target. The door hung off its hinges, the wall beside it smashed. A shaft of sunlight cut through the swirling dust from a hole in the roof.

He jumped up. The guard was closest to him, breaking out of his daze as he saw the prisoner move and standing clumsily, raising his gun—

Eddie grabbed his arm and wrenched it up behind his back as he fired. The bullet smacked against the door.

The sound shocked the governor back to life. He fumbled for his own holstered weapon, broad face contorted in panic and fury.

Eddie twisted the guard's arm even harder, jamming the gun's muzzle into his lower back—and his own index finger on top of his captive's. Four shots burst gorily through the guard's abdomen. Even mangled and smashed by their passage, the rounds still had enough force to tear into the governor's flesh. He screamed, gun forgotten as he writhed in agony from the mortal wounds.

Pulling the gun from the dead guard's hand, Eddie dropped the corpse and whirled to face Boodu. The Zimbabwean was on his hands and knees. As he squinted in pain and disorientation, his gaze fell upon his machete, the ornate handle just inches away. He grabbed it—

Eddie's foot stamped down on the blade.

Boodu looked up to find the smoking, blood-dripping gun pointed right at him. "All right, face-ache," Eddie growled. "Let go." Boodu withdrew his hand and backed away. The Englishman bent to retrieve the machete. Outside, an alarm bell started ringing—just as another round of far-off thumps reached the prison. "Oh, and if I were you, I'd duck."

Boodu shielded his head as another round of mortar shells struck their targets. These explosions were farther away, but still shook dust from the ceiling as guard towers were blasted into fragments and the prefabricated administration block blew apart, the remains collapsing on top of the prison staff inside.

Eddie jabbed Boodu with the machete. Another noise rose: the helicopter, its pilot desperately trying to take off. "Okay, get up. Get up!" He gestured with the gun toward the broken door. "Move."

Boodu had no choice but to obey, though his voice seethed with defiance. "Where are you taking me?"

"Long term? Botswana. Short term," Eddie went on as the other man responded with confusion, "we're going to do what I came here for—get Strutter. Lead the way."

"You can't get out of here," Boodu spat as they exited the cell. Through the hole in the ceiling, they heard the Alouette's roar as it left the ground. "The main gate is shut, and mortars won't break it—I know, I attacked this place during the war. You need a tank. And you don't have one."

"Let me worry about that," said Eddie. He prodded him again, far from gently, with the machete's point. "Come on, shift your arse."

Making an angry sound, Boodu stepped over the rubble littering the floor and moved down the passage, Eddie a few paces behind. Another explosion outside: a secondary detonation, one of the vehicles inside the compound. There would be a last round of shelling, then after that everything depended on getting the main gate open . . .

Frantic yelling and thumping came from a cell as they passed it, a man inside begging in the Shona language. Eddie checked the door, but it needed a key. Shit! He should have taken the set from the dead guard—

Another guard ran out from a junction ahead, gun in hand. He looked relieved to see Boodu—then realized that the militia leader was not alone and whipped up his pistol.

Eddie was quicker. A single shot and the guard fell backward, blood gushing from a bullet wound in his forehead.

Boodu spun, intending to take advantage of the distraction and tackle Eddie, but the Englishman had already brought the gun back to cover him. "Get his keys and open the cell," he ordered.

Boodu glared venomously at him; then after a moment, a calculating expression formed on his face. "Why don't you just kill me?" he asked, more rhetorically than in concern. Cunning replaced calculation. "You can't, can you? You need me alive."

"Not quite," said Eddie. "I *want* you alive, 'cause I'll get paid extra."

"And you said you weren't a mercenary anymore," Boodu scoffed, before the implications of Eddie's words sank in. "Paid? By who?"

"Oh, just the people I got across the border last time I was here. And some other Zimbabweans who escaped." His voice hardened. "People who had to leave family behind. Family you got hold of. They're pretty keen to see you again—on their terms." A flicker of genuine fear replaced the arrogance in Boodu's eyes. "Strutter's the main reason I'm here, but giving you to them's a bonus. Don't get me wrong, though—if you try anything again, I'll blow your fucking head off and give 'em what's left of it in a carrier bag. Now open the door."

Boodu did as he was told. The door swung open and a haggard man, face swollen with bruises, rushed out—only to retreat in fear when he saw who had released him.

"It's okay, come out," said Eddie, bringing his gun to the back of Boodu's head to show the terrified prisoner that the balance of power had changed. He glanced into the cell and saw that the man was not alone; there were five others, all showing signs of recent beatings, in the cramped, sweltering space. He tossed the keys into the room. "Get everyone out, and be ready to run when you see the signal."

"What signal?" a prisoner asked.

Eddie grinned. "You won't miss it." He swatted Boodu with the machete as the men in the cell hesitantly emerged, as if expecting some cruel trick. "Keep moving."

"You are setting these traitors, these *scum*, free?" Boodu hissed through clenched teeth. "You'll die for this, Chase!"

"Yeah, yeah," Eddie replied with a shrug. "But first, let's set another scumbag free and get Strutter, eh?"

Trying to mask his concern, Boodu continued down the passageway, Eddie behind him. More people were quickly released from other cells. Another series of explosions shook the old fort: the final mortar attack. If things were going according to plan, the prison would now be in chaos, with communications and most of the defenses smashed. The next phase—creating an escape route—should now be under way.

But while freeing Zimbabwean political prisoners would be a great humanitarian feat, it wasn't why Eddie was there. Only one prisoner concerned him.

The man behind the steel door they had just reached.

Keeping Boodu at gunpoint, Eddie listened at the grille set into it, straining to make out anything over the clamor of alarm bells. That the opening was there at all spoke volumes. Torture chambers designed for the purpose of extracting information were generally sound-proofed, the atrocities committed within witnessed only by the torturers and their victims. This, though, let everyone in the cells hear the screams. Another form of torture, more insidious, one that didn't even require the abusers to lay a hand on their other victims.

Through the door, he heard muted gasping. Anything else was masked by the bells and his own less-than-perfect hearing, damaged by years of exposure to gun-fire and explosions. "Open it," he muttered to Boodu.

The Zimbabwean glowered, but pushed the door open. "It's Boodu," he announced.

There was no answer. Surprised, Boodu stepped cautiously into the chamber. Eddie followed a couple of steps behind. On the far side of the shadowed room he saw the man he had come to rescue: Johnny Strutter, an overweight Kenyan man in his forties. Strutter was shackled face-first against the wall, his bare back marked with savage weals and bleeding lines where he had been whipped. There was also a strong, sickly smell like scorched meat. Burn marks dotted across Strutter's shoulders and upper back told Eddie that it wasn't from a barbecue. A bench beside him was home to numerous instruments of torture, some of which had been demonstrated to—and upon—Eddie the previous day.

Their user was gone, however. The torturer had fled like a coward at the first sign of danger. Whips and hooks and soldering irons were no defense against bombs and bullets.

Eddie gestured at Strutter. "Get him down."

At gunpoint, Boodu unlocked the shackles. The overweight man collapsed when the last one was released, moaning. "Into the corner," snapped Eddie, signaling for Boodu to back away as he checked the prisoner.

Strutter forced open his pain-clenched eyes. "Chase?" he rasped in disbelief. "Eddie Chase! God above, it *is* you! I almost didn't recognize you with the beard . . ."

"Can you walk?" Eddie demanded curtly.

Strutter flexed his legs and grimaced. "I don't know. I've been through a lot since I was arrested, old friend. You'll have to carry me."

Eddie fixed him with a cold glare. "Let's get this straight, Strutter. I'm not your *old friend,* and I'm not fucking carrying your fat arse anywhere. I want one thing out of you—information—and if you can't move, I'll chain you back to that wall and carry on where the last guy left off to get it."

Strutter hurriedly got up. "On the other hand, I could walk."

"Glad we're on the same page." Eddie turned back to Boodu. "All right, dickhead, let's go. Strutter, take this machete. If he tries anything, stab him."

Strutter took the blade and eyed Boodu. "It would be a grand thing for the entire world if I just stabbed him anyway."

"I know, but I'll get a few quid for handing him over."

"You are back in the mercenary business? I thought you left for good."

"It's just temporary," Eddie said as he returned to the door. The only people he saw outside were prisoners, a few of whom had acquired weapons from the guards and were exchanging intermittent fire through a door to the courtyard. Fort Helena was still in turmoil.

But even with the governor dead, there was a chain of command. Somebody would soon take charge; every minute brought a counterattack closer. The armory might have been destroyed, but the guards still had firepower on their side.

Boodu knew this too. "You can't get out," he said, sneering at the prisoners. "You think these starving dogs can break through the gate?"

"Nope," said Eddie, heading for the exit. "But I know someone who can."

As if on cue, more gunfire erupted outside—though from the prisoners' confusion, it was clear that it wasn't being aimed at them. Eddie cautiously peered into the courtyard. The watchtowers were smoldering wrecks, and a column of black smoke rose from the remains of the administration block. A car nearby was also ablaze. But what about the guards?

He saw several uniformed men race across the courtyard to scale the steps built into the fort's thick defensive wall, joining others along the ramparts—and firing on something outside the prison.

Something getting closer.

A deep rumbling growl filled the air. Boodu's eyes went wide. "You *do have* a tank!"

"Not quite," said Eddie, "but the next best thing." He smiled. "Check out my killdozer."

The great gates burst apart.

Roaring through a cloud of dust and black diesel smoke was a large bulldozer, its front blade raised like a battering ram—but this was no ordinary construction vehicle. The engine compartment and cabin were covered by steel plates. The guards' bullets clanked harmlessly off the armor as the behemoth ground over the ruined gates into the courtyard.

The killdozer was not simply an impenetrable bullet magnet, however. It had weapons of its own. Slots in the cabin's shields dropped open—and the muzzles of machine guns poked out, firing up at the fort's defenders. Guards flailed and fell under the hail of fire. The machine rumbled on, flattening a car into unrecognizable scrap.

Eddie called to the prisoners. "Okay! That's your way out of here—there are trucks coming to the gate. When I tell you, run for it!"

Boodu raged impotently. "English *bastard*! You're helping these traitors escape? You'll die for this—no, you'll *beg* me to kill you after I'm finished with you!"

The prisoners' own fury rose as they realized who he was. Eddie reasserted who was in charge by cracking his gun against Boodu's head. "Keep your fucking mouth shut—or I'll give you to this lot. We'll see who's begging then." Seeing the vengeance-filled eyes of the men surrounding him, Boodu wisely decided to stay silent.

A thunderous explosion shook the building, and the lights went out. Eddie saw the killdozer backing away from the blazing remains of the prison's generators. Through the gates, he spotted a pickup truck barreling down the dusty road to the fort. "If you've got a gun, get ready to use it!" he called. "If you haven't, then run for the gate . . . *now*!"

He broke from the doorway into the courtyard, gun at

the ready. Strutter followed, forcing Boodu along at
machete-point. The prisoners spilled out behind them.

The killdozer was growling back to the gate, but Eddie
was only concerned with the remaining guards. A man
leaned around a corner and fired into the fleeing crowd—
then dropped with a spurting chest wound as Eddie returned the favor.

Another two guards rose from cover behind a wall
and opened up with rifles. There were screams as prisoners were hit. Eddie turned to deal with the new threat,
but the men in the killdozer beat him to it, the machine
guns unleashing furious bursts of automatic fire. The
wall pocked and splintered under the barrage, both
guards tumbling amid bright red sprays of blood as bullets ripped into their bodies.

Shots cracked out from the escapees. The other guards
realized they were overmatched and tried to retreat.
Spitting lines of fire from the killdozer tracked them.

Eddie was almost at the gate. The pickup had stopped
outside, more vehicles pulling up behind it. Inside them
were resistance members opposed to Zimbabwe's brutal
government, many of whom had been driven to direct
action by the imprisonment of family or friends in places
like Fort Helena. A man jumped from the pickup and
waved frantically to him: Banga Nandoro, one of those
with whom Eddie had planned the whole operation.

"Come on, hurry!" Banga yelled as Eddie charged
through the gate, the prisoners following him. More
men jumped from the arriving trucks to help pile the
escapees aboard.

Eddie ran to Banga, gun still raised as he watched the
fort's walls for snipers. "Glad you could make it," he
told the Zimbabwean as Boodu and Strutter caught up.

Banga nodded, eyes fixed on the men emerging from
the gate. At the sight of one in particular, he gasped.
"Chinouyazue!" he cried, running to his brother.

Eddie patted his heart. "Makes you feel all warm in
here, doesn't it?" Boodu's expression twisted into a
glower.

The killdozer reached the gate, the remaining prisoners streaming past as it turned on its tracks to prevent any surviving vehicles from leaving the compound. A steel slab dropped from the cabin's side, hitting the ground with a bang. Two Zimbabweans holding machine guns emerged, followed by a huge Caucasian man who unfolded himself from the cramped confines and squeezed out. He saw Eddie and gave him a cheery wave, then hopped down and produced a hand grenade, pulling the pin and tossing it over his shoulder into the killdozer as he jogged away. An explosion ripped apart the controls, turning the makeshift tank into an extremely solid barricade.

"Little man!" Oleg Maximov called as he approached Eddie. "You okay, *da*?" The bearded Russian scooped him up in a crushing embrace.

"Yeah, I'm fine," Eddie grunted. "Okay, okay, that's hurting now!" Grinning, Maximov released him. Eddie saw numerous red marks on his face and arms: He had been scorched by the spent bullet casings pinging around inside the cabin. "Did you get burned?"

"*Da*, a little," said Maximov, tugging out a pair of silicone earplugs; without protection, the gunfire inside the metal-walled cabin would have been deafening. He smiled. "It felt good."

"You're weird, Max." Years earlier, the muscular giant had survived a bullet to the head, with the side effect that his pain response had become scrambled. Getting hurt now actually gave him pleasure, making the ex-Spetsnaz mercenary an extremely dangerous opponent, as Eddie had discovered.

But they were on the same side for this job. "Nice work," he told Maximov before turning his attention back to the escapees. Almost a hundred prisoners had been freed, he estimated—so many that it might be touch and go whether they could all fit in the waiting trucks. "Come on, move it!" he shouted, waving for the stragglers to hurry.

"And where do you think they will all go?" Boodu

demanded with condescending sarcasm. He glanced to the west; Botswana was only ten miles away. "The border is too well guarded—they will never get across it. And if they stay in Zimbabwe, we will find them. There is nowhere they can hide."

"That's not gonna be your problem," said Eddie. The last of the men squeezed aboard the trucks, some dangling from the sides, held by their former cellmates. The first vehicle started to lumber away. "Right, Banga, we'd better shift. I don't want to miss my flight."

Banga helped his weary brother into the pickup's cab, then climbed into the driver's seat. Eddie hopped into the rear bed, keeping his gun on Boodu as the Zimbabwean, Strutter, and Maximov followed suit. The pickup set off, but instead of following the other trucks back along the dirt road, it angled away into open scrubland. Shots from the fort followed them, but they were quickly beyond the range of the guards' weapons.

Banga kept driving across the windy plain. After a few minutes, structures appeared ahead. Skeletal frames rose from the ground like hands clawing from a grave, the part-built beginnings of what had been planned as a cement works before Zimbabwe's ruined economy forced construction to be suspended. The killdozer, in its original peaceful guise, had been one of the pieces of equipment abandoned in situ.

A long road ran from the site to a highway a few miles to the south, widened and flattened to allow the passage of heavy machinery. Eddie hoped it would also be wide enough for another form of transport . . .

"There she is!" shouted Maximov, pointing into the sky. Eddie looked up to see a bright yellow aircraft approaching at low altitude.

It wasn't the one he had expected, however. "What the bloody hell's that?" he demanded as the large, ponderous biplane made a lazy descent toward the road. The closer it came to the ground, the slower it moved, to the point where it seemed to be hanging impossibly in the air. Then, with an upward twitch of its nose, it dropped the last few feet and bounced along the dirt track before trundling to a stop near the unfinished buildings.

Banga drove the pickup to meet it. Strutter prodded Boodu out of the back with the machete as Eddie jumped out and ran to the aircraft. A hatch opened in the biplane's rear flank. "TD!" he yelled over the engine's sputtering growl. "What the fuck's this piece of old crap?"

Tamara Defendé looked offended. "And it's nice to see you too, Eddie," she said in her melodious Namibian accent.

"What happened to the Piper?" He had expected her to be flying her Twin Comanche air taxi.

"Didn't I tell you? I've got two planes now—my business is expanding. I thought you might need something bigger for this." She nodded at Maximov as he accompanied Strutter and Boodu to the aircraft. "I don't think he would even fit in the Piper."

Eddie was still far from impressed. "But . . . but it's fucking *prehistoric*! It's a biplane, for Christ's sake. Who built it, the Wright brothers?"

"It's Russian," said TD, pouting in defense of her plane's honor. "It's an Antonov—"

"Antonov An-2, yeah, I know." Eddie's military training had included aircraft recognition. He clambered into the surprisingly capacious hold, moving aside to let the three other men in. "I meant, why the hell would you buy this thing? It must be sixty years old!"

"Hah! It's only thirty-nine, so it's younger than you—"

"It's the same age, actually," he protested. "I'm not forty yet."

"—and it's cheap and simple and I can repair it with a wrench and a hammer out in the bush if I need to. And it can carry a lot of cargo and land just about anywhere, so it's perfect for my work."

"Main thing I want to know is: Is it fast?" Eddie asked as he waved good-bye to Banga and shut the hatch.

"Not really, but this is Africa. Things don't happen in a rush here."

"They will once the government finds out what just happened at the prison."

The attractive young pilot took the hint and hurried up the cabin to clamber through an arched opening into the cockpit. Eddie checked on the other passengers. Strutter, evidently as unconvinced by the Antonov's supposed airworthiness as Eddie, had already strapped himself firmly in. The only thing keeping Boodu down, however, was Maximov's scowl from the neighboring seat.

"You'll never get away," the Zimbabwean snarled as Eddie took the seat next to Strutter, facing him across the cabin. "Not in this antique."

"Ten miles and we're across the border," Eddie reminded him. "Even this thing can make it before any of your fighters reach us."

TD revved the engine, applying full rudder to turn the elderly aircraft back down the road. The Antonov lurched over the bumps. Strutter nervously pulled his straps even tighter. "*If* it can make it," said Boodu.

"I heard that," TD snapped from the cockpit. She straightened out, braking and checking the instruments before pushing the throttle to full power. The engine roared, the entire fuselage vibrating and rattling.

"I should have kept earplugs in," Maximov complained. Eddie had to agree; the Antonov betrayed its Soviet military heritage by its utter lack of creature comforts such as soundproofing.

"Hang on," TD warned. The jolting increased as the biplane picked up speed. Eddie looked out through the row of circular portholes, gripping the arm of his seat with one hand as he kept the gun aimed at Boodu with the other. They were doing forty miles per hour, fifty— then abruptly the juddering eased and the plane tipped back sharply as it took to the air. Antiquated though it might be, the Antonov still had low-speed performance that almost no modern planes could match.

"How long to the border?" Eddie shouted to TD as she banked to head west toward her current home country.

"Less than ten minutes."

"Okay." Once the An-2 reached Botswanan airspace—passage had already been secured—another fifteen minutes of flight would bring them to a bush airstrip.

Where the relatives of some of Boodu's victims awaited his arrival.

Boodu had realized this, his attempt at a neutral expression not hiding the concern on his scarred face. His gaze flicked to the machete, which Strutter had shoved point-down into the frame between his and Eddie's seats. "Don't even think about it," Eddie warned, with a jab of the gun for emphasis. The militia leader leaned back in his seat, eyes narrowed.

Now that they were in the air, Strutter started to relax. He wiped sweat from his forehead, then turned to the Englishman. "You say you are not my friend, Eddie, but for getting me out of that place, you have a friend for life. Whether you like it or not!" He beamed, but the smile faded at Eddie's unimpressed look. "Whatever you need, whatever you want, you'll have it."

"Just information'll do," said Eddie. "I'm trying to find someone."

"If anyone can find them, I can," Strutter said proudly.

"That's why I rescued you. In fact, that's the *only* reason I rescued you." The Kenyan looked somewhat deflated, so Eddie softened slightly. "You get me what I want, Johnny, and as far as I'm concerned we're all square, and you're free to go. Sound good?"

Strutter nodded. "It does. Thank you." He offered his hand. "I promise you, I will find—"

A line of ragged holes burst open in the fuselage, shards of aluminum showering the passengers.

Wind shrieked into the cabin. "Shit!" Eddie gasped as TD threw the lumbering plane into an evasive turn. They were being fired on—but how?

The Alouette. Boodu's helicopter was equipped with a

pair of .303-caliber Browning machine guns—and after fleeing the prison, it must have withdrawn to a safe distance before its crew spotted the incoming Antonov and deduced that the highest-value escapees would be taken aboard. Eddie didn't know the Alouette's top speed, but suspected it would match—or beat—the old biplane.

Another burst of machine-gun fire punctured the hull, the shots ripping along the length of the plane—

Into the cockpit.

TD screamed. Eddie saw blood on the windshield. The plane lurched. "TD, are you okay? TD!"

Her reply was a barely coherent wail. "Oh God, my arm!"

Eddie jumped up and was about to enter the cockpit to help her when the nose tilted upward, sending him staggering back down the cabin . . .

Boodu lunged for his machete.

Off balance, Eddie took a shot at him that went wide, adding another hole to the Antonov's puckered fuselage as Boodu yanked the blade from the seat frame—

More of the Alouette's bullets struck the biplane. It pitched up almost vertically, dropping Eddie and Boodu toward the rear bulkhead as the other two men struggled to hold on to their seats.

The sheet metal buckled under Eddie as he crashed against it. Boodu slammed down beside him, the machete clanging against the bulkhead just inches from the Yorkshireman's chest.

Boodu swept the weapon as Eddie rolled away. The machete's sharp edge caught his arm—only a glancing blow, but still deep enough to draw blood. He tried to bring the gun around, but Boodu lashed out with one leg and kicked his hand, sending the pistol flying across the hold.

The plane's nose tipped back down. Even wounded, TD was still fighting to keep control of her aircraft. Eddie thumped to the deck as the Antonov came out of its climb. Over the engine's roar, he heard the clatter of the helicopter's machine guns. Bullets clunked into the wings.

"Max!" he shouted. "Get into the cockpit and help her!" Maximov gave him a thumbs-up and squeezed through the cockpit entrance.

More bullet impacts, this time against the fuselage. One of the portholes blew out—then the cabin hatch burst open and fell away behind the plane. Strutter screamed in terror.

Eddie clung to a structural spar as the slipstream tried to drag him out after the hatch. The horizon tipped sharply, the Antonov now in a steepening plunge. The engine note rose in pitch.

Boodu braced his feet against another spar and swung again, Eddie ducking just in time to avoid a machete blow to his face. The blade clanged against the hull above his head. He retaliated with a punch, but only caught the Zimbabwean's shoulder as he drew back the machete for another attack.

A churning sensation in Eddie's stomach told him that he was in free fall. The Antonov was picking up speed in its dive.

Which gave him a new dimension in which to fight.

Boodu slashed at him—but Eddie had already kicked away and shot toward the ceiling, grabbing a flapping cargo strap and using it to somersault himself around. The plane's occupants were now effectively in zero g, the Antonov's power dive matching the speed at which gravity was dragging them down. From Boodu's expression of shock—and sudden nausea—it was something he had never experienced before.

Eddie had, however. He kicked off again and propelled himself at the Zimbabwean like a missile. Before Boodu could react, the Englishman had plowed into him, sending both men tumbling weightlessly across the hold. He drove a punch into Boodu's face, breaking his nose. Globules of blood whirled in the air. Another powerful blow, then he grabbed the African's arm and tried to pry the machete from his grip.

The engine note changed again, the cabin spinning around them as the plane turned. They were running out of sky . . .

Eddie finally broke Boodu's hold on the machete—as Maximov pulled up, hard. No longer in free fall, the two men crashed heavily to the deck. Gravity went from zero to double as the An-2 continued its roller-coaster ride. The machete slammed down with sledgehammer force, embedding its tip an inch into the floor beside the open hatch.

The ground outside was frighteningly close—

An explosion of dust whirled into the cabin as the Antonov pulled out of its headlong dive mere feet above the plain and began another steep, rolling climb. Eddie and Boodu, still grappling, slid back down the hold . . .

Straight at the hatch.

Eddie realized the danger and let go of Boodu, clawing at the spars. He snagged one with his fingertips, but lost his grip almost immediately and continued to slither toward the opening. Boodu, just ahead of him, screamed as he fell into nothingness—

And caught the back edge of the frame, dangling outside the ascending aircraft.

Eddie flailed his arms helplessly, sliding out into the void . . .

His left hand slapped against one of the wrecked hinges. He grabbed it. Torn metal cut into his palm, but he had no choice but to cling on as his free hand hunted for purchase—

Boodu's hand clamped around his throat.

The militia leader pulled himself higher. Choking, Eddie looked down at him, seeing his face twisted into a defiant snarl. Behind the Antonov's tail, the pursuing Alouette came into view as it climbed after the biplane. "If I die," Boodu roared into the wind, "so do you, Chase!"

He squeezed harder, trying to force Eddie away from the hatch. The hinge's sharp edges dug deeper into the Englishman's hand. He tried to push Boodu back down, but didn't have enough leverage. Instead, he groped inside the cabin for a handhold . . .

His fingers found sharp, thick metal.

The machete!

He tugged at the handle. The blade shifted, but didn't come loose, still stuck in the floor like a crude Excalibur. Boodu dug his thumb harder against Eddie's windpipe, hauling himself higher. Another few inches and he would be able to get an elbow over the edge of the hatch to pull himself inside.

A last desperate yank—and the blade came free.

Supported by only one hand, Eddie swung farther out of the hatch. Boodu shot him a look of triumph—which abruptly vanished as he saw what his opponent was holding. "No, don't!" he cried.

"Hands off!" Eddie shouted.

He brought down the machete in a savage slash—and lopped the Zimbabwean's clutching arm off at the wrist.

With a horrible shriek, Boodu plummeted away in the Antonov's wake—

And fell into the helicopter's rotor blades.

The lower half of his body burst into a thick spray that repainted the olive-green military camouflage in a gory red, the upper smashing screaming through the cockpit windows. The Alouette slewed round, rapidly losing height—then hit the ground and exploded in an oily fireball.

Eddie stabbed the machete into the plane's side and dragged himself back into the cabin as the Antonov leveled out. He lay gasping for several seconds before realizing that Boodu's severed hand was still gripping his neck. He pulled off the appendage and was about to toss it through the hatch after its former owner when he took in the ring on its finger, the emerald still gleaming in its gold setting. A moment's thought, then he wedged it in a seat frame and staggered to the front of the compartment. Strutter was still clutching his chair, petrified. Eddie leaned into the cockpit. "TD! Are you okay?"

Maximov had the controls, hunched in the copilot's

position with a look of laser-beam concentration. Beside him, TD was very pale, her left hand tightly squeezed around her bloodied right bicep. "Not—really," she managed to say through her pained grimace. "Oh God, it hurts!"

"Let me see." He carefully lifted her hand. She cried out, but he saw enough of the injury to know that it wouldn't be life threatening if she got prompt medical attention. "Okay, it's okay," he said, trying to sound reassuring. "Just keep hold of it. We'll fix you up when we land. How far to the border?"

She squinted at the instruments, then out of the window. "We'll be . . . across it in a minute."

"I have a question," said Maximov, gripping the controls so hard that the tendons stood out like brake cables on the backs of his hairy hands. "How do we land? I don't know how to fly!" He gave Eddie a hopeful glance. "Do you?"

"Nope—it's been on my to-do list for about five fucking years!" He looked back at TD. "Can you talk him through it? I don't want to have been in *three* plane crashes in eleven bloody months."

She managed a feeble smile. "No problem. Another reason I bought . . . an Antonov. If you turn into the wind, the stall speed is . . . zero knots. So much lift it can just—float down."

"You're kidding." Another attempt at a smile through her pain. "You're not. Wow. I guess Russian stuff isn't as crap as I thought."

"Hoy!" Maximov protested.

Eddie grinned and retreated into the main cabin. Strutter's rictus look of terror had finally relaxed, and he was hesitantly loosening his seat belt straps. "I'd keep 'em fastened," Eddie warned him. "This might be a bit bumpy."

* * *

Twenty minutes later, the Antonov was on the ground, in more or less one piece. Eddie had radioed ahead to alert the reception committee that they needed medical help; it turned out that no fewer than three of the waiting Zimbabwean expatriates were doctors, educated professionals being high on the list of targets for the government's thugs. Two of them took TD to the nearby bush farmhouse for emergency treatment. The third wanted to check Eddie's injuries, but he had business to attend to first.

Maximov followed the Englishman from the plane. "That was easy!" he crowed. "Maybe I should become pilot, *da*?"

Despite TD's claims, the An-2's touchdown had been far from feather-light. Eddie tried to crick the stiffness out of his sore neck and spine. "You might need a bit more practice." Maximov laughed.

"Mr. Chase?" Waiting for Eddie was Japera Tangwerai, one of those whom he had helped escape from Zimbabwe several years before. Although she was only in her early thirties, the lines of stress and loss on her face made her appear middle-aged, for she had seen nearly her entire family murdered by Zimbabwean militia forces. Her only surviving child, a boy now eight years old, looked up at Eddie nervously from behind her skirts. "What happened? Did you free the prisoners from Fort Helena?"

"Yeah," he told her. "Don't know exactly how many, but a lot, about a hundred. Banga and his people got them out of there."

"And what about . . ." Her voice dropped. "What about Boodu?"

Even as a whisper, the hated name still caught the attention of others nearby. More people approached Eddie. "Did you catch him?" a man demanded. "Did you bring the Butcher?"

"Some of him. Here." Eddie brought something out from behind his back. "Let me give you a hand."

Everyone recoiled in instinctive shock and disgust before they realized the significance of the distinctive ring on one stiffening finger. "It . . . it's his," said Japera softly. "It's the Butcher's hand." She raised her voice to her companions. "It is the Butcher's hand!"

The man who had spoken stared at it; then his mouth widened into a grin. He took the lifeless hand and held it aloft. "You killed the Butcher! He's dead! The Butcher is dead!" The call was taken up by the others, delight and relief spreading through the little crowd.

Japera's response was more muted, a tear beading in one eye. "You killed Gamba Boodu," she said quietly to Eddie. "Thank you. My family . . . can rest now. Thank you." She squeezed his hand. He nodded in silent acknowledgment. After a moment, she released him. "I will get your money."

"Don't give it to me," he said, to her surprise. "TD can have most of my share—I don't think getting her plane fixed'll be cheap. And Max can have the rest." He nodded toward the huge Russian, who was surrounded by cheering Zimbabweans and looking bemused but pleased by the attention. "All I need is enough to cover some expenses. Plane fares, mainly."

Japera tried to hide her disappointment. "You are leaving? So soon?"

"I've got somewhere to go. All I need is to find out where. Excuse me." He headed back to the plane to meet Strutter, who had just planted both feet on solid ground with huge relief.

"Eddie, Eddie, Eddie!" said the Kenyan, rubbing his brow. "We made it—you saved me!"

"Yeah, well, don't expect me to make a habit of it. Like I said, if you tell me what I need to know, we'll be all square."

"No problem. I will find your friend, don't you worry."

"He's not a friend," said Eddie, expression turning cold. "You know Alexander Stikes?"

Strutter nodded. "Of course. Ex-SAS like you, runs his own PMC—although I heard he suddenly shut it down not long ago and started working for someone full-time. I had some dealings with him; arranged for him to hire mercenaries for certain jobs, people like Maximov. But he's a dangerous man. In honesty, I'm happy he's gone." He regarded Eddie curiously. "You've gone to a lot of trouble for someone you don't like. Why do you want to find him?"

Eddie's face became even harder. "So I can kill him."

TWO

New York City

Nina Wilde looked disconsolately out across her hometown from her office in the United Nations Building. Today marked a date she had no desire to celebrate: It was exactly three months since she had last seen her husband.

With a quiet sigh, the redhead turned away from the view and returned to her desk. A framed photograph beside the phone was a reminder of far better times: herself and her partner at an infinitely less depressing anniversary, the party thrown to mark the first year of their marriage. The picture was less than two years old, but a lot had happened since then.

A lot of people had died.

One of them was the subject of the email she had just received, the grim reminder prompting her melancholy reflectiveness at the window. It was from an Interpol officer named Renée Beauchamp, in charge of investigating the death of another member of the multinational police organization. The victim was Ankit Jindal, head of Interpol's Cultural Property Crime Unit—and also a friend who had worked with Nina on two of her previous archaeological expeditions.

The prime—in fact, the only—suspect was Eddie Chase. Her husband.

That would have been bad enough on its own. But things were worse: She had been a witness. And despite her unwillingness to believe it, the only conclusion she could draw, no matter how many times she replayed events in an attempt to find evidence to the contrary . . . was that Eddie had cold-bloodedly murdered Kit.

The memory returned, unbidden. Peru, three months ago to the day. A gas pipeline in a pumping station south of Lima had ruptured, and flames spread rapidly to the rest of the facility. The catwalk on which Eddie and Kit were standing had partially collapsed, leaving the Indian dangling above a searing jet of fire. As Nina reached the scene, she saw Kit struggling to hold on, grasping for a handhold on a pipe—

And Eddie kicking Kit in the face and sending him plunging into the inferno below.

She snapped back to the present. The image was as clear and vivid as if it had just happened.

No gun.

Eddie had insisted that Kit had tried to kill him, that he had been going for a gun. But there was no gun in her memory, just Kit trying to save himself from a deadly fall. A fall that came anyway, moments later.

Beauchamp's email was an update on the search for the wanted man. Somehow her murder suspect had managed to escape Peru undetected and been sighted in England, India, South Africa, and most recently Zimbabwe—but never in time for local Interpol agents to catch him. He was always a step ahead: a shadow, a ghost. It hadn't taken long for the investigators to suspect that he was receiving help.

That didn't surprise Nina in the least. From their first meeting, Eddie had astonished her with the sheer number of his friends and contacts around the globe, all of whom seemed willing to do him favors far beyond simply picking him up at the airport. Some would be more useful in his current situation than others: The forger, for example, an Australian ex-military colleague, could have provided him with a fake passport. But she couldn't bring herself to pass on her suspicions to Interpol.

Eddie was still her husband. And she knew him well enough to be sure that whatever she had witnessed, he'd *believed* that Kit had a gun. Since he wasn't prone to hallucination or confabulation, this had provided her with the seed of doubt she needed to think that he was telling the truth. That he was innocent.

And if he *was* innocent, she couldn't help his hunters track him down.

Other facts had arisen in Beauchamp's investigation suggesting that more had been going on than anyone had realized. Kit had told Nina that he was going to the pumping station on Interpol authority to meet a representative of mercenary leader Alexander Stikes. The British former soldier had stolen archaeological treasures from the ruins of the lost city of El Dorado; according to Kit, he was willing to return them in exchange for legal immunity.

Kit had been lying. Interpol knew nothing about it.

Eddie had gone to the gas plant after him because he believed Kit and Stikes were working together—thereby directly involving Kit in the murder of Eddie's friend and mentor, Jim "Mac" McCrimmon. And Nina herself had glimpsed a man who might have been Stikes fleeing the burning station in a helicopter. *Could* Kit have been corrupt? It seemed unlikely—Stikes had tortured him for information after doing the same to Nina to learn more about the search for El Dorado—but now that the seed had been planted . . .

She leaned forward, head in her hands. Suspicions didn't help Eddie. While he was ahead of the police for now, they were catching up. Eventually he would be caught. Charged with murder. Tried.

And based on the evidence to date, found guilty.

Her phone rang, an internal call. With another sigh, she picked it up. "Yes?"

"Nina?" Lola Gianetti, her personal assistant. "Matt

asked me to tell you that they're waiting for you in the conference room."

She looked at her watch. Damn! There was an important meeting scheduled on the hour, and it was now ten past. "I'll be right there."

One good thing about being the director of the International Heritage Agency, she mused as she hurried from her office, was that meetings had to wait for her rather than the other way around. All the same, she tried to hide her embarrassment as she entered the conference room. "Sorry I'm late."

"No worries," said Matt Trulli. Of the group, the tubby, unkempt Australian, on secondment from the UN's Oceanic Survey Organization, knew her best and was well aware of the stress she had been under.

Another man was decidedly less sympathetic, his impatience clear. "Thank you for coming," said Dr. Lewis Hayter with barely restrained sarcasm as Nina took her seat. "So, if we're all ready?"

"Go ahead," said Nina. "Anything to do with these excavations always gets my full attention. Once I've dealt with my other IHA responsibilities," she added, a little poke to remind the thin-faced archaeologist that she was his boss. "So, you've found something exciting?"

"We've found something *very* exciting." Hayter picked up a remote control and switched on a projector. A screen displayed a map of a number of buildings. Even in simplified cartographic form it was clear that they were ruins, the illustration showing where parts of the structures had collapsed and strewn debris nearby.

These were no ordinary ruins, though. Even through her gloom, Nina felt her heart quicken with a thrill of expectation. The map was of the very heart of the lost civilization of Atlantis—the sunken capital she had discovered five years before.

Her work at the IHA had since taken her down other historical roads, leading to more incredible archaeological discoveries. But there was something special about

Atlantis. It had vindicated her theories, catapulted her to international fame . . . and allowed her to finish the journey her late parents had begun.

Simply locating the city was far from the end of the work, though. Atlantis had more secrets yet to be uncovered—even if she now had to rely on others to discover them vicariously. Hayter indicated one of the ruined buildings with a laser pointer. "We used the new high-resolution sonar to look through the sediment at the palace's western wing. We found the entrance to what we think is a royal burial chamber. My recommendation is that this be our next primary objective."

Nina checked her notes. "What about the Temple of the Gods? I thought you were planning a full excavation of that." The small ruin, close to the palace, had so far been explored only to a limited extent.

"It was an option," Hayter said sniffily, "but to be honest, I doubt it'll be worth the effort. It's much more badly damaged than most of the other buildings, and the initial survey didn't turn up anything particularly unusual."

"You don't consider a single structure dedicated to every single god in the pantheon, even the ones who already have temples of their own, unusual?"

"I'd call it a minor mystery, nothing more. The burial chamber is a much bigger prize, certainly for this leg of the expedition."

Nina considered his words, then reluctantly nodded. "I'll want to see the list of alternatives, but okay, yes, the burial chamber it is." With the archaeological dig taking place eight hundred feet beneath the surface of the Atlantic, most of the work had to be done from submersibles; ensuring that the expensive-to-run machines made the best possible use of their time was crucial. "Matt, will your subs need any extra equipment to get in there?"

"Nah, we'll be able to handle it," said the maritime engineer. "*Sharkdozer Two* should be able to clear most of the rubble, and even if it's too tight for divers in deep suits, *Gypsy*'s still got the two ROVs. We'll find your crowns and scepters, or whatever they hid down there."

"Great. What timescale are we looking at?"

"I think we'll have got as much as is practical from the Temple of Poseidon in another few days," said Hayter. The red dot of his pointer moved to another, larger structure, one with something considerably younger than the eleven-thousand-year-old ruins overlaid upon it: the wreck of a ship. "Which brings me to this."

A click of the remote and the map vanished, replaced by an underwater photograph. A stone chamber, badly damaged, huge slabs from the semi-collapsed ceiling jutting down into the space. Nina knew it immediately: the altar room within the enormous Temple of Poseidon. She had never been inside it personally, something that still bugged her, but she had seen live video footage of it shot by Eddie before its partial destruction. The ship that had crashed onto the structure was the research vessel *Evenor*, from which the first underwater expedition had been launched. It had taken over four years before other explorers managed to clear away enough of the wreckage to find that some sections of the smashed temple had survived.

Atlantean artifacts and treasures had been recovered from the altar room by the IHA, but by far the most valuable of its contents was still in place. Parts of the walls gleamed in divers' spotlights. The chamber had been lined with sheets of precious metal, a gold alloy known to its builders as orichalcum, but even they paled in worth against the words inscribed upon them. The room recorded the entire history of Atlantis, from its earliest beginnings right up to its fall—and one of the hopes for Hayter's expedition was that it would find those last words and solve the final mystery of one of humanity's greatest legends.

Why Atlantis sank.

The pointer jittered over crumpled metal protruding from beneath a fallen block. "As you can see," Hayter went on, "a lot of the panels have been lost. More than half of them are completely buried, and short of taking apart the temple stone by stone, it's unlikely we'll ever be able to recover them."

"*Sharkdozer* could do it," Matt chipped in. "The heavy lifting arms can easily shift that lot. It's just a matter of time."

"And money," Hayter said patronizingly. "Now, around two-thirds of the accessible panels are damaged to some extent." The laser spot danced over gashes and twists in the orichalcum. "Fortunately, one of the larger ceiling slabs only collapsed at one end, and as you can see here"—he indicated a rubble-choked gap beneath a long block of stone lying at an angle—"it protected the texts beneath it to a degree. Once we cleared the debris, we were able to view them."

Another click. The new picture was closer in on the now accessible space. More orichalcum sheets gleamed, words in a long-dead language discernible upon them. The chronicles of the Atlantean empire ran around the room, added day by day, line by line.

"Our translation team started work on this section as soon as the divers returned to the surface," said Hayter. "Most of it's similar to the other texts in the temple—accounts of the actions of the king and queen and other political leaders, military activity, and so on. Talonor's expeditions are mentioned several times." The Atlantean explorer's unearthed records had led Nina to discover an ancient—and spectacular—Hindu vault high in the Himalayas the previous year. "But the part I think you'll be most interested in is this."

He used the remote to display a close-up of one particular section of the scribed texts. Nina examined it thoughtfully. "I recognize some words," she said. "Something about . . . keys? The keys of . . . strength, it looks like. No, of power."

Hayter seemed put out that she could understand any of it without his help. "I'll save you some time," he said, highlighting a line. "Beginning here: 'Nantalas, high priestess of the Temple of the Gods and keeper of the sky stone, showed the magic of the keys of power to the royal court. In the hands of others they were nothing more than simple statues, but in hers they blazed with heavenly light.' "

Nina stiffened, immediately realizing the significance of the words. Matt cocked an eyebrow at her reaction, but said nothing as Hayter continued: " 'Nantalas told the king that the keys had given her a vision of the sky stone'—we're not sure whether that's referring to an actual meteorite or something more metaphorical, by the way—'with its power unleashed, a power to destroy the enemies of Atlantis.' "

"These keys," Nina asked. "Is there a description of them?"

"Yes, here." Hayter indicated another part of the text. " 'Three figures of purple stone, in height less than one foot. When apart, the touch of the priestess lights one to point the way to the others.' There was probably more, but the sheet was damaged."

Nina ignored him. She had already heard enough to confirm her suspicions.

The artifacts Alexander Stikes had taken were three small purple statues. The first had been found inside the buried Pyramid of Osiris in Egypt; the second, hidden with other stolen historical treasures in a secret bunker owned by the insane billionaires Pramesh and Vanita Khoil. The third, split into two halves, she had discovered in the lost cities of Paititi and El Dorado in South America, where the Incas hid the riches of their toppling empire from the rapacious Spanish. A trio of crudely carved, seemingly innocuous figures.

Yet they had been found in places separated by continents, by millennia. There was no known connection between the empires of the Incas and the predynastic Egyptians. But both had hidden their statues in their most secure locations.

And now it seemed that the link was . . . Atlantis. A great empire that eleven thousand years ago had spread from a now submerged island as far east as Tibet, as far west as Brazil. They had apparently created the statues, then dispersed them to the farthest reaches of their dominion, to be passed down from one successive civilization to the next.

The question was: Why?

She fixed Hayter with an intense, all-business look. "Have you dated this section? How long before the fall of Atlantis was it written?"

Hayter was caught off guard by her abrupt change of attitude. "It, ah, let me see . . ." He flicked through his documents. "Based on your original report from five years ago, this section is, ah, around six feet along the wall from where the texts stopped. So it would have been written less than a year before Atlantis sank."

"And that section hasn't been excavated?" Her tone was almost accusing.

"You can see for yourself how big the slab blocking it is," said Hayter defensively. "It must weigh tons. And there's more debris on top of it."

"*Sharkdozer* could have cleared it if you'd let me try," said Matt.

"It would have taken too long, and the effort would be far out of proportion to the value of the find. I had to prioritize. The more time we spend bulldozing, the less there is for actual archaeology, and we could do more digging for less effort in other parts of the temple—"

"I want it cleared," said Nina firmly.

Hayter gawped at her. "W-what?" he finally spluttered. "But if we do that, we won't be able to explore the burial chamber. The support ship can only stay on station for another two weeks before it has to return to port, and if we waste time—"

"This is my decision as director of the IHA," Nina said, standing. "I want all resources dedicated to clearing the rest of that area so I can see the final texts." She turned to Matt. "How long?"

"I dunno," said the Australian, as surprised as Hayter by the turn of events. "A week, maybe more? There's a fair old pile of stones that needs to be shifted."

"Then shift them. This is top priority." She turned to leave.

Hayter jumped up. "This—this is absolutely insane! You can't reprioritize an ongoing dig on some personal whim. I know the description of these statues matches the two that Donald Bellfriar examined for the IHA, but that doesn't mean they're really the key to god-like powers!"

"If you won't do it, Lewis, I'll replace you with somebody who will. The IHA is about more than just archaeology, remember? It's also got a global security mandate, and like it or not the second of those trumps the first. I need to see those last texts. Are you with me?" Hayter could only respond with silent shock. "Good." She opened the door.

"I'm—I'll take this higher."

"You do that. But in the meantime, you'd better get back to the site. There's a lot of work to do, and I want it done fast." She left the room, the team staring after her in stunned bewilderment.

* * *

An hour later, Nina's phone rang. She jabbed at the speaker button. "I told you not to disturb me."

"Sorry, Nina," said Lola, "but Mr. Penrose is here. He says he needs to see you urgently."

Nina frowned. While Sebastian Penrose worked for the United Nations, not the IHA, his position as liaison between the UN and its cultural protection agency gave him a certain degree of authority. "Okay," she said reluctantly, "send him in."

The prim, bespectacled Englishman entered. "Afternoon, Nina."

"Sebastian. I can guess why you're here."

"I imagine everyone in the Secretariat Building heard Lewis Hayter throwing a wobbly. But as soon as he said you claimed it was a security issue, I told him to shut up until I'd had a chance to look into it. Not quite that bluntly, of course." He sat facing her. "So what's going on?"

Nina turned her laptop so he could see the screen. She had already accessed all of Hayter's research data on the ongoing excavations and was reading the full translation of the uncovered texts. "The three statues. They're Atlantean."

Penrose's eyes widened. "Are you sure?"

"Positive. They're described here . . . along with a display of something that can only be earth energy." She gave him a précis of what was written on the temple wall and how it related to the strange, not yet fully explained lines of power coursing through the planet, the effects of which she had experienced—and barely survived—on some of her previous adventures.

Now his eyes were almost larger than the lenses of his glasses. "Well. I see why you made it a security issue."

"Damn right. We know that earth energy can be incredibly dangerous in the wrong hands—and it looks like the Atlanteans knew about it eleven thousand years ago. Considering what we know about them now, that they were a race of ruthless conquerors, I don't consider *their* hands particularly safe."

Penrose rubbed his chin, thinking. "So how do you want to proceed?"

"For now, I want to do exactly what I told Lewis. We need to excavate the rest of the altar room and find out what's written in the final texts—the last records of Atlantis before it sank. If there is an earth energy connection, then we *have* to find the statues. They're too dangerous to be left in the open—especially in Stikes's hands."

"You think he might find a way to use them?"

"I'm more worried that he might sell them to someone who can. We know the Russians have the ability to build an earth energy weapon—and so does the United States, for that matter." Both nations had developed systems that could collect and focus the natural power and unleash it on a faraway target with the force of an atomic blast. "It won't work without a natural superconductor to channel the energy, but I have a horrible feeling that the statues might be exactly what they need."

"But the superconductor won't work on its own. They would also need a person who can activate the effect."

Nina knew exactly what he was suggesting. "Yeah. Someone like me."

"You know, that might . . ." He stopped.

"What?"

He hesitated before answering. "If someone did build another earth energy system, to make it work they would need the statues—and you. And if another party wanted to *stop* them from developing it, well . . ."

"They might try to kill me?" said Nina, suddenly feeling very cold even in the warm room.

"I'm just saying that this could be dangerous on a personal level, not simply as a global security issue. You're the only person in the world who is known to be able to channel earth energy. That makes you potentially extremely valuable to some people . . . and possibly a great threat to others. You need to be careful. Very careful."

"Careful?" Nina said. "After everything I've been through, it's lucky I'm not completely paranoid! But judging from what's written in the temple texts, I'm not the only person who's ever been able to channel earth energy. There was a priestess, Nantalas, who could apparently do the same thing. I guess that proves Kristian and Kari Frost were right—I really am a descendant of the Atlanteans."

"Personally, I wouldn't place much stock in the beliefs of a pair of genocidal lunatics," said Penrose. The IHA had been created in the wake of an attempt to use "pure" recovered Atlantean DNA to genetically engineer a virus that would be lethal to anyone not of that descent. The agency's task since then had been to ensure that nobody else exploited Atlantis—or any other archaeological discoveries—for similar gain. "But the idea that Atlantis could hold the key to using earth energy . . . you're right, it's definitely a concern. And I absolutely agree with your decision to make it a security matter. If there is any more information in that temple, it needs to be found."

"We need to find the statues too. And Stikes."

"I'll speak to the UN intelligence committee and try to prod its members into stepping up the search. And I'll talk to the State Department as well, make sure the CIA and National Security Agency get a reminder." He shook his head. "All those thousands of agents, billions of dollars, computers, satellites . . . and they can't find one man."

More than one, thought Nina, glancing at the photo of herself and Eddie.

She gave Penrose what additional facts she had; then the Englishman departed, leaving her alone with her thoughts. She continued reading Hayter's files, but anything further the Atlanteans had recorded about the statues remained hidden in the Temple of Poseidon . . .

The phone rang. Lola again. "Nina, there's a phone call for you."

" 'Do not disturb' is still in effect, Lola," Nina replied testily.

"I know, but I think this could be important."

Something in Lola's tone made Nina's heart pound. *Eddie!* Was it someone with news about him? Or even her husband himself, finally making contact? "Put it through!"

She waited in tense anticipation for the call to be transferred. A click of the line . . . then a voice.

It belonged to a man called Chase. But not the one she had hoped to hear.

Larry Chase, Eddie's father.

THREE

Mozambique

The bar was dimly lit at best, and the haze of smoke made it murkier still. Most of the miasma was from cigarettes, but it was bolstered by the tang of cigars and even whiffs of hashish from the darkest corners.

Eddie shot a disapproving glance toward one of the shadowed users as he stubbed out his cigarette. Secondhand smoke was one thing; secondhand narcotics, another entirely. He flicked another Marlboro out of its pack and was about to light it when he paused, gazing at his reflection in his Zippo. He had quit smoking years ago, during his first, short-lived marriage, but the strain of being on the run, perpetually alert for the approaching hand of the authorities, had seen him take up the habit once more.

He shook his head and lit the cigarette. *Nina would be furious if she knew,* he thought, a sudden gloom settling over him. There was a cellular phone on the scratched table before him, and he could talk to her with a couple of key presses . . . but he knew it wasn't possible. For one thing, any contact—on a line that was almost certainly being monitored—could see Interpol eyeing Nina as an accomplice rather than a witness.

For another, from what she had said the last time he saw her, in Peru . . . she thought he was guilty. She might not even *want* to speak to him.

So he had to prove his innocence first. Which meant finding Stikes. And doing whatever was necessary to force the truth from him—before his much-deserved death.

He looked at his watch. Strutter was, as expected, late. Tracking down contacts and wheedling information out of them, especially on a subject as risky as Stikes, wasn't something that could be done on a timetable. But the Kenyan had said earlier that he had a promising lead, so Eddie was willing to wait.

The phone rang. Strutter? No—the number on the screen was British. There was only one person in his home country who knew how to contact him. Nevertheless, he was still cautious and terse when he answered, putting a finger to his other ear to block out the tinny music coming from a tape deck behind the bar. "Yeah?"

"It's me." He knew the voice. Peter Alderley, an officer of MI6, the United Kingdom's foreign intelligence service. Not a friend, exactly—in fact, Eddie rather disliked him—but for now an uneasy ally. The murder of Mac had instilled them both with the need to uncover the truth. Alderley had given Eddie a sporting head start to escape the law in London following their comrade's funeral, and since then had provided surreptitious updates on Interpol's search for him during their intermittent contacts.

In return, Eddie had provided Alderley with what information he had uncovered on his travels, and was hoping he had managed to do something useful with it. "What've you got?"

"First thing: Interpol is getting closer to you. They know you were just in Botswana."

"Do they know where I am now?"

"No, but if I were you I'd move on. Sharpish."

"That's the plan anyway—I'm just waiting to find out where to go. What else?"

"That paper you found in Jindal's flat, the one with a number and some Hindi text. I've had it checked out—on the quiet, obviously, which is why it took so long. The number could mean anything, of course, but my best guess is the international code for a Greek phone number."

"Greek?" Eddie was surprised. He couldn't imagine any possible link between Kit and Greece.

"Yeah. I tried ringing it, but it's a dead number. The thing is, though, the text with it translates as 'and the best of the greatest.' I think what we've got here is a fairly simple code. The 'best of the greatest' is probably another number, so if you add that to the one you already have, you get the real result."

"So what's the other number?"

"Damned if I know. Something significant to Jindal, at a guess. You knew him far better than I did—any idea what it might be?"

Eddie thought about Kit. Youthful, handsome, an idealistic Indian cop who had specialized in the investigation of art thefts before transferring to Interpol to do the same thing in a worldwide jurisdiction. Cheery and good-natured but with steely determination behind his smile, a cricket fan, a Hindu, not as stylish a dresser as he thought he was. A friend.

A friend who had killed another friend in cold blood. Eddie hadn't witnessed it personally, but when he pieced together everything seen by others there was only one possible conclusion.

Kit had murdered Mac in order to let Stikes escape from El Dorado. He had shot the elderly Scot twice in the back and left him to die.

What Eddie couldn't fathom was *why*. Why had the Interpol officer suddenly turned against his friends and the law he had pledged to uphold? Why had he struck a deal with Stikes, a man who just days earlier had tortured him? Blackmail? Brainwashing? Eddie didn't know.

And Stikes wasn't the only one of Eddie's enemies

with whom Kit was involved. When Eddie confronted him at the pumping station, he had found not only Kit making a deal with Stikes, but also someone he thought was dead. His ex-wife, Sophia Blackwood. Aristocrat, murderer, terrorist . . . and seemingly in charge, negotiating with the mercenary and giving Kit orders.

Eddie couldn't reconcile the friend he thought he knew with the man who had tried to kill him. The contradictions made it impossible for him to get a handle on Kit's thought processes. "I dunno," he told Alderley at last. "I just don't know."

"Well, keep thinking about it. Maybe you'll come up with something. I'll have another poke through Interpol's file on him to see if anything suggests itself."

"Just don't attract any attention. If you get busted, it'll make it a real pain in the arse for me to stay ahead of the cops."

"Glad you've got my best interests at heart," Alderley snarked. "But I want to know what happened as much as you do. If I find out something new, I'll be in touch—and you do the same if you hear anything."

"Will do. And . . . thanks."

"I can't exactly say it's my pleasure, for all sorts of reasons, but I appreciate hearing that. Don't get caught, okay?"

Alderley disconnected. Eddie put down the phone, then tapped the growing length of ash from the end of his cigarette and took a drag. *The best of the greatest.* But who or what *was* the greatest in Kit's mind?

He thought back three months. One of his first ports of call after fleeing Peru, and then England after paying his last respects to both his late grandmother and Mac, had been India. Eddie had broken into the young cop's apartment to find it had already been searched by Interpol officers trying to learn more about the circumstances of his death. Suspecting that Kit would have kept his secrets hidden in a way his colleagues wouldn't expect, he had eventually discovered something concealed in plain sight. Interpol had taken Kit's laptop and printer but left the latter's paper . . . and written on the bottom sheet, Eddie found words in Hindi and a number.

Alderley had to be right. It was a code, one that could give him the answers he wanted. But without the clue he needed to crack it, it was worthless . . .

The music changed: the opening bars of Lynyrd Skynyrd's "Free Bird." One of Eddie's favorite records, but on this occasion it filled him with an unexpected melancholy. At one time, it had been a symbol of his wanderlust and desire for action when he felt stifled by the demands of his relationship with Nina and an office job at the IHA. Now, though, a life of everyday domesticity with her was the thing he wanted most in the world. Longing pulled at his heart . . .

"Eddie, my friend!" Strutter's voice jerked him back to grim reality. He looked around to see the middleman approaching, wearing an electric blue suit and a purple silk shirt beneath it.

"You found some new threads, then," said Eddie as Strutter sat opposite him.

"I have an image to maintain." He regarded Eddie's beard. "You should consider yours too."

Eddie shrugged. "I dunno, I like it. Makes me look distinguished."

"More like disreputable. But as for myself, I wouldn't attract many clients in prison rags, would I?"

"Lose much business while you were away?"

"In Africa, there is *always* business for mercenaries. I'm already getting back into the heart of the storm. It takes more than Zimbabwean thugs to keep down Johnny Strutter!" Registering Eddie's thoroughly unimpressed expression, he became more muted. "But you no longer want to be part of that world, do you, my friend? A shame—you always were a very good fighter. Still, there will be plenty of work for Maximov." He tapped his forehead. "Not too smart, but the man is like a walking tank!"

"I'm only interested in Stikes," Eddie said impatiently. "Do you know where he is or not?"

Strutter leaned closer. "No. But," he added quickly, "I know someone who does. I put the word out to my contacts, and I heard back from a man in Yemen, who had spoken to another man in Pakistan—"

"I don't care who talked to who. I just want to know what they said."

The sharpness in Eddie's voice warned Strutter to stick to the facts. "Okay, okay. There is an American called Scarber, Madeline Scarber, in Hong Kong. She knows where Stikes is."

"So where is he?"

Strutter shifted uncomfortably. "Well, the thing is, my friend . . . she would not tell me. She will tell you—but only in person."

Eddie had never heard of Madeline Scarber, and didn't like that the reverse was apparently not the case. "Why?"

"I don't know. But that's what she told me."

"How do you know she's not working for Interpol? Or Stikes, for that matter?"

Strutter shook his head. "People I trust have vouched for her."

"The only people you trust are on banknotes, Strutter," Eddie said scathingly. "You've spoken to her?"

"Yes."

"Recently? Like, just now?"

"Before I came here, yes."

"Call her. I want to talk to her."

The Kenyan wasn't happy at the prospect. "I don't know if that is a good idea."

"Flying all the way to Hong Kong to meet someone I don't even know on your say-so isn't a good fucking idea either. Make the call."

Strutter reluctantly acquiesced. After a brief exchange, he held his phone out to Eddie. "She'll talk to you."

"Good." He took it. "Madeline Scarber?"

"Speaking" came a dry, rasping voice. Scarber was clearly a chain-smoker; she sounded quite old.

"I'm told you've got some information for me. About Alexander Stikes."

"You betcha. I know where he is now, and where he'll be for the next couple of days."

The silence that followed became long enough for Eddie to think that the connection had been lost, until he heard Scarber cough faintly. "So . . . you going to tell me, or what?"

"Or what, I'm afraid. For now. I'll tell you how to find Stikes, but I want you to do something for me in return."

"My rates are two hundred quid an hour, and you provide the condoms," Eddie said irritatedly. "Kissing costs extra." Scarber made a sound that could have been a laugh. "Whatever you want me to do, I'm sure you could find someone to do it in Hong Kong. All I want is information."

"And you'll get it. But only face-to-face. And I'd get here pronto, if I were you. When Stikes leaves, I don't know where he'll go. Call me on this number when you arrive. See you soon, kiddo."

"Arse," Eddie muttered as the phone went silent. He wrote down the number, then returned it to Strutter. "Was she the only lead you had on Stikes?" The other man nodded. "I might have fucking guessed."

"What did she say?"

"She wants me to do some job for her before she'll tell me anything."

"What job?"

"I don't know. And I doubt it'll be anything good either." He blew out a frustrated breath. "Looks like I'm going to Hong Kong. Phooey."

FOUR
New York City

Nina entered the restaurant with some trepidation. The last time she shared a meal with Larry Chase, the evening had not gone well. Eddie had been estranged from him for over twenty years, the reunion taking place only at Nina's urging . . . and father and son immediately resumed old hostilities, to the point of almost coming to blows.

And according to Eddie's sister, Elizabeth, when the two men briefly met again shortly after Eddie had gone on the run, their conflict indeed became a physical one.

Nina knew that Eddie had met Larry in the Colombian capital a few days before the fateful night at the Peruvian pumping station. Whatever they had discussed, though, he kept to himself. But despite his closed mouth, it was clearly something Eddie had considered very serious.

In all honesty, if not for this black hole in events, Nina probably wouldn't have agreed to meet her father-in-law and his second wife at all. While she found Julie Chase pleasant enough, Larry's arrogance was far less appealing. But there was the possibility of learning what had happened in Bogotá, which might provide new insight into subsequent events . . . and there was also a chance, however small, that Larry could have news about Eddie.

Larry and Julie were already seated, and the maître d' guided Nina to their table. "Nina, hi!" Julie chirped. "Great to see you again."

"Hi, you too," she replied as Larry stood to greet her. She somewhat awkwardly accepted his kiss on the cheek, then sat facing the couple. Even the restaurant's low lighting couldn't hide the age gap between them; Julie was over twenty years younger than her husband. "This is, uh . . . kind of a surprise."

"We're here on holiday," Larry announced. "Doing a quick tour—New York, New England, San Francisco."

"Sounds like fun. Though I'm not sure you picked the best time of year for it. September would have had much better weather than November."

"Well, to tell the truth," said Larry, leaning closer in an exaggeratedly conspiratorial way, "I'm attending an international logistics conference in Frisco, but I'm claiming the whole trip as a business expense. Just don't tell the taxman, eh?" He laughed, Julie joining in with a giggle. Nina put on a thin smile.

"But I've wanted to come to the States for ages," added Julie. "We're going skiing in Vermont, which sounds lovely."

"I'm flying us to the lodge," Larry bragged.

Nina was surprised. "You're a pilot?"

"Oh yes. Helicopters. Tremendous fun."

"He's *not* a pilot," said Julie, teasing. "I bought him a flying lesson for his birthday last year, and now he thinks he's Airwolf. He's only done it four times."

"Five times," Larry corrected.

"No, I'm sure it's—wait, did you go on a flight without me?"

"Yes, when I took Jim and David from the golf club up for a spin last month. I told you about it." Julie's slightly hurt expression suggested to Nina that he hadn't. "Anyway, yes, I'll be flying us up there."

"I'm sure it'll be great," said Nina, not especially caring. "But you came to New York first?"

"You have to see New York when you visit the States, don't you? I think it's mandatory now, like having your fingerprints taken at immigration." He shook his head. "The stories I've heard from American immigration officers about how useless that whole system is . . ."

"I'm sure Nina's not interested in talking shop, love," chided Julie. She turned to the redhead. "So what have you been doing since we last saw you?"

Despite her best efforts, Nina couldn't hold back her sarcasm. "Well, I discovered the lost city of El Dorado, and then my husband disappeared and is now wanted for murder."

There was an awkward silence.

"I'm . . . I'm sorry," Nina eventually said. "It's just that the last three months have been . . . stressful. To say the least."

"No, no, don't apologize—I shouldn't have asked such a silly question," Julie said sympathetically. "It must have been horrible."

"It still is. But thanks."

"Have you . . . have you heard from Eddie? Or anything about him?"

"No. Not directly," Nina replied, the sudden bitterness behind the words surprising even her. "According to Interpol he's alive, but beyond that I don't know."

"I'm sorry." Julie looked at her husband as if expecting him to follow up her question, but he offered nothing.

A waiter glided over to the table, asking if they were ready to order. Larry shooed him away. Nina turned her gaze to her father-in-law. "You actually last saw Eddie after I did, in England. Elizabeth told me about it, but . . . what about you? Why did Eddie hit you?"

Larry was annoyed to be reminded. "He caught me off guard," he said, unconsciously raising a hand to rub a long-faded bruise on his jaw. "Unbelievable. Right after Catherine's burial service, too. I can't believe he was so disrespectful."

Nina knew that was the last thing Eddie would have wanted to do; of all his family members in England, he had been closest to his late grandmother by far. "He must have had some reason to be so angry at you."

"God knows what," Larry said huffily. "He shows up out of the blue, starts ranting on at me, and then *pow!* Smacks me in the mouth."

Nina raised a quizzical eyebrow. "Ranting? About what?"

"About some friend of his who'd died."

"Do you mean Mac? Jim McCrimmon?"

"Yeah, him. He blamed me for it, for God knows what reason."

She gave him a deeply suspicious look. "And why would Eddie do that? Was it anything to do with when he met you in Bogotá?"

Larry said nothing, but Julie rounded on him. "Wait, you met Eddie in Colombia? You didn't tell me about that!"

"I'm sure I mentioned it," Larry said uncomfortably.

Scowling, the blonde turned away from her husband to address Nina. "I'm trying to remember what Eddie said—I'm sorry, I was so surprised to see him, and the whole thing happened so fast, I didn't really get it all. But he said . . ." Her frown deepened with the effort of mental dredging. "He said Larry talked to someone about you, about El Dorado—and then this guy turned up there."

"Stikes?" Nina suggested.

"Yes, that's it! Stikes."

Now it was Nina's turn to round on Larry. "You talked to *Stikes*? About me?"

"He was a client of mine," Larry replied defensively.

"He was *what*?" The last word came out as an angry yelp, drawing the attention of other diners. She dropped her voice to a furious whisper. "You were working for Alexander goddamn Stikes?"

"I told Edward the same thing I'm going to tell you," said Larry, bristling. "He was just a client who asked me to arrange the shipping of some goods on behalf of *his* clients. His company was a legitimate British business, and none of the goods were illegal or on any international watch lists. So I did nothing wrong." He slapped both hands down on the table for emphasis. *"Nothing."*

Nina was already putting the pieces together, and not liking the picture they formed. "And these clients of his: They wouldn't have been General Salbatore Callas and Francisco de Quesada, would they?"

The answer emerged with considerable reluctance. "Yes."

"A murderer who tried to overthrow the Venezuelan president, and a drug lord?"

"What they do for a living isn't my business," Larry protested. "Do postmen carry out background checks before they give someone their mail?"

"Postmen don't pick and choose who they deliver to," Nina countered. "You do." She thought for a moment, still fuming. "I didn't know about any of this—but Eddie must have, before he saw you in Bogotá. What happened?"

The waiter reappeared. "Not now," Larry snapped before continuing with bad grace: "All right, yes, I made a delivery to de Quesada in Colombia."

"Let me guess," Nina cut in. "Two Incan artifacts, one of which was made of solid gold and weighed about two tons?"

"It was a hell of a job to transport, let me tell you," said Larry almost with pride, before the glares of the two women reminded him to stick to the point. "But I made the delivery and de Quesada was impressed at how quickly I'd arranged everything, so I gave him my card in case he might put any future work my way. But I didn't think any more of it—until Edward turned up at my hotel. With my business card. He threatened that if I didn't give my entire fee to charity, he was going to turn the card—with my fingerprints on it, obviously—over to

Interpol and have me implicated in whatever the hell was going on."

"That would be murder, robbery, an attempted coup, and drug smuggling," Nina reminded him. "Just to start with."

"None of which had anything to do with me! But do you have any idea how much being accused of involvement in that sort of thing could damage my business? Obviously I was worried—and I don't take threats lying down, especially not from my own son. So I called Stikes to see if there was anything he could do to fix the situation."

"And . . . what? You told him that we were searching for El Dorado in Peru?"

A pause, Larry choosing his words with care. "It came up," he admitted. "Stikes asked about you—I didn't think anything of it," he said defensively as Nina's look darkened. "He wanted to know where you were. I assumed it was because he might want to straighten things out with you."

While for the most part Larry did not resemble his son physically, being taller and thinner-faced, their eyes were all but identical, and Nina knew one of Eddie's subtle expressions well enough to recognize the same on his father: He was dissembling. "But you must have known that Eddie and Stikes weren't exactly old army buddies."

"Not until Edward told me," Larry insisted. "When Stikes first contacted me, he said he was actually a friend of his, and that Edward had recommended me to him for a job."

"And you believed him? After what happened when we had dinner at your house?"

"I thought that maybe Edward was trying to apologize by sending me a potential client. Clearly I was wrong."

"But after Eddie told you, you still spoke to Stikes anyway?" Nina's voice became accusing. "Did you think that he might, I don't know, make your problem *go away*?"

It took Julie a moment to realize what she was implying, and when Nina's veiled meaning struck her she gasped. Larry, on the other hand, got it immediately; the reason for his delayed response was pure outrage. "Of *course* that's not what I thought," he said in a low growl. "That's just— Christ, no, that's not it at all! I can't believe you'd even—"

Nina's own anger was rising. "That's what happened, though. People *died* in Peru, Larry, a lot of people— because *you* told Stikes that I was there. Eddie's friend— my friend too—was killed. Murdered." She rose from her seat, once again attracting the attention of other diners, but ignoring them. "So now do you know why Eddie was so mad at you? It was *your fault,* Larry! If you hadn't called Stikes in order to cover your own ass, all those people would still be alive!"

"But how could I *know*?" Larry cried, the words somewhere between a demand and a plea. "I had no idea any of that would happen!"

"Well, of course you didn't. Because that would have meant thinking beyond yourself, wouldn't it?" She shoved back her chair. "Julie, every time we've met dinner's ended in an argument. I'm sorry, it's not your fault. But you, Larry . . ." She gave him a look of utter disgust. "What you've done, it's . . . unforgivable." Without a further word, she turned and walked away.

Julie blushed crimson under the eyes of the other patrons, leaving Larry to shift awkwardly in his seat. The waiter hesitantly returned. "I, er, think we'll call it a night," the Englishman told him, tossing a couple of bills on the table. Julie was already on her feet as Larry stood up to leave.

FIVE

Nina emerged from the elevator and made her way to the IHA's offices, still angry about what she had learned the previous evening. All the deaths at El Dorado, the destruction of a priceless archaeological site . . . everything had happened because of Larry Chase. A few words to the wrong person had ended dozens of lives. And for what? Nothing more than money. The mere thought stoked her fury once more.

"Uh-oh," said Lola Gianetti from the watercooler.

Nina stopped. "Uh-oh what? What is it?" She gave Lola a worried look; her assistant was seven months pregnant and, judging from the size of her bump, the baby was impatient to leave its increasingly cramped accommodation. "Was it a kick? Or a contraction? It wasn't a contraction, was it?"

Lola laughed. "No, I'm fine. The *uh-oh* was for you. You've got that look again."

"What look?"

"The look that warns everyone they should stay out of your way."

"I don't have a look," Nina protested as the big-haired

blonde padded back to the reception desk. "Do I? What does the look look like?"

"That was almost a tongue twister," said Lola, sitting. "But . . . well, you'd know it when you saw it. Everyone else does."

"*Everyone* thinks I have a look? Oh, great," Nina said, exasperated. "I thought I was a half-decent boss, but apparently I'm some terrifying flame-haired Medusa stalking the halls with her deadly *look*."

"Only occasionally," Lola said with a teasing smile. "By the way, Mr. Penrose asked me to call him when you arrived. He wants to see you."

"Tell him I'm here," said Nina, starting for her office.

"Okay. Oh, by the way, how was your dinner with Eddie's dad?" Nina glowered at her. "There's the look again," Lola said, hurriedly picking up the phone.

Penrose was in Nina's office less than ten minutes later. "There's been a development regarding the statues."

"What kind of development?"

"They've been found."

Her eyes widened. "Stikes has been caught?"

"I'm afraid not. But they're secure, and apparently intact. They're in Japan."

"Japan? Who's got them?"

"Do you know of a man called Takashi Seiji?" Nina shook her head. "He's a Japanese businessman, the head of Takashi Industries."

"Never heard of it."

"I'm not really surprised—it's the kind of company that owns dozens of other companies that you probably *have* heard of. But that's not important. What does matter is that he has all three statues. Here." He handed her a color printout; it showed the trio of crudely carved figurines inside a display case.

Nina examined the picture closely. As far as she could tell, the statues were in the same condition as when she had last seen them. "What's his interest in them?"

"He owns one of them."

She was startled. "What?"

Penrose gave her another picture. In this there was only a single statue, the one discovered in the Khoils' underground vault in Greenland. There was a date stamp in one corner: over ten years earlier. "He also supplied all the necessary certificates of ownership. It was stolen from him last year. Apparently by the same group that stole Michelangelo's *David* and the Talonor Codex."

"Working for the Khoils," Nina remembered. "But wait—Interpol tried to track down the owners of everything they'd stolen, and nobody ever claimed the statue. If he'd reported the theft, they would have returned it to him. Why didn't he say anything?"

"No idea. But there was a Japanese connection, as I recall—that exporter in Singapore got something out of the country for the Khoils."

"The statue?"

"Possibly. But this is why Mr. Takashi wants to meet you."

"He's coming here? Is he bringing the statues?"

He hesitated. "Ah . . . actually, no. He wants you to see him. In Japan. He's a recluse who doesn't like traveling. Supposedly, he rarely leaves his penthouse."

"Who does he think he is, Howard Hughes?" Nina frowned, weighing up her options. On the one hand, she was already busy enough without adding a trip across the Pacific; on the other, it meant the possibility of finally uncovering the secret of the statues . . . "How did he get hold of them?"

"Via the black market, it seems."

Disgust entered her voice. "Can we even trust this guy? Buying stolen antiquities on the black market isn't exactly ethical."

"Mr. Takashi might be reclusive," said Penrose, "but he's also a major contributor to a number of United Nations charitable programs. The UN certainly trusts him. Besides, he's told us that he'll return the other two statues to their countries. But first he wants you to examine them, to confirm that they're genuine—and also to tell you what he knows about his statue."

"There are these marvelous new inventions called telephones. Has he heard of them?"

Penrose smiled. "What can I say, Nina? Maybe he's just a fan of yours. But we definitely think you should go. Securing the statues will ease the minds of a number of concerned people, and you might even learn something new about them."

He was right, Nina decided reluctantly. "He's definitely willing to give the other statues back to Egypt and Peru? No conditions?"

"Apparently that's so. His main concern was reclaiming his own property, but he said he bought the others as well to get them back into the right hands."

"How much did he pay for them?"

"I don't know, but . . . a large sum, I imagine."

"Which is probably now in Stikes's pocket. Great," she said glumly. "When does he want to see me?"

"He said that's up to you," said Penrose, "but from the IHA's point of view, the sooner the better. If the statues are off the market, that's one security issue we no longer need to worry about."

She considered it. "Okay, I'll go see him. Once this is wrapped up, I can focus on the Atlantis excavations."

Penrose nodded. "A sound choice. I'll let Mr. Takashi know."

He left the office, and Nina picked up her phone. "Lola. I need you to book a flight for me."

* * *

Half a world away, Eddie had completed a flight of his own, and was making a taxi journey through the bustling streets of Hong Kong. He had visited the former British colony several times before, and was always amazed by the island's energy and vibrancy, a hothouse for deal making and fast action. It was a vanguard for the new China, raw entrepreneurial capitalism working at a merciless pace that shocked even Americans. Anyone who wasn't constantly clawing their way up like the ever-climbing skyscrapers very quickly got trampled.

But this time, the city's rush was nothing more than a background hum. There was only one thing on his mind. The taxi deposited him at a corner near the address he had been given, and he carved his way like an icebreaker through the crowds filling the narrow, advertising-banner-filled street to reach one particular door. He found the buzzer for the apartment and pushed it. After a pause, a female voice spoke in Cantonese.

"It's Eddie Chase," he said.

The voice switched to English. "You made it. Come on in. Sixth floor, on the left." The door latch clacked, and he entered the building.

There was no elevator, so he pounded up the cramped stairwell to the sixth floor. A woman opened the door as he reached it. "Come inside."

There was no mistaking Madeline Scarber's sand-paper-throated voice, but its owner was very different from Eddie's preconceptions. For a start, her name had led him to assume that she was Caucasian, but the short, skeletal woman with the helmet like black bob was of Chinese descent. She was also younger than he had imagined, around fifty rather than the pensioner her gravelly growl suggested. "Not what you expected, huh?" she said as she ushered him inside. "My mother was Chinese German, and she married a Dutch American. I'm a one-woman melting pot."

More like a one-woman ashtray, Eddie thought as the all-pervading reek of stale cigarette smoke hit him, but he kept it to himself. Scarber closed the door and followed him into a lounge. The room was expensively furnished in stark black and white, a glimpse of the harbor visible through the window between two much taller apartment blocks. She waved for him to sit on a stylish but, as it turned out, not especially comfortable leather couch. "So you're here, kiddo. I guess you want to know what I want from you in return for telling you how to find Alexander Stikes."

"It'd crossed my mind."

Scarber lit a cigarette, then almost as an afterthought offered him one. "We'd like you to do something for us."

"*We?*" Eddie asked as she held out her expensive lighter.

"The people I represent. We have a mutual enemy."

"Stikes?"

She shook her head. "Stikes is part of it, but no big deal to us."

"He is to me."

"I know. Which is why my proposal will benefit us both."

He leaned back and blew out smoke. "So get to the point, then. What's the job?"

Scarber slowly paced across the lounge, a line of smoke trailing behind her. "Stikes stole something from your wife—three stone figures."

Eddie stiffened. "Those statues?" he snapped. "For fuck's sake! You know how many people have died because of those fucking things—and now you want me to get them for you?"

"No. We don't want you to get them. We want you to *destroy* them."

It took him a second to get over his surprise. "Now, that's more like it."

"We both know that the statues have unusual properties—properties that could be very dangerous if they fall into the hands of the wrong people. That can't be allowed to happen."

"And how do you know that?"

"I've got access to certain classified information. Including the IHA's files on earth energy."

He shot her a mistrustful look. "You're a spook, aren't you? CIA?"

"Former spook," Scarber replied. "Now I'm what you might call a freelancer."

"Not a big fan of spooks. Been fucked over by them a few times. They tend to lie about what they're really doing."

The accusation didn't bother her. "Nature of the business, kiddo."

"So what *is* your business? Why're you so keen to destroy the statues? Who are you working for?"

"That doesn't matter."

"Oh, it bloody does."

She abruptly crossed back to him, face hardening. "Do you want to know where Stikes is or not? This is the situation: We want the statues destroyed. Stikes has the statues. You want to kill Stikes. It's a simple enough proposition—we tell you where he is, you find him, destroy the statues . . . and then you can do whatever you want with him. We'll even pay you. How does half a million dollars sound?"

"I'd kill Stikes for free . . . but yeah, half a mil sounds pretty good," said Eddie. He had spent the last three months hunting for Stikes, and this was by far the closest he had come to tracking down his nemesis. However, there were too many aspects of the deal he didn't like, not least Scarber's secrecy about her employer. "But . . ."

"There's something else we can offer," she said, seeing his hesitancy. "We can make the charges against you go away. Completely. You'll be able to go home. To your wife."

Eddie was silent for a long moment. "How can you manage that?"

"Let's just say my employers have a lot of influence."

His suspicion returned. "Then why do they need me to do this job?"

"Because you're very highly motivated. I've read your IHA file too; you're extremely good at what you do. If anyone can get to Stikes, you can."

"So I take it he's not just hanging out by a pool somewhere. Where is he?"

"Do we have a deal?"

He considered it . . . then nodded. "Where's Stikes?"

"Japan. Tokyo, specifically. But he'll be hard to reach. We can get you into the building, but you'll have to make your own way to him from there."

"What building?"

Scarber finished her cigarette. "The headquarters of Takashi Industries."

SIX

Tokyo

It was Nina's first visit to Japan, and she looked out at the sprawling city from the limo that had collected her from Narita Airport with great interest. As a New Yorker, she was no stranger to tall buildings, but the differences between those of her home and Tokyo intrigued her, not least the way that some rooftops were home to so many garish billboards and advertising banners that they resembled clipper ships, about to set sail across the urban sea.

One building stood out—not because it was festooned with signs, but instead because several wind turbines rose gracefully above its roof. She guessed it to be around fifty stories tall, nothing remarkable by New York standards, but enough to put it in the upper ranks of this earthquake-prone country's structures. An illuminated logo stood out near its summit. A stylized *T*, the letter drawn with the flowing strokes of Japanese calligraphy.

The same logo appeared on the letter the bowing limo driver had presented to her at the airport. A greeting from Takashi Seiji, apologizing for not meeting her in person. Instead, the industrialist had written to humbly request—the exact words of the letter—that she meet him at his penthouse.

To her surprise, it turned out that the penthouse was above the corporate headquarters. Takashi was apparently so dedicated to his work, he literally lived at the office.

The skyscraper was set back from the streets, surrounded by an expanse of perfectly manicured lawn. Knowing that Tokyo real estate was among the most expensive in the world, Nina recognized something so simple as a patch of grass as making a subtle yet powerful statement: *Yes, we can afford this.* Having done a little research during the flight, she knew that Penrose was right about the company's being a major force in Japan. Takashi himself was the third-generation leader of the business, and in the forty years he had been in charge he had taken it to heights that even his successful father and grandfather could not have dreamed of.

The limo pulled up at one of the building's entrances, the driver opening the door for Nina and bowing again as she got out. A young Japanese man in a crisp Italian suit came to meet her, bowing even lower before extending his hand. "Good afternoon, Dr. Wilde," he said. There was a faint West Coast accent to his English. "I'm Kojima Kenichi, Takashi-san's secretary. I hope you had a pleasant journey."

"A little short notice, but yes, thank you." She'd had an extremely nice surprise at JFK when she discovered she had been upgraded to first class, courtesy of Takashi.

"I'm glad to hear it. Please, follow me—don't worry about your bags, you'll be taken to your hotel after the meeting." Another bow, then he started for the entrance. Nina followed.

Kojima led her to a marble reception desk in the lobby—where she was startled to discover that the figure behind it was not human. The receptionist was actually a robot, designed to look like a young and pretty Japanese woman. The illusion was convincing enough for Nina to have reached the desk before noticing something was amiss, but now that she knew, she found the replicant's slightly stiff movements and glassy eyes unsettling. The robot turned toward her and spoke Japanese in a high, girlie voice.

"Uh . . . what do I do?" she asked Kojima, who appeared amused by her discomfiture.

The robot bowed its head and spoke again, this time in a distinctly lower register. "My apologies, madam. I did not know you spoke English. May I take your name, please?"

"Nina Wilde?" Nina offered hesitantly.

The robot's mouth pulled into a smile. "Thank you, you are expected. Mr. Takashi is waiting for you. If you will please take your visitor's pass and wear it at all times while you are in the building?" Its hand gestured toward a slot set into the marble desktop, from which emerged a laminated card bearing Nina's name and photograph—which, she realized with unease, must have been taken just moments before by a camera in one of the robot's eyes. She picked up the card, finding it still warm from whatever gadget had produced it, and clipped it to her jacket. "Please go to elevator number one," the simulacrum told her. "Have a nice day."

Nina stepped away from the desk with haste. "Well, that was . . . creepy," she said. "Aren't there any, y'know, *real* people who could do that?"

Kojima smiled as they crossed the lobby. "Takashi is a world leader in robotics. One of the best ways to test our new technology is to put it on the front line, so to speak. Also, Takashi-san only employs the best and brightest people, and believes that hiring such people for menial work would be a waste of their potential."

"Uh-huh," said Nina noncommittally, wondering how Lola would react to having her job described as "menial." To her mind it seemed better to provide a person with work and a wage than to spend God knew how much money building a freaky robot to do the same thing, but then, she reflected, that was probably why she wasn't the head of a multibillion-dollar company. "So, before I meet Mr. Takashi, is there anything I should know? I haven't had much time to brush up on Japanese etiquette."

They approached a bank of elevators, one of which was separated from the rest and guarded by two uniformed men—who were, to Nina's relief, genuine human beings and not robots. "Don't worry about it, Dr. Wilde," said Kojima. "You are Takashi-san's honored guest. You would have to work very hard to offend him."

"I'll try not to anyway," she said as they reached the guards. She expected them to check her identity, but instead a line of laser light from a sensor above the door danced briefly over a barcode on her pass. The absence of alarms and sirens satisfied the two men that she was approved to enter, and they bowed to her before moving aside.

"This is Takashi-san's private elevator," said Kojima as the doors opened and they entered. Despite the building's height, there were only three buttons on the control panel. He pushed the topmost. "It only serves the parking garage, the lobby, and the penthouse. But," he continued as the car started to rise, accelerating quickly enough for Nina to feel it in the pit of her stomach, "he rarely uses it these days."

"So it's true he hardly ever leaves the penthouse? Why?"

"I wouldn't presume to speak for Takashi-san. But I'm sure he will tell you if you ask."

Nina was indeed curious, but she had more important questions for the reclusive industrialist. Before long, the elevator stopped. "Follow me, please," said Kojima.

The hallway of Takashi's penthouse was decorated with pale wall panels intercut with beams of contrasting dark hardwood, the floor varnished and polished to a lacquered shine. It was austere and minimalist, yet clearly extremely expensive. Windows to one side looked out across the sunset sprawl of Tokyo, the white peak of Mount Fuji visible in the distance. "That's a hell of a view," she said, feeling a twinge of vertigo.

They passed several doors before arriving at the end of the hall. Kojima knocked on the double oak doors there, waiting for several seconds until hearing a reply from within and opening them. With another bow, he gestured for Nina to enter.

The room beyond ran the entire width of the sky-scraper, windows on three sides providing a panoramic view of the city. Despite its size, it was sparsely appointed, with more potted plants than items of furniture. A large desk was the focal point, a single elegant chair placed before it.

Behind the desk was Takashi Seiji.

The official photograph Nina had seen on the company website was considerably out of date. She guessed him to be in his seventies, at least twenty years older than his public face. He was bald but for thin gray wisps above his ears, wrinkles and bags narrowing his eyes to sleepy slits. However, there was nothing remotely tired about his gaze, which locked on to Nina as she entered the room. He stood, revealing a hunched, but still strong, figure.

Kojima guided Nina to the desk, then spoke to Takashi in Japanese. She recognized her name among the words. The old man said nothing, but bowed deeply, so far that she thought his head would touch the desk. When he straightened again, he spoke, his secretary translating. "Welcome to Japan, Dr. Wilde. I am most honored by your presence."

"Thank you, Mr. Takashi," she replied. "It's my pleasure to be here."

Kojima relayed this to his boss, who sat back down and nodded at the solitary chair. "Please take a seat," Kojima told her.

Nina did so. The plain wooden chair looked as ascetic

as the rest of the room, but turned out to be surprisingly comfortable. "Would you care for any refreshment before we begin?" Kojima asked. "Tea, coffee?"

"No, thank you, I'm fine," she said. "I'd like to get down to business."

Takashi made a small sound of amusement before Kojima could translate for him. He understood English? "Takashi-san appreciates your attitude," the younger man told her after his boss spoke. "The Japanese obsession with protocol slows down business and wastes too much time."

"And at my age, time is a more precious resource than money," Takashi added. Though he had a strong accent, his English was precise. He smiled slightly. "My apologies, Dr. Wilde. Speaking through a translator is another protocol that is expected. But now that I see you have as little patience as I for such things, we can continue in a more efficient manner."

"What would you have done if I'd asked for coffee?" Nina asked mischievously.

"Since a leisurely pace would have made you more comfortable, I would have continued speaking through my secretary. But no matter. You are here on business, so now we can discuss it." He nodded to Kojima, who bowed and retreated to the outskirts of the room. "I imagine you have many questions."

"I do," she replied. "First, you said that you own one of the statues. Where did it come from?"

"Kojima-kun can provide you with a full written account of its known history, but to summarize, it came from Tibet into China during the reign of the Chenghua Emperor, in the Ming dynasty."

Tibet: where one of the farthest—and last—outposts of the Atlantean empire had been established. That tied in with her theory that the Atlanteans had, for whatever reason, dispersed the statues as widely as they could. "Fifteenth century, I believe?"

"Yes. It remained in the possession of successive emperors until the Japanese occupation of China before the Second World War. It was brought to Japan along with other treasures, where it passed through the hands of several private collectors before I obtained it in 2002."

"What was your interest in it?" Nina decided to tread carefully and avoid mentioning anything about the statue's special properties unless Takashi himself brought the subject up. The United Nations might have trusted him, but she was still going to reserve judgment for the moment.

"There is a legend about the statue, Dr. Wilde," said Takashi. "It is supposed to contain great power, but a power that can only be used by a chosen few. The power of the earth itself."

The intensity of his gaze suggested to Nina that he was expecting a response from her, confirmation that she knew exactly what he was talking about. She kept her expression and voice neutral. "What kind of power?"

"It has many names in different cultures. Inyodo, Feng Shui, dragon lines, ley lines, telluric currents, chi . . . all are the same thing. A network of lines of power generated by the earth itself, a natural source of energy. Just as blood flows through our veins, so this energy flows through the world around us. The life force of the planet, you might say. I have been fascinated by the concept ever since I was a child, and I first heard the legend of the statue over thirty years ago. When the statue came on the market, I had to have it. I had to find out if the legend was true."

"And what did you find?"

"Nothing." He shook his head. "I had the stone analyzed. It was unusual, apparently a meteorite, but it did not possess any special properties. At least, not that *I* could find."

Again, Nina refused to take the bait. "So you bought it and kept it . . . until it was stolen."

A grunt of annoyance. "Yes. I had a second property at the time where I kept my collection of antiquities. It was robbed, very professionally—but the robbers took only the statue and left other items of far greater value. I believe you also encountered these thieves."

"Yes, I did," she said, recalling a mad chase through San Francisco to recover a stolen Atlantean artifact. "They were employed by Pramesh and Vanita Khoil."

Takashi nodded. "I was told they used their Internet technology to intercept people's private communications. I imagine that is how they learned about my statue. But that raises a question."

"Why they wanted it in the first place?"

"Yes. For them to have gone to such lengths to steal it, the statue must be of greater importance than it appears to be."

Nina had another question. "Why didn't you report it stolen? When it was recovered from the Khoils, you could have gotten it back from Interpol. Rather than buying it on the black market."

"You do not approve, Dr. Wilde?"

"No. It just encourages the illegal trading of antiquities—if thieves know they can get a high price for what they've stolen, they'll keep on doing it."

"On this occasion, I had no choice. There were other interested parties, and I could not let the statue—the statues, all three—fall into their possession."

"Which other interested parties?"

"That is no longer important. What matters is that I now have them." Takashi stood. "In answer to your question," he told her as he slowly walked around the table, "I did not report the theft of my statue because even though I have rightful ownership, there are those who want it taken from me and returned to China. For the sake of diplomacy—and their own political ambitions. If the statue had been brought to me through Interpol, they would have interfered, or even attempted to seize it." He gestured to Kojima, who went to another set of doors and opened them. Takashi started for the exit. "Please come with me, Dr. Wilde. I am sure you are keen to see the statues for yourself."

Unable to deny that, she followed him. Near the door, set against the outer wall, was a wood-and-glass booth that she had assumed was some sort of display cabinet. Closer up, she saw that it contained an orange sphere around five feet tall. Takashi noticed her curiosity. "My escape pod."

Nina couldn't believe her ears. "Your *what*?"

"In case of a major earthquake." Seeing her still incredulous expression, he went on: "You do not have escape systems in American skyscrapers?"

"No—or if we do at the UN, nobody's ever let me in on the secret."

Now it was his turn to look disbelieving. "I hope it is never needed," he said as they left the office.

To Nina's surprise, the next room contained a beautiful rock garden, shrubs and miniature trees carefully arranged among large rounded stones, all surrounded by gravel precisely raked into wave-like patterns. She wanted to stop for a moment to admire it, but before she could even offer any praise Takashi had moved on to the next set of doors. They went down another hallway, passing more rooms of the penthouse. Outside, a tall white mast rose from a tier a few stories below: the tower of one of the wind turbines she had seen from the limo. Light from the setting sun flickered off the rapidly turning blades above. "That's something else I've never seen on an American skyscraper," said Nina, looking up at the structure.

"They generate up to ten percent of the building's energy needs," said Takashi with pride. "I would like more, but I must battle with the city planners over such things." He stopped, turning to face her. "This is why I am so interested in the earth's natural energy. Renewable sources like wind and wave power are a beginning, but the world's energy demands are growing faster than they can be met. We need more, and it must be nonpolluting, or we shall all choke. If earth energy can be harnessed, it could be the key to the future of humanity."

"It could be dangerous, though."

"All energy sources are dangerous, if used wrongly. That is why they must be kept in the right hands."

The obvious question was somewhat rude, but had to be asked. "Yours?"

"Not mine alone. But those who are seeking global stability and security." He set off again. "This way."

He led them into a large, softly lit gallery, the walls of which were home to numerous paintings and woodcuts. Nina didn't recognize any, but from their style and condition took them to be the work of Japanese artists dating back at least two centuries, some of them clearly much older. At the room's far side was another set of double doors. Takashi signaled to Kojima, and the secretary pushed a button on the wall. The doors were paneled in dark oak, but the hum of powerful machinery as they slowly swung open suggested that there were heavier and more secure materials behind the façades.

"My strongroom," said Takashi. "After the statue was stolen from me, I had the rest of my collection made as secure as possible. It is why I live here now, at the top of my own skyscraper. No intruder can reach this place without being caught. My guards see to that."

Nina was dubious. "What, the two guys all the way downstairs?"

A knowing smile. "They are not my only guards. But come, come." He beckoned her through the doorway. Lights came on as they entered.

Her eyes went wide at the sight within. The industrialist had an incredible collection of antiquities. Most were Japanese, which was not her area of expertise, but she recognized other items as being from China, India, Tibet, and more. Scrolls bearing gorgeous calligraphy; exquisite carved statues of ivory and jade; a full set of ornate samurai armor; jewelry in gold and silver, precious stones glinting from the settings. The value of the room's contents was easily tens of millions of dollars, perhaps even hundreds.

Kojima's phone trilled. He spoke briefly to the caller, then bowed to Takashi and Nina. "My apologies, but there is a matter I must see to. I will be back soon."

Takashi nodded, then continued into the room as his secretary departed. He paused as he reached one item. "Do you recognize this, Dr. Wilde?"

Nina examined it: a sword, the white blade long and notched in places with the scars of battle. "I'm afraid not. What is it?"

He looked disappointed, apparently expecting her to be more impressed. "This is Kusanagi-no-Tsurugi, the sacred sword of the great warrior Yamato Takeru. It is one of the three Imperial Regalia of Japan."

The sword's name dredged up a vague memory from her childhood, when her parents had taught her the legends of other countries. "Kusanagi . . . that's the Japanese equivalent of Excalibur, isn't it? I thought it was kept in a temple."

"The Atsuta Shrine in Nagoya, yes. That is what the priests there claim. It is good for business." A brief, grunting laugh. "But I have owned it for more than thirty years."

"If it's part of the Imperial Regalia, doesn't it really belong to the emperor?"

Takashi struggled to conceal his irritation. "A few politicians have suggested that. But they are now *former* politicians." He moved on, keen to change the subject. "Here, Dr. Wilde," he said, standing before one particular display case. "Here is what you have come to see."

Nina gazed at the objects within. They seemed unremarkable: crude figures, primitive carvings made from an unusual purple stone. One had been bisected vertically, the left and right halves put back together and held in place by thin elastic bands. Compared with the treasures around them, they appeared all but worthless.

She knew that was far from the case, however. They were conductors of earth energy, which in certain hands— her hands—produced extraordinary effects. When separated, each statue glowed, brighter bands of light pointing in the direction of its two companions. When all three were brought together . . .

That was the main reason she had come to Japan. To find out. She had never had the chance to complete the set before they were stolen by Stikes.

Now, that chance had come.

SEVEN

Dressed in a cheap suit from Hong Kong, Eddie entered the Takashi building.

Scarber had provided the information he sought. Stikes was in the building right now, meeting the company's boss on the fiftieth floor. The first obstacle he would have to overcome was getting up there. The penthouse—apparently the guy lived right above his headquarters, which Eddie supposed was one way to cut down on commuting—was only serviced by a single elevator, which was permanently guarded. He could see two uniformed men standing at a set of doors away from the other elevators, and guessed they were backed up by electronic surveillance.

But that wasn't the elevator he would be taking. Scarber had also given him the name of a contact within the company who could get him up to the thirtieth floor. That left another twenty, but one step at a time . . .

Feigning casualness, he strolled to the reception desk. "Hi, I'm here to see—whoa!" He flinched as he realized he was talking to some sort of mechanical mannequin rather than a young woman, and looked around to see if he was being secretly filmed for some elaborate practical joke. "What's this, Realdoll HQ?"

The robot's response was to bow its head, then say, "My apologies, sir. I did not know you spoke English. May I take your name, please?"

"Ed—er, Barney Phelps," he stuttered, thrown by the disconcerting encounter.

"I'm sorry, I did not hear you correctly," said the robot apologetically. "Could you repeat that, please?"

"Barney Phelps," he said again. "Look, no offense, but I'd rather talk to a real person. Wait," he added, "why am I apologizing to a fembot?"

A lifeless smile spread across the robot's face. "Thank you, you are expected. Mr. Jiro is waiting for you. If you will please take your visitor's pass and wear it at all times while you are in the building?" The machine indicated a slot in the desktop. Eddie hesitantly took the pass that slid out and attached it to his lapel. "Please go to elevator number twelve and exit on the thirtieth floor. Have a nice day."

"I might, if this wasn't fucking Westworld," Eddie muttered as he headed for the elevators. "Okay, number twelve . . ."

He was the only person waiting; at this time of day, Takashi employees were just starting to leave for the evening. Once the elevator had disgorged its occupants, he entered and rose up through the building alone. The doors opened, and he stepped out into a small lobby area. Another of the unsettling robot receptionists was waiting at a little desk, but to his relief an actual human being came to meet him before it could speak. "Mr. . . . Phelps?" said the thin-haired Japanese man. Despite the air-conditioned cool, sweat was beading on his forehead.

"That's right," Eddie answered. "You're Jiro?"

"Yes, yes." He gave the Englishman a perfunctory bow, glancing about to check that nobody was watching. "Come with me, please."

Eddie followed him down a corridor into a small office. Jiro quickly closed the door behind him, then pulled open a drawer and, hands shaking, took a holdall from it. "I will be fired if anyone learns of this," he said. "Or worse. Give me your pass."

Eddie took it from his jacket. "What're you going to do with it?"

"I will log you out of the building. On the computer, it will look as though we left together. I don't want to be connected with whatever you're doing." He exchanged the holdall for the pass.

Eddie opened the bag. Inside was a gun, a Russian Makarov PMM automatic. Considering Japan's extremely strict gun laws, it must have taken some work to obtain. He eyed his contact. "Doesn't sound like you're too happy about helping me."

"I don't want to. Scarber is making me. *Busu ama!*" He almost spat the insult.

"So how do I get up to the penthouse?"

"You will have to get into the central core. Only two elevators go to the top of the building—Takashi-san's private elevator, and one for maintenance. But the maintenance elevator is controlled by computer, so you will have to climb up."

"There are security cameras on the stairs, I take it." Jiro nodded. "So how do I get into this central core?" Eddie asked as he checked the gun. It was fully loaded with twelve nine-millimeter rounds.

"There is a door used by the cleaning robots. You will—"

"Wait, the what? Jesus, is everything in this place robotic?"

"You will have to be careful," Jiro continued impatiently. "The door only opens for the robots, and they stop if a person gets too close. For safety." He scribbled a rough map from the office to the service entrance. "When you are inside, there is an elevator that goes to the maintenance hub on the forty-fourth floor. From there . . . you are on your own."

"Looks like I already am," Eddie said scathingly as

Jiro hurriedly prepared to leave. "What if I run into any-body on the way?"

"There is a fake pass in the bag, so put it on. If you look as though you know where you are going, no one will be suspicious."

Eddie took out the laminated pass. He couldn't help noticing that its picture was not of him; the grinning youth with extravagantly styled hair seemed to have been clipped out of a magazine advert. "Only way this could've looked less like me would be if you'd used a photo of Pamela Anderson."

"All you *gaijin* look the same. I am going now." Jiro donned his coat and scurried out. "Be sure no one sees you leave my office."

"Not going to wish me luck?" Eddie called after him. He examined the crude map and memorized the route, then affixed the bogus pass to his jacket. He opened the door a fraction. Nobody was in the corridor. He pock-eted the gun and set out.

The stereotype of the long Japanese working day seemed to have some truth to it; even though it was clocking-off time, there was plenty of activity in the of-fices he passed. A moment of concern as a door opened ahead of him, but the woman who emerged, carrying a large bundle of documents, hurried past without even giving him a glance.

A couple of turns, and he saw the service door ahead. It was lower and wider than he had expected, less than four feet high—and had no handle. It bore a large NO ENTRY logo. The system was fully automated. In that case, he needed a robot . . .

One presented itself as he reached the junction at the corridor's end. He had half-expected a mop-wielding android French maid, but this was merely a large rounded-off box, a simplistic "face"—two dots for eyes and a smiling curve of a mouth—picked out by glowing lights on its front. Rotating brushes whirled under its bumper-car-like skirt, leaving a damp trail on the floor in its wake. It slowly hummed toward him. When it was a yard away, it stopped. A voice came from the machine, speaking in Japanese with a subservient tone. He guessed that it was asking him to get out of its way.

Eddie stepped back. The robot set off again, heading for the service door. He followed. This would be easier than he'd expected—

The robot stopped once more. Its sensors apparently scanned in all directions. He retreated a step. It resumed, the hatch sliding open as it approached. There was barely an inch of clearance on all sides. He would have to wait for it to get all the way through before he could enter . . .

The door snapped shut the moment it was inside.

"Buggeration and fuckery!" Eddie growled. He poked at the hatch, but it was almost flush with the wall, giving him nothing to grip. And attempting to force it open would definitely attract attention. He would have to find another robot and try again. Trying to look purposeful, he headed down one of the corridors.

It didn't take long for him to spot a telltale polished trail on the floor. He followed it, quickly catching up with another machine. It was heading away from the hatch, though; no telling how long it might take to do its rounds. If he delayed too long, Stikes might leave. How could he force it to speed things up?

The rear of the robot, he noticed, had a large flap on its top and a vertical row of little blue LEDs, the uppermost one of which was unlit. Above them was the symbol of a stylized wave. An indicator of how much water the automated cleaner had in its tank . . .

"*Domo arigato*, Mr. Roboto," he said as he strode up to the machine, which halted. He lifted the flap to find a dustbin-sized water tank, about three-quarters full. The robot spoke, but he ignored it, circling to look for controls. There was a small panel of touch-sensitive buttons on one side. One of them, he guessed from the symbol, was its main power switch.

A plan was forming, but he needed somewhere private

to carry it out. He looked at the doors along the corridor. One was a restroom. Perfect.

He retreated, letting the robot continue along its route until it was level with the restroom door—then caught up and, as it asked him to move, jabbed at the power button. The machine fell silent, its lights going out. Glancing about to make sure nobody was coming, he grabbed it and, with considerable effort, pushed it to the door. "Can't believe I'm mugging Artoo-Detoo," he muttered as he manhandled it into the room.

The bathroom was large and had a tiled floor, both of these facts being good; it would give him space to work, and the people on the level below wouldn't be immediately alerted by gallons of water coming through the ceiling. He strained to tip the robot on its side. The flap burst open as it thumped down, water sluicing out. He pulled the now considerably lighter machine back upright and checked that the corridor was still clear before hauling it outside.

Eddie clambered into the empty tank. He leaned over the side and pushed the power button again, then curled himself into a ball in the confined space and lowered the lid.

Nothing happened for several seconds. He was starting to worry that he had damaged the machine when it completed its self-test routine and abruptly turned to head back the way it had come. As he'd hoped, the robot had registered that its water supply was drained—and was going for a refill.

He raised his head, pushing the lid up just enough to risk a peek. Someone walked past, but far enough away not to trip the machine's sensors—the office workers were clearly so used to the robots that they ignored them.

A turn, and the machine rolled toward the service door. Eddie hunched down again and waited. He heard the hatch open. The robot started through it, hesitated as if belatedly becoming aware of the stowaway . . .

Then went through. The hatch closed. Eddie looked

out again, but found only darkness. Robots didn't need light to see. He had a small torch in one pocket, but there wasn't enough room for him to fumble it out. All he could do was go along for the ride until he reached the forty-fourth floor's maintenance hub—and hope he could climb out before the water tank was refilled.

He heard the rumble of other machinery over the robot's electric whine. It made its way through the dark, then bumped over a threshold. A pause, then Eddie felt a different kind of movement. He was in an elevator, going up.

The ascent soon stopped and the robot reversed out of the elevator on a new floor. Eddie lifted the lid. This time there was light, even if it was only dim. Other robots trundled between various machines, having their supplies of cleaning fluids refreshed and wastes flushed away before returning to the elevator and being taken to a new floor to continue their endless drudgery.

He climbed out and made his way to an area bounded by yellow lines: a safe path through the hardware for maintenance workers. Once happy that he wasn't about to be decapitated by some swinging mechanical arm, Eddie looked around. He was in the skyscraper's central core, so he couldn't be far from the elevator shafts. The metallic rumble of a high-speed elevator car came from nearby. He followed the path toward the sound and opened a door—to find himself at the edge of a man-made precipice.

"Shafted," he said, peering at the vertiginous drop beyond the safety railing. A bank of eight elevator shafts descended into darkness, the saucer-sized maintenance lights between the doors across the rectilinear crevasse shrinking to pinpricks far below.

The hiss of fast-moving cables and a rising rush of displaced air prompted him to move back from the edge as a car rocketed up the shaft, stopping a few floors above. Eddie looked up. He was six levels from the fiftieth floor, but this block of elevators only went as high as the forty-ninth. He needed one that went all the way . . .

A short distance along the narrow walkway, he found a guide in the form of a floor diagram on an electrical switchbox. The text was Japanese, but the numbers were self-explanatory. There were two main banks of elevators, eight shafts in each—and another two shafts set apart from the rest. Number one, he assumed, was Takashi's private elevator, making the other the maintenance access to what he took to be a machine floor above the penthouse. He got his bearings and set out for the latter.

This shaft turned out to be narrower than the others. The car, out of sight somewhere below, would hold three or four people at most. The cables were stationary, which was a relief—he could use the girders forming the shaft's framework to climb up the remaining six floors. Or, a thought striking him, *seven* floors. If he went to the machine level rather than the penthouse, there would be far less chance of being spotted by surveillance cameras or tripping an alarm, and there could be air vents or access hatches that would allow him to pick the best entry point.

Seven floors it was, then. He carefully clambered over the guardrail and edged across a girder until he reached one of the vertical struts, then started his ascent. It took less than half a minute to reach the next floor. Six to go. The next stage took the same amount of time, the third a little longer as his body began to feel the strain. It wasn't the climb itself that was wearing, but the effort of maintaining a grip on the featureless steel. Only the pressure of his hands and feet kept him from a very long plunge.

Three floors to go, and he paused to let the aching in his muscles fade. He took out the torch and shone it upward. There were the doors to the penthouse . . . which had extra wiring around them. Alarms. Going the extra floor to the machine level was the right decision.

He set off again. Grip the strut, push his feet against it for support, bring up his hands one at a time, hold tight, raise his feet, repeat. The cramp in his hands returned—

An echoing metallic *clack* from below, the grumble of machinery building up speed . . . and the cables started to move.

The elevator was rising.

Shit! He looked down, seeing the tiny pinprick lights going out one by one as the car blotted them out. It was maybe twenty floors below him—and picking up speed.

He was halfway between levels. There was no way he could climb up to the next before it reached him, but if he dropped back down, the slightest mistake would pitch him down the shaft.

No choice. He swung sideways, let go, fell—

The drop was about eight feet, onto unyielding, narrow steel. Even bending his legs to absorb the impact, Eddie still felt pain slam up through his feet into his knees and hips. He wobbled, grabbing at the strut as he pivoted to push himself back against the wall . . .

One foot slipped.

Fear shot through him. He clawed at the metal frame, fingertips desperately searching for purchase on the bare steel—

And finding a dent where it had been banged against a neighbor during construction. He rasped his nails against the imperfection, finding just enough grip to steady himself.

Both feet back on the girder, but now the car was only a couple of floors below, and still racing upward . . .

Eddie straightened and flattened himself against the wall just as the elevator reached him. He sucked in his stomach and held his breath, head turned sideways as it passed. There was so little clearance that his shirt buttons rasped against its side. Then it was past, decelerating sharply to stop at the forty-ninth floor. The clattering cables fell still.

He let out a gasp of relief, tempered with frustration. The car now blocked his path. All he could do was wait and hope that whoever was using it wasn't settling in for a long night shift.

Fortunately, it took only half a minute before another clack of brakes being released warned him that the elevator was about to move again. He squashed himself against the wall once more, wincing as the car scythed back past him—this time actually tearing off a button. It could have been worse, he decided: It might have lopped off a nipple, or an even more important protuberance farther down his body. Suppressing a shudder, he waited until the elevator was safely distant before gathering himself and resuming his ascent.

Fiftieth floor, a brief rest . . . then on to the top.

He climbed to the doors, shining his torch over them. No alarms that he could see. A closer look revealed a locking bar; he pulled it downward. A clank, and the door shifted slightly. He worked his fingers into the gap between the two sliding sections and forced them apart.

Like the maintenance hub, the skyscraper's uppermost story was sparsely lit, but Eddie could see well enough. In common with many tall buildings, the topmost level was dedicated to mundane but vital functions such as supplying air-conditioning and water to the floors below. He moved deeper into the maze of humming machinery, sweeping the torch beam from side to side. What he needed was an access panel, some way into the crawl space between this and the penthouse . . .

A hatch was set into the floor beside an air-conditioning unit. He opened it and shone his torch inside.

The space below was cramped and dusty, about two feet high and a nest for numerous snaking ventilation hoses serving the penthouse. A squeeze, but he had been in much tighter confines. He climbed down and crawled toward the nearest air vent.

He found on reaching it that it was too small for him to fit through, but a quick survey with his light revealed fatter hoses nearby—presumably serving larger vents. He followed one of the larger lines until it curved down to attach to a slatted grille set into the floor. That was more like it! Once he disconnected the hose, he could either unscrew or simply kick out the grille and drop down into the penthouse.

Voices reached him as he arrived at the vent. Someone was in the room below. This particular entrance wasn't a good choice, then, but there would be others. He was about to move on when he realized the speakers were talking in English. Curiosity got the better of him, and he peered through the slats. He was above a rather spartan lounge, a young Japanese man in an expensive suit addressing someone out of sight. "That should not be an issue," said the man. "We are all working for the same goal, so there's no need to be concerned about details of overall responsibility."

"Being concerned about details is how I stay alive," said another voice.

Eddie froze, a sudden surge of anger and adrenaline rushing through his body. *Stikes!* There was no mistaking the measured, arrogant tones of the former SAS officer.

Scarber had told him the truth: His enemy was here, right now. He felt the weight of the gun inside his jacket, and almost without conscious thought reached for it. One shot through the grille would see his enemy dead . . .

He forced himself to stay his hand. Yes, he could kill Stikes, but he didn't yet have an escape route short of groveling back through the crawl space and climbing down fifty floors. Besides, he now had an obligation to Scarber. The ex-CIA agent had lived up to her side of the bargain by giving him Stikes's location; he should do the same by trying to destroy the statues.

He shifted position to get a look at his target. Stikes sat nonchalantly in a leather armchair, a glass of whiskey on a small table beside it. His haughty, smug expression as he spoke was just as Eddie remembered—though the Yorkshireman took a small amount of satisfaction from seeing that his aristocratic features were disfigured, the vivid scar of a grazing bullet wound running from his forehead up through his blond hairline.

Stikes had made himself comfortable, so Eddie guessed he would be here for a while. Good; that gave him time to locate the statues before settling old scores. He started to move away to find another vent—

"Dr. Wilde is with Takashi-san at this moment," said the Japanese man.

Eddie was so shocked that he almost yelped *What?* out loud, managing to clamp his mouth shut before he gave himself away. Nina was *here?* The thought sent a thrill of longing through him—tempered by caution. Why would she be here with Stikes? He leaned closer to the grille, straining to hear every word.

"She will soon put the statues together for us," the man continued. "Then we'll finally see their power—and the plan can begin."

"It took you long enough," Stikes replied. "I gave them to the Group three months ago."

"We were exploring other options."

"But you already knew she could make them work, so you wasted time looking for someone else with the same ability. I told you she was the best choice, and that she wouldn't be able to resist the chance to find out more about the statues. She's an obsessive—it's what drives her. Her work always comes first."

The other man nodded. "She will be very valuable to the Group, then."

Stikes sipped his drink. "If the statues do what they're supposed to."

"We'll soon know. Takashi-san will see you afterward. In the meantime, I must get back to him." He bowed and left the room. Stikes took another sip, then with a look of sardonic amusement stood and walked out of sight.

Eddie remained still, mind racing. Nina was working with Stikes's new paymasters? He couldn't believe it. But much as he hated to admit it, Stikes was right about her being obsessive about her work. It was something that had prompted him to everything from teasing to outright anger in the past. Even so, he couldn't accept that her lust for knowledge was so great that she would throw in her lot with Stikes to satisfy it. It wasn't possible.

Was it?

Either way, he had to find her. He resumed his search for another way down.

EIGHT

Takashi opened the display case. "Here, Dr. Wilde. Let us see if the legend is true. Please, pick them up."

Nina realized as she stepped up to the case that her heart was racing. She knew what to expect of the statues individually, but the effects of putting them all together she could only imagine.

In a few moments, though, she wouldn't *have* to imagine. She would see for herself.

She held out a hand, hesitating before picking up the statue she had discovered within the Pyramid of Osiris. It glowed strongly.

The industrialist didn't appear surprised, only intrigued. "As I told you, all my life I have been fascinated by ideas such as Feng Shui," he said. "This skyscraper was built according to its principles, on an intersection of dragon lines. It is a place of great power. As you can tell."

Nina examined the statue. As she had seen on previous occasions, the shimmering light running over its surface was strongest in the direction of its companion pieces. The effect was a pointer, allowing those who could use it—those like her, some aspect of their body's bioelectric field allowing them to channel the strange energy—to find the other crude figurines.

And now that they were finally together . . . their secret would be revealed.

She picked up Takashi's statue. It too glowed. She brought the pair shoulder-to-shoulder, carved arms interlocking. The glow intensified, the brighter bands merging and pointing toward the last figure. Cradling them in one hand, she reached for it . . .

It also lit up: Its being split into two parts had not affected its mysterious properties. Excitement rose in her, as did an urge to complete the triptych—an almost electric thrill of imminent discovery.

Literally electric, she realized. There was a faint but definite tingling in her hands, as if a low current was running through them. Not painful, or even unpleasant, but a clear sign of something extraordinary.

She glanced back at Takashi. His gaze was fixed on the glowing stone figures, his expression one of rapt expectancy. He whispered in Japanese, anticipation so great that he momentarily forgot his guest did not understand the language. "Put them together," he said. "I must see!"

Nina felt the same. Carefully shifting the split statue in her hand, she brought it closer to the other two, turning it to join up with them for the first time in untold centuries . . .

They touched.

And Nina's senses were thrown into another world.

The effect was only brief, her shock causing her to break the link between the statues, but the results were almost overwhelming. Just for that moment, she felt as though her mind had left the confines of her body. Not a dislocation, but an *expansion,* spreading into the room, down through the building, into the city and the land beneath it.

And somehow, she also felt . . . *life.*

She sensed Takashi's presence a few feet from her, and

others farther away—above, around, below. And not just people. Birds roosting amid the machinery atop the skyscraper, the plants in Takashi's office, insects and rats in their hiding places within the building's structure. The lawns around its base—and beyond them the mass of living creatures of every kind within Tokyo. She was connected to them, some strand among all the different forms of life linking them in an inexplicable unity, a feeling of oneness.

And there was another sensation, equally strange, like a tugging at her soul. Something far away, yet also a part of her—and of everything else. She could feel it without touching, knew where it was without seeing—

Then it was gone, her consciousness snapping back to reality as her shock made her stagger. She instinctively grabbed the display case for support, letting go of the statues . . .

They didn't fall.

Before, the figures had always stopped glowing the instant they left her touch. Now, though, they continued to shimmer as they hung impossibly in the air, slowly drifting apart. Both Nina and Takashi stared at them, she in astonishment, the tycoon with . . .

Vindication?

The glow quickly faded. The figurines dropped, at first in slow motion but rapidly picking up speed—

With a stifled shriek Nina grabbed two of them, Takashi lunging to catch the last as it fell. Suddenly breathless, she leaned against the case. The pair of statues in her hands were glowing again, but the incredible experience did not return. "What the hell was *that*?" she gasped.

Kojima hurried back into the room and went to his boss's side, but his urgent and concerned questions were waved away as Takashi kept his gaze fixed on Nina. "You felt it?" he said urgently. "You must tell me! What did you feel?"

"I dunno," she said, bewildered. "It was . . . I don't know how to describe it, just—just *overpowering*. But the statues . . . they were floating! How is that even possible?"

"Diamagnetism," said Takashi.

Nina blinked. "What?" Considering what he had just witnessed, he seemed remarkably composed. "What do you mean? I'm an archaeologist, not a physicist."

Kojima provided a partial explanation. "All materials can be affected by magnetic fields, even ones we don't think of as magnetic. You can levitate a train with magnets—but with enough power you can levitate an animal, even a person. Diamagnetism is the name of this property."

"You charged the statues with earth energy," continued Takashi. "For just a few seconds, they held that charge—and were levitated against the energy fields of the planet itself. It was an effect we had predicted. But," he admitted, "seeing it for myself was . . . startling." He regarded the figure cradled protectively in his hands.

"Wait, you predicted this?" Nina demanded. Her initial amazement was already being tempered by a growing feeling that she had been played: Takashi knew far more than he was letting on.

He lowered his head. "I apologize, Dr. Wilde. We thought we knew what to expect, but there was no way to know exactly what would happen when you brought the statues together."

"There's that *we* again," she said. "Who else knows about this?"

Takashi ignored her question. "What did you feel while you were holding the statues?"

"You answer me first."

A flash of anger crossed his face at being challenged in his own domain, but he quickly regained control. "I am a member of . . . a group that believes earth energy is the key to the world's future. We seek to use its unlimited power for the benefit of humanity, while keeping it from those who might misuse it. People like Jack Mitchell."

Mitchell—supposed friend turned betrayer, using the IHA as the means to his end of constructing a devastat-

ing weapon powered by the planet itself. She felt a
twinge of phantom pain from her right leg, where he
had shot her to force her to do exactly what Takashi had
just manipulated her into—channeling earth energy. Her
eyes narrowed in suspicion. "How do you know about
him?"

"We have access to a great deal of information, from
all over the world. We do not represent any one nation—
we are above politics, you might say. Our goal is
simple—peace, stability, an end to conflict. And with
your help, we can achieve this goal."

"Well, that all sounds very laudable. Unfortunately,
Mitchell said pretty much the same thing."

"All I can do for now is ask you to trust us, Dr. Wilde.
We will prove our good intentions in time. But for now,
as I have answered your question, I ask you to answer
mine. When you brought the statues together, you had
an . . . experience. I would very much like to know what
you felt."

Nina was reluctant to respond. She was now convinced that she was part of some larger game, but had
no idea which side—if any—she should run with. Still, it
was clear that Takashi knew more than she did about
the statues, and if she gave him some new information,
perhaps he would reciprocate. "It's hard to explain,"
she began. "I felt . . . I don't know, *connected*."

"To what?"

"To everything. To life, I guess." She struggled to recall the sensation, but much of it had already faded, like
a half-remembered dream. "And there was something
else, a feeling like, like . . ." The words refused to form.

Takashi offered them, however. "Something calling to
you?"

"Yes, exactly!" She regarded him in surprise. "How
did you know?"

"As I told you, we have access to much information."

"Someone else already knew about this? Who?"

"A person from a long time ago. But," he went on,
before she could ask any follow-up questions, "there is

something you might not have seen. When you brought the statues together, their glow changed. Before, they pointed to each other, but for just a second the light moved to . . ."

He indicated a direction, then gave an order in Japanese to Kojima, who took out his phone and brought up an app—a compass, Nina saw. "About two hundred and sixty degrees west," the young man reported.

Takashi nodded. "Is that from where you felt this call?"

"Yes . . . at least, I think." Nina rubbed her forehead. "I'm not sure. The whole thing happened so quickly, and now it's fading away."

"There is a way to experience it again." Takashi held up the figure in his hands almost reverently. "Dr. Wilde, would you be willing to place the three statues back together?"

She hesitated. Nothing about her extraordinary experience had felt remotely harmful—if anything, quite the opposite—and her innate scientific curiosity was now crying out to learn more. On the other hand, for all Takashi's fine words, he still had to provide any proof that he intended to back them up with deeds. His true goal might be identical to Mitchell's.

But . . . she *had* to know. The same part of her psyche that had driven her to find Atlantis and all her other discoveries was now fully in control and demanding answers. Even though she had no idea where this path might lead, she knew she had to follow it.

Whatever the cost.

"All right," she said at last. "I'll do it. Just make sure you're ready to catch me *and* the statues this time, huh?"

"We will be very careful," said Takashi with a small smile. "Are you ready?"

Nina took a breath to settle herself. "No time like the present."

Takashi held out the third statue to her. She linked the other two together in one hand, then reached for it—

A loud crash came from the adjoining room, the clang

and clatter of metal followed by the thump of something heavy landing on the thickly carpeted floor. Nina, Takashi, and Kojima whirled, the statues momentarily forgotten. A figure stepped into the vault.

"Ay up," said the new arrival.

"Eddie?" Nina gasped, if anything more shocked than she had been by her mind trip. "What are— How did— *Huh?"* was all she could manage to say.

Kojima's hand darted into his jacket, but Eddie snapped up the Makarov. "Don't do anything stupid, mate. Just keep still. You an' all," he added, flicking the gun toward Takashi. "And you, Nina."

His harsh tone sent a chill through her. "Eddie, what are you doing?"

"What're *you* doing?" he shot back. "I spend three months hunting for Stikes, and it turns out he's right here with you!"

"Stikes? What are you talking about? I wouldn't—"

Takashi spoke calmly yet defiantly in Japanese. Kojima translated for him. "Takashi-san apologizes for interrupting a personal discussion, but he would very much like to know what you are doing here."

"Oh, he would, eh?" said Eddie. He indicated the statues. "I'm here for them—that's part of the reason, anyway."

Kojima relayed that to his boss, then provided another translation. "Takashi-san regrets that he will not allow you to take the statues, and also warns that the consequences if you try will be severe."

"Tell him he doesn't get a say in it," Eddie replied, aiming the gun at the old man. Kojima began to translate this back into Japanese.

"Oh, knock it off," Nina snapped. "You speak perfect English!"

Takashi sighed. "I was trying to buy us time, Dr. Wilde."

"Well, time's up," said Eddie. "So first, give me the statues. Then take me to Stikes. He's the rest of the reason I'm here—I'm going to kill that bastard."

"Stikes is here?" asked Nina, shocked.

Eddie regarded her doubtfully. "You didn't know?"

"Of course I didn't! That son of a bitch *tortured* me—do you seriously think I'd be here if I'd known he was too?" She glared at the Makarov. "And are you actually holding me at gunpoint? My God, Eddie! I can't believe you think I'd turn against you!"

Slightly shamefacedly, Eddie lowered the gun, just a little . . .

Enough for Takashi to risk making a move. A bony finger firmly tapped the face of his watch.

An alarm shrilled. Eddie whipped the gun back up, making even the normally implacable Takashi flinch, but he didn't fire. "That was a fucking stupid thing to do," he growled, stepping farther into the strongroom and gesturing for the trio to move past him to the exit. "Okay, old-bloke-san, you lead the way. Hands up where I can see 'em. All of you. Sorry, Nina," he added, "but I need to get out of here."

"Why are you doing this?" she demanded as they filed past him. "And why do you want the statues?"

"I don't want the bloody things—they've caused enough trouble already. But somebody else wants 'em smashed, which is fine by me."

Takashi looked back at Eddie with a calculating expression. "*Who* wants them smashed?"

"No idea—someone who really hates purple, maybe."

"You do not know who sent you here, or why?"

"All I know is that they told me how to find Stikes, and killing that bell-end's all I'm bothered about right now. Okay, move. Go through the—"

A flurry of movement in the next room, figures appearing seemingly from nowhere in a whirl of dark cloth and the flash of drawn weapons. They flanked Takashi and Kojima, narrowed eyes staring coldly at Eddie.

The foursome were dressed entirely in midnight blue, their faces mostly concealed behind balaclavas. Each had a different weapon at the ready: a *katana,* a traditional curved Japanese sword; a long black wooden *bo* staff banded with metal; *nunchaku,* two hefty wooden handles connected by glinting steel links; and a *kusari-gama,* a malevolent-looking sickle with a ball and chain attached to its handle. The wielder of the last spun the weight with one hand, making a low and threatening *whoosh* with each revolution.

Eddie almost laughed. He pointed the gun at each in turn. "Let me guess—Leonardo, Michelangelo, Donatello, and Raphael?" He looked back at Takashi. "Seriously, fucking *ninjas*? You're joking, right?"

"You will find that the joke is on you," Takashi said. A small nod . . .

"*Hai!*" The *katana*-wielding ninja lunged with astonishing speed, his blade a silver line slicing at its target's throat—

"Bye!" Eddie shot him. The ninja slumped to the floor with a bullet hole in his chest and a distinctly surprised expression.

He turned to his other new opponents, ready to give them the same treatment if they were dumb enough to bring swords to a gunfight . . .

Donatello released one of his *nunchaku*'s handles, his free hand whipping something from a bandolier across his chest. A flash of steel through the air—and Eddie yelled in pain as a throwing star thunked into his upper arm.

Another *shuriken* was already spinning at him, this one slashing through his sleeve as he dodged and brought up his gun—

Something heavy smashed into his hand, chain whipping around the Makarov. Raphael's *kusarigama,* the ninja using his weapon like a metal lasso. He yanked it back. The gun was torn from Eddie's stinging hand, flying over the remaining three ninjas and landing in the gallery as they rushed into the strongroom.

Takashi was already making a remarkably rapid exit for a man of his age, barking orders. Kojima pulled Nina with him, ignoring her protests. "Eddie!" she cried, but the secretary practically scooped her up and ran after his boss.

Eddie reeled backward as Michelangelo charged, his

staff sweeping and stabbing. One metal-tipped end caught his forearm, sending another bolt of pain through the already wounded limb. He slammed against a display case. The glass cracked—and a moment later shattered as the *kusarigama*'s spiked ball hit it, Eddie barely jerking out of its way.

The man with the *nunchaku* was racing around the edge of the room, trying to flank him. If he didn't find a way to fight back quickly, he would be attacked from three sides at once—and unlike the ninjas in martial arts movies, these didn't seem inclined to stand back and wait patiently for their comrades to be dealt with one at a time.

The *bo* staff thrust again, this time hitting him in the sternum. Crackling agony spread through Eddie's ribs. Gasping, he stumbled back—and collided with the samurai armor, tumbling to the floor amid a clattering avalanche of ornate pieces of metal. Another intense stab of pain as the *shuriken*, still embedded in his arm, was driven deeper into the muscle.

And more of the lethal throwing stars were about to come his way, Michelangelo spinning his staff in one hand as his other went to his bandolier—

The armor's elaborate breastplate was beside Eddie. He snatched it up and rolled to raise it like a shield. A *shuriken* flying straight at his head clanged off it.

Something else shot toward the armor—and punched right through it with a bang. Eddie flinched as the *kusarigama*'s razor-sharp sickle blade slammed to a stop inches from his face.

Raphael hauled on the weapon's chain again, whisking the shield away.

Leaving himself briefly open to attack—

Eddie pulled the bloodied *shuriken* from his arm and hurled it. It hit the ninja in the throat with a solid *chut* and a crimson spray. He collapsed, twitching and gurgling.

Both remaining ninjas froze, exchanging glances as they reassessed their opponent. Eddie scrambled up.

The pain in his chest made every breath hurt, and his arm was now damp with blood. He glimpsed his gun on the floor of the next room, but he would have to get past the staff-wielding Michelangelo to reach it.

And now Donatello was whirling his *nunchaku* from hand to hand as he advanced from the opposite direction.

Trapped—

* * *

"Let me *go*!" Nina yelled, striking at Kojima with her heels and elbows as he dragged her into Takashi's office. "He's my husband! I can talk to him, find out what's going on!"

Takashi had no interest in debate. Instead he went to a cabinet and took out a sturdy impact-resistant case. He opened it, revealing that it was lined with foam rubber, inset with three recesses in the exact shape of the statues.

"Put them in here!" he ordered. Still holding the struggling Nina with one arm, Kojima tugged one of the statues from her grip as Takashi placed his own figurine in the case. "Dr. Wilde, the statues must be kept from any harm. And so must you."

"You're the one who should be worried about harm!" Nina cried as she finally broke loose, giving Kojima a solid kick in the shins. He yelped. "Call off your—your ninjas," she said, not quite able to believe what she was saying. "I can get Eddie to—"

The door opened. She turned, hoping to see Eddie . . . but saw instead his most deadly enemy.

Alexander Stikes.

She backed away like a cat facing an aggressive dog. "What the hell is *he* doing here?"

The industrialist didn't appear pleased to see him either. "I told you to wait until we were finished."

"Sorry," said Stikes with a sarcastic smile, "but the alarm going off was rather a clue that something was wrong." He turned to Nina. "A pleasure to see you again."

"No it goddamn isn't," she growled. She addressed Takashi. "This son of a bitch tried to kill me!"

"He is only here because he delivered the statues to me," said Takashi. But there was a flustered quality to his reply that made Nina suspect he was concealing the whole truth, if not outright lying. "Please, Dr. Wilde, you and the statues must be protected." He pointed at the stone figure still in her hand. "Put it in the case. If necessary, we will use the escape capsule to get them—and you—safely out of the building."

Nina glanced at the booth containing the spherical pod. "You're not shooting me fifty stories into the air in that thing."

"It is for your own safety," Takashi insisted as Kojima hobbled to her and took the last statue, then put it in the case and closed the lid.

"I can look after myself."

"Don't worry," said Stikes. "I'll take care of her."

The malice behind his supercilious smirk was impossible for Nina to miss. She had seen it before, as his prisoner. As his *victim*, tortured for information with scorpion venom. Fear rose at the memory, her fight-or-flight instincts kicking in with a rush of adrenaline.

Fighting was out of the question. She knew she couldn't win.

Which left—

She burst into motion, shoulder-barging Kojima aside and snatching up the case before sprinting through the doors.

"Dammit!" Stikes spat as they slammed behind her. He reached into his jacket and drew a gun, a nickel-plated Jericho 941 automatic, and ran after her.

"No!" Takashi's command made him freeze mid-stride. "Put your gun away. She is too valuable to the Group. She must not be hurt."

The Englishman gave him a baleful look. "She must not be *killed*. That isn't quite the same thing." He flicked off the Jericho's safety. "Don't worry, Mr. Takashi. I'm a very good shot."

Before Takashi could say anything further, he threw open the doors and rushed out after Nina.

* * *

Eddie's gaze flicked back and forth between the two ninjas as they closed in. Donatello was still twirling his *nunchaku* with dangerous ease, trying to intimidate him into retreating—into range of Michelangelo's poised staff.

His eyes moved to the exit—and the gun. If he could knock down or even distract one of the ninjas for as little as a second, he had a chance to round the other and reach the Makarov. But he would have to pick the perfect moment . . . and it wasn't here yet. Both men needed to be closer, but not so close that they could make an unstoppable strike.

The ninjas knew what he was thinking. They exchanged another look, silently agreeing on a plan of attack. Eddie stepped back. Even if they had figured out what he was about to do, he had no option left but to chance it.

The staff, though less showy, was more likely to fell him than the *nunchaku*. Donatello was his target, then. The ninja was still approaching, more cautiously. Another couple of feet.

One more step—

Eddie bumped into something. Caught off guard, he instinctively glanced at the obstruction—a display case containing a sword.

Donatello darted forward, the *nunchaku* whipping up at Eddie's face. He raised his arms, taking a fierce crack to the elbow from the wooden handle—

The staff swung like a baseball bat, slamming across his stomach and pitching him backward against the case. The whole thing toppled and fell, glass exploding beneath Eddie as he landed on top of it. Shards stabbed into his shoulders. He rolled sideways to get clear of the debris as the *nunchaku* lanced at his head. More glass splintered as it missed by barely an inch.

Michelangelo raised his staff again, bringing it high over his head to crush Eddie's skull like a watermelon—

Eddie grabbed Kusanagi and swung it upward as the staff lashed down. A sharp crack of wood against metal—and the *bo*'s end was neatly chopped off by the sacred sword, its edge still keen even after centuries.

Even with his weapon reduced to two-thirds of its length, the ninja struck again. This time, Eddie used the sword not to parry but for leverage, shoving himself out of the wreckage and rolling onto his feet. Michelangelo's thrust fell short. Another attack, but this time Eddie was prepared.

He swung the sword as hard as he could at the ninja's neck.

Swordsmanship was not one of Eddie's combat skills, fists and firearms the majority of his military training. The blade caught the ninja flat-on instead of with its edge.

But that was enough. The sword made an almost musical ringing note as it hit the side of Michelangelo's jaw like a hammer. Spitting blood, the ninja crashed through another display, shattering jade figurines.

Eddie had no time to celebrate. The other ninja made another charge, *nunchaku* flailing so quickly they were a blur. One of the handles clanged off the sword as the Yorkshireman defensively snapped it up. Donatello instantly adjusted his movements to send the next strike past the ancient blade, the chain looping around it. He pulled back sharply, trying to yank the weapon out of Eddie's hands.

This time Eddie kept a firm grip. He charged, driving the blade at the ninja's stomach.

Donatello was too quick, twisting out of the way. He braced himself as Eddie collided with him, then with a rapid movement freed the *nunchaku* from the sword and turned to strangle his adversary with its chain . . .

Eddie headbutted him in the face.

The dark blue of the ninja's balaclava suddenly blossomed with a damp purple patch around his mouth and nose. Even with his eyes screwed shut, he still tried to attack again. The *nunchaku* swished through the air—

Hitting nothing. Eddie had ducked.

Now it was his turn again—and with a roar he thrust the imperial sword with his full strength, transfixing the ninja through the stomach all the way to the hilt. Donatello gasped, mumbling in Japanese before collapsing face-first into the broken glass of Kusanagi's shattered display case.

"Cowa-fucking-bunga," Eddie rasped, forehead throbbing from its impact with the ninja's nose. He straightened and looked around. Michelangelo was still alive, on all fours and clutching his truncated staff. But the way to the door was now clear—and his gun was just outside.

He ran. The last ninja scrambled up, but Eddie was already past him. The Makarov had landed about ten feet beyond the door. He crossed the threshold, bending to snatch up the weapon—

Something shot past him just before he reached it. The *bo* staff, hurled like a javelin—not at him, but at the gun. It hit the Makarov and sent it skidding through a set of open doors into an adjoining room.

Eddie looked back at Michelangelo, who was now searching for something on the ground . . .

Leonardo's *katana*. Michelangelo seized the sword and pointed it angrily at Eddie—then sprinted toward him with a howling battle cry.

"Oh, fuck!" Eddie himself ran, racing after the gun. The doors had been closed when he dropped down from the vent; the ninjas must have entered through them. Beyond was a traditional Japanese dining room, rows of low tables with tatami mats on which the diners would sit lined up along the polished wooden floor.

Where was the gun? It had skittered over the slick wood—and ended up beneath one of the tables.

But which one?

He reached the first table and flipped it over. No gun. Next table. Still nothing. The ninja's padding footsteps were rapidly closing. Third table, nothing. He grabbed the next in the row and flung it back toward the door. Still no sign of the Makarov, and from behind came a crack of wood as the *katana* slashed the little table in two.

He threw another place aside—and saw the glint of steel beneath.

The ninja was almost on him—

He dived for the gun, grabbing it and twisting to bring it to bear. The blade flashed down—and the ninja took two bullets to the chest as Eddie fired at point-blank range. The Englishman rolled to avoid the bloodied corpse as it fell, the *katana*'s point stabbing into the wood floor to leave the weapon standing beside the body like a tombstone.

"Jesus," Eddie gasped, regaining his breath as he shakily stood. "Fucking ninjas, they're like cockroaches!" He checked the room, trying to get his bearings. There were two exits: the one to the gallery and the vault, and another opening onto a windowed hallway. He hadn't seen the direction Takashi had gone, so a split-second instinctual decision sent him toward the latter.

At the hall's far end to his left was Takashi's private elevator, an illuminated indicator showing that it was stationary at the penthouse level. Takashi hadn't taken Nina and the statues out that way, then. In the other direction was a set of imposing oak doors. The industrialist's inner sanctum?

He ran toward it, gun at the ready.

* * *

The case in her hand, Nina raced into the gallery. "Eddie?" she cried, uncertain—fearful—about what she might find.

She discovered corpses, which in some grim way was hardly a surprise, but to her relief none was her husband. Three in the strongroom, and a fourth in a dining room through another doorway. Eddie must have gone that way. She ran after him.

More doors led into the hallway to Takashi's office. She went through them. Beyond the windows, Tokyo was now a glittering sea of lights beneath the twilight winter sky. She looked around. The elevator was to the left; to the right—

"Eddie!" she called again, running after him. Her husband slowed, turned, saw her . . .

And raised his gun.

NINE

Nina froze, shocked—and afraid. Eddie's expression was one of pure hatred. "What are you . . . ," she started, but her mouth had gone dry.

Then she realized that he wasn't looking at her, but something behind her. "Nina, move," he growled.

She whirled. Stikes had just come from the dining room—and also had a gun raised. She was directly between the two men, blocking their lines of fire. A standoff.

"Yes, step aside," said Stikes. "I should have known you'd turn up sooner or later, Chase. It's a bad habit of yours." A smile of cruel anticipation twisted his mouth. "One I look forward to breaking."

"Move, Nina," Eddie repeated. "I've been hunting this shitbag for three months. He's not getting away this time."

"Why don't you just shoot, Chase?" taunted Stikes. "I gather you've been having marital problems—it would save you the cost of a divorce."

Eddie clenched his jaw angrily, about to risk darting sideways for a clear shot in the hope of catching the other man by surprise . . . before a thought struck him. Why didn't *Stikes* shoot?

Nina started to step aside. "Wait!" Eddie snapped. "Stay still."

"Uh, Eddie," she said with a nervous glance between the two guns, "what're you doing?"

Eddie's gaze remained fixed on Stikes, whose eyes began to betray his frustration. For whatever reason, he couldn't risk killing Nina, even if that cost him the chance to eliminate one of his enemies.

Now it was Eddie's turn to smile slightly, confusing Nina and infuriating Stikes. "Nina, come over here. Trust me," he added, seeing her hesitancy.

"I dunno if you noticed, but the guy who hates us both is aiming a gun at me," she pointed out.

"He won't shoot. He *can't* shoot. He needs you alive. Come on."

"Alive isn't the same as unharmed," said Stikes as she started to move.

Nina cringed. "Oh, I was so hoping he wouldn't say that."

"He wounds you, you fall, I kill him," Eddie told her. "He loses."

"I don't exactly come out a winner either!" She was now two-thirds of the way between the former SAS men.

A faint sound from the other end of the hall. The elevator was descending. "That'll be more of Takashi's security," said Stikes, his arrogance returning. "You can't get away. I'll tell you what—just drop your gun and I'll make it painless. One bullet, right in the forehead. For old times' sake."

"How about I give you one bullet right in the bollocks? For old times' sake." But Eddie knew Stikes was right—he was rapidly running out of time before reinforcements arrived. He needed to break the deadlock . . .

A bright light suddenly filled the hallway.

From outside.

Eddie looked around in alarm as an approaching helicopter's spotlight swept over the penthouse. He whipped back to face Stikes, but the mercenary was just as surprised as he was—

The windows shattered as gunfire raked the building.

Nina shrieked and ran to Eddie, who dived on top of her to shield her from the flying glass and bullets. Stikes also threw himself to the floor. Wood panels splintered, the drywall behind erupting with great sprays of fragmented plaster as more shots carved through the hallway.

The firing stopped. Eddie raised his head, seeing the helicopter hovering about fifty yards from the skyscraper. The glare from its light meant that he couldn't identify the type, only that it was painted black—and had a machine gun protruding from an open hatch in its side.

But the aircraft was now turning to face the building head-on. The gun wasn't its only weapon . . .

Eddie flattened himself over Nina again as a flash of orange fire streaked out from the chopper. A rocket hit the building above the hallway and exploded, the remaining windows shattering. Debris cascaded from the ceiling between the couple and Stikes.

Nina screamed as a second missile struck overhead, the floor pounding like a drumskin. "Holy *shit*! Who the hell are they?"

"They're shooting at us, so bad guys!" Eddie shouted back. He shook off lumps of fallen plaster and lifted his head. They were dangerously exposed here. If they ran toward the elevator, the building's central core might provide some protection. But that would mean covering almost the entire length of the hallway, making them an easy target for the gunner—

The floor shook again. Not from an explosion, but a deep, ominous creak of metal and concrete. The helicopter hurriedly retreated. The sound grew louder, joined by the groans and cracks of failing structural supports . . .

Nina realized the cause with horror. "Oh, crap! Eddie, move, *move*!"

One of the wind turbines outside toppled like a felled redwood, scything down through the ceiling and tearing a great gash out of the skyscraper as the enormous steel tower ripped through story after story before finally being dragged to a halt by the sheer mass of tangled wreckage.

But the danger wasn't over. Nina and Eddie suddenly found themselves sliding toward the widening hole as the floor, its supports severed, sagged beneath them. They slithered helplessly down the polished wood—

Another loud crack—a floorboard springing up at one end as it buckled. Nina grabbed it, Eddie catching her legs and clinging on.

She was still holding the case in her other hand. "Get rid of that fucking box before we both fall!" he ordered.

"Not a chance!" After what she had experienced earlier, there was no way Nina was going to give up the statues now. Instead she tossed the case back up the sloping floor to land in the corner near the doors. For a moment, it looked as though it was going to slide back down again . . . then it wedged against another warped board.

She clawed at the wood with her now free hand until her fingers found purchase. "Okay, just hang on," Eddie grunted as he stuffed the gun into his jacket and began to pull himself up her body.

"Oh, ya think?"

He held back a sarcastic response of his own, concentrating on survival. Boots scraping against the floor, he brought himself high enough to reach the board. "Got it," he said, releasing Nina and edging sideways to support his foot against a cracked plank. As she squirmed up, he twisted to locate the other threats.

The helicopter was shining its light into Takashi's office. As for Stikes—

His former superior officer was on the far side of the gap, scrambling back to level ground. He straightened, brushed off dust, then looked back. His gaze met Eddie's. A brief twitch of anger, then he smirked and reached for his gun . . .

It wasn't there. His look changed to outright anger as he realized he had dropped it—and it had fallen into the hole. All he could shoot at Eddie was a scowl, which he delivered before turning and running for the elevator. A flashing red NO ENTRY symbol on the display warned that it was no longer in operation; the fire alarm had been sounded, and the elevators were programmed to stop in response. Instead, Stikes rounded a corner and passed out of sight, heading for the emergency stairs.

Eddie cursed at having missed his chance to kill Stikes, then clambered back up the slope to join Nina. They exchanged relieved looks—which were instantly replaced by concern as the machine gun fired again.

* * *

In the office, Kojima desperately tried to push Takashi into the open escape capsule. "You've got to get out!" he cried as the piercing spotlight sliced across the windows.

Takashi resisted, shouting into a cell phone, "Two hundred and sixty degrees west! Have you got that? Two hundred and sixty degrees!" Receiving confirmation, he finally addressed Kojima. "The statues, and Dr. Wilde—they must be saved! The plan is more important than any one member of the Group. Find them and get them to safety!"

"No, Takashi-san! You have to—"

The beam locked on to them, pinning the two men in its harsh gaze. Eyes narrowed against the glare, Takashi stared back with a mix of defiance and acceptance. "Glas," he said. "That traitor Glas is behind this—"

The machine gun spat fire. The windows shattered, a storm of bullets shredding Takashi and his secretary into bloody chunks.

* * *

Eddie regarded the oak doors with concern as the gunfire stopped. "Definitely don't think we want to go in there." The pitch of the helicopter's engine changed, suggesting that it was circling the building.

Looking for more targets.

"That doesn't leave us with many options," Nina replied. There was another, single door in the corridor wall on their side of the chasm, but reaching it would require going back down the dangerous slope before hopping onto the stub of a beam at what had been floor level. She retrieved the case. "Keep hold of my hand until I can jump across."

"For Christ's sake, just leave the case, will you?" He frowned. "Wait, what's in it? It's those fucking statues, isn't it!"

"Yeah, and after everything I've been through to get them, I'm not letting go of them now."

"After all the trouble they've caused, the world'll be well rid of them," he countered. "Give 'em here."

"*No,* Eddie," Nina insisted, clutching the handle more tightly. "I don't have time to explain right now, but they're a part of something big—something *amazing.* I have to find out what it is."

He shook his head. "No, you—"

"You asked me to trust you a minute ago," she cut in firmly. "Well, trust *me.* Please, Eddie. It's very important."

"All bloody right," he said after a moment. "I won't smash 'em, I promise. Now get moving, will you? If that chopper comes back—"

"I'm moving, I'm moving," she protested, extending her free hand to him and starting down the slope. He held on to her, leaning forward as far as he dared. She neared the broken beam and took a deep breath, swinging the case in her hand. "Okay, and a-one, a-two, and a-*three*!"

He let go and she jumped as the case reached the end of its upward arc, its momentum helping carry her all the way to the stub in the wall. She landed—and wobbled, waving her arms before steadying enough to hop across to the open door. The room beyond was a lounge, minimalistically furnished. Nina entered as Eddie made a running jump onto the beam, then without a pause leapt the rest of the way into the room. "All right, now what?" she asked.

"Try to find another way out of here." He recognized the room as where he had seen Stikes earlier; that meant there was a way back to the maintenance shaft through the ventilation grille overhead, but it would take more time than they could afford. There was a second door across the lounge, however. "You know where that goes?"

"No—but Takashi took me through the rooms on the other side of the building," she remembered. "If we carry on past the vault, we might be able to get to the stairs from there."

"Probably run into trouble coming up 'em, but it's better than being stuck here." He drew the gun and went to the door. Beyond was what appeared to be a conference room. More doors led off it, but the one that seemed the best prospect was in the opposite wall. "Okay, come on," he said, crossing the room. Nina followed, the case in her hand.

Eddie opened the door a crack and cautiously peered through. Beyond was the Zen garden. The white spire of another wind turbine was visible through the windows, the lights of Tokyo beyond. "Okay, it's clear," he said. "Which way?"

"That door," Nina said, pointing to the right. They jogged toward it—

And were dazzled by the spotlight beam as the helicopter descended outside.

They both dived for cover as the gunner opened fire. Wind shrieked through the windows as they burst apart in a crystalline spray, trees shattering under the pounding onslaught. "Shit, shit, *shit*!" Nina wailed as she scrambled behind a boulder. "Why do people in helicopters always try to kill me?"

The gunfire stopped. Eddie peered out from behind a

rock and saw what he had feared—the chopper was turning to bring its rockets to bear.

"Stay down!" he shouted as he ran to the windows, opening fire with the Makarov. The gunner ducked back into the cabin as a bullet clanged off the fuselage, but the helicopter was almost a hundred yards away, and the Russian gun was sighted for much closer ranges—he couldn't aim it accurately enough to hit a specific target.

The chopper's nose came around, the spotlight dazzling him. He could now barely make out the aircraft itself through the glare, never mind its pilot.

But there was something closer that he *could* see, and hit . . .

He snapped up the pistol and emptied the magazine into the wind turbine's hub.

Machinery blew out in a shower of sparks. The whirling blades juddered, their vibration rapidly increasing, loud clangs rising even over the helicopter's roar. Another burst of sparks from the crippled generator—then with a screech the rotor sheared away from the hub.

Still spinning at high speed, it dropped to the tier below—and bounced away into the night sky.

Straight at the helicopter.

The horrified pilot tried to take evasive action as it arced at his aircraft, but it was too late. The hefty blades sliced off the chopper's tail boom as if it were made from damp paper. Without its tail rotor, the helicopter immediately went into an uncontrollable spin. Wobbling like a top, it whipped around faster and faster, losing altitude as it careened toward the skyscraper—

Eddie hurled himself back into the garden as the tumbling aircraft crashed through the building's outer wall six floors below and exploded. A huge fireball surged up the tower's side behind him. He scrabbled to join Nina, shielding his face from the heat as the roiling inferno ascended. "You okay?"

She nodded, still stunned by what had just happened. Oily black smoke boiled upward beyond the broken windows, leaving the edge of the carpet aflame. "Oh my

God!" she cried. "What about all the people down-stairs?"

"Soon as the fire alarm sounded, they'll have evacu-ated," said Eddie, hoping that the Japanese reputation for efficiency extended to Takashi Industries' emergency procedures. "And I think we ought to join 'em."

He helped her up, and was about to head for the exit when the ceiling sprinklers burst into life, drenching them. "Great," Nina moaned, flicking strands of wet hair from her eyes. "What next, an earthquake?"

The building shook.

Eddie shot her an accusing glare. "That was *not* me tempting fate!" she protested as she retrieved the case. "I'm not a fate-temptress!"

Another jolt. The sound of more windows splintering came from below—followed by a deep groan of buck-ling metal and crumbling concrete. The sprinklers died as pipes were severed. They both felt another move-ment, their inner ears warning them that they were lean-ing over—even though they were standing still. Through the smoke, the glowing Tokyo skyline slowly began to tilt. "The whole fucking *building's* going over!" Eddie yelled.

More noises of imminent collapse reached them as girders broke from their joints and concrete slabs sheared apart. The doors through which they had been about to leave creaked in distress as their frame warped—then they shattered, chunks of wood flying into the room. The ceiling behind the exit collapsed, ventilation hoses thrashing angrily amid the falling rubble.

They were cut off from the stairs.

The floor of the now visibly tilting room trembled. Another deep destructive boom from below and the lights flickered, then went out. The burning carpet pro-vided enough illumination for Eddie to see, but even with that they still had nowhere to go . . .

Nina grabbed his hand. "This way!" She pulled him down the ever-steepening slope toward Takashi's office.

"How's that going to help?"

"He's got an escape pod!"

"He's got a *what*?"

"Yeah, that's what I thought too!" She reached the door and tried to open it. It didn't move. Like the set at the other end of the room, the frame was warping under the structural stress. "Dammit!"

Eddie solved the problem by kicking the doors open. "Go on!"

Nina recoiled at the sight of what was left of Takashi and Kojima in the firelight. Suppressing her nausea, she crossed the blood-splattered floor to the booth. The bright orange capsule was still inside, door raised and a light glowing within. To her dismay, the padded interior only looked big enough for one person.

"Get in!" Eddie barked, pushing her toward it.

"I'm not leaving you behind!"

"Too bloody right you're not! I meant get in and *shove over*!"

She clambered through the hatch and lowered herself onto a thickly cushioned seat. Eddie followed her. He bashed the case. "Can't you just dump that fucking thing?"

"No, I—aah!—can't," she grunted as he squeezed into the cramped space. "Okay, so how does this work?"

Eddie spotted a small control panel. It had two buttons, the top one flashing. The crash of another section of collapsing ceiling told him that there was no time to figure out what they did. Instead, he jabbed at the lit button. The clamshell door descended with a mechanical hum, pressing him even more tightly against his wife.

"Well, not quite the reunion I'd hoped for," she mumbled into his butt—

Eddie pushed the second button.

Rockets set around the capsule's door fired. More pyrotechnics on the window behind it shattered the safety glass a fraction of a second before the pod blasted through and sailed out into open air. The g-force squashed Eddie hard against the door, Nina screaming as she was jammed against him.

A moment later, the skyscraper crumbled.

A wedge-shaped chunk eight stories high sheared away from the top of the tower, sliding diagonally down the fault line created by the exploding helicopter before plunging toward the ground in a trail of smoke and dust. Evacuees ran screaming across the lawns as it fell. The mass of steel and concrete and glass smashed down, the shock of the impact destroying every window on the bottom twenty floors and sending a choking cloud of pulverized debris across the grass after the fleeing workers. More office detritus rained down on the mangled girders and rubble.

The escape pod was also falling—but far more slowly. The rockets had burned out in seconds, their job of propelling the capsule away from the building completed. After a brief but terrifying period of free fall, a trio of parachutes deployed. Twirling gracefully like a sycamore seed, the orange sphere descended and thumped down on one of the lawns well clear of the scene of destruction.

The door opened. Eddie fell out backward, a dizzied Nina crawling after him and flopping onto the grass. She regarded the smoking wreckage with horrified amazement as people staggered out of the billowing cloud like walking ghosts. "I think . . . I want my office moved to the first floor," she gasped.

Eddie sat against the pod, recovering his breath. "Are you all right?"

"Yeah. Somehow." She looked up at him, taking in his bruised face and torn, bloodied clothes. "My God! You look . . ."

"Like I got beat up by ninjas?"

"I was going to say *weird with a beard.*"

"Tchah!"

"But yeah, you need to get to a hospital."

"They might be a bit busy tonight." He nodded toward the fleeing workers. "And anyway, that could cause me a few problems if the police want to ask me any questions."

Nina sat up. "*I've* got some questions. Where have you been for the past three months? What have you been doing? And why are you here—I mean, this exact place, right now, at the same time as me?"

"In order? All over the place, tracking down Stikes—" He stopped midsentence, instantly angry.

"Stikes?" Nina looked around nervously, as if the mercenary might suddenly appear and try to finish the job, but there was no sign of him.

Eddie shook his head. "He'll be gone. He'll be fucking gone! Bastard, that—*fuck*!" He banged a rage-clenched fist against the pod. "I *had* him, I had my chance to fucking kill him, and I missed it!"

"*That's* why you were here?" said Nina in disbelief. "To kill Stikes? Not—not what you told me in Peru, that you were going to prove you didn't murder Kit?"

Her disappointment, almost disgust, immediately poured cold water on his burning fury. Several moments passed before he spoke again, more calmly. "It doesn't matter, 'cause I think I've been set up. We both have."

"What do you mean?"

"Someone told me Stikes would be here—in return for me doing something for them."

"Destroying the statues." Nina pulled the case from the pod and opened it. The three stone figures inside were all intact.

"Yeah. Only I don't think it's a coincidence, that chopper showing up as well. Somebody wanted all of us dead—Takashi, Stikes, you . . . and me. I need to find out who." Flashing lights caught his attention, emergency vehicles racing along the nearby roads. Ambulances, fire trucks—and police cars. "Can't talk about it now, though. I've got to go."

"No, Eddie, you can't! Look, Interpol knows that Kit was up to something—if you come in, we can try to clear you—"

"Sorry, love, but I can't. Not yet." He stood, searching for an escape route. The wind turbine's rotor had stabbed into the grass like an enormous lawn dart; be-

yond it, streets led into Tokyo's urban maze. "I need to
have words with somebody." He turned, about to run—
then, before Nina could react, snatched the case from
her hand.

She jumped up, but he was already sprinting. "Eddie!"

He looked back. "Remember something else I said to
you in Peru? The *last* thing? I still mean it!"

Nina was too shaken to pursue him. All she could do
was slump against the pod and watch as he disappeared
into the night.

She did indeed remember his parting words as he fled
the gas plant. They were *I love you.*

"Oh God, Eddie." She sighed. "What have you gotten
involved in?"

It was a question she could also ask of herself.

TEN

The *shinkansen*—better known in the West as the bullet train—was as much a symbol of Japan as Mount Fuji, the streamlined expresses hurtling between cities with incredible speed and clockwork precision. This particular one was heading southwest out of Tokyo, the last train of the night from the capital to its final destination of Hakata on the country's west coast, five hours and seven hundred miles away.

Eddie wasn't going that far. His stop was Nagoya, a third of the way along the route, from where he would leave Japan via the international airport; security would be at a lower alert there than at Narita. His exit had been arranged by Scarber. Considering what had happened at the Takashi building, he was not the least bit surprised to learn when he called her that she was in the country. She had almost certainly been within sight of the skyscraper to observe events personally.

And report the outcome to her bosses.

A scrolling LED display overhead told him that the time was almost midnight. Scarber's instructions had been that they not meet until then, after the train departed Shin-Yokohama station. Nagoya, the next stop, was an hour and fifteen minutes away. Plenty of time, she had said, for an undisturbed discussion.

He had his own suspicions about why she didn't want to be interrupted. And had taken precautions.

In the meantime, his thoughts returned to what Nina had said to him after their landing. His relief and delight at seeing her again had been followed by dismay at her reaction on learning *why* he was there. She had been appalled to learn that his goal had been to kill Stikes . . . and, he now accepted, rightfully so. He *had* set out from Peru with the intention of proving his innocence, but somehow over time that had fallen away, replaced by a simpler, cruder, *easier* motivation. Vengeance, nothing more, taking his revenge on Stikes for everything he had done. He had always thought of such payback as unprofessional, but over the last three months he had fallen into the emotional trap. Uncovering whatever plot connected Kit, Stikes, and Sophia had proved harder and so far fruitless, and he had allowed another goal chosen by some reptilian, bloodthirsty part of his psyche to drive him instead.

Now, though, his objective was investigation once more. He was going to find out who had set him up, and why.

But when he did, he might well indulge the reptile within.

There was something else to kill first, however: the last few minutes before his meeting. He flipped through the English-language edition of the *Asahi Shimbun* newspaper he had bought before boarding. "Interpol Widens Search for Fugitive Billionaire" was a minor headline that caught his eye; the name Harald Glas stirred his memory as being connected to the IHA in some role. The Dane had apparently fled his native country when faced with charges of fraud, money laundering, and drug smuggling. Eddie imagined that Glas's life on the lam was considerably more luxurious than his own.

Midnight. He put the paper aside and headed for the

middle of the train, the "green"—first-class—section. Another reason to be wary: The more expensive carriages would be less busy, especially at this hour. More privacy—or fewer witnesses.

There was another reason why the former spook had chosen her particular seat, as Eddie found when he entered car number ten to be greeted by the acrid smell of tobacco. Smoking was still permitted in certain parts of the *shinkansen,* and this was one of them. He had retrieved his belongings from a subway station locker and, after some rough-and-ready first aid to his injuries in a restroom cubicle, changed out of his torn and filthy suit into something more comfortable. Taking a pack of Marlboros and his lighter from the breast pocket of his leather jacket now, he moved down the aisle, looking for his contact.

He found her quickly; there were only a handful of other people in the carriage, suited and bored-looking Japanese men. "There you are," rasped Scarber from a window seat in the center of the coach, blowing out a line of blue smoke. "Come on, sit down."

Eddie dropped into the seat facing her and lit his own cigarette, then returned the lighter and pack to his pocket. "So, you're here in Japan, eh?"

"Keeping an eye on my employer's interests."

"I don't need to tell you what happened, then."

"No, I got a pretty good idea. Jesus, what a cluster fuck." She took a long drag, the cigarette's glowing tip crackling. "The main thing I want to know is: Did you destroy the statues?"

"Not yet."

She frowned. "The deal was that you destroy them, kiddo."

"The deal was that I kill Stikes."

"We told you he was there, he was there. Not my problem if you fuck up the hit. Where are they?"

"Safe."

"They're not supposed to be safe. You had a bag when you boarded—are they in it?"

Eddie shrugged. "I've got some questions myself first."

"I don't give a crap. Where are the statues, Chase?"

He fixed her with a cold stare. "Why'd you try to have me killed, Scarber?"

She was silent for a moment, smoke wafting from the cigarette. Finally, she gave him a smile of patronizing admiration. "Figured it out, huh?"

"The bit where some twat fired rockets at me was sort of a giveaway."

"Yeah, that wasn't subtle, was it?" The smile chilled—then her right hand whipped into her handbag.

Eddie was faster, snatching out the Makarov and aiming it at her chest. "Ah-ah."

"Would you believe me if I said I was just getting a tampon?" Scarber asked, slowly withdrawing her hand.

"Not really. Now take out the gun. Slowly, thumb and little finger."

Glaring, she reached into the bag and extracted a pistol. Eddie saw that it was a Smith & Wesson SD9, a compact automatic—yet not so compact that Scarber could have easily smuggled it into the country. She must have picked it up in Japan, which meant she had associates.

Associates who could bring modern weapons from the United States through the strict Japanese customs checks . . .

"Eject the mag, then chuck 'em under the table," Eddie ordered. She did so, the gun and its magazine clunking to the floor. He kicked them under his seat. "Former spook, my arse. You're either still active or you've got close mates in the CIA. So who are you working for—and why'd you go to all this trouble to put me in the building when your chopper started shooting it up?"

Scarber sneered, parchment skin drawing tight. "You really think I'm going to tell a punk like you?"

"If you don't, that'll be your last smoke." The Makarov remained locked unwaveringly on her heart.

She took the cigarette from her mouth and looked at it ruefully. "I was planning on quitting anyway . . .

Okay, kiddo, strap yourself in. The people I work for wanted Takashi dead—your wife too—and the statues destroyed. Stikes was just an incidental bonus."

Eddie clenched his jaw. "Why do they want to kill Nina?"

"Hell if I know. I'm just an operator—I don't make the decisions. They're on one side, my employers are on the other, it's that simple. As for why they want *you* dead . . ." Scarber returned the cigarette to her mouth, a final lengthy draw burning it to ash all the way to the filter. She smiled like a skull. "Seems one of my employers has a beef against you personally. When he found out there was a chance to get you into the building with your wife, he asked me to arrange it. I guess you really pissed him off at some point."

"There's a long fucking list of people I've pissed off," said Eddie. "Shorten it. Who is he?"

Instead of answering, she glanced down the aisle. Eddie turned his head—to see one of the other passengers pointing a gun at him. Another SD9. A second man approached from behind Scarber, similarly armed. "You took your goddamn time," she snapped.

"Sorry, ma'am," said the first man. His accent was American. "We didn't have a clear line of sight on the subject. If you'd sat in the aisle seat, as we suggested . . ."

"Don't you try to give me fieldcraft tips, kid," Scarber said, irritated. "I was working undercover in China while your dad was still in diapers."

"More like his granddad," Eddie said, grinning.

With an angry look she took the Makarov from him. "Son of a bitch," she muttered, ejecting the magazine and finding it empty. "It wasn't even loaded."

"What do you want us to do with him, ma'am?" asked the gunman.

"Gee, what do you think? Deal with him."

His gun still locked on Eddie, the man slipped into the seat beside him. The other goon took the empty seat next to Scarber, also fixing his weapon on the Englishman. "You're just going to shoot me?" said Eddie, feigning casualness even as his mind raced to figure a way out of the situation. "I think the other passengers might notice."

"Everyone in this car is with me," Scarber announced smugly. "We booked every seat."

"Oh. Glad I bought shares in Japan Rail, then," Eddie replied, his affected nonchalance rapidly fading. The remaining "passengers" headed for the exits at each end of the carriage, presumably to stop anyone from passing through while Scarber's people completed their work. "Be a bit hard for you to hide a body with a bullet hole in it for another hour, though."

"Don't worry, kiddo, we thought of that." She nodded to the man beside Eddie, who cautiously holstered his weapon—the other gunman pointedly raising his SD9 toward Eddie's face to discourage him from trying anything—and took out a shiny metal tube with a nozzle on one end. "Gas injector," Scarber explained. "No needle marks, no noise, and you'll be dead in twenty seconds. We get off at Nagoya, and by the time someone tries to wake you up at the end of the line we'll be out of the country."

"Well, hoo-fucking-ray for Japanese politeness," said Eddie. Blocked in, with the man across the table covering him, he could neither fight nor run. "Do I at least get to finish my ciggy?" He raised it to his mouth.

Scarber shook her head. "Those things'll kill you." She gestured to the first goon, who turned in his seat to face the Englishman, bringing up the gas injector—

Eddie spat the cigarette into his eye.

Sparks flew, the blinded man screeching and clapping a hand to his face—and Eddie yanked him over the armrest. The startled agent opposite found his line of fire blocked by his partner.

The anguished operative was still clutching the injector. Eddie clamped a fist around his hand and twisted it to jam the nozzle up against the goon's jaw. There was a sharp hiss. The man's shrieks turned to pure horror as he realized his death was just seconds away.

But the same would be true for Eddie if he couldn't get clear . . .

He bodily shoved the dying man across the table, then snatched at a lever on his chair. The first-class seat slammed into its reclined position as Eddie threw himself back against it. The other man stood to bring his gun above his spasming partner—only to have the Smith & Wesson kicked from his hand as his target rolled backward.

Eddie crashed down in the next set of seats and scrambled to his feet. He had to get out of the carriage—the presence of witnesses would drastically limit Scarber and her men's actions. He leapt into the aisle, about to sprint for the door at the end of the coach—

It opened. Another suited Asian man came through, gun raised.

Eddie dived across the aisle as he fired. A dull thump of lead against flesh and a choked scream came from behind him. The man beside Scarber had moved to retrieve his gun, only to take the bullet in his chest.

Another shot smacked into the seat back above Eddie. The new arrival was charging down the carriage for a clear shot. He needed a weapon. The dead goon's gun had landed on the seats across from Scarber's table. Eddie flung himself over the row of chairs. Another shot hissed overhead as he landed heavily.

The gun! Where was it?

He looked frantically about, hearing footsteps rapidly closing.

If it had fallen under the seats, he was doomed—

There, against an armrest. He snapped it up, firing blind over the seats. The running man ducked for cover.

Eddie jumped back into the aisle. Scarber was still in her seat, but had hooked her gun with one outstretched foot and was reaching under the table for it.

He pointed the SD9 at her and pulled the trigger—

It clicked. Empty.

Scarber nevertheless flinched as if she had received an electric shock. A brief exchange of hostile glares, then

Eddie vaulted the dead man and ran for the rear of the carriage. "Get Jun and kill that bastard!" Scarber shouted.

The door automatically slid open as he approached. He darted into the boarding compartment. Two sets of doors ahead marked the connecting passage between this coach and the next—and through the glass he saw another man hurrying toward him.

Nowhere to go. The outer doors were sealed, controlled by the *shinkansen*'s crew and opening only when the train was stationary.

But there was another door, a NO ENTRY sign on it. He shoulder-barged it, but the lock held firm. The man was almost at the connecting passage.

Another slam—

The door burst open. Eddie fell into a cramped guard's compartment, hip barking against a shelf-like desk on the back wall. A telephone was fitted above it, but there was no time to call anyone for help. He shut the door, jamming the handle with the empty gun.

Not that it mattered, as the compartment was too small to provide any cover. All the gunman had to do was fire through the door. He looked about in desperation. Nothing he could use for protection, no panels in the walls or floor—

A small hatch in the ceiling.

Eddie didn't know where it led, or care. He scrambled onto the little desk and tugged at the hatch's inset handle. If it was locked, he was dead. The handle rattled, but didn't move.

Noises outside. The door juddered, clanking against the wedged gun. A kick, then another, harder. The panel around the catch buckled.

He gripped the handle with both hands, his entire weight on it. Metal creaked. A third strike from outside—

Something inside the hatch snapped—and it dropped open, wind screaming into the cubicle. Eddie grabbed the frame above and pulled himself up.

Onto the bullet train's roof.

The slipstream mashed him against the opening's rear edge with hurricane force. In the darkness the *shinkansen*'s white-painted carriages were little more than dim blocks shrinking into the distance ahead and behind, the only illumination the glow of the train's internal lights on the concrete trackside—and the dazzling blue flashes of electrical sparks where a pantograph arm touched the overhead high-tension cables.

The roof was smooth except for a pair of parallel ribs running its length, about two feet apart. Eddie lay flat between them, palms and toes pushing against the low aluminum ridges, and crawled forward. Moving toward the train's rear would be far easier, but it would leave him completely exposed, whereas the pantograph's raised base was just a few yards ahead. Getting over it would give him some protection against bullets.

However small.

The exposed top of his head stung and prickled as dust and grit snatched up by the train's wake hit him at the takeoff speed of a 747. He kept moving. Even though the pantograph's base was streamlined, it still disrupted the airflow, blasting a swirling tornado into Eddie's face as he got closer. He had to turn his head and bury his chin into his shoulder just to draw a breath.

Movement behind—a man emerging from the lit rectangle of the hatch.

The sight of the agent galvanized him. He scrambled along the roof like a gecko, the airflow trying to tear him off with every movement. Another sharp stab as something hit him above one eye, then he reached the pantograph and pulled himself over its base, careful to avoid the arm itself—

A gunshot!

He flattened himself against the roof, not sure how the gunman had missed from such close range. Another shot—but still he didn't feel the agonizing slam and burn of a bullet impact. He grabbed the rooftop ribs again and pulled himself onward, risking a look back. A flash from the power line revealed the agent halfway out of the hatch, anger clear even through the force of the wind on his face.

That same wind had saved Eddie. The gunman's aim was thrown wildly off as the 180-mile-per-hour gale lashed his arm.

But now the agent was climbing out after him. No matter how strong the blast, he couldn't miss from a distance of two feet. Eddie set off again, muscles already aching. He squinted ahead. Machinery was set into the smooth aluminum expanse of the roof, but at the very far end of the carriage. He had a long way to go before knowing if it would help or hinder him.

And his opponent was younger, faster, not sore from multiple injuries. He was already slipping past the pantograph, smoothly avoiding the electrified arm like liquid metal. All Eddie could do was keep going, knowing that the other man would be close enough for an unmissable shot in seconds—

A sudden bolt of pain—but in his face, not from behind. The shock almost made him lose his grip.

An insect, he realized. He had just hit a bug, the unfortunate creature splattering against his forehead.

If something so small could hurt so much . . . what about something larger?

Even as the idea blazed through his mind, he was already shifting position, bringing one hand to his jacket pocket. It found hard, cold metal—his lighter.

He drew it out, looking back. The agent was mere feet behind him. The man brought up his gun, took aim—

Eddie tossed the lighter over his shoulder.

Instantly caught by the slipstream, it shot backward and hit the gunman's face with the force of a punch. He screamed as blood streamed from his nose—then Eddie's boots cracked against his head as the Englishman deliberately raised his hands and let the wind whip him back along the smooth metal surface. The agent lost his hold and tumbled along the roof—

Into the overhead cable.

Tens of thousands of volts surged through him, his hair instantly bursting into flames. A fiery halo surrounded his head as the cable sliced vertically down through his skull like a cheese wire. Friction dragged him backward—into the arm, which collapsed under his weight.

Registering a dangerous loss of power from one of its pantographs, the train's computers immediately applied the emergency brakes.

Eddie had just regained his grip on the rooftop, but even had he been equipped with suckers on his hands and feet he wouldn't have been able to hold on against the abrupt deceleration. Momentum hurled him forward. The low ridges weren't enough to channel him— he bumped over them, sliding toward the edge and a lethal plunge to the tracks below—

One hand caught a protruding section of the air-conditioning machinery set into the end of the roof. He jerked to a halt, crying out as his shoulder joint crackled.

Brakes squealing, the *shinkansen* dropped below a hundred miles per hour, sixty, thirty. A final shrill, and it lurched to a standstill on a concrete flyover above the surrounding countryside. Eddie painfully dragged himself back onto the roof and started a staggering run toward the head of the train, looking for another access hatch. He had to get back inside before Scarber and her remaining goon found the statues . . .

* * *

Scarber didn't need the update from her man Jun to know that something had gone seriously wrong; the sudden braking that threw her to the floor of the first-class car had been clue enough. Any stoppage of a bullet train was considered an emergency by the authorities, and with at least two corpses aboard and clear evidence of a gunfight there would be a massive police presence very shortly. It was time to bug out.

But there was something she had to do first. "Never

mind that," she told Jun as he started explaining where the Englishman had gone. "We've got to find the statues. You saw the bag Chase had when he boarded—it must be somewhere forward of here. Find it, then evac the train."

Jun nodded. "Where do we meet?"

Scarber looked through a window. There was nothing visible in the darkness outside; the train had stopped somewhere between the towns along Japan's south coast. "Hell if I know. Just get the statues, then once you're off the train call me—we'll rendezvous when I've got a GPS fix."

"Okay. What about you?"

"Never mind about me, just get the bag. Go on!"

Jun turned and jogged from the carriage. Scarber raised her recovered and reloaded gun and fired three shots at the nearest window, splintering the toughened glass.

* * *

The other carriages were scenes of confusion and rising concern. The *shinkansen* were renowned for their efficiency and safety; an emergency stop far from a station was almost unheard of. The train's staff were making their way through each coach in turn, trying to reassure the passengers that the delay was only temporary, the problem would soon be solved, and they would be moving again as quickly as possible.

Jun pushed through the worried commuters, eyes sweeping from side to side as he searched the luggage racks. Chase had boarded the train carrying a nondescript black holdall, and a couple of passengers had already protested when he examined what turned out to be false positives. But he was running out of time to worry about raising suspicion; the operation had already gone to hell, and he wanted to get out of the confines of the train as quickly as possible.

He spied another black bag on the luggage rack. The fact that nobody was sitting in the seats immediately beneath it made it a likely prospect. None of the passengers nearby paid him any attention as he took it from the rack, more concerned with questioning the guard about the delay. He unzipped the holdall. Inside was a polycarbonate case. He opened it—and smiled.

Three crude statuettes of purple stone gazed dumbly back at him. Why they were important, he didn't know, or care. His superiors wanted them, and that was all that mattered. He closed the case, refastened the bag, then squeezed back down the aisle.

The door to the boarding compartment slid open, and he went through. Those to the connecting passage were push-button-operated rather than fully automatic, so he tapped the control and waited for them to hiss apart—

An arm locked around his throat from behind, pinning him in a brutal choke hold as a clenched fist pounded paralyzingly into his kidneys. A voice growled in his ear: "I think that's *my* bag."

The fist rose to his head, opened, clamped around his face—

There was a horrible crackling snap as Eddie twisted hard and broke the man's neck. He let the limp body drop, ignoring the helpless choking gurgles from the agent's crushed windpipe as he took the SD9 from inside his jacket, then collected the bag before moving at speed into the next carriage.

He headed for the first-class coaches. The body would soon be discovered, so he had to get off the train as quickly as possible. But he also had to find Scarber.

One way or another, she was going to give him answers.

He reached car number ten, immediately noticing a breeze as the sliding door opened. A window had been smashed. Scarber's escape route. He hurried to it, gun at the ready. The train was on a long viaduct over a bowl of farmland. The lights of towns shimmered in the distance ahead and behind, but he was searching for something nearer . . .

Movement on the tracks, a scurrying figure picked out

by the glow from inside the train. Scarber. Eddie jumped down and ran after her. She was crossing the other line, heading for the broad concrete maintenance path along the viaduct's edge.

He followed, closing quickly. He would catch up well before the end of the bridge, leaving her with nowhere to run.

Which meant she would fight. The former agent wouldn't give up easily.

He passed the *shinkansen*'s streamlined nose, now only a hundred yards behind her. Tough and resourceful Scarber might be, but she was a decade older than Eddie, and a chain-smoker to boot. Fifty yards. With the rumble of the train's motors fading behind her, she would soon hear him . . .

Forty yards—and Scarber looked back.

Eddie dropped the bag, taking careful aim as the woman spun and raised her gun. He couldn't risk killing her, not yet.

Scarber had no such restraints. She fired three rapid shots. Bullets cracked against the concrete, closer to him each time—

Eddie pulled the trigger. One shot, but it was all he needed. Scarber shrieked and staggered, dropping her gun and clapping her left hand to her right shoulder.

Keeping the SD9 fixed on her, he ran the rest of the way. "You fucking little *shit*!" Scarber hissed.

He kicked her gun away. "You'll live—*if* you tell me who you're working for. Otherwise I'll shoot you right here."

Her voice became tremulous. "You'd shoot a defenseless woman?"

Eddie almost laughed. "Defenseless? You just tried to fucking kill me!"

The tremor disappeared. "No, I didn't think you'd buy that." She screwed up her face in pain, looking down at her injured arm. "All right. But do I have your word that you'll let me go if I tell you?"

"Yeah. I just want to know who wants me and Nina

dead." Behind her, a new light appeared in the far distance—another bullet train, coming the other way. The service path was wide enough for them to keep safely clear, though he expected it would be horribly loud. "Think we should move back a bit first, mind." He retreated a couple of steps.

Scarber followed, coming closer to him. "There are two people. One of them is only interested in seeing your wife dead—you're not even on his radar. It's the other who has a personal grievance."

"Who?"

"Victor Dalton."

The name sent a shock running through him. Victor Dalton—the ex-president of the United States. The man who two years earlier had tried to have Eddie and Nina killed to cover up his involvement in a conspiracy, and in return had been forced to resign from office in utter humiliation when a video of him having sex with Eddie's ex-wife Sophia Blackwood hit the Internet.

Which would explain his grudge, certainly.

"Dalton?" echoed Eddie, stunned.

Scarber took her hand from the bullet wound. "Hell of a thing, huh, kiddo?"

All kinds of questions sprang to his mind, but one was far and away at the head of the list. "So who's the other per—"

A flat *snick,* and Scarber's hand suddenly slashed at his throat. He instinctively whipped up his gun arm to block it—then jumped back with a pained yell as something stabbed into his forearm. Before he could recover, another swipe knocked the Smith & Wesson from his hand with a clack of metal against metal.

The former agent still had a trick up her sleeve—literally. A slender blade jutted out from beneath her wrist: a spring-loaded weapon strapped to her arm. She jabbed it at Eddie's face again, forcing him to stumble back or be blinded.

The approaching train was now much nearer, racing toward them at full speed, but Scarber's focus was entirely on the fallen gun. She bent to retrieve it, then whirled and pointed it at Eddie—

He drove a fearsome spin-kick into her stomach, sending her flying backward—into the path of the oncoming train.

The *whump* as its pointed prow hit her at 180 miles per hour was audible even over the thunder of motors and the scream of displaced air. The *shinkansen*'s white nose suddenly became a bright red.

Eddie dropped to the concrete, shielding his ears as the train blasted past. Even if the driver reacted instantly to the collision and slammed on the emergency brakes, it would still take a mile for the express to come to a stop. The moment the rearmost car passed, he hurried back to collect the bag, then ran for the end of the viaduct. With two bullet trains now halted and bodies littering the scene, a major police operation would soon begin, and he needed as big a head start as possible.

Once he was clear, though, he knew his next step. He had to get back to the United States.

And deal with Victor Dalton.

ELEVEN

Rome

Returning to New York via Italy hadn't been Nina's plan, but she had been left with more than enough time while waiting to deal with the Japanese authorities to think about the full implications of the events in the Takashi building.

Foremost on her mind was her husband. Three months without even an attempt to communicate, then he appeared out of the blue? She didn't know whether to be overjoyed or furious—though his accusing her of being in league with Stikes tipped her feelings a little toward the latter.

Stikes's presence was itself a concern. She was sure Takashi had lied about the mercenary's being a mere delivery boy; he was involved with whatever was going on. As for what that might be, though . . .

Could she believe Takashi's claims about the goals of his mysterious organization? That Stikes was connected to it at all made her doubt its true commitment to ending global conflict, for a start—as a gun for hire, his livelihood depended on that. But someone else was opposed enough to take action to stop him. Drastic action.

The helicopter attack had been intended to kill her, Takashi, and Stikes alike.

And Eddie. Somebody wanted him dead too. But why? What was the connection?

The statues were the key, she was sure.

Takashi had known what to expect when the figures were brought together. But nothing Nina knew of suggested even remotely that the statues could use the planet's own energy fields to counter the force of gravity—to say nothing of her extraordinary mental experience.

Which meant that someone, somewhere, had information that outstripped even the IHA's discoveries. She only knew one group that might fit the bill. And that was why she had come to Rome.

"Dr. Wilde," said Nicholas Popadopoulos, turning her name over in his mouth like a piece of slightly unpleasant food. She had dealt with the stooped old man before. The Brotherhood of Selasphoros possessed an enormous trove of ancient texts concerning Atlantis; the organization's purpose had been to suppress knowledge of the lost civilization.

It had done so by trying to kill anyone who got too close to the truth, which was why Popadopoulos's antipathy was more than matched by Nina's. She had been targeted, as had her parents. She had survived. They had not. The thought still caused a knot of anger to tighten within her.

She tried to suppress it. Her life might now depend on something in the Brotherhood's archives. "Mr. Popadopoulos," she replied, voice studiedly neutral. "Good to see you again."

"And you," he said, less than convincingly. "This visit is unexpected, though. We have cooperated fully with the IHA in providing anything it requested, so why you felt the need to come here in person . . ."

"Your definition of *full cooperation* isn't quite the same as ours," Nina said with a thin smile.

"We are doing everything asked of us!" Popadopoulos's resentment was clear in every word. "We are the only people who know everything in the archives. It would take outsiders years just to understand how it is cataloged. Perhaps you think you can do it without us?"

Her smile turned colder. "I dunno, maybe we should try. You could have a nice long vacation . . . paid for by the state. What do you think?"

He glowered at her through his little round spectacles. What was left of the Brotherhood after the battles leading to Atlantis's discovery had been forced to open its records under threat of being held to account for the organization's past crimes. "I will see if things can be done more . . . expediently," he conceded.

"Thank you. Although that isn't actually why I decided to pop in."

"What? Then why *are* you here? Just to bully and harass us?"

"No, I want some information. Expediently."

The old man was annoyed at having his words turned back at him. "What information?"

"I want to know if you have anything in the archives about Nantalas."

"The priestess?"

Nina arched an eyebrow. "Then I guess you *do* have something."

"She was an important figure prior to the sinking of Atlantis." He leaned thoughtfully back in his seat. "She claimed to have visions, I remember. Of war, usually, but that was the major occupation of the Atlanteans. She also claimed to have magic powers."

"These powers—they wouldn't have been connected to three statues, by any chance?"

Popadopoulos sat back up, surprised. "Yes. How did you know?"

"We excavated some of the texts from the Temple of Poseidon."

"Ah, I see." His face tipped into a frown. "It would be nice to receive updates on the IHA's progress in Atlantis. Anyone would think you did not trust us."

"Really," said Nina scathingly. "So what else do you know about the statues?"

"It is many years since I last read the text, but I think they were how she received her visions. They were the keys to her powers . . . No, the powers were not actually hers. The statues were how she channeled them, but they came from something else, a stone . . . Wait, the *sky* stone, that is it."

"And what were these powers?"

He shrugged. "I don't remember. It was all magic, nonsense. I paid it no mind."

Nina fought to keep her frustration in check. "And you didn't think it might be worth telling the IHA this? You must have known that we had two of the statues."

"We provide exactly what is asked for," Popadopoulos told her. "Nothing less—and nothing more."

"Well, you might want to feel a bit more of the volunteer spirit in future," she snapped. "But in the meantime, I want to know everything about the statues. Even the stuff you think is nonsense."

"I told you, I would have to read the text again."

"Well, I'm not busy right now, and if you've got time to see me you can't be either. So let's go."

"You want to see the original text? In the archive?" He appeared horrified by the suggestion.

"Yep, pretty much."

"That was never part of the deal! It was agreed that the Brotherhood could maintain the secrecy of its archives."

"I don't give a damn about your secrets. What I do give a damn about is that somebody else knows about the power of these statues—at least two groups of somebodies, in fact, and they're already fighting over them. Did you see the news about that skyscraper in Tokyo?"

"Yes, of course. They said it was attacked by a helicopter."

"I was in the penthouse!" He regarded her in astonishment. "I had the statues, all three of them, in my hands. And something happened, something I didn't understand—but something incredible. I need to know what it means. I think the answer's in your archive."

Popadopoulos sat back again, deep in thought. At last, with a decidedly conflicted expression, he stood. "Very well, Dr. Wilde. But these are exceptional circumstances, yes? I am not willing to have other members of the IHA *pop in,* as you say, whenever they want."

"Just show me what you've got on the statues and I'll be out of here."

For the first time, he liked something she had said. "Come with me."

The Brotherhood's activities in Rome were hidden behind the cover of a law firm, its offices within sight of the high walls of the Vatican. Popadopoulos led her through the narrow corridors to one particular door on the ground floor. "In here."

Nina eyed the interior dubiously. "Seriously?" It was a closet containing shelves of cleaning products, a tiny barred window high on one wall.

He sighed and entered, waving her inside. She squeezed into the cramped space as the Greek closed the door and reached for a light switch. Instead of flicking it, though, he took hold of the casing and gave it a half turn. A click, a muted hum from somewhere below—and Nina gasped as the floor began a slow descent of a shaft of dark old bricks.

Popadopoulos chuckled at her uneasiness. "Do you like our elevator?"

"It's, uh . . . different."

"It was installed over a hundred years ago. The Brotherhood has owned the building since it was constructed in 1785—but the archives have been here for far longer. I hope you appreciate that I am actually giving you a very rare privilege," he went on. "The number of outsiders who have seen them in, oh, the past five hundred years can be counted on both hands. Even members of the Brotherhood were rarely allowed to enter if they were not involved with record keeping."

The elevator stopped around thirty feet below street

level. A passage led off to one side, dim bulbs strung along its length. Heavier-duty electrical cables ran along the walls. "Follow me," said Popadopoulos.

After twenty yards the brickwork gave way to older and rougher stone. The tunnel continued ahead for some distance. Nina tried to get her bearings. "It's a catacomb," she realized. "We're going under the Vatican?"

"Yes. The catacombs beneath the Holy See stretch for tens, maybe even hundreds of kilometers—they have never been fully mapped. These sections were sealed and donated to the Brotherhood in the ninth century by a cardinal who was also a supporter of the cause."

Nina was impressed. "Your own version of the Vatican Secret Archives."

"Yes—although our records contain material that even the *Archivum Secretum* does not."

"I'm guessing that the scope of your records is more limited, though."

"You would be surprised by the scope of our records," he said smugly. "But yes, Atlantis is its focus. The Atlantean empire, its rulers, its society . . . and the threat it poses."

"*Posed,* surely," Nina corrected. "Past tense. Unless you're saying there are more genocidal nuts like the Frosts plotting to resurrect it?"

"You were the one who was attacked over the statues," he pointed out. "But here we are." Ahead, the passage was blocked by a heavy steel door. Beside it was a keypad; Popadopoulos, after making sure Nina couldn't see over his shoulder, tapped in an entry code. The door rumbled open, bright lights shining behind it. The low hum of ventilation machinery became audible.

Popadopoulos went through and called out in Italian. "The librarians may be deep in the archives," he added for Nina, before shouting again. "Agostino!"

An echoing reply came from down one of the other tunnels leading from the large room. "He is on his way," said the Greek. Nina nodded, looking around while they waited. Two entire walls were taken up by the stacked wooden drawers of a card index system; while there was also a PC on a desk that apparently served the same function, she suspected from the contrast between the lovingly polished old hardwood and the rather dusty computer that the librarians preferred the traditional method of locating a specific document. The electrical cables branched out to power other pieces of equipment: air conditioners, dehumidifiers, pumps, everything needed to keep conditions throughout the underground labyrinth as dry and stable as possible.

After a minute, shuffling footsteps heralded the librarians' arrival. Two men emerged from a tunnel—one an old, white-bearded man with a bulbous nose, behind him a somewhat overweight, shaggy-haired youth. The elder didn't appear pleased to have been interrupted, and his look became one of outright hostility when he saw Nina. He snapped in Italian at Popadopoulos, who gave him a resigned placatory response before making introductions. "Dr. Wilde, this is Agostino Belardinelli, chief archivist of the Brotherhood, and his assistant, Paolo Agnelli. Agostino, this is—"

"I know who she is!" Belardinelli said angrily, jabbing a gnarled finger at Nina. "You brought *her* in here? It is a, a . . ." Another burst of outraged Italian as he mimed stabbing himself in the heart.

"Agostino's son was also a member of the Brotherhood," Popadopoulos told Nina awkwardly. "He, ah . . . lost his life in Brazil."

"Did he now," she said coldly. That meant Belardinelli's son had been one of those trying to kill her and the team searching for a lost Atlantean outpost deep in the jungle.

"Yes, well," said Popadopoulos, "it would be best if we got this over with. Agostino, Dr. Wilde needs to see everything concerning the Atlantean priestess Nantalas and the three statues that she said granted her powers."

That provoked another highly emotional outburst from the archivist. Popadopoulos listened with growing impatience before finally cutting in. "Agostino! Once she has seen what she needs, she will leave, and then we can discuss this. But for now, let us find it as soon as possible, hmm?"

Muttering to himself, Belardinelli crossed to one of the ranks of drawers. "Nantalas, Nantalas," he said, finger waving back and forth like a radar antenna. "She was mentioned in one of the Athenian annals. Now, was it Akakios, or . . ."

Agnelli spoke for the first time. "It was Kallikrates," he said hesitantly. "One of the parchments in the fourteenth arcosolium."

"Kallikrates, yes." Belardinelli had evidently memorized the intricacies of the index, as he went to a particular drawer and flicked through the hundreds of cards within. Taking one out, he donned a pair of reading glasses and peered at it. "Ah, his ninth text. I thought so. And it is in the fourteenth arcosolium."

"Well done, Paolo," said Popadopoulos. "It seems we really do not need a computer after all."

"I, uh—I have been memorizing the catacombs," said Agnelli.

Nina wondered why he seemed so nervous about the admission, but Belardinelli's irritable words gave her an explanation. "Yes, he is always wandering off when I need him!" He returned the card to the drawer, giving the computer a contemptuous glare. "Still, at least he is learning for himself. Better than being told the answer by a machine. I never use it myself. If God had meant machines to think for us, why give us brains?" He jabbed distastefully at the mouse to the left of the keyboard.

"The text?" prompted Popadopoulos.

The old man grunted in annoyance. "Down here."

He led the others into one of the tunnels. Unlike the route from the elevator, these were more than mere access passages. Carved into the walls were long, low niches, stacked as many as four high. Loculi, Nina knew:

burial nooks, in which the ancient Christians had placed the bodies of their dead.

There were no corpses present now, to her relief. Instead, the niches were home to shelves holding wood and metal boxes, carefully wrapped bundles of thick cloth, sealed glass tubes containing rolled papers and parchments. A great repository of ancient knowledge.

Stolen knowledge. Not even famous historical names had been safe from the Brotherhood's attentions; one of the items in the archive had been *Hermocrates,* the lost dialogue of the Greek philosopher Plato. She wondered what secrets were contained in the documents she passed—and how many people had been killed for them.

But there were more important issues than her disgust at the Brotherhood. They went deeper into the catacombs, Belardinelli turning without hesitation at each junction to lead them to their destination. "Here," he said, stopping at a larger, arched niche, reliefs of figures and Latin text carved into the stonework. "The fourteenth arcosolium."

Within the ornate burial nook was a tall grid of shelves, upon which were dozens of cloth-wrapped objects. Books, but very large ones; Nina had seen a similar example when Popadopoulos brought the original text of *Hermocrates* to her in New York. The "pages" were actually sheets of glass, the fragile parchments carefully preserved between them and the whole thing bound together by metal.

Belardinelli squinted up at one of the higher shelves, then looked around and spotted a little stepladder not far away. He waved for Agnelli to bring it. "Shall I get the book for you?" the youth asked as he set the ladder in place.

"No, no," the bearded man insisted. He ascended the steps, stretching to reach the uppermost shelf. He had to hold on to the old wood with his left hand for support, leaving a print in the dust as he strained to pull the heavy book from its resting place. Nina cringed as it tipped over the edge, its weight almost too much for Belardinelli to support with one hand, but he managed to catch it before it fell.

He clambered back down. "This is what you wanted to see," he told Nina, unfolding the thick cloth. Compared with the other wrapped volumes, there was surprisingly little dust. The cover was of thick burgundy leather, framed in scuffed brass. "The texts of Kallikrates."

"I've never heard of him," she admitted.

"You wouldn't have," said Popadopoulos. "The Brotherhood made sure of that. But he was a student of Theophrastus—"

"One of Plato's students."

That seemed to elevate her, very slightly, in Belardinelli's eyes. "Yes. Kallikrates was intrigued by the history of the wars between Athens and Atlantis. These texts"—he tapped the book—"contain his writings on the subject."

"Well, let's see what he said about Nantalas, shall we?" said Nina.

Belardinelli placed the book on the stone slab at the base of the arcosolium and opened it carefully, the binding creaking as he turned each glass "page." At a particular one, he put his reading glasses back on. "This is it."

A discolored sheet of parchment was pressed between the glass plates, the bottom part raggedly torn away and the remainder showing clear signs of damage from water and time. Tightly packed Greek text was written in faded brown ink. "What happened to the rest of it?" Nina asked.

"Nobody knows," the old man replied. "When Kallikrates died, there was a dispute over his possessions. The Brotherhood took these texts from one of his brothers, but the rest were lost."

She imagined that the taking had been by force, but was more eager to read the ancient document than criticize. Her parents had taught her Greek as a child, so the only problems were the occasionally poor legibility of the text and the low light. From what she could tell, the previous part of Kallikrates's writings concerned the Atlantean royal court, before discussing the high priestess's part in its affairs. "Seems she was quite the warmonger," she said. Most of her supposed prophecies were more like thinly veiled entreaties to lead Atlantis into yet another battle against its many enemies.

"All Atlanteans are warmongers," said Belardinelli accusingly. "Violence is in their blood."

"And in the blood of their enemies too, apparently," she shot back. "Where's the part about the statues?"

Belardinelli indicated a section farther down the page. Nina read it out loud. " 'When Nantalas held the statues, a great light would fill the Temple of the Gods, giving the high priestess visions as the stone called out to her. She said that such visions let her see through the eyes of all the watching gods, and that she could feel all life in this world.' That's what I . . ."

She trailed off, not wanting to let the members of the Brotherhood in on her secrets. "What I expected based on our new excavations," she continued before quickly reading on until she found another relevant piece of text. " 'The high priestess requested the presence of the king at the Temple of the Gods. She told him again that the power of the sky stone would make the empire invincible. When he demanded proof, she brought the statues together and touched them to the stone. The king was astounded when it . . .' "

That was the end of the text, nothing more than the occasional letter discernible at the torn bottom of the parchment. "That's all there is?" she asked Belardinelli.

"Nantalas appears in a few other texts," he replied, "but only as a name—nothing more is said about her."

She turned to Popadopoulos. "The Brotherhood is the only organization that has this information, yes? There's nobody else who might have copies of it, or another source?"

"Not that I am aware of," he said.

"And you haven't shared anything from the archives with anybody but the IHA?"

"We would not even have done that if we had not been forced," said Belardinelli, affronted.

"Why are you asking?" said the Greek.

"Because," she said, "I think somebody has information about Atlantis that not even the Brotherhood of Selasphoros possesses."

Belardinelli shook his head. "Impossible! The Brotherhood has been dedicated to its task for hundreds of generations. We have found everything there is to find about Atlantis."

"Except Atlantis itself," Nina reminded him. "You needed me to do that."

The Italian seemed about to explode with anger, but Popadopoulos waved him down. "What are you suggesting, Dr. Wilde?"

"When I put the three statues together in Tokyo," she said, "I had . . . an experience."

"What kind of experience?"

"Let's just say that Nantalas might not have been a fraud. But the thing is, Takashi—the guy who had the statues—knew what to expect, as if he'd read this text." She indicated the parchment.

"Impossible," Belardinelli said again.

"I dunno—this could very easily be interpreted as what I experienced, certainly from the point of view of someone living eleven thousand years ago. But the thing is, that wasn't the only thing he was expecting. There were . . . other effects, is all I can say right now, when the statues were put together. Physical effects, that . . . well, the only way I can describe them is *extraordinary,*" she said, with a helpless shrug. "But Takashi wasn't at all surprised—by any of it. Not only did he know about what's written here, but he also knew something you don't."

Popadopoulos was stunned. "You think this man Takashi had read the missing parts of Kallikrates's texts?"

"Maybe. Maybe more than that. Is there *anyone* else

who might have information about Atlantis that the
Brotherhood doesn't? Governments, other secret societies?" She glanced up at the ceiling. "Religions?"

"There is nothing in the *Archivum Secretum* about
Atlantis," said Belardinelli firmly.

Popadopoulos was more doubtful. "Several governments have vast secret archives of their own," he admitted. "But we have never shared our knowledge with
anyone, except the IHA."

"So, if you're so sure that this parchment is the only
copy of Kallikrates's work, how could Takashi know
what it describes?" Nina asked.

Belardinelli took off his glasses and paced across the
narrow tunnel before whirling on his heel to face Nina.
"The other part of the page repeats the same information, obviously," he said, punctuating his words with
more jabs from his finger. "Someone else possesses it—
and that is where Takashi read it."

"Parchment could be expensive," Nina countered. "I
mean, look how many words Kallikrates crammed onto
this. You don't waste it by repeating yourself."

"But that—that is the only possible explanation," said
Agnelli. Nina had almost forgotten he was there.

"No, there's another one. You won't like it, though,"
she told the two older men. "Someone inside the Brotherhood passed on the information to Takashi's organization."

The silence told her that her theory had not been well
received. "No!" barked Belardinelli at last. "It is not
possible. Every single member of the Brotherhood is
completely loyal to the cause!"

"You don't *have* a cause anymore! Atlantis has been
discovered, the Frosts and their followers are dead, the
Brotherhood's been exposed—and it's now got the UN
and several governments watching over it. Maybe someone decided it was time to get out, and thought that
selling secrets would be the best way to set up a retirement fund."

"It is . . . hard to believe," said Popadopoulos slowly.

"Agostino is right—loyalty to the Brotherhood is very important."

"And besides," said Belardinelli, "there are only three people who know the full contents of the archives: myself, Nicholas, and Paolo." He crossed his arms as if that settled the argument.

"Well, that narrows the list of suspects, doesn't it?" Nina said. As the three men exchanged glances, she looked up at the shelf from which the preserved parchment had been taken. "Huh."

"What is it?" asked Popadopoulos.

She pointed to the left of the empty spot. "That's Mr. Belardinelli's handprint there in the dust."

"Yes? So?" Belardinelli snapped. "I made it when I took down the book. You saw me do it."

"So whose is that on the other side?" She indicated another mark in the gray layer.

"You never touched that part of the shelf, Agostino," said Popadopoulos, moving for a better look. "But someone has—and recently. There is hardly any new dust."

Nina turned to Belardinelli. "Are you right-handed?"

"Yes," he said, puzzled and angry. "What has that to do with anything?"

"When you climbed up, you used your left hand for support while you pulled the book out with your right hand—your stronger hand. But that mark was made by someone's right hand . . . meaning they moved the book with their left."

"I am right-handed," Popadopoulos told her.

"Yeah, I thought you would be." Now she faced Agnelli. "The computer was set up for someone left-handed. And Mr. Belardinelli here said he never uses it, so that only leaves you." Prickles of sweat blossomed across his broad face even in the climate-controlled cool of the catacomb. "*You're* left-handed, Mr. Agnelli. And you knew where the parchment was without having to check—and the ladder was even right here." She looked back at the other men. "How does that sound?"

Their faces betrayed shock—which, she quickly realized, was far greater than her deduction deserved. She turned to Agnelli once more.

And froze. "Oh, crap."

The young Italian was pointing a gun at her.

TWELVE

Agnelli was shaking, the small silver automatic trembling in his hand, but his index finger was tight around the trigger. "D-don't move," he stammered.

A chilling fear coursed through Nina. In his frightened, agitated state, Agnelli might shoot her by accident. "Okay, let's, ah, let's all stay calm, huh? Nobody wants to get shot. I have been before, and I didn't like it."

"Paolo!" exclaimed Belardinelli. "What is this?"

"I—I am sorry," said the sweating Agnelli. "I needed the money, and they gave me fifty thousand euros for a picture of the parchment. Only that one page! I didn't give them anything else. I didn't betray the Brotherhood."

"And yet you are pointing a gun at us," Popadopoulos said in an acid tone.

"Why were you even carrying a gun?" Nina asked. "Expecting to get caught, were you?"

"Shut up!" cried Agnelli, almost hyperventilating. "Everyone shut up! Move back."

Nina willingly retreated a couple of steps, as did Popadopoulos, but Belardinelli stood his ground. "What are you going to do, Paolo? Kill us? Is that how you repay the Brotherhood for everything it has given you? Is that how you repay *me*?"

"No, no, I—I don't want to hurt anyone, I just want to get out of here," said Agnelli, wide-eyed. "Please, Agostino, move back!"

Instead, Belardinelli held out his hand. "Give me the gun, Paolo." He stepped forward. "We can—"

The gunshot was almost deafening in the confined space.

Belardinelli staggered, clutching feebly at his chest. He looked up at the younger man, face shocked and hurt . . . then slowly crumpled to the floor. Agnelli's own features conveyed equal disbelief.

Silence and stillness for a moment. Then Popadopoulos fled down the tunnel.

The gun roared again. The Greek crashed against a wall, knocking items from a loculus.

Agnelli brought the gun back around to Nina—

She too was moving—but not running. Instead, she swept up the little stepladder and flung it at him. He reeled, pulling the trigger, but the bullet went well wide of its target.

Now Nina ran, leaping over the moaning Popadopoulos and sprinting down the tunnel. Behind her, Agnelli's shout warned her that his fear had turned to anger.

She threw herself down a curving side passage as Agnelli fired again. Where it led she had no idea, but she had no choice except to follow it.

The Italian set off in pursuit. He reached the side passage, turned—

And stopped in momentary surprise. The tunnel was in near darkness.

Still running, Nina passed beneath another lightbulb and, fist clenching her jacket's cuff, reached up to smash it. Even with the material protecting her hand, she still winced as a glass splinter stabbed into the flesh.

But that pain was infinitely preferable to the burning hammer blow of a bullet. She was in Agnelli's domain, the Italian knowing every twist and turn of the tunnels. Her only hope of escape was to confuse him long enough for her to get past and make a dash for the elevator.

The passage twisted around to a four-way intersection. She carried on straight ahead, breaking another light—then doubled back into the left tunnel. A boxy dehumidifier grumbled away on the floor; she jinked past it and continued on, straining to pick out Agnelli's pounding footsteps over the machine's noise. How close was he?

Too close, almost at the intersection.

She flattened herself into the shadows of another arcosolium as Agnelli reached the junction. He glanced to each side before continuing ahead into the darkened tunnel. Nina held her breath. His steps faded—but was it because he was getting farther away, or just that he was slowing?

It was hard to be sure over the dehumidifier's thrum. She leaned out from her cover and looked back. Had her ruse worked? If she made a dash for the intersection, she might have a clear run to the entrance—or she might find herself face-to-face with Agnelli if he had realized her deception.

The longer she stayed in the catacomb, the greater her chances of her being cornered. She had to risk going back. She moved out of the shadows—

Agnelli reappeared at the junction.

Nina scrambled to reverse direction as he saw her. The gun snapped up, but in his haste he fired without aiming, the shot chipping the ancient stone wall several feet short. By the time reason overcame panic and he raised the automatic higher to look down its sights, she had rounded another corner.

More broken bulbs tinkled into the growing darkness as she ran through the archive's ancient tunnels. The passage ahead split into two. On impulse she went left, smashing another light. She was outpacing the overweight Italian, the tunnel's turns preventing him from lining up another shot, but if she found herself in a dead end he would catch up very quickly.

Or not. It sounded as though he were slowing down. He might be tiring . . . but Nina somehow knew that wasn't the case. Dread rose inside her. He had stopped running because he no longer needed to.

She had nowhere left to go.

Even with that frightening knowledge, she kept moving, destroying more bulbs. The passage bent around, another light ahead. She reached up to break it—

And saw the end of the tunnel as it opened into a chamber lined with burial niches, all packed with ancient records. A cool breeze from an air conditioner wafted around her as she skidded to a halt.

No way out.

And no hiding places either. The room was cramped enough for Agnelli to find her even in the dark. She would have no choice but to fight—against a much larger and heavier foe armed with a gun. Despite having been taught the basics of unarmed combat by Eddie, she didn't like the odds.

But it was that or stand there and wait to be shot. She was about to hit the bulb when an idea came to her.

The air conditioner. Its power cord snaked back down the tunnel . . .

Nina burned its position into her mind—then smashed the final light.

* * *

Agnelli blinked as the passage ahead went completely dark. He slowed to a cautious walk. The only remaining illumination was a dim glow from far behind him, and even that would be gone when he rounded the next bend.

But he knew exactly what lay ahead. "You can't hide from me!" he called, growing more confident despite the adrenaline making the blood hiss in his ears. "And— and I can tell the Brotherhood that you shot everyone before I stopped you. They'll believe me—they know you hate us!"

"You've got to find me first," came an echoing voice from the end of the tunnel. "You fat fuck!" it added, New York accent becoming more pronounced.

Agnelli's face tightened with pricked pride. She was *insulting* him? "Give up and—and I'll make it quick for you," he said, dredging up half-remembered dialogue from some movie in an attempt to sound more threatening.

It didn't work. "You couldn't be quick if you tried, you fucking greaseball! Come on, get your fat ass down here—if it'll squeeze through the door!"

Anger rising over his anxiety, Agnelli started to jog, right hand stretched out to feel his way along the tunnel wall as he held the gun at the ready in his left. There was no way she could slip past him in the passage, so she would be trapped in the end chamber. He went around the last turn, total darkness enshrouding him. Now he'd show her that he had more muscle than fat—

Something snagged around his ankles—and he went flying over the makeshift trip wire Nina had made from the air conditioner's power cable, slamming down facefirst in the small room. Before he could recover a foot drove into his side, followed by another kick that caught his elbow. He yelled, then panic returned as he realized he had let go of the gun.

Nina heard the clatter of metal on the floor. Run while Agnelli was down, or go for the gun and turn the tables? She chose the latter, crouching and fumbling in the blackness. Stone and dirt were all she felt. She heard the Italian also groping blindly for his fallen weapon. Where was the damn thing?

Cold, angular steel. She grabbed the gun, trying to flip it around to get a proper hold—

Agnelli gripped her wrist.

He was too strong for her to pull free, dragging her toward him. She lashed out with her other hand, hitting the side of his face, but before she could go for his eyes he bashed her hand against the floor.

She gasped in pain. Agnelli pounded her hand down again, harder. The pistol jolted loose and clacked onto the stone. The Italian batted savagely at her body with his other arm, then scrambled for the weapon—

A bell sounded, its clamor echoing through the catacomb.

Agnelli let out a gasp of horror as he realized what it meant. The wounded Popadopoulos must have managed to drag himself to the archive entrance and set off the alarm. More members of the Brotherhood would be on their way—and the old man would tell them everything.

He abandoned the gun and leapt back to his feet, scrambling down the tunnel. Ribs aching where he had hit her, Nina found the pistol in the blackness, then quickly followed the panicked Italian.

She soon reached the lit junction and paused, listening. Agnelli was heading deeper into the tunnels. She ran after him. Where was he going?

Another exit, maybe one even Belardinelli didn't know about. The old man had said that Agnelli spent a lot of time exploring the catacombs.

The bell faded as she moved farther into the maze. She noticed that some passages were unlit, their loculi empty. Not even the Brotherhood's vast collection of stolen records could fill the space donated to them. But the running man was following the lights, with a specific destination in mind . . .

She slowed sharply as she realized she could no longer hear Agnelli's steps. But he couldn't be far away; she had been gaining on the lumbering youth. Cautious, gun raised, Nina advanced. There was a room ahead, a larger chamber than any she had seen so far—and straining sounds of movement came from it.

A glance through the entrance simultaneously told her the room's purpose and excited her aesthetic and archaeological sensibilities. It was a crypt; not the dank Gothic tomb of vampire lore, but a high-ceilinged space decorated with elaborately carved pilaster columns and painted friezes, tiers of large burial nooks built for the members of an entire family around the walls.

But no Agnelli.

Confused, she warily entered. The crypt was lit by only a single bulb above the entrance, the farthest corners in shadow. She aimed the gun at each in turn, but still saw no sign of the Italian—until a noise from above made her whip the weapon up.

Despite his size and weight, Agnelli clearly had some skill at climbing. He had scaled the loculi before pulling himself up one of the pilasters, and was now more than twenty feet above and still ascending. "Stop!" Nina shouted, taking aim.

He ignored her, toes scrabbling at footholds as he headed for a dark opening where a block had either fallen or been removed from the vaulted roof. She repeated her command, but knew she couldn't shoot an unarmed and terrified man—and also that if he died, which a gunshot wound and the subsequent fall would all but guarantee, there was no way to discover who had paid him to photograph the Kallikrates text. All she could do was watch in impotent frustration as he reached the opening and squeezed inside.

"Son of a *bitch*!" she spat as she realized where his escape route led.

Into the Vatican.

The city-state's own catacombs—those that had been mapped, at least—were centered beneath the vast basilica of St. Peter. If Agnelli had discovered a way into the Vatican's lower levels, from there he could enter the basilica itself . . . and then simply walk out into the streets of Rome.

Nina shoved the gun into a pocket and started after him. "Two places in two days where I've been shot at," she muttered as she climbed. "If I get back to New York and someone tries to kill me *there,* I'm gonna kick their ass so hard . . ." She reached the uppermost niche and took hold of the column set into the wall. It didn't look the least bit safe—though the fact that someone of Agnelli's bulk had scaled it without breaking it apart gave her some limited reassurance.

Without the secure footing of the loculi, her ascent was now much slower. As she inched her way closer to the opening, the muffled sounds of Agnelli's passage through the narrow tunnel faded. He was getting away from her.

"No you goddamn don't," she growled, pulling herself higher and refusing to succumb to the awful temptation to look down at the ever-increasing drop. Instead she fixed her eyes on the dark hole as she brought herself within reach. It was a few feet to the pilaster's side—she would have to stretch across to it, taking her weight on one hand.

No choice. Nina took a deep breath, then clutched the ancient stone as tightly as she could with her left hand as she reached out with her right, hooking her fingers over the lip of the new passage—

Her left hand slipped.

She screamed, clawing desperately at the wall. Her right foot jolted from its hold, leaving her suspended and straining between two very precarious points like a human tightrope. She scraped her toe against the ancient stonework for a terrifying eternity before finally finding purchase on a jutting brick. That gave her just enough leverage to bring her left hand up to the hole and grip the edge. A few seconds to recover her breath, then she pulled herself into the low passage.

Heart rate dropping from that of a frightened rabbit, she looked ahead. The passage, what she could see of it in the dim light from below, was about thirty inches wide and slightly lower, angling upward into darkness. She could hear a distant rustle as Agnelli crawled up the incline.

The gun was a hard lump pressing into her side. She drew it and headed after him.

Very quickly she was in total darkness. An instinctual fear rose: simple unreasoning terror at being in a confined space, unable to see. "If he can fit," she whispered to herself in an attempt at reassurance, "so can I. I don't have a fat ass. Well, it's not *huge* or anything. I mean, I work out. Kind of. When I have the time . . ."

The distraction did its job, the encroaching panic retreating. Looking ahead, she saw a faint glimmer of light marking the tunnel's end. It was mostly obscured by the silhouetted form of Agnelli—who as she watched pulled himself out and disappeared.

Her anxiety returned, but now for a more concrete reason. Agnelli might be waiting in ambush at the top of the shaft. She slowed as she drew nearer, listening intently. Nothing. Had he already fled—or was he preparing to smash a brick down on her head?

She hesitated a foot short of the exit . . . then scrambled through as quickly as she could.

No stones dashed out her brains. Agnelli had already left the softly lit chamber. It appeared to be an archaeological excavation, crumbled walls having been dug out of the pale brown soil. But there was no indication that the dig was an ongoing project; instead it seemed frozen in time, as much a part of history as the ruins it had unearthed . . .

Nina suddenly knew where she was.

Beneath the Vatican, uncounted tombs and burial chambers dated back as far as Imperial Rome, layer built upon layer over centuries. The passage from the Brotherhood's maze of archives emerged in the Scavi, a necropolis hidden under St. Peter's Basilica. It had been unearthed in the 1940s at the instigation of Pope Pius XII during a search for the tomb of St. Peter himself. Since then, the site had been left largely untouched—partly out of reverence, and partly for the more pragmatic reason that it was directly below the magnificent bronze baldachin of St. Peter within the basilica, and further excavations ran the risk of damaging the foundations. Agnelli must have discovered the passage during his explorations of the catacombs—and now he had his own private emergency exit into the Vatican.

That thought spurred her back into action. She clambered over the ruins to a low opening in one wall. Drifting dust motes told her that Agnelli had squeezed through the gap not long before, dislodging chunks of crumbling plaster. She followed with more care, emerging in a narrow brick-lined passageway. Holes in the walls led to other ancient chambers, including St. Peter's tomb, but Nina's concern was something of more recent construction. A doorway led to a flight of metal stairs, heading upward. Between the necropolis and the basilica were the Vatican grottoes: the tombs of the popes.

Nina pounded up the stairs. A sound reached her—the low echoes of many voices speaking in hushed reverence. The Scavi was only opened for a handful of visitors each day, but the tombs above were a destination for pilgrims from all over the world. At the top, a door was swinging closed. She flung it back open and rushed through.

Agnelli had clearly been through here—several people on their way to view the nearby Clementine Chapel were staring in shock down a hallway, having just been barged aside by the fleeing Italian. Nina added to their outrage by following suit. "Excuse me! Sorry," she called out as she ran down the hall, weaving among the visitors.

Agnelli was leaving an audible trail of protesting voices. She followed it, emerging from the hall into a larger and more spacious section of interconnected chapels and shrines. This part of the grottoes was much busier: the tomb of John Paul II, a recent and highly venerated pope, was situated within.

Nina slowed, scanning the throng of pilgrims. Where was Agnelli? Trying to blend in with the crowd—or using them as cover to escape?

A woman's cry told her it was the latter. She saw an

elderly lady in black lying on the pale marble floor, her companions still reeling. Agnelli's path was as clear as a ship's wake.

"Let me through!" Nina shouted as she ran after him. Even giving a warning, she still had to sweep an arm ahead of her like a snowplow to push past the startled mourners—until a shriek of *"Pistola!"* told her that someone had seen her gun.

The chamber erupted into chaos, frightened people scattering in all directions. Nina cursed. She had briefly spotted Agnelli's distinctive haircut over the crowd—now it was lost again in the confusion.

A man called out ahead. From his authoritative tone he was clearly a member of the Vatican's staff, trying to restore order. A woman shouted behind her; Nina's Italian was limited, but she knew enough to pick out *capelli rossi*—red hair. Two attendants in dark uniforms swung in her direction, yelling *"Scostare, scostare!"* as they pushed people out of their way.

Nina ducked lower, angling away from the guards into the milling mass. She could no longer afford to be polite—if she were caught, by the time she explained the situation Agnelli would have escaped.

A broad set of steps ahead. She jumped them, almost slipping on the marble as she landed and careering against a burly man. The gun was snagged from her grasp by his camera strap and clattered to the floor. Shit!

No time to stop and pick it up. All she could do was keep running. Another glimpse of Agnelli. He was heading along the right side of the new room, passing the tombs set into the alcoves along it.

He rushed into one of them. Nina glanced back. One of the guards had tripped on the steps, bowling over a tourist as he fell. His comrade was lost to sight behind a knot of panicking people.

She reached the alcove, home to a stone sarcophagus, and charged through the doorway behind it. Ahead was a museum, archaeological discoveries from beneath the Vatican on display behind glass. No time for sightseeing;

she continued to chase Agnelli through the rooms. He now had something in his hand—*a phone,* she realized.

Who was he calling? And was he trying to get help—or backup?

* * *

The panting Agnelli ran up a flight of stairs, thumb clumsily swiping over his phone's screen. Once he got outside into the Piazzetta Braschi, he would finally have cell reception and be able to call the number his contact had given him for emergencies.

Until now, his idea of what might constitute an emergency had been the Brotherhood becoming suspicious that he had secretly passed on information from the archives—not a madwoman chasing after him with a gun. The Brotherhood had killed her parents, and tried to kill her; after the ferocity with which she had attacked him in the catacombs, he had no doubts that she wanted to return the favor.

The thought sent a resurgent wave of fear through him, blowing away his fatigue. He glanced back. She was gaining. *Oh God, help me!*

Even in this holiest of places, God couldn't assist him directly—but there was someone who could. He reached the top of the stairs and threw open a heavy door, tapping furiously at the screen as the phone finally got a signal. "Come *on!*" he gasped as he ran into the square, turning to head for an archway that would take him out of Vatican territory back into Rome—

He stopped abruptly. Beyond the arch, two men in brightly colored uniforms and black berets were sprinting toward him: Swiss Guards. Their elaborate, old-fashioned clothing might have looked ridiculous, but anyone who took the soldiers themselves lightly would quickly regret the mistake.

That escape route blocked, he ran for another. Nearby was an entrance to the basilica itself. He could get away through St. Peter's Square—

A voice from the phone. "Yes?"

"Copel!" Agnelli cried in relief. "It's Paolo, Paolo Agnelli! I'm in trouble—I need your help, now!" Another look back as he reached the doorway. The redhead had just burst from the grotto entrance, the Swiss Guards veering to follow her as they passed through the archway.

"Where are you? What's happening?"

"I'm in the Vatican," he said as he raced down a narrow connecting corridor. "The Brotherhood know what I did for you—and Nina Wilde's chasing me!"

Another voice in the background, a woman's, said something in English with a tone of aggrieved disbelief. "Paolo," said Copel after a moment, "get to the Piazza del Sant'Uffizio. We can meet you there in three minutes."

Even through his panic, Agnelli was surprised. "You're that close?"

"Just get there." The line went silent.

He had no further time to think about the oddness of the situation. Instead he hauled open another door and entered the great basilica of St. Peter.

* * *

Nina pounded down the corridor. She was gaining on Agnelli—but the two Swiss Guards were closing on her much more rapidly. She had to slow them down . . .

A fire extinguisher was mounted near the door into the basilica itself. She plucked it from the wall as she ran past, tugging out the safety pin, then spun to wedge it in the doorjamb as she pulled the heavy door shut.

Its weight forced down the lever—and a choking gush of carbon dioxide gas spewed from the nozzle. The Swiss Guards retreated from the freezing cloud, coughing and hacking.

Nina didn't wait to see if her improvised smoke screen had worked. Instead she pursued Agnelli through the basilica. Even in her flight, the building's sheer scale and magnificence were awe inspiring, the ceiling so high and the supporting pillars so huge that people seemed nothing more than toy figures beneath them. Glorious statues and paintings flashed past, altars and monuments to saints and popes, but she couldn't afford to give the antiquities more than the briefest glance as she fixed her gaze on the Italian ahead. The two running figures were drawing attention, but the commotion from the grottoes hadn't yet reached the vast church, the worshippers bewildered rather than scared.

Agnelli reached the doors, swatting aside an attendant who tried to block his path. He ran out into the open. Nina hurdled the fallen man and followed, finding herself looking out across the huge expanse of St. Peter's Square. The name was something of a misnomer; the western end in front of the basilica was a trapezoid, beyond it a great elliptical plaza, at the center of which was a towering Egyptian obelisk. The nearer part of the square was hemmed in by the walls of long galleries, but the plaza was in the embrace of towering colonnades to the north and south—through which could be reached the streets of Rome.

Agnelli was running for the southern colonnade, having knocked down a barrier to cut diagonally across the square instead of being channeled around its edge. She raced after him, startled tourists watching her. Some had cameras and phones raised. *Great,* she thought, *I'm going to be in the news again . . .*

That was something to worry about later, after catching Agnelli. He was about thirty yards ahead, gaining a second wind now that escape was in sight. The Italian ran for another section of barrier. Much to Nina's astonishment, the overweight youth successfully hurdled it with barely a break in his stride. Reaching it a few seconds later, she was forced to halt and scramble over the metal obstacle, losing precious time. By the time she cleared it, Agnelli had reached the colonnade and ducked between its great stone pillars.

She followed. When she regained sight of him, he was

on a wide street, the Piazza del Sant'Uffizio—outside Vatican territory, a gate to her right marking the boundary of the Holy See. The Italian looked about frantically, apparently expecting to see someone in particular. The person he had phoned must have arranged to rescue him.

"Agnelli!" she tried to shout, but it came out as a strangled croak. In her adrenalized state she hadn't realized how tired she was becoming, but her muscles were now rebelling against their endocrinal manipulation. "Stop!"

If he heard her, he showed no sign. Instead the Italian kept running, himself showing growing fatigue that not even fear could overcome. He was still searching the street with increasing desperation—

Tires screeched. Nina leapt for the sidewalk as a glossy black Range Rover with darkened windows skidded around the corner behind her and swept down the street, engine roaring. Agnelli turned toward it, face filled with relief.

The Range Rover didn't stop.

Its blocky nose hit him square-on, sending him flying into the air, broken limbs flailing. He smashed down on the tarmac in a heap—and the four-by-four drove right over him with a horrible crunch of bones. Pedestrians screamed and ran for cover as the big SUV made a skidding handbrake turn to power back the way it had come.

Straight at Nina.

She had stopped in horror at the sight of Agnelli being mowed down, but now she broke back into a sprint, terror overpowering her body's protests. The only place that offered even the slightest protection was the doorway of a nearby building. She ran to it, grabbed the handle—

Locked!

Nina turned. The Range Rover was rushing at her, about to smear her along the wall—

It abruptly veered off and came to a squealing stop. Even though the windows were tinted, she could see figures inside. The passenger was apparently as surprised by the maneuver as she was. He remonstrated with the shadow in the driver's seat, then opened the door and jumped out.

The man, blond, wearing an expensive suit and sunglasses, had a gunmetal automatic in his hand. He regarded Nina coldly and raised the pistol—

His chest erupted with bloody exit wounds as the Range Rover's driver fired several shots into his back.

The man crumpled to the sidewalk, a crimson pool rapidly forming around him. Shocked, speechless, Nina tore her gaze from the corpse to see who had saved her.

It was the last person she had expected.

The driver was Sophia Blackwood.

Sociopath, killer—and Eddie's first wife, from a time before her insane rage at the system that had bankrupted her father and wiped out her inheritance had seen her try to destroy the West's economy by nuking Wall Street. The last time Nina saw her, Eddie had thrown her off the top of a waterfall.

Clearly, she could swim.

She had not survived the experience unscathed, though. Even through the shadows, Nina made out a long scar running down the left side of her face and neck. There was also something *different* about the rest of her features, a hard-to-define yet impossible-to-miss shifting of shapes and proportions. Plastic surgery?

Not that it mattered. Sophia held a gun in a black-gloved hand, its smoking muzzle now fixed on the American. Their eyes met, locked. Nina was frozen, knowing that the instant she moved, the raven-haired aristocrat would kill her.

She waited for the shot . . .

The gun flicked up, and Sophia dropped it almost casually onto the passenger seat. As the stunned Nina watched, she smiled, then raised a finger to her lips. The meaning of the gesture was unmistakable.

Shh. This is our little secret.

Then she floored the accelerator, spinning the wheel to peel the Range Rover away. The door slammed shut as it turned, Nina's last sight of Sophia that same unfathomable smile. It roared into the crowded streets of Rome, leaving Nina standing there, utterly lost, as police sirens rose in the distance.

THIRTEEN
Maryland

The house overlooking the Potomac River had once been Victor Dalton's vacation retreat. Since the divorce, it had become his home, and his ex-wife had made it very clear that he was lucky to have kept even that. A small part of him couldn't really blame her for the angry separation—he had, after all, been caught on video in flagrante with a woman who was not only someone else's wife at the time, but also turned out to be the mastermind behind a terrorist plot against the United States.

The rest of him, however, still burned with fury at the injustice. All his achievements as president had been obliterated from the public mind by that one lapse of judgment, and he had been hounded out of office. The holder of the most powerful position on the planet could not be a man whose defining moment was rated NC-17.

Sitting alone in his kitchen, Dalton clapped down his glass with a bang that echoed like a gunshot. As it faded, the thought occurred that his Secret Service bodyguards—even disgraced presidents were still entitled to protection for ten years after leaving office, though his team was considerably smaller than that of his more honored predecessors—probably wouldn't even bother to leave their surveillance trailer to investigate the noise. Though they were always stone-faced and professional in their duties, he was sure they mocked him behind his back.

He knew exactly who was to blame for his expulsion from power: Nina Wilde and Eddie Chase. He had personally awarded them the Presidential Medal of Freedom for their role in saving New York from nuclear attack—and they had repaid him by plastering the Sophia Blackwood video all over the Internet. Merely thinking about them made his jaw clench with involuntary anger.

And to make matters worse . . . they had somehow survived the events in Japan.

At least Takashi was dead. That was one small diamond in the mound of shit. The Group would endure his loss, of course, but it would cause them considerable disruption.

The Group. Another silent snarl. They had helped put him into the White House, and could have kept him there; they possessed the influence to have swayed the media and other politicians back behind him. But instead they had left him to flounder in the Washington piranha tank.

Bastards! Well, they'd regret that decision. It was a shame he didn't dare let them know that he had been a part of that payback . . . but he valued his freedom, and his life even more.

He swallowed the last slug of bourbon, then stood. It was approaching midnight, and the habit of late nights and early mornings developed in years of public office was hard to break, even with no work waiting for him the next day. He shook his head. Victor Dalton, *unemployed*! The word was like a personal insult. But nobody would touch him, even former friends who should by all rights have been offering him board seats and lucrative consultancy posts failing to return his calls. "Cocksuckers," he muttered, heading upstairs.

In his bedroom, Dalton disrobed and went into the

adjoining bathroom. He was supposed to wear a panic button on a thong around his neck at all times, but the damn thing only got in the way while he was washing, so he put it with his watch on a shelf and pulled the curtain on the shower cubicle. A quick burst of hot water and creamy suds helped ease his tension a little. He toweled himself down before donning a bathrobe, then reached for the panic button.

It wasn't there.

He stared at the shelf. His watch was exactly where he had left it, but the teardrop-shaped device was gone. No sign of it on the floor. Confusion growing, he returned to the bedroom, wondering if it had somehow fallen and bounced into there . . .

"Lookin' for this?" said a voice.

Dalton froze in petrified shock. Eddie Chase, bearded and scruffy, sat casually in a chair, the panic button in one hand—and a silenced gun in the other.

It took a couple of seconds for Dalton to force out any words. "How—how did you get in here?" he croaked. "How did you get past the Secret Service?"

"By being bloody good at what I do." There was dirt on the Englishman's dark clothing: he had crept and crawled through the grounds to reach the house undetected. "Now sit on the bed, and keep your voice down. You give me any trouble, and I'll put a bullet through your fucking head."

Dalton moved to the bed, struggling to control his fear. "How did you get back into the country?" he asked as he sat, playing for time. "Interpol has you on a watch list—you should have set off every alarm in the airport when they took your fingerprints."

Eddie smiled coldly. "US citizens don't get fingerprinted."

"You're not a US citizen."

"Amazing what you can do with a fake passport, innit? Now"—the smile vanished—"my turn to ask questions. Biggest one: What the fuck is going on?"

"That's . . . rather too broad for me to answer."

"You'll manage." The gun angled up toward Dalton's face. "Scarber told me you were her boss, and that you set everything up in Japan. Why were you trying to kill me and Nina?"

"I have no idea what you're—"

Eddie shifted the gun slightly and pulled the trigger. The flat *thump* of the bullet exiting the oversized suppressor was echoed by the sound of it blowing apart one of Dalton's pillows in an explosion of goose down. The ex-president jumped in fright. "Next one won't miss. Why were you trying to kill us?"

Shaking, Dalton stammered out a reply. "It—it should be obvious, shouldn't it? Even to a grunt like you. I wanted you dead, Chase. You destroyed my life, you and your wife. I was the president of the United States, and what am I now? A laughingstock! An international joke! But," he went on, some of his arrogance returning, "I'm not powerless. There are still some people who are loyal to me."

"Like Scarber?"

"Yes. She left the CIA to work as my private operative. As soon as she heard what you were after, she told me. I knew you wouldn't be able to resist the chance to clear your name."

Eddie gave him a look of resigned annoyance. "Yeah, I thought that offer was too good to be true. So you set me and Nina up to settle old scores—but why was Takashi involved? What's your problem with him?"

Dalton leaned forward conspiratorially. "Have you ever heard of . . ." He glanced about as if afraid of being overheard. "The Group?"

"Weren't they Bob Dylan's musicians?"

Now it was Dalton's turn to express annoyance. "No, that was the Band. The Group is—how best to put it? The people *above* the people who run the world. They're a cabal of exceptionally powerful and influential figures—businessmen, bankers—"

"Presidents?"

The gray-haired man snorted. "Only one US president

has ever been a member—and it wasn't me, I might add. But nobody *gets* to be president without the Group's approval."

"They fix the elections?" said Eddie dubiously.

"They don't need to. Anyone they don't like is eliminated from the process long before then. All those scandals that come out of the woodwork during the primaries? The Group sees that they're exposed, leaving only the candidates they approve of. From both parties."

Eddie's interest in American politics was limited, but even he was shocked by Dalton's revelation. "Wait, so when you were president . . . you were working for these guys? They told you what to do?"

He shook his head. "It's nothing that blatant. It's more like they make . . . suggestions. Advise that one policy direction would be preferable to another. From their point of view, at least."

"So what have they got to do with Takashi?"

"You haven't worked that out?" Dalton said with a cutting laugh. "He was one of them!"

"You wanted him dead?"

"I want them *all* dead, to be honest. Those bastards could have saved my presidency. But instead they left me to twist in the wind, and that jackass Leo Cole took my job. That backstabbing son of a bitch."

"So Takashi was one of them," said Eddie, waving the gun to focus Dalton's mind on the matter at hand. "Who are the others?"

Another snort. "If I gave you their names, I'd be dead within twenty-four hours."

"You could be dead a lot sooner if you don't. And you gave me Takashi's."

"Anything that might have connected him to the Group will already have been wiped from existence. You don't know how powerful these people are, Chase. Or what they're capable of doing. What they're actually *planning* to do—with your wife's help."

Eddie narrowed his eyes. "Meaning what? What do they need Nina for?"

"It's something to do with those statues. She—"

"I want more than fucking *something*, mate. What?" There was a lengthy silence. "Well?"

"I . . . don't actually know, precisely," Dalton admitted. "Only my partner does."

"Doesn't sound like much of a partner if he keeps secrets from you," Eddie scoffed. "More like a boss."

"It's an alliance of convenience," said the politician, prickling. "We have a mutual enemy—the Group."

"What's he got against them?"

"They tried to kill him."

"Well, yeah, that does tend to piss people off. Why?"

Another pause. "He was a member," said Dalton. "The statues are part of their plan—something to do with earth energy, I assume. He was opposed to it, so they tried to eliminate him. But he escaped, and has been in hiding ever since. He arranged the helicopter attack in Tokyo. The statues and your wife were the primary targets, Takashi was the secondary, and you were . . . Well, he didn't even know you were there. That was entirely down to me."

A frown creased Eddie's brow. "You know, I'm having a really hard time thinking of reasons why I shouldn't just shoot you in the face."

"I can think of one very good one," said Dalton, with a smug smile. "Nina."

"What about her?"

"You think this is over? She's the key to the Group's plan—they can't achieve it without her. So I'm afraid my partner will still be trying to have her killed. Instead of threatening me, you should be trying to protect her. And you won't be able to do that without my—"

Eddie exploded from his seat, lunging across the room to grab Dalton by his throat and slam him backward on to the bed. He thrust the gun hard against the ex-president's cheek. "I want this fucker's name in five seconds, or you *die*! Four, three, two—"

"Glas!" Dalton squealed. "His name's Glas, Harald Glas!"

To Eddie's surprise, he knew the name. "But he's something to do with the IHA . . ."

"One of the—non-executive directors," Dalton managed to gasp. "He has a lot of involvement with the UN. He's in the energy business—oil, gas, coal, even nuclear."

"So where do I find him?"

"I don't know—*I don't know!*" he repeated with considerably more fear as the silencer was rammed harder against his face. "I told you, he's in hiding. And I don't know how to contact him—he always contacts me. But I do know that he's already tried to kill your wife again. In Rome, earlier today. One of my people in the State Department told me."

Cold shock froze Eddie. "Is she . . ."

"She's all right. She has the same damn charmed life as you." He sat up and rubbed his bruised cheek as the Englishman pulled back. "But it won't last forever. He'll keep sending people after her, and sooner or later one of them will succeed. Unless . . ."

"Unless what?"

"You'd like to go home, wouldn't you, Chase? Be reunited with your wife?" The smarminess of a politician making promises returned at full slimy intensity. "I can arrange it. Bring the statues to me, so I can show Glas that they've been destroyed, and I'll get him to call off his dogs. I'll even do what I can to get you off the hook with Interpol."

Eddie stared at him for a long moment. "Nah, I don't think so."

It wasn't the response Dalton had expected. "What?"

"I trust you about as much as I could shit an elephant. Soon as I go, you'll scream for the Secret Service, and then either I'll be dead or every cop and government agent in the country'll be looking for me." He regarded the gun. "Unless I make sure you can't."

Dalton went pale. "No, no, wait. There's no need to kill me—I can help you, I really can! Whatever you need, I can get—I still have the connections. I do!"

Another silence, the gun fixed on the trembling man . . .

then unexpectedly Eddie let out a sarcastic chuckle. "You're right, I don't need to kill you. I can do something worse."

"W-worse?"

Eddie crossed the room to a dresser, on top of which was a collection of framed photos of Dalton in his presidential days—and picked up a phone that had been propped, half hidden, behind one of the pictures. "Did you get that?" he said into its camera.

"Came out great, mate," said an Australian voice from the other end of the line. "Bluey" Jackson, the friend who had provided Eddie with his fake US passport.

"Cheers. You know what to do." He turned the phone around and tapped its screen to disconnect.

Appalled realization hit the former president. "You *recorded* this?"

"Worked last time, didn't it?" Eddie said cheerily as he pocketed the phone. "That was a live video call to a mate of mine in another country—the same mate who helped me make you into a YouTube star a couple of years back. He was recording it, and right now he's copying it and sending it to *his* mates for security. You just confessed to conspiracy and attempted murder and Christ knows what else, so it'd be a real shame if the video got sent to, I dunno, the Justice Department. And *The New York Times*. And the BBC. And—"

"I get the picture, damn you," spat Dalton.

"So will everyone else. Fool you twice, eh?" His voice became harsher. "So first off, you keep quiet about me being here. Second, next time this Glas bloke calls, you tell him to call off anyone he's sent after Nina."

"I don't know when he'll contact me next," said Dalton, sweating.

"You'd better hope it's soon." Eddie tossed the panic button onto the chair. "Anyway, I'll be off. You have a nice night." He opened the door, then paused halfway through it. "You've got more to be scared of than this

Group, Dalton. You've got me." The door closed behind him.

Dalton stared after him for several seconds, then scurried to the chair. He picked up the panic button . . . but didn't dare use it. Instead, trembling with fear and anger, he threw it down on the carpet and returned to sit on the bed, head in his hands.

FOURTEEN

New York City

The arrivals area of John F. Kennedy Airport's Terminal 7 was far from welcoming, but to Nina reaching the huge, impersonal structure felt oddly like coming home. Since joining the IHA five years earlier, she had done so much international travel that she imagined her total mileage would stretch to the moon—yet no matter how far-flung her travels, at the end the comforting sight of Manhattan was always waiting for her.

There was the usual rigmarole to endure first, however. Standing in line at immigration control, the interminable wait for her baggage . . . and then she would still have to battle for a cab.

Which was why the sight of a card reading DR. NINA WILDE was such a pleasant surprise when she reached the concourse. It was held by a mustachioed man in a chauffeur's uniform and dark glasses, who stepped forward as she approached. "Dr. Wilde?" he said. His accent had a European tinge, but she couldn't place it precisely. "Mr. Penrose sent me to bring you to the United Nations."

"Oh. Huh. Y'know, I was kind of hoping to go home first. I've had a long couple of days." She had attempted to sleep on the flight, but despite her exhaustion from the chase in Rome her rest had been fitful. And now Penrose probably wanted to drag her into another lengthy meeting with senior UN officials to explain how death and chaos had followed her to two foreign capitals . . . "Well, guess not," she said, on the chauffeur's silence. "Okay, let's go."

She waited for him to take her luggage, but instead he started to turn away before halting, as if belatedly remembering that his duties extended beyond simply driving a car. "May I . . . take your bags?"

"You certainly may." Nina relievedly passed them to him, then followed him through the concourse.

He led her to the sprawling parking structure beyond the AirTrain light rail station. Nina stifled yawns on the way. Fortunately, her chauffeur didn't seem inclined to be talkative.

* * *

The chauffeur had his own reasons for not wanting to engage her in conversation. Large among them was that he was not actually a chauffeur.

His left arm nudged with every step against the gun concealed beneath his jacket. He was sweating, the perspiration due in varying degrees to the weight of the bags, the wig and false mustache he was wearing to shield his identity from the airport's surveillance cameras, and the enormity of what he was about to do. He was no stranger to violence, but straight-up assassination was something new and troubling.

He knew it had to be done, though. He had complete faith in his boss, and if Harald Glas said that the innocent-looking redhead was a threat to the entire world, he believed him.

She was famous, wasn't she? Some kind of scientist. Pretty, too, for an egghead . . .

He forced himself not to think about her. All he had to do was get her into the back of the blacked-out limo, then draw the gun and fire. Three shots to the head would do it. She wouldn't even have time to be scared.

They descended through a stairwell. He had parked in a quiet corner with limited CCTV coverage—the limo was soundproofed and his gun silenced, but anything unusual could still attract attention. A couple of people passed them on the stairs, but neither gave a second glance to a driver and his passenger.

His heart began to race as they reached the lower level. The limo was a long dark shape in the concrete gloom about fifty yards away. He headed for it, the gun hard against his ribs.

＊ ＊ ＊

"Jeez, could you have parked any farther away?" said Nina, trying to hold in another yawn. She had expected her ride to be waiting near the terminal's entrance with the buses and cabs.

The chauffeur mumbled a vague apology, then opened the rear door for her. She climbed inside. "Thank you." He didn't acknowledge her, instead closing the door and putting her bags in the trunk. Nina checked her watch. If the traffic were favorable, she might reach the UN in around forty minutes. No telling how long Penrose's meetings would drag on, though . . .

The trunk lid slammed. The chauffeur walked back to the driver's-side door. He opened it, but didn't immediately get in, instead reaching inside his jacket with a gloved hand.

＊ ＊ ＊

Turning away to make sure his target couldn't see what he was doing, the assassin drew his gun. He started to enter the limo—

Someone hit him hard from behind, smashing his face against the edge of the roof.

＊ ＊ ＊

Nina jumped as a loud metallic bang echoed through the limo. The driver was struggling with somebody—

She glimpsed a gun as the two men fought.

Jesus! It was a carjacking!

She tried to open the door—and found to her horror that the handle refused to move. Child-locked. The other door was the same. She stabbed at the window switch to lower it, but without the key in the ignition the mechanism was inert.

The driver slammed against the limo's side, his attacker delivering a punch to his stomach before grabbing his arm. The gun clacked against the rear window. A *thwat* as it fired, the bullet hitting the concrete floor and ricocheting away with a whine. Another shot and a car's windshield shattered, setting off the vehicle's alarm.

The chauffeur struck back, and the other man lurched away. The gun came up—but not pointing at the assailant.

It was aimed at Nina.

Trapped, all she could do was dive into the foot well—

The gun fired—just as the second man hurled himself bodily at the chauffeur. The window shattered from the force of the bullet at point-blank range, the round tearing into the leather upholstery beside Nina. She shrieked.

The new arrival twisted the chauffeur's right arm savagely behind his back. The driver let out a strangled cry of pain, free hand clawing over his shoulder at his opponent's eyes. The wig slipped off his head as he tried to break loose, knees bashing against the limo's door—

Another muffled *thwat,* a spent casing clinking off the floor. The chauffeur convulsed, face twisted into an anguished grimace by the pain of the bullet that had just ripped into the back of his calf. Before he could even scream, the other man slammed him face-first against the top of the door frame. He dropped to the concrete, unconscious.

The victor stepped over him and tugged at the door handle. The lock released with a clunk. Nina stared up at her savior.

"So this is what you get up to while I'm away, is it?" said a Yorkshire voice.

She gawped at the disheveled, bearded figure. "Eddie?"

Her husband smiled. "Last time I checked. Come on, open the boot so I can dump this twat in it before anyone sees him."

He extended his hand. She hesitantly took it, and he helped her out of the limo. The chauffeur lay at her feet. "Son of a *bitch*!" she suddenly cried, booting him again and again.

Eddie pulled her back. "What the hell are you doing?"

"I'm kicking his ass, like I promised I would!"

"Er . . . okay," he said, bewildered. "Now you've done that, can we shift him?" He glanced warily toward the stairwell in case anyone was coming to investigate the alarm.

Nina opened the trunk. Eddie dragged the driver to the limo's rear and dumped him inside. He quickly searched his pockets, producing the car keys, then slammed the lid and retrieved the gun. "There might be more of them—we need to get out of the airport." He got into the driver's seat and started the car.

Nina joined him in the front passenger seat. "Eddie?"

"Yeah?"

"What the *fuck* is going on?"

"That's a bloody good question," he replied as he put the limo into gear and made a hurried exit from the car park.

* * *

An hour and a half later, having abandoned the limousine—after wiping it clean of fingerprints—in Queens and taken a cab into Manhattan, the couple faced each other over a table in a darkened corner of a Midtown bar. "We should have gone back to the apartment," Nina grumbled.

"Trust me, there's nothing I'd like more," said Eddie. "But it might not be a good idea me being seen around there." He shook his head. "Christ, what a mess."

Right now, Nina didn't want to think that far ahead. She took in her husband's less-than-pristine appearance. "That's not the only thing that's a mess."

Eddie gingerly touched his jaw where the assassin had landed a blow. "That guy got in a couple of punches."

"No, I meant in general. What *is* with the beard?"

"You don't like it?"

"Would you be offended if I didn't?"

"N—"

"I hate it," she said, before he could even finish the word. "I don't know if you were trying for a Commander Riker look or something, but it's definitely more toward the Charles Manson end of the beard spectrum."

"First chance we've had for a proper chat in over three months, and that's all you want to talk about?"

Her change of expression warned him that was far from the case. "God, no, Eddie," Nina said with a long sigh. She spread her fingers, putting the tips to her temples. "There's so much I want to say that it feels as though it's all going to burst right out of my skull. I mean, Jesus Christ, Eddie. Jesus *Christ*!" She hit his arm, far from gently.

"Ow," he said. "What was that for?" She did it again, harder. "Ow!"

"What was *that* for?" she echoed incredulously, voice rising in both volume and pitch. "For God's sake! You disappear and leave me for three months, not a word the whole time, the police and Interpol and God knows who else are scouring the globe for you—then you turn up out of nowhere at the top of a Japanese skyscraper, which then gets blown up with me inside it, and when I finally get back home after being chased and shot at in Rome, you pop up again as if by magic to save me from some asshole who was apparently trying to kidnap and murder me! The least I deserve is some kind of goddamn explanation!"

"Oh. Yeah. All that. So what happened in Rome?"

"Don't change the subject!" she snapped, raising her fist once more.

"All right, fucking hell! Just don't hit me again, okay? I've had people laying into me for the past week, and I'm getting pretty pissed off with it."

"Sorry," she muttered. "I'm just . . . I'm so happy to see you again, you wouldn't believe it. But I'm also so *mad* at you."

"Okay, so stick with the happy part for now, all right?" said Eddie. "You want to know what I've been doing? I've been looking for Stikes, for one thing. I had to bust someone out of a Zimbabwean prison to track him down, but I finally found him . . . and you were there with him."

"I was not *with* him!" she protested.

"Yeah, I know that now. But he got away, and I'm not going to get any more help from the person who told me how to find him. Seeing as she tried to kill me."

Nina sighed. "What is it about us? Why are we incapable of having a normal life that doesn't include regular assassination attempts?"

"Dunno. But I don't remember breaking any mirrors, walking under ladders, or not saluting magpies, so it must all be your fault." He managed a half smile at her outraged look, then became serious again. "But as well as that, I was trying to find out what happened in Peru. I didn't murder Kit, Nina. He was trying to kill me. What I did, it was self-defense . . . whatever you thought you saw me do."

She said nothing for several seconds, causing an unexpected apprehension, even fear, to rise within him. But her reply made it vanish. "I believe you."

His face lit up. "You do?"

"Yes. I believe you're innocent. But . . ." The single word instantly crushed his elation. "I need to *know* you're innocent. And so does everybody else—Interpol, the IHA, everyone. Otherwise, what? You go on the run again? Or you get caught and sent to prison—or worse? Eddie, I . . ." She buried her face in her hands. "I can't go on like this. Without you. It's just . . . destroying me." A tear rolled down her cheek.

"I'm not exactly keen on it either," he replied. But despite his attempt at forced levity, he too felt his eyes welling. "Oh Christ, look at me. Getting all emotional."

"You do that a lot more than you like to pretend," Nina told him, wiping her face.

"I've had a lot to *get* all emotional about lately," he admitted. "Losing Mac, losing Nan . . ." Now it was his turn to rub his eyes. "Losing you."

She shuffled around the booth to sit beside him. "You didn't lose me, Eddie. I lost you. For a while. But I got you back."

"Thanks," he managed to say, almost overcome. He put his arm around her. "Thank you."

"I'm still completely furious with you, obviously," she said after a pause.

He half-laughed. "So what else is new? You're always furious about something. Bloody redheads."

"Yeah, we're the best." They sat in silence for a while, simply enjoying being together again.

"So what changed?" Eddie eventually asked. "When I left you in Peru, you . . . well, you flat-out accused me of murder. Why do you believe me now?"

Nina straightened. "A few things. First, Kit lied to me about Interpol authorizing him to negotiate with Stikes to get the statues back. So that made me start wondering if he'd lied about anything else. And the second thing is . . . well, you."

"Me?"

"I *know* you, Eddie. I think pretty well by now. And the more I thought about it, the more it seemed . . . *wrong*. I know how angry you were that night—but kicking a helpless man to his death? I know the things you can do when you feel you have to, but that's not one of them."

"I was actually trying to get Kit *out* of there," he said, thinking back to the chaos of the impending conflagration. "He was the only way I could prove what was going on. But he would have shot me if I hadn't . . . well, you were there. Even if you didn't see the gun."

"It wasn't on the video either," she told him glumly. "The angle was wrong, and it was too dark. I watched it over and over, but I couldn't see anything. Interpol didn't either."

"There's a video?"

"Yeah, from a surveillance camera. Renée Beauchamp sent me a copy to see if I could tell her anything new."

Eddie became thoughtful. "How long is it?"

"Ten or twelve minutes, maybe. Nothing happens for a lot of it, though; you climb up onto the catwalk, then you're out of shot until you and Kit are fighting."

"I'll need a look at it. But there wasn't anything showing Stikes or Sophia?"

"Afraid not. Oh, oh!" she added excitedly. The shock of the attack at the airport had pushed events in Italy to one side. "Sophia was in Rome!"

"*What?*"

"I don't know what she was doing—I don't even know how she's still alive. But she was there, and she . . ." Nina trailed off, still not quite able to accept what had happened.

"What did she do?" he demanded.

"She, ah . . . You're not going to believe this, but she saved my life."

He stared at her. "You're right, I don't believe it. How?"

She explained what had happened outside the Vatican. "So," said Eddie when she was done, "she shot her own man in the back to save you, then got all cutesy and 'don't tell anyone' about it? Why would she do that? She hates you even more than she hates me!"

"Thanks for that, Eddie. I always like being reminded that a murdering psychopath has a grudge against me. But no, I don't know why she did it. I'd guess she was there to make sure Agnelli didn't blab to me about whoever paid him to raid the Brotherhood's archives. And so was the other guy—only she double-crossed him."

"Sophia stabbing someone in the back? No!" said Eddie sarcastically.

"But whose side is she really on? Apart from her own,

obviously. She didn't save me because she wants a bridge partner—she needs me alive for something."

"Something to do with those bloody statues, probably. Even Dalton mentioned them."

"Dalton?" said Nina in surprise. "As in, out-on-his-ass president?"

"Yeah. Turns out he set me up to be killed in Japan. Sophia's not the only person who holds grudges. I popped around to his house to have words."

She put her head in her hands again. "I need the Cliffs-Notes to follow all this. What the hell is going on?"

He patted her shoulder. "Well, you tell me what you know, I'll tell you what I know, and maybe between the two of us we'll get a clue."

"I'd be happy with even *half* a clue," she said.

*   *   *

It took some time to exchange stories, long enough for the barman to cast annoyed looks in their direction, compelling Eddie to buy some drinks to justify their stay. But eventually they had all the pieces.

Not that they made much sense.

"Okay," said Nina, still turning over what she had learned in her mind, "so this . . . this Group has some plan in mind that requires the statues—and me—in order to work. Harald Glas was a member of the Group, turned against them, and is now trying to sabotage their plan."

"By killing you," said Eddie.

She smiled thinly. "Again, thanks for that. But Takashi was a member of the Group, Stikes gave them the statues, and Sophia . . . I honestly have no idea how she fits in. You said that in Peru she seemed to be working for the Group—so why was she with a guy who tried to kill me? And then she killed him. So is she with them, against them, or just taking a murder vacation in Italy?"

"Buggered if I know," he said. "I suppose if we knew what this plan was, it'd help."

"Takashi said it was about bringing peace and stability to the world, whatever that means. But I don't know how the statues would accomplish that."

"You said something weird happened to you when you put them together," Eddie reminded her. "Like what?"

"It's hard to describe. Just that I felt . . . *connected* to the world somehow. And that I knew where to find something important. But it's gone now—it's hard to remember."

"The Group probably wants this important thing, then."

"And Glas and Dalton want to stop them."

"Which makes them the bad guys, I guess."

"Stikes is working for the Group," she reminded him. "And based on past experience, when billionaires start making plans for the entire world I get a bit nervous." She gazed into her drink. "They knew what would happen when I brought the statues together. Part of that they got from the Brotherhood . . . but what about the other part? Where did that come from? Popadopoulos said that some governments have their own secret archives, and you said Dalton told you that the Group has influence over governments . . ." She looked up at her husband. "Maybe that's how they got the rest of their information."

"Dalton might know," Eddie suggested. "I could have another little chat."

Nina shook her head. "It's too risky. Hell, you're taking a huge risk just coming back to New York—back to the States, even. All it takes is one cop to recognize you from a watch list . . ." She sat up, determination entering her voice. "We've got to clear your name—prove that you were acting in self-defense when you killed Kit. Otherwise you'll be spending the rest of your life running. And I'm not going to let that happen."

"I like the thought, love," Eddie said gloomily, "but fuck knows how we'll do it. We've got a video that doesn't show the important bit, those numbers I found in Kit's flat in Delhi that don't mean anything without solving some puzzle . . ."

"What did it say again?"

"Something like *and the best of the greatest.* Alderley thinks that if you add the answer to the original number, you'll get whatever Kit was trying to hide."

"So all we have to do is figure out *what* Kit thought was the greatest. Or who."

"He was a Hindu," suggested Eddie. "Who's the greatest Hindu god?"

"Shiva, I think. Although actually he's considered to be one of a triumvirate—Brahma and Vishnu are equally powerful. But . . ." Another shake of her head. "It'll probably be something more personal, something only Kit would know. The clue isn't a riddle—it's more like an aide-mémoire. The answer must be something he would immediately know, a significant number. A date, a time, an address . . ."

"A score," said Eddie quietly.

Nina could tell that he thought he was on to something. "What kind of score?"

"A *cricket* score. Kit was mad keen on cricket, remember? Him and Mac were always banging on about it." The thought of Kit's murderous betrayal of the Scot caused a flare of anger inside him, but he suppressed it. "They were once arguing about who was the greatest player of all time—Kit thought it was an Indian guy. Can't remember his name, though."

Nina took out her iPhone. "Well, that's why we have the Internet. Let's have a look . . ."

A brief search produced an answer. "Sachin Tendulkar," Eddie read. "Best score in a test match, two hundred and forty-eight runs. So if we add two hundred and forty-eight to the number I found . . ." He took the phone from her and switched to its calculator, tapping in a figure.

Nina looked at the screen. "You remember the number?"

"Something that important, I burned it into my fucking mind. Okay, so add two hundred and forty-eight . . ."

"The last three numbers are six-zero-nine," she said before his finger reached the EQUALS key.

"Smart-arse." But she was correct. "Okay, Alderley said it might be a Greek phone number. Let's give it a try."

He entered the new number and made the call, switching the phone to speaker. But to their disappointment, the only result was a flat, continuous tone: number unobtainable. "Well, cock," Eddie muttered.

"Maybe there's a different score we could have used," said Nina, taking back the phone.

"No, I don't think so. Kit thought Tendulkar was the greatest player, and two hundred and forty-eight was his best score. Maybe it isn't a phone number at all."

"Then what is it?"

"No idea." He swilled the last dregs of beer around in his glass before downing them. "Let's go back to that video for now. Where is it?"

"On my laptop at the UN."

"Probably not the best idea for me to stroll in and watch it there," Eddie said with resigned amusement.

"Well, we probably can't risk going to the apartment either. But we need somewhere private. Who is there in the city that we can trust not to run screaming to the police the moment they see you?" She thought for a moment, then smiled. "I think I know . . ."

FIFTEEN

"Nina?" said Lola as she opened her apartment door. "My God, where've you been? We heard what happened in Rome—everyone's been so worried! Are you okay?"

"Yeah, I'm fine," Nina replied. She glanced along the corridor to make sure nobody was around. "Listen, there's a really huge favor I need to ask you, but first, Don isn't here, is he?"

Lola's fiancé was a firefighter. "No, he's working night shifts at the moment."

"Okay, good. Now, I need you to promise me that you will keep this an absolute secret for now. You can't tell anyone, not even Don—and definitely not the police. If you think that's going to be a problem, then don't worry, I'll just leave."

"Nina, it's me," Lola said firmly. "You know you can trust me. You saved my life! We Gianettis, we remember that kind of thing."

Nina smiled. "That's good to know." She checked the corridor again, then waved her increasingly intrigued PA back from the door. "Okay," she called, "come on."

The stairwell door opened and Eddie poked his head

out before hurrying down the hallway into the apartment. "Hi, Lola," he said casually as he passed her.

Lola stared openmouthed after him. "Oh, my God. Oh my God!"

"Yeah, yeah, yeah," said Nina, following Eddie inside and closing the door. "Now you see why you need to keep this quiet?"

"Uh-huh," Lola said, nodding. She went to Eddie, regarding him with amazement. "Where've you been? What have you been doing? How did you get back here without the police catching you?" A more quizzical look. "Why did you grow a beard? It doesn't suit you."

"There's nowt wrong with my beard," Eddie insisted jokily. "Tchah! Anyway, they don't give you razors in Zimbabwean prisons."

Lola's eyes widened. "You were in—"

"Let's save the travelogue for later, huh?" Nina cut in. "There's something more important to deal with first— namely, Eddie's innocence." She extracted her MacBook Pro from a bag.

"I *knew* you were innocent!" Lola exclaimed.

"Well, we've still got to actually prove it," Eddie admitted. "But thanks." He looked down at her baby bump. "So, either the pregnancy's going well, or you've been eating a lot of pies."

"Eddie!" Nina chided.

Lola giggled. "Both, actually."

"How far along are you now?"

"Seven months."

"You know if it's a boy or girl?"

"No, we want that to be a surprise."

"If it's a boy, Eddie's a good name," he said with a grin before turning to his wife. She had put the laptop on a table and opened it. "You all set there?"

"Nearly," she replied. "Lola, we need to watch a video. It might help prove Eddie's innocence, but . . . you probably won't want to see what happens in it."

Lola looked uneasy. "Is it the one Interpol sent you?"

Nina nodded. "Oh. Okay, yeah, I *definitely* don't want to see it."

"I'm sorry about this."

"It's okay. I'll be in the bedroom. Or the bathroom. It's where I seem to spend half my time anyway." She glared at her belly. "Bad baby! Very bad baby! Stop squishing Mommy's bladder, okay?" She headed for another room. "If you need me, just shout."

"Will do," said Nina as she left. "Wow, Lola's gonna be a mom. That's such a weird thought. Exciting, though."

"We could have tried for one by now if you'd wanted," Eddie said.

She snorted sarcastically. "Are you kidding? Can you imagine me going through what I have lately if I'd been pregnant?"

"You'd have survived. And so would the baby. I've seen pregnant women in war zones who've been through Christ knows what, and still gave birth to healthy kids. People are always panicking about every little thing that might go wrong, but the whole pregnancy process is pretty reliable. If it wasn't, humans would have died out before we even got out of Africa."

"Thank you, Dr. Chase, ob-gyn. Bet you wouldn't be so casual if it were *your* baby," Nina said, giving him a sly smile. "Anyway, this is the video."

Eddie regarded the screen. It showed a grainy still frame from the Peruvian gas-pumping station, a catwalk with a multitude of pipes and valves beneath it cutting diagonally across the camera's view. Near the left of the screen, a ladder ran from ground level to the gridwork walkway.

He remembered the scene well. "That's where I climbed up," he said, pointing at the ladder. "Kit and Stikes were farther along here"—he indicated a point out of frame—"talking to Sophia." There was a time-code at the bottom right. "How long before I turn up does it start?"

"Not long." She tapped the trackpad, and the video started to play. It was immediately clear that the pipeline monitoring system was not employing the latest technology. The image occasionally flickered with lines of static, looking as though it had originally been recorded on a well-used VHS tape rather than digitally.

The only things that moved for several long seconds were video glitches—until a figure, bent low and creeping stealthily through the shadows, appeared at the left of the frame. "There, that's me," said Eddie.

"Yeah, I kinda guessed that," Nina replied. He made a rude sound.

The Eddie on the screen, carrying a SCAR assault rifle, reached the base of the ladder and began to climb. "There isn't any sound, is there?" his present-day counterpart asked. Nina shook her head. Past-Eddie cautiously peered over the top of the ladder, watching something off-screen, then made a quick ascent to the walkway and brought up the rifle as he disappeared from view.

"It's a few minutes before anything else happens," said Nina. She was about to fast-forward through the recording, but Eddie stopped her. "What?"

"If there's anything in this that can help me, it has to be in the boring bits everyone skips through. Otherwise someone would have seen it by now."

"Interpol will have watched the entire thing."

"I've done surveillance work. It's the most bloody mind-numbing thing imaginable, and it's easy to miss something, even with other people looking as well. You can go over a tape again and again, and not catch something until the third or fourth time. So let's keep watching."

They did so. Apart from video flickers, nothing seemed to happen for over two minutes, and then a wash of light swept over the scene. "That's me and Macy arriving," said Nina. "And—"

"And now everything kicks off," Eddie said as two figures came back into view: himself and Kit, wrestling for control of the SCAR. Staccato flames burst from its barrel as it fired down into the pumping machinery. The pair continued their desperate brawl—then the image was momentarily wiped out by an explosive flash from below, video afterimages fading to reveal a jet of bright flame blasting out horizontally from a damaged pump.

Both Eddie and Kit had been knocked over by the blast, the Indian landing on top. He landed a couple of blows on Eddie's head, then finally managed to pry the gun away from him, turning it around to fire—but Eddie kicked it upward as he pulled the trigger, the last bullets searing just over his head.

Even though she had seen it before, Nina still winced. "Jesus, that was close."

"Feels even closer when you have a gun fired in your fucking face," said Eddie.

Another explosion flared as a second pump blew apart, starting the chain reaction that would soon consume the entire gas plant. The men on the screen were still fighting, Eddie slamming Kit's head against a railing—then the section of catwalk on which they were battling suddenly collapsed, tipping like a trapdoor to drop them toward the burning gas jet below. Eddie hit a stanchion and swung for a moment before pulling himself up.

Kit had fallen farther before catching the edge of the catwalk, dangling above the flames near a cluster of pipes. He tried to haul himself higher, but couldn't get a firm enough grip. Eddie hesitated, then used the stanchions like stepping-stones to get closer.

"I was going to pull him up," said Eddie. "Honest to God. I needed him alive to find out what the hell was going on."

"I believe you," Nina reassured him. On the screen, her husband reached Kit, who had at last managed to find a more secure hold.

Eddie started to bend down, extending his hand—

Then abruptly drove a boot into Kit's face, sending the Interpol officer plunging into the inferno below.

The sight shocked Nina as much as when she had witnessed it in person. And despite what Eddie had told her, she still couldn't see a gun in Kit's hand. She looked at him questioningly.

"Wind it back," he said. She did so. "Okay, watch his right hand . . . now!"

Nina paused the recording. "Eddie, there's . . . I can't see anything." Shadows and the camera angle, coupled with the low quality of the video, made it impossible to discern anything clearly among the pipework.

"It's there, I tell you." He leaned toward the laptop until his nose was almost touching the screen.

"I told you, not even Interpol found anything, and they gave it the full *CSI* treatment."

Eddie sat back. "Buggeration. I'm fucked, then. The only way I can prove it was self-defense is showing people that gun."

"I'm sorry." They sat in glum silence—until a question occurred to Nina. "Where did the gun come from? You and Kit were fighting over that rifle, so presumably he didn't have one of his own."

"No, it was Stikes's gun. I made him and Sophia chuck theirs over the edge. It must have landed in the . . . ." He jerked upright. "It landed in the pipes! Wind it back to when I went up the ladder."

His sudden hope was infectious. "What are we looking for?" Nina asked as she scrolled back through the recording.

"I climbed up the ladder—Sophia and Stikes were talking, and they didn't see me coming." On the laptop, past-Eddie acted out his current self's narration. "Sophia had a bodyguard who pulled a gun, so I took him down"—muzzle flash from offscreen—"and then, and then . . . ." He tried to remember the precise sequence of events. "Stikes dissed Mac, so I shot him—"

"You *shot* him?" exclaimed Nina, pausing the playback. "He seemed pretty spry in Tokyo for a dead man!"

"I only clipped him. Gave him a nice scar to remember me by." Eddie tapped his forehead in the same spot as Stikes's wound. "Kind of wishing I'd just blown his fucking head off now. Anyway, after that I told him and

Sophia to get rid of their guns. Stikes lobbed his over the side, past me . . ." He pointed at the shadowed pipes on the screen. "It *had* to end up where Kit could reach it. Play it."

Nina tapped the trackpad. "How long was this after you climbed onto the catwalk?"

"Not long—a minute, maybe less."

She glanced at the timecode. Twenty seconds passed, thirty. Her attention went back to the pipes. Any moment now . . .

A video glitch rippled across that part of the screen for a fraction of a second. Nina's heart sank—anything the video might have revealed was lost in the distortion— but Eddie's shout was one of triumph. "There! You see it?"

"No, I only saw the—"

"It's there, it's there," he said excitedly. "Take it back and play it frame by frame." He indicated a specific spot. "Right there, keep watching."

Nina replayed the video in extreme slow motion, eyes fixed on the pipes. Each frame chugged past, the only movement the shimmer and crawl of analog video. Then—

Eddie stabbed at the trackpad to pause the recording. "That's it!"

Nina stared at the screen. It was at the very edge of the picture, blurred by its motion and just barely catching one of the pumping station's lights, a silvery shape among the shadows.

But that shape was instantly recognizable. A gun.

"My God," she said quietly. "It's there, I can see it."

"Told you, didn't I?" He advanced to the next frame— and the falling gun was consumed by the bolt of static. It only lasted for another three frames, less than an eighth of a second, but by the time the image cleared the gun had vanished into the darkness between the pipes. "That's why nobody saw it. One frame's not long enough for your brain to pick it up consciously, so the only thing anyone registered was that glitch."

"You saw it, though."

"I knew it was there."

Nina looked at him, a smile spreading across her face. "Eddie, this proves your story. We've got to tell Beauchamp, let Interpol know what we've found. This'll get you off the hook!"

"You mean *you* let Interpol know. Until this is all sorted out, I'd better keep a low profile."

"The main thing is, we've got proof." She took the recording back to the frame showing the gun. "All we have to do is give Beauchamp that timecode, and you're in the clear!"

Lola came back into the room. "What happened? Did you find something?"

"We found something," Nina told her happily. "We definitely found something."

SIXTEEN

It wasn't enough.

Eddie stood silently listening as Nina held an increasingly dismayed phone conversation with Renée Beauchamp at Interpol. "I don't understand," she said. "You've watched the video, you've seen the gun at the exact timecode I gave you—you just *told* me you saw it! Kit grabbed it, so Eddie was clearly acting in self-defense. Why doesn't that clear him?"

"Because it still does not establish any motive for Kit to do what Eddie accused him of," the French officer replied.

"But you know he was doing *something*. He lied about his reason for meeting Stikes."

"That is not proof of wrongdoing. If we had any evidence of that, it would help Eddie's case, perhaps even clear him outright, but we have found nothing. All we know is that he and Kit were fighting, and that Kit found a gun and was apparently about to use it when he was killed. You say Eddie was acting in self-defense, but Kit may have gone for the gun for the same reason. Your husband has, ah . . . a reputation for violence, after all."

"So what *would* count as proof?"

"Something that links Kit to illegal activities. Falsifying evidence, accepting bribes, passing classified information to outside parties, abuse of power . . ." Beauchamp sighed. "But we have found none of these. There is nothing to suggest that Kit was anything except an exemplary police officer who was dedicated to the pursuit of order."

"So even though you've got new evidence, it doesn't help Eddie at all?"

"It would help his case if he turned himself in. But does it clear his name? No, I'm afraid not."

"Well, that's great," said Nina, struggling to contain her angry disappointment. "Thanks anyway, Renée." She put down the phone with more force than she intended.

"That didn't sound like it went well," said Eddie.

"It did not."

"Bollocks. I really thought it'd be enough."

"So did I. Oh God." She slumped back in her chair, looking out of her study window at the midmorning Manhattan street scene outside. They had left Lola's and returned to their apartment after midnight, Nina surreptitiously letting Eddie in through a fire exit to avoid the attention of the doorman. "I don't know what else we can do."

"There isn't anything else we can do. But there's something *I* can do."

"Which is what?"

"Leave." He walked out.

Nina jumped up and followed him into the lounge. "What? Wait a minute, what do you mean *leave*?"

"You know, go out through the front door and don't come back."

"Why?" she cried.

"Same reason I didn't call you while I was on the run. For Christ's sake, Nina, I'm wanted by bloody Interpol for murder! If I'd talked to you on the phone that would have been bad enough, but if I'm found here, that makes you an accessory for harboring a fugitive, or whatever it's called." He started for the bedroom to collect his belongings.

"So what are you going to do?" she demanded, moving to block him. "Just run off around the world again and try not to get arrested? Or killed?"

"I *have* to."

"No! No, you don't! We found Kit's gun on the recording, we can work out his code as well. Beauchamp said if we found evidence that proved Kit was doing something illegal, it'd clear your name. All we need is time."

"The longer I hang around here, the more chance there is of us both getting caught. And I'm not going to let you get dragged into this. Come on, let me past." He tried to move around her.

"It's a bit late for that, Eddie. Someone blew the top off a skyscraper trying to kill me, remember? And if you leave, then what? You want them to come after me again?"

That stopped him in his tracks. "Of course I bloody don't!"

"It's what'll happen. For God's sake, I would probably have died in Tokyo if you hadn't been there—never mind what happened at JFK! And from what Dalton told you, Glas won't give up. I *need* you, Eddie."

"You could hire a bodyguard. I've still got Charlie's number; he's got a couple of guys I'd trust to keep you safe."

"I don't mean I need you as a bodyguard." She stepped closer, looking into his eyes. "I need you as a *husband.* You know: best friend, soul mate . . . lover?" She held his hands. "I want you back, Eddie. I want my husband back. Not on the run in God knows what part of the world."

"Christ, believe me, that's what I want more than anything!" Eddie replied desperately. "But I don't have any choice. I've got to go. Otherwise—"

He broke off at the sound of someone knocking at the

door. Nina jumped. "Shit!" she whispered. "What if it's the cops?"

"They'd be knocking with a battering ram." He moved her aside. "Get rid of them. I'll hide in the bedroom."

"Don't you *dare* pack your things," Nina warned as she went to the door, waiting for Eddie to get out of sight before looking through the peephole.

It wasn't the police. But she was still startled by who she saw.

The visitor was Larry Chase.

"It's your dad!" she hissed to Eddie.

He poked his head around the door frame. "What the fuck's *he* doing here?"

"I don't know."

"Then get rid of him!"

Eddie retreated, leaving the bedroom door fractionally open so he could listen as Nina let the unexpected visitor in. "Larry, hi. This is, uh, kind of a surprise." He was alone. "Where's Julie?"

"Shopping," Larry replied. "She's on a pilgrimage to Bloomingdale's, so I thought I'd leave her to it."

"When are you flying back to England?"

"Tonight. Not trying to get rid of me, are you?"

"It's kind of an awkward time."

"That's okay, this won't take long." He looked around the apartment. "Nice place you've got. Very tasteful." He spotted one of Eddie's possessions on a shelf, a pottery cigar-box holder in the shape of a smiling Fidel Castro. "Well, mostly."

"So what can I do for you, Larry?" Nina asked, moving around the room so that by facing her, Larry would have his back to the bedroom door.

"I wanted to fix things up between us. When we had dinner, it didn't end well. Which made it two out of two, and I'd like dinner number three to at least reach the dessert course without any fireworks!" He laughed a little, but stopped when he saw Nina's stony expression.

"That's assuming that you're willing for there to *be* a dinner number three, of course."

"It's not something I'd given a great deal of thought, to be honest. Look, Larry, this really isn't a good time—"

"Please, it'll just take a minute!" He was silent for a moment, composing himself. "I wanted to apologize. For what happened in South America. I've been thinking about what you told me, and . . . you were right. I shouldn't have talked to Stikes."

"No," said Nina coldly. "You shouldn't."

"But I didn't know, I didn't *know*!" Larry protested, hands spread wide. "Yes, Callas and de Quesada weren't the kind of clients I'd actively seek out, but I didn't know what they were planning. When Edward turned up in Bogotá afterward and started threatening to tie me in with their attempted coup, I . . . well, I admit it, I panicked. I needed reassurances that I wasn't going to end up embroiled in the whole mess—and Stikes was the only person who could provide them, since de Quesada and Callas were both dead."

"And because you called him—"

"I know," he interrupted. "And I'm sorry, I really, really am *sorry* about it, and I know that if I hadn't spoken to Stikes none of it would have happened. If I'd known, if there had been any possible way I *could* have known, I wouldn't have done it."

"That doesn't change what happened, though," said Eddie, stepping out of the bedroom behind him.

Larry whirled, face a mixture of shock, relief—and nervousness. "Edward? Oh my God! You're all right!"

"Yeah, I'm okay," Eddie said with a shrug, before fixing his father with a cold gaze. "So, did I just hear that right? You actually apologized to someone?"

"If I make a mistake, I own up to it," his father replied stiffly.

"So I guess that must have been the first mistake you ever made in your life, seeing as I don't remember you doing that before."

"Eddie, for God's sake," said Nina, stepping between

the two men to prevent yet another family argument. "The point is, he *did* come here to apologize. Maybe now that you're here too . . ." She gave the elder Chase a pointed look.

"Well?" said Eddie, folding his arms and regarding his father expectantly.

It took considerably more effort for the words to emerge this time. "Okay. Edward. What I wanted to say was . . . I made a mistake, and I regret it. I'm sorry."

A sarcastic smile split his son's face. "Well, fuck me. I can die happy now that I've finally heard that."

"Jesus Christ, Eddie!" Nina snapped. "Will you just listen to him, please? For me, if nothing else?"

"I'm sorry, I'm *sorry*," Larry repeated, with growing emotion. "Look, I'm . . ." He paced in agitation across the room, then turned back to Eddie. "I'm not a soldier like you. I've never been in any situation where people's lives were in the balance. How do you think I feel about learning that something I did ended up getting people killed? It's—it's appalling! I don't know how to deal with something that huge. I really don't." He went to a chair and sat staring miserably down at the floor. "I'm sorry."

"That doesn't bring back Mac," Eddie rumbled. "Or any of the other people who died."

"No, it doesn't. But . . ." He looked up, meeting his son's icy gaze. "I did what I did because I was trying to save my own arse. I admit that. And now I completely understand why you took a swing at me in England." He shrugged not disdain, but a kind of acceptance. "To be honest, I can't help thinking now that you showed remarkable restraint."

"If Holly hadn't put herself in front of you," Eddie told him, "I wouldn't have stopped."

"And I would have deserved it. Well, up to a point." A faint attempt at a smile. "But when your granddaughter's braver than you are, it's probably a sign that you need to reassess some things in your life. Like . . ." He sighed. "Like your relationship with your son."

Eddie remained silent, compelling Nina to speak up. "In what way?"

Larry was not relishing whatever admission he was about to make. "I, er . . . I think I've misjudged you, Edward. I always thought of you as the boy you used to be—not the man you've become. But, well . . . you've changed. You grew up, you took on responsibilities for things bigger than just yourself. And . . . it's made me realize that maybe I never did."

He turned his eyes back down to the floor, not awaiting approbation but simply mentally worn from having forced out the confession. Nina looked between the two men, wondering which would speak first.

It was Eddie. "That's something I never thought I'd hear." But there was no malice or criticism to it, merely a statement of fact.

"It's something I never thought I'd say," replied Larry. "But I have, so, there you are. I hope you'll accept it."

Eddie held him in suspense for several seconds before delivering his reply. "I'll think about it."

His father had clearly been wanting more, but more or less managed to cover his downhearted look. "I suppose that's the best I could hope for."

A noncommittal sound, then Eddie tried to change the subject. "How is Holly? And Lizzie?"

"Elizabeth's fine; you know her, she always pushes on no matter what. Holly was very upset about losing your grandmother, as you can imagine, but she's a strong kid. She's handling it. What about you?"

"Me? Well, obviously I was upset about Nan too. I should have been there with her." He considered that, then gave Nina an apologetic look. "I mean, I wish I *could've* been there to see her one last time."

"She would have liked that," said Larry, "but I meant what about *you*, personally? You disappeared for three months, and it looks like you've been in the wars. What with the cuts and bruises, and the . . ." Larry indicated his chin. "The face fungus."

"Why does nobody like my beard?" Eddie said with a

sigh. "But yeah, I've had a few scrapes. Par for the course when you're on the run because you've been accused of murder. Speaking of which, I need to get going."

Nina hurriedly blocked the entrance to the bedroom once more. "Eddie, I'm not going to let you go again."

"We've been through this—I've got to. I can't clear myself without that code of Kit's, and I'm not going to bring you down with me as well."

"*No*, Eddie," she insisted. "Whatever happens, we're going to deal with it *together*, okay? If you think I'm going to let you go again now that I have you back, you're really, *really* mistaken."

"How are you gonna stop me? Tie me to the bed? Not that you haven't done that before, but—"

"We have company," Nina hurriedly reminded him, blushing.

"Well, maybe *I* should get going," said Larry uncomfortably. He went to the door, then hesitated, curious. "There's something that can clear you, Edward? Why don't you tell the police?"

"Because we don't know what it means," said Nina. "It's a number, a code. We think it's important, but we don't know why."

"What number?"

"What, *you* think *you'll* be able to work it out?" Eddie said in a cutting tone. "A mathematical genius"—he nodded at Nina—"and an MI6 agent couldn't find the answer, but a bloke who works in shipping can?"

"Maybe it's a shipping number," Larry replied defiantly.

"Ah . . . that's actually not a bad idea," Nina had to admit. "And really, it's not like it could hurt."

"All right, whatever," Eddie muttered. He wrote down the number while Nina gave Larry a potted account of how it had been calculated. "We thought it might be a Greek phone number, but it doesn't work." He gave the paper to his father.

Larry looked at it and frowned. "Hmm. Twelve digits, starting with three and zero . . ."

Nina's eyebrows shot up. "You know what it means?"

"Maybe. Thirty is a Swiss bank code. For banks in Bern, I think."

Eddie regarded him in disbelief. "You just know that off the top of your head?"

"Quite a few of my clients have Swiss accounts, so yeah. I deal with this stuff all the time. Let's see . . ." His brow crinkled in thought. "A full Swiss IBAN code would be twenty-one characters, but the first four are basically a computer checksum, so you can ignore them. Then it's five for the bank code and twelve for the account number, but account numbers are almost never that long, so any blank spaces are just padded out with zeros. Most Swiss bank codes are only four digits, so three-oh-two-one gives you the bank . . . and whatever's left is the actual account number."

"If we told Interpol what you just said," Nina asked cautiously, "would they be able to find out who the account belonged to?"

Larry nodded. "Swiss banks aren't like super-secret fortresses anymore. The United States strong-armed them into opening up after September 11. If you want to keep your money hidden nowadays, you take it to a bank in Andorra or Macao or—well, that's not really important," he said, noticing Eddie's disapproving look. "But if this is a Swiss account number, this would be enough information for its owner to access it—or Interpol to investigate it."

"We have to tell Beauchamp," said Nina, heading to the phone. Without looking back, she pointed at Eddie. "Don't you even think of leaving."

"I'm not," he replied. "Not until I see how this pans out, at least."

"Well, it looks like this'll get complicated, and I was going anyway, so . . . ," said Larry.

"Are you sure?" asked Nina.

"I should catch up with Julie before she melts my credit cards," he said with a small laugh. "But, ah . . . if

I was right about that number, you'll let me know, won't you?"

"Of course we will. Won't we, Eddie?"

"I suppose," said Eddie, rather dismissively.

"Okay, then. And about the money Stikes paid me? You were both right; it's . . . *tainted*, I suppose. As soon as I get back to England, I'll donate it to one of those charities you mentioned, Edward." He looked hopefully at his son, but no praise was forthcoming. "Well, I'll, ah, see you again sometime. Both of you." Larry gave Nina a brief embrace and Eddie an awkward nod, then departed.

Nina rounded on her husband. "That's *it*? That's all you had to say, *I suppose*?"

"What were you expecting?" Eddie replied sarcastically. "Big backslapping hugs and manly tears and the whole *I love you, son, I love you too, Dad* thing? We're not Americans. Besides, even if he's right about Kit's code, it doesn't change the fact that he fucked up. He can apologize as much as he likes, but it'll take a lot for me to get over that."

"Even if he helps clear your name?"

He huffed. "Stop asking me things I don't want to answer and call Renée."

Nina smiled and picked up the phone.

SEVENTEEN

"Welcome back!" cried Lola, embracing the newly shaven Eddie as he entered the reception area. Several other IHA staffers gave him a round of applause.

"Thanks! Thanks, everyone. It's good to be back," Eddie replied. "Steady on, the wife's right behind me," he added as Lola kissed him.

A grinning Nina followed him into the IHA offices. "It doesn't take long for word to spread around here, does it, *Lola*?"

"I could hardly keep it to myself, could I?" Lola replied without a hint of contrition as she released Eddie. "It was bursting to get out. Like I wish this little guy would." She looked down at her stomach.

"He'll have his freedom soon," Nina assured her. "Or she'll have hers, whichever it is. Anyway, thank you, everyone."

People congratulated Eddie and shook his hand, then returned to their offices and labs. He and Nina had work of their own to deal with. "Mr. Penrose is waiting for you," Lola told them. "And Ms. Beauchamp is ready to take your call when you are."

They went to the conference room. Sebastian Penrose

stood up to greet them as they entered. "Ah, Eddie! Glad to see you again, alive and well and a free man. It must be a huge weight off your mind."

"You're not kidding," said Eddie as he shook hands with the older Englishman. "Although let's make sure I actually *am* free first, eh? I still keep thinking a SWAT team's going to burst in at any moment."

"I think this will just be a formality," Penrose said, smiling. "Now, I understand that Renée is ready for us, so let me set this up . . ."

The conference room was equipped for videoconferencing. Penrose tapped at a remote control to switch on a large screen on one wall. A view of another conference room appeared, this one at Interpol's headquarters in Lyon. Renée Beauchamp looked back at them. "Good afternoon, Sebastian," said the tall Frenchwoman. "Or whatever time it is there."

"Good morning," Penrose replied, amused. "Now, I have two people here who are very eager to hear what you have to say, so . . . I hope it's good news."

Beauchamp sighed a little. "It is good news for Eddie; not so much for Interpol, I am afraid. Nina, you were right about the number being a Swiss account code. We made a priority check with the bank in Bern, and found that it was indeed registered to Ankit Jindal."

Eddie noted her formality in using Kit's full name; she was upset and disappointed in her former friend. "When was it opened?"

"Over two years ago. And a considerable sum of money had been paid into it during that time—over three hundred thousand euros."

"Paid in by whom?" Nina asked.

"A company in the Cayman Islands, which turned out to be a shell. It ceased trading three months ago—just after Ankit's death. But I had our Financial Crime Unit check it, and they found that the company was originally created as a subsidiary of a business owned by Harald Glas."

"Glas?" echoed Eddie, exchanging a brief but knowing look with Nina. "He was involved with Kit too?"

Beauchamp tipped her head quizzically. "There is some other connection?"

He decided not to let her in on his nocturnal visit to Dalton's house. "His name came up when I was trying to find out who attacked the skyscraper in Tokyo. But I didn't know he had Kit on his payroll."

"Nor did we. It is embarrassing to Interpol; Internal Affairs will have to investigate further." She shook her head. "Of all people, I never would have believed he would be corrupt. He fought *against* corruption in India before joining Interpol, and he was always very firm on the need for order. I don't know . . ." Another shake.

"What about Glas?" said Nina. "Is Interpol any closer to tracking him down?"

"No. It is as if he has disappeared from the face of the planet. Even though Eddie stayed ahead of us, we knew where he had been, and we were catching up."

"You didn't get me, though," Eddie couldn't resist pointing out.

Beauchamp's lips briefly twitched into a hunter's smile. "We would have. In time. But Glas . . . he has completely disappeared. An international red notice was placed on him, but he has not been seen since the warrant for his arrest was issued. We think he was tipped off. More corruption. But," she went on, "as for another red notice . . . Eddie, you will be very pleased to know that the one issued against you has been formally rescinded. The new evidence against Ankit proves that he had something to hide—which, with the gun found on the video footage, makes your claim of self-defense more valid."

"Thank God," said Nina.

"There will still have to be further investigation into what happened in Peru—and the Peruvian government has outstanding charges against Eddie for assaulting two police officers. But"—another slight smile—"I have persuaded them this is not a matter that calls for extradition."

Eddie counted names on his fingers. "So that's Zimbabwe, Syria, and now Peru I can cross off my holiday list, then. And Monaco, too."

Beauchamp's look of curiosity returned. "What happened in Monaco?"

"Uh, nothing," Nina said quickly, not wanting to remind Interpol of the couple's involvement in the crashing of a multimillion-dollar yacht into the middle of the wealthy principality's annual motor race. "But we'll be happy to cooperate with Interpol to make sure Eddie is fully cleared. Won't we?"

"No arguments here," Eddie assured her.

"For now, though," Beauchamp continued, "Eddie, you are a free man."

Eddie let out a long sigh of relief. "I'm bloody glad to hear that, Renée. Thanks."

The Interpol officer nodded. "I will speak to you again, no doubt. Good-bye."

She disconnected. Nina turned to her husband. "How do you feel?"

"Relieved. As. *Fuck*." He slumped in his chair. "Being on the run really bloody takes it out of you."

"Well, now you can stop running," said Penrose. "So, they found a connection between Jindal and Harald Glas? Interesting."

"You knew Glas," said Nina. "Can you think of any reason why he might have been paying Kit to obtain the statues?"

He shook his head firmly. "I wouldn't say I was exactly a close friend—I knew him through the United Nations, that's all. But no, I can't think of anything."

"Kit was on his payroll before we even found the first statue in Egypt, though," Eddie noted. "So Glas must have been looking out for the statues even then."

"I suppose having someone inside the Cultural Property Crime Unit would give you a heads-up if they turned up on the black market," Nina said thoughtfully.

"But how would he even have known about the statues in the first place?" asked Eddie.

"I wish I knew," said Penrose. He stood. "I have to go and brief the UN bigwigs on all this; Nina, I'll forward you the minutes. And Eddie . . . congratulations."

"Thanks." The two men shook hands again, then Penrose departed. "So," said Eddie, "now what?"

"First of all, before anything else . . ." Nina leaned over, placed both hands on Eddie's cheeks, and kissed him deeply. "That."

He was startled—but appreciative. "No tongue? Ah," he added as she returned for a second helping, this time with an open mouth. He was slightly breathless when she finally released him. "No sex on an office table?"

She grinned. "Don't push your luck. But I just wanted to show that now that I've gotten you back, I'm not letting you go again. From now on, we stick together, no matter what. You and me, always and forever. Okay?"

He pretended to give the matter deep thought. "I can cope with that. So we're back?"

"We're back, baby."

"And we're not going to have any more arguments?"

"Well, let's not say anything *crazy*." They both smiled. "Anyway, second of all—"

"Bollocks! I knew you'd be straight back to work."

"Second of all," she repeated, touching a finger to his lips before becoming more serious, "we need to decide how we're going to deal with all this. Glas and the statues."

"The statues are safe, for the moment," Eddie told her. "I left them with a mate of mine in Chinatown. But if Glas wants 'em destroyed, maybe we should just do that and get him off our back for good."

"Maybe. But he might still want me dead, no matter what. We need more information; we need to find out *why* the statues are so important. The Brotherhood had some, but it was incomplete."

"Who else'd know?"

"A very good question. And . . ." Realization lit up her face. "I think I know who could have the answer. Popadopoulos told me that the only organizations that

might have more information than the Brotherhood
would be certain powerful governments. And which is
the most powerful government on the planet?"

"Liechtenstein?"

"No, they're number two. Come on."

They left the conference room and headed back to the
reception area. Lola did a mild double-take. "Eddie, are
you wearing lipstick?"

"Damn, the secret's out," he said, wiping his mouth.

"Lola, I need you to contact someone for me and put
them through to my office," said Nina.

"Sure, no problem," the blonde replied. "Who?"

Nina paused before answering. "Victor Dalton."

* * *

"Mr. President!" said Nina with a big fake smile. "So
good of you to agree to see us."

Victor Dalton waited until the Secret Service agent
who had just searched the two visitors—and made sure
they were not using any recording equipment—left the
study before replying. "It seems I didn't have any goddamn choice," he said, giving Eddie a glare of deep
hatred. "But I'll warn you right now—I don't take well
to attempted blackmail."

Nina's smile vanished as if a switch had been flicked.
"And I don't take well to people trying to kill me. So I
think we understand each other."

Dalton put his elbows on his large oak desk and stee-
pled his hands as his guests sat. "All right. What do you
want?"

"Information."

"About what?"

"About why Glas wants me dead. About the three
statues I found that Stikes gave to Takashi."

Dalton made a dismissive sound. "I don't know about
any of that."

"But you're working with Glas. How can you not
know?"

"My interest is in getting payback against the Group.

I don't really give a damn what Glas is up to. Parts of our objectives coincided, and we were in a position to provide mutual assistance, that's all. I already told Chase as much as I know." His gaze became piercing, dangerous. "You want to know what I said? Just watch his damn recording."

"Maybe some more people ought to watch it," said Eddie.

Dalton jabbed a finger at him over the desk. "I warned you, Chase—"

"Okay, then," Nina cut in, "tell me about archives instead. The Group apparently knows more about the statues than anyone else. They found out some of it from the Brotherhood of Selasphoros in Rome—where did they learn the rest? Does the US government have any records concerning the statues? Anything connecting them to earth energy, Atlantis, the Kallikrates text—"

The ex-president's eyes flicked wide at that last. "You know what it is?" Eddie asked.

Dalton considered his words carefully before answering. "I don't know what it is, but I've heard of it, yes. When I was president, the Group would occasionally make requests for information from our top-secret archives. That was something they wanted to see, the Kallikrates file. I remembered it because it's an unusual name. But I have no idea what's in it."

"I need to read it," said Nina. "How would I go about that?"

"There's a facility in Nevada called Silent Peak. A lot of highly classified material is stored there. The kind of material that's so secret, they don't let it out of the place—not even for presidents. If you want to read it, you have to go there." A faint smile. "And they don't appreciate uninvited visitors."

"Well then," she said, "you'll just have to get us an invitation, won't you?"

Dalton shook his head. "Out of the question."

"I dunno," Eddie said, "you still had the connections

to send assassins halfway around the world to try to finish me off in Japan. So I'm pretty sure you should be
able to get me and Nina into some library." He reached
into his jacket and took out his phone. "Unless you
want me to make a call that gives *The New York Times*
their next big headline?"

"Wait, wait," said Dalton hurriedly. "Let me think.
It's a military facility, so access would have to be arranged
via the Pentagon . . ." He mused for a few seconds. "I
know some people who might be able to do it—so long
as they can arrange deniability. They wouldn't just be
risking their career by doing this. They could go to jail."

Eddie waggled the phone in his hand. "They wouldn't
be the only ones."

The angry lines on Dalton's face deepened. "You're
asking me to get people who have nothing to do with
our differences to risk everything to help you. These are
loyal Americans. Patriots."

"So patriotic they were the first people you thought of
when you needed someone to break the law," Nina remarked, voice cutting. "Look, I'm not asking to see nuclear launch codes, or the names of our spies abroad, or
the damn X-files. The Kallikrates text was written over
two thousand years ago, so it can hardly be a threat to
national security. That's the only thing I want to see. If
you can arrange that, then I'm willing to . . ." She looked
at Eddie. "*We're* willing to call a truce. We'll keep the
video quiet and make sure it never sees the light of day."

Eddie's expression told her that he was dubious about
giving up their leverage, but his silence was sign enough
that he was willing to go with her judgment. Dalton's
own visage was calculating. "Do I have your word on
that?" he finally said.

"Yes. If we have yours that you'll get us access to this
Silent Peak place."

"*Safe* access," Eddie added pointedly. "In and out."

Another pause for thought, then: "I'll see what I can
do—it should be possible." He leaned back in his chair,
the dismissive shift in his body language a clear sign that

he considered the meeting over. "You'll forgive me if I don't seal the deal with a handshake."

Eddie stood, returning the phone to his pocket. "Damn, I wasted a perfectly good stinkpalm."

"Gross, Eddie," said Nina as she rose. "We'll see ourselves out. Good-bye, Mr. President."

Dalton watched impassively as they left the room. Once they were gone . . . a tiny but devious smile curled the corners of his mouth.

EIGHTEEN
Nevada

"I don't like this," Eddie muttered as he and Nina walked toward the security station.

"Well, yeah, we're taking a hell of a risk," she whispered. "We're trying to get into a top-secret government facility under false pretenses—and that's assuming we can trust Dalton not to have set us up to be thrown into prison for the rest of our lives."

"No, I don't mean that." He tugged irritably at the too-tight collar of his US Air Force uniform, rented from a high-end theatrical costume house in New York. "I meant me, dressed as a fucking crab!"

"A what?"

"It's the army nickname for flyboys."

"Why crabs?" Nina asked, puzzled.

"Because their uniforms are the same color as the ointment they used to put on soldiers' tackle if they caught crabs."

"I wish I hadn't asked. Okay, here we are."

They were inside the Janet facility at Las Vegas's Mc-Carran Airport, which served a private airline used to ferry workers to the military testing grounds in the desert far north of the city. *Janet* was a jokey acronym from the days when the US government routinely denied that any such facilities existed: "Just Another Non-Existent Terminal." Since it was now overlooked by the enormous black glass pyramid of the Luxor hotel, that degree of cloak-and-dagger secrecy had been rendered pointless—but the terminal was still off-limits to all but authorized personnel.

So far, the passes grudgingly arranged by Dalton had got them through the main gate, but more stringent checks awaited. Two armed security men manned an X-ray conveyor and body scanner; another pair of large guards lurked near the door leading to the tarmac. All eyes were on the new arrivals as they crossed the concourse. At this time of day, they were the terminal's only visitors, the current shift's workers having departed for the desert hours before.

They reached the checkpoint. "Can I see your passes and flight documentation, please?" a guard rumbled, giving them both looks of institutional suspicion.

"Certainly," said Nina brightly, taking out her paperwork. "I'm Dr. Nina Wilde; this is Captain Tyler. We're both going to Silent Peak." She said their destination as casually as if she commuted there regularly, but in truth, not only did she not know exactly what she would find at the facility, she didn't even know where it was. Silent Peak did not exist on any maps—at least, not ones available to the public.

The guard took her papers, then turned to Eddie. "And you, sir?"

"Here ya go," drawled Eddie in an abysmal attempt at a Texan accent as he produced his documents. Nina forced herself not to wince visibly. Fortunately, if the guard had any acting critiques, he kept them to himself as he ran a light-pen over the passes. His companion's eyes flicked between the couple and his computer; after a moment, he nodded. Dalton had been good to his word, at least so far: The documents had been backed up by the government's computer network.

"Everything's in order, sir, ma'am," said the first

guard, returning their papers. "If you'll put your case on the belt and step into the scanner?"

Nina placed her briefcase on the conveyor, then walked through the arch of a millimeter-wave body scanner. Again, the second guard scrutinized a monitor before giving a nod of approval. Eddie followed her, with the same result. "Okay, I'll let your pilot know that you're here," said the first man, picking up a phone.

"Thank ya kaahndly," said Eddie. Nina wanted to deliver a sharp kick to his ankles to make him stop talking, but since they were being watched she could only give a pointed glare.

The guard finished his brief call. "Your pilot'll meet you at the gate in a minute. Have a nice flight."

"Thank you," said Nina as she and Eddie headed for the exit. As soon as they were out of earshot, she hissed, "Will you stop that?"

"Stop what?" asked Eddie.

"Your goddamn John-Wayne-with-brain-damage voice!"

"I can't exactly talk normally, can I? Might be a bit of a giveaway that I'm not really a Yank if I'm all *Ay up, by 'eck, look sithee.*"

"Then don't talk at all! Honey, you can't do accents. Just accept it."

Eddie huffed, but fell silent as they reached the gate and waited, the other two guards watching them. After a few minutes, a middle-aged black man in a civilian pilot's uniform arrived. "Dr. Wilde? Captain Tyler?"

"That's right," said Nina, with another warning glance at Eddie, who limited his answer to a nod.

"I'm Samuel Abbot—I'll be flying you today." He shook their hands. "Okay, if you'll follow me?"

He led them out onto the parking apron. At this time of year the temperature in Vegas fell far short of the blistering heat of summer, but the combination of the high sun and an unbroken expanse of concrete meant that a wave of hot air rolled over them as they left the air-conditioned terminal building. Eddie tugged at his collar again.

Nina had bigger concerns than personal comfort. She looked around for any signs that their cover had been blown. No security vehicles screamed toward them; no guards raised guns. They had passed the first hurdle.

But there would be more to come.

A Boeing 737 airliner, white with the red stripe of the Janet fleet, was parked nearby, but Abbot took them to a smaller plane in the same livery, a Learjet 35A. Its twin engines were already idling. "Private jet," said Nina. "Nice to get the VIP treatment."

"Yeah, but if this goes pear-shaped," Eddie reminded her quietly, "our next flight'll be with Con Air."

The door was open; Abbot showed them inside. The plush six-seater cabin was empty, but Nina saw a copilot already in the cockpit. "If you'll take your seats," said Abbot, closing the hatch, "we'll get this show on the road." He joined the other man up front.

Eddie listened warily to the pilots and their radio communications, but heard nothing that suggested potential danger. He relaxed, slightly. The engine noise rose. "Okay, fasten your seat belts," Abbot said over the intercom as the plane began to move. Nina nervously pulled her restraint tight, but Eddie left his belt loose—just in case he needed to make a move in a hurry.

The crew didn't seem about to turn against them, however. Takeoff was swift, the Learjet quickly ascending to ten thousand feet and heading north. A barren landscape of desert and mountains spread out below. "Hey," said Eddie after a while, indicating something through a window. "Guess what that is."

Nina saw a stark, almost circular expanse of pale sand against the russet-browns of the surrounding terrain. A dry lake bed, she guessed; on its southern edge was what looked like an airfield, a long runway stretching all the way across the flat plain. "I don't know. A military base?"

Eddie chuckled. "Yeah, you could say that. That's Area 51!"

"You're kidding. What, *the* Area 51? Where they're supposed to keep the aliens and flying saucers?"

"That's the one. I'd love to poke around there, just to see if any of the stories are true."

"You might get the chance," said Nina as the plane tipped into a descent. "You think that's where we're going?"

He pressed his cheek against the window for a better view ahead. "Don't think so. Looks like we're heading for the hills east of it." A frown. "Weird, I didn't think there was anything out there."

"Oh, so you're an expert on Area 51?" Nina asked, teasing.

"Had a bit of an interest back when *The X-Files* and all that kind of stuff was big," he admitted. "Used to buy magazines called things like *Alien Encounters*. Hey, come on!" he added, seeing her smirk. "Military secrets are a lot more boring in real life than on TV. It's loads more fun to imagine you're guarding a crashed UFO than a warehouse full of broken radio gear. And yes, I had to do that once. For a whole month."

"Poor baby. So what *is* down there?"

"That's the thing: nothing. That's why they put Area 51 out here in the first place, 'cause it's fifty miles from anybody who might be watching."

The plane slowed, engines easing back as it continued its descent. "Okay, folks," said Abbot over the intercom, "we'll be landing at Silent Peak in five minutes. Put your seats and tray tables in the upright position, huh?" He laughed a little at his aeronautical joke.

Nina wasn't amused, though. The message had hammered home the reality of what they were about to do. "God, if something goes wrong while we're out here . . ."

"Bit late to start worrying now," said Eddie. "But we got this far okay. All we can do is keep pretending we know what we're doing."

"Isn't that what we always do?"

The Learjet kept slowing, dropping toward the rugged hills. Eddie looked for their destination. They were heading into a closed valley, a single large rocky peak beyond, but there was no sign of anywhere they might land . . .

He blinked as the truth suddenly sprang from the background like the hidden image in a stereographic puzzle. The valley floor had at first glance appeared desolate and empty—but as the plane drew closer the giveaway parallel lines of human activity were revealed. A runway ran along it, partly hidden beneath sand and dust. The concrete had apparently been made from that same surrounding sand, the colors matching almost perfectly.

Such camouflage wouldn't conceal it from the infrared vision of satellites, though. That probably meant it had been built before they came into common use. Some kind of Cold War facility?

They would find out soon enough. The Lear adjusted its course for the final descent, lining up with the long runway. "This'll be bumpy," Abbot announced, "so hold on tight."

Nina's nails were already digging into the leather of her armrests. "If I hold on any tighter, I'll merge with the damn chair!"

The pilot had, if anything, underplayed the roughness of the touchdown, bumps and cracks in the dusty concrete making the jet judder like a bicycle riding over cobblestones. "Christ, I think I've lost a filling," Eddie said as the shaking eased to merely uncomfortable levels.

Nina took in the view outside. "Where are we going?" she wondered aloud. There were no buildings along the runway, just the rising valley sides. "I don't see anything here."

"Must be something," said Eddie. "If there isn't, this is a really, really expensive version of the Mafia taking people out into the desert to kill them."

"Thanks, Eddie. You're always so reassuring." But there were still no structures in sight . . .

The answer came as the Lear slowed to taxiing speed

and made a turn, bringing the cliff at the end of the valley into view. Set into the rock at its bottom was a door.

A very large one.

It took Nina a moment to take in its sheer scale. An opening at least three hundred feet across and sixty feet high had been blasted out of the mountain. "Jesus," she gasped. "That's a big-ass door."

"You should see their draft excluder," said Eddie, impressed.

The jet came to a stop. "Ladies and gentlemen," said Abbot, "welcome to Silent Peak."

• • •

A military jeep took the couple from the stationary plane to the base's entrance. The door itself didn't open; rather, a part of it did, a smaller section hinging upward like a cat flap to let the vehicle through. Even this opening was on a giant scale, easily large enough to have accommodated the Learjet. Worryingly, a sign beside the entrance warned of the sanctions that would be taken against unwanted visitors: USE OF DEADLY FORCE IS AUTHORIZED.

But that concern quickly took second place to amazement. It was all Nina could do not to gawp at what lay behind the door. They had entered a vast underground hangar, at least seven stories high and lit by rank upon rank of lights in the ceiling, made so small by height that they looked like perfectly aligned stars. Several C-130 Hercules transport aircraft were parked along one wall, almost lost in the cavernous space. "Wow. This is incredible!"

The jeep's driver took them to a clutch of portable cabins opposite the line of aircraft. Men in the blue berets of the USAF Security Forces stood waiting for them. "Ay up, it's the goon platoon," Eddie whispered to Nina.

"Don't talk unless you absolutely have to—and even then, don't!" she replied.

The jeep stopped, the military policemen surrounding

it. Another man, a lanky officer in wire-rimmed glasses, stepped forward to greet the passengers. "Dr. Wilde, welcome to Silent Peak Strategic Reserve," he said, holding out a hand to help Nina from the vehicle. "I'm the base CO, Colonel Kern—Martin Kern. It's a great honor to have you here."

"Thank you, Colonel," Nina replied. Eddie climbed from the jeep beside her, remembering military protocol and saluting his superior officer. "This is my liaison from the Pentagon, Captain Tyler."

"Sir," said Eddie, making Nina cringe inwardly once more. Even that one short word sounded incriminatingly fake in his terrible accent.

But Kern was only concerned with his female guest. "Captain," he said with a noncommittal salute of his own, before turning back to Nina. "I read about the role you played in saving President Cole's life in India last year. That's true heroism, if you don't mind my saying. Something every American can be proud of."

"Ah, thank you." Nina's awkwardness at the gushing praise was increased by the certainty that Kern would have a very different opinion of her if he knew the real reason for her visit. She changed the subject by presenting her pass. "Here's my paperwork."

"This'll just be a formality—I know who you are," said Kern with a smile. He briefly scanned the documents, then returned them before giving Eddie's pass slightly longer scrutiny. "Okay, I imagine you're keen to go down to the repository."

"Down?" said Nina, surprised. She indicated the nearby cabins. "I thought those were . . ."

"These? Oh, no, these are just the administration facilities. You don't know about the base?"

"No, everything was arranged at very short notice, and I didn't think to ask. So, there's even more of this place?"

Kern grinned. "Oh, there's more! I'll give you the tour personally. Log them in," he told one of the men nearby, before beckoning for Nina and Eddie to follow him.

"Normally we'd take your phone and any other electronic devices, but you've got top clearance, so no need to worry." That raised a warning flag in Nina's mind: Why would Dalton have gone the extra mile for them? "This way, please. I think you'll be impressed."

He led them to a golf-cart-like yellow buggy nearby, the guards heading back to the cabins. Nina sat in the front passenger seat beside the officer, Eddie behind her. "So just how big is this place?" she asked as Kern set the little electric vehicle in motion.

"This level? One point two million square feet of floor space, more or less. And it's not even the biggest. There are twelve levels in all."

"Fu—Gee, that's a hell of a size," said Eddie—though it came out as *a hail arf a sars*.

Nina shot him a sharp look. "When was it built? For that matter, *why* was it built?"

"They started construction in 1954," Kern told her. "It was designed as a way to ensure that the United States had a second-strike nuclear capability—no matter what the Soviets managed to achieve with a first strike against us, we'd have a backup bomber force able to be launched against them from a hidden base days or even weeks later. Problem was, by the time Silent Peak actually came online both sides had put ICBMs into service, making long-range nuclear bombers obsolete. So the base became a strategic reserve." He indicated the aircraft across the hangar. "Basically, it's a storage facility."

"Lark the boneyaahds in Arizonah," said Eddie, referring to the huge desert ranges filled with mothballed planes.

"Not quite—the vehicles there are just as likely to be scrapped or stripped for parts as returned to service. Everything stored here at Silent Peak can be made combat-ready within forty-eight hours, if needed. You'll see our inventory on the way down."

Nina looked ahead past lines of trucks and Humvees, but didn't see anything that looked like a ramp or elevators, only a large black square on the hangar floor.

"How do we get— Oh." Her eyes went wide as she realized what she was looking at.

The square wasn't on the floor, but set into it, a separate entity. A gigantic elevator shaft.

"Isn't that something?" said Kern, pride in his voice. "It's two hundred and sixty feet on a side, and can bring a fully laden B-52 up from the lowest level in under five minutes. So I'm told, anyway. I've never seen it move anything that big myself—I only took command here last year."

"That's . . . quite a thing, yes," Nina agreed. She wondered what future archaeologists, as far removed from the present as she was from the heyday of Atlantis, would make of Silent Peak. Would they have any comprehension of its original deadly purpose and the ideological conflict that spawned it?

She put such musings aside as Kern steered the buggy toward one corner of the open shaft. A metal cage marked a section roughly ten feet square. "Passenger elevator," the colonel explained as he pulled up alongside it. "There's one at each corner of the shaft. It can be a bit unsettling, but it's a lot easier than taking the emergency stairs. Okay, step aboard." The trio dismounted from the buggy, Kern opening a gate in the cage and walking through onto a platform with handrails around its edge. Once Nina and Eddie were on the platform, he closed the gate and went to a control panel. "The repository is on the lowest level."

"The depths of the earth," Nina remarked.

"Yeah, you could say that. Some people say that if you listen hard enough, you can hear Satan himself at work underneath." Kern laughed briefly, then pushed a button. "Okay, here we go. Hold on."

The platform dropped from the cage into a massive vertical shaft that fell away into oblivion. Nina instinctively recoiled from the edge, vertigo rising.

"Don't worry, Dr. Wilde," said Kern. "It's perfectly safe. Nobody's fallen down it—at least, not on my watch!"

"I think I'd still prefer more solid railings," she said. "Or, y'know, walls . . ."

The elevator continued its journey. Great vertical tracks ran down the shaft's sides; guides for the as-yet-unseen main elevator platform. At widely spaced intervals below were bands of light in the darkness marking the entrances to the base's other levels. From the looks of it, the repository could be almost half a mile underground. Even in the vastness of the shaft, the thought gave Nina a claustrophobic shudder.

The first level was approaching. "Take a look at that," said Kern, gesturing toward the hangar as it came into view.

It was full of aircraft. Bombers, the long, sinister charcoal-gray forms of a dozen, two dozen, more, B-52s packed into the space like lethal sardines. The eight engines of each plane were shrouded, the sleeping giants awaiting a new call to action.

"That's . . . that's a lot of planes," Nina said. She hadn't taken in the full meaning of the term *strategic reserve* until now. Just because a weapon was old didn't mean it was useless.

"That's only one level. We've got another three floors of Buffs—"

"Buffs?"

"Big Ugly Fat Fu—uh, Fellows," Eddie told her.

The colonel smiled. "Three more floors of them, plus we've got Eagles, Hornets, Warthogs . . ."

"Sounds more like a zoo than a military facility," said Nina.

"Ha! Yeah, I guess. And then we've got choppers, and a lot more general equipment—trucks, jeeps, bulldozers, that kind of thing. And more tanks than you can shake a stick at."

"My tax dollars at work." Even in 1950s money, the cost of excavating Silent Peak must have been as huge as the base itself.

They passed the hangar and continued down. The next level contained more B-52s, with Huey utility helicopters nestled in among the colossi; the hangar below was packed with fighter aircraft. Then more bombers, this time joined by a trio of coal-black SR-71 Blackbird spy planes. Never mind the base, Nina thought—the value of the mothballed hardware it contained was equally mind blowing.

A sound reached them from below, the echoing rumble of an idling engine. Its source was revealed as they approached the eleventh level. The main elevator platform, an enormous metal expanse almost filling the width of the shaft, waited here; the hangar itself was filled with precisely lined rows of M60 tanks. One of the armored vehicles was surrounded by portable lighting rigs, a pair of men working on its open engine compartment. Wide flexible hoses snaked across the floor, drawing its exhaust fumes into a large extractor vent. "Routine maintenance," Kern explained as they continued to descend, passing through the complex web of girders forming the platform's supporting structure. "Like I said, everything here is kept ready for action. If we needed to, we could have a couple dozen of those babies rolling out of here by tonight."

"Let's hope we never need to," said Nina. The elevator drew closer to its final destination. She moved back to the railing, eager to see what the lowest level contained . . .

The sheer scale of what met her eyes was astounding. Despite the size of the rest of the base, it was in essence nothing more than a very large parking structure. The twelfth floor, however, was home to something vastly more complex.

The repository was a library—but beyond anything Nina had ever seen. The stacks were arranged in a grid, stretching away seemingly to infinity. And the shelf units were not built on a human scale; they were easily thirty feet high.

It quickly became clear that the whole place was not intended to be directly accessed by humans at all. Between the stacks ran a network of tracks, along which ran towering robotic forklifts. She had seen similar devices before: automated storage and retrieval systems, designed to collect specific items from large archives and deliver them to a central point. But the system at Silent Peak was several orders of magnitude larger and more complicated than anything she had encountered in academia.

"My God," she said, genuinely awed. "How big is this place? There must be miles of shelves!"

"Something like three hundred miles, if they were all laid end-to-end," said Kern as the platform stopped. "But Dr. Ogleby can give you the exact details. I just work here." He opened another gate so they could exit the elevator, then led them to one of several cabins nearby. It was marked with a sign: READING ROOMS 01–08. Kern entered, Eddie and Nina exchanging *what the hell have we gotten into?* glances behind him. Another man in Security Forces uniform sat by the door, looking utterly bored. He stood and saluted them, then returned to his blank-eyed torpor. Kern called out, "Dr. Ogleby! Are you here?"

A bald man popped up like a groundhog to peer at them over a cubicle wall. "Oh, it's you, Kern," he said, annoyed at being disturbed. He padded out to meet the new arrivals. Unlike the other base personnel, he was a civilian, wearing a threadbare suit and a garish yellow bow tie.

Kern started to make introductions. "This is Dr. Nina Wilde from the International Heritage Agency, and Captain Tyler—"

"Yes, I know, I know," said Ogleby dismissively. "I read the email." Beady eyes scrutinized Nina. "Waste of time and money your coming here in person. The material you want may be Eyes Only, but we could still have couriered it to you in New York."

"Really? We were told we could only view it here," said Nina, concealing her sudden nervousness. Dalton had been very specific that they would have to travel to Silent Peak to see the file.

"Not for something of that classification. You were obviously misinformed." He turned his grouchy gaze to Kern. "Something else I can help you with, Colonel?"

Kern was evidently well used to Ogleby's attitude. "Apparently not. Well, Dr. Wilde, Captain, when you're finished here I'll arrange for someone to bring you back to the surface."

"Thank you," said Nina. Kern exited, leaving her and Eddie alone with the sour-faced librarian. "So, Dr. Ogleby, this is a remarkable archive you have here."

He didn't even respond well to a compliment. "It would be if they gave me the staff and money to run it properly. Right, let's see your papers, then."

The pair produced their documents. Ogleby read them, then went to a computer to double-check their details. "No need for you to come here at all," he muttered as he pecked at the keyboard with one finger, logging the new arrivals into the system.

"I'm curious about that myself," said Nina. "I mean, what we're here to see is of historical importance, but it's hardly a national security matter. Why keep it so highly classified?"

"It's not the material itself, it's where it came from," Ogleby replied, still tapping away at the computer. "In this case, the Nazis."

"Nazis?" said Eddie, in his surprise using his normal accent before hurriedly correcting himself. "Uh, I mean, Nat-zees."

Fortunately, Ogleby didn't pick up on it. "It was part of a scientific archive seized by US forces at the end of the war, some of which had been stolen from Greece during the German occupation there. A lot of the other material concerned what you might call 'ethically questionable' Nazi experiments"—he gave them a decidedly ghoulish smile—"so the whole collection was classified, including the material you want to see."

"Why?" Nina asked. "It couldn't possibly be connected to anything the Nazis did."

"It was connected just by association," said Ogleby in a patronizing tone. "The Nazis were very good at filing. You release one file, people want to know where the others are, and what's in them. It's simpler just to classify everything so only people with a need to know can see it. That way, we still have the information without bleeding hearts bleating about our benefiting from 'immoral knowledge.' There's no such thing." He finished typing. "We can't put the genie back in the bottle, but at least we can stop people from whining that someone removed the cork."

Nina agreed with him in principle that knowledge itself could not be immoral—as far as she was concerned, the cliché that "there are some things man was not meant to know" was an anti-intellectual crock—but that hadn't stopped her from quickly developing a dislike for the librarian. "Well, we're in the need-to-know club now, so if we could see it?" she said spikily.

Ogleby's nod was distinctly disapproving, but he signaled impatiently toward one of the cubicles. "Go on, in there. You can get a good view of the system at work."

As well as a well-lit reading desk, the cubicle contained something that reminded Nina of a smaller-scale version of an airport's baggage carousel. A large flap set into the cabin's outer wall opened onto a set of steel rollers that would channel anything coming down it into a flat collection area; another set of rollers at the opposite end led back through a second flap. A window looked out into the hangar and its miles of shelves. "Your material is on its way," said Ogleby. "The shuttle should be here in a minute."

Eddie and Nina moved closer to the window. The tracks crisscrossed the vast space between the stacks, points at alternate intersections allowing the shuttles to follow the most efficient course through the grid. As they watched, one of the towering machines trundled past, carrying a large container resembling a bank's safety deposit box. Sparks crackled from its bumper-car-like overhead power grid. It clattered through a set of points and turned down an aisle, disappearing from view. Other shuttles were at work farther away.

"The place looks busy," said Nina.

"It always is," Ogleby replied. "We send out at least three hundred retrieval requests per day—and new material arrives all the time, of course. The Pentagon, CIA, NSA, even the White House—everybody has files down here. And we keep track of every single one." Pride briefly overcame grumpiness. "Nothing's ever been leaked or stolen from Silent Peak. Not so much as a Post-it." His abrasive attitude returned. "How long will you need?"

"I don't know," she said with a shrug.

The gesture irritated their host even more. "Well, this isn't a social club, so don't waste time chatting about it. As soon as you've got what you need, put everything back in the box and push it down the belt, then you can leave. In the meantime, I have work to do, so if you need anything, ask the zombie over there." He cast a disdainful look toward the mind-numbed man by the entrance, then stalked out of the cubicle.

"Thank fuck he's gone," said Eddie.

"I know. What a jerk!"

"No, I meant I can finally talk again."

"With you, silence is golden," Nina told him. "Especially with that god-awful accent you were using. Seriously, what the hell was it? You're *married* to an American—how can you not know what we sound like?"

"Oh, I know what you sound like. Sort of shrill, and annoying—ay up." Their discussion was interrupted as another shuttle stopped outside the window. A hydraulic whine as it raised its cargo to the drop-off point, then the flap opened with a bang and a metal container skittered down the rollers to stop in the collection area before them.

Nina examined the delivery. It was somewhat larger

than a standard box file, a barcode laser-etched on the brushed steel. Beneath it was a large label bearing an identification number, along with the cryptic line SCI(G3)/NOFORN. The more readily understandable EYES ONLY was printed beneath it in red. "What does that mean?" she asked, tapping the jumble of letters.

"*NOFORN* means 'no foreign nationals,'" said Eddie. "I'd better look away, then. Don't want to break any rules."

"I think we're past the stage of worrying about that," Nina said with a halfhearted smile.

"Just a bit. And *SCI* stands for 'sensitive compartmentalized information.' Super-top-secret, basically. The *G3* part's probably some particular need-to-know clearance. Which Dalton arranged for you, so you'd better start using it. The quicker we're out of here, the better."

She took the box to the reading desk. "Yeah. I didn't like what Ogleby said, that we could have had this brought to the IHA. You think Dalton's trying to set us up to be caught red-handed?"

"I'm surprised we haven't been arrested already, to be honest. Or shot."

"There's a pleasant thought." Nina sat and opened the box, Eddie leaning over her shoulder to see what was inside.

It didn't contain a great deal: a manila folder with thirty or so typewritten pages within, and a large padded envelope housing a flat and heavy object. She flicked through the folder first. The opening pages were a summary of where and when US forces had acquired the material from the Nazi archive at the end of the Second World War, and the bureaucratic decision-making process that had kept it hidden to this day. Following them were translations—from German to English, of the Nazis' own records, and then from ancient Greek to English—of the material itself.

Nina put them aside and picked up the envelope. Inside was another folder, but this was metal bound in thick black leather, not a simple card sleeve. A brass zipper ran around three sides. She carefully unfastened it and opened the cover.

She immediately recognized the contents.

It was the rest of the torn parchment she had seen in the Brotherhood of Selasphoros's archives in Rome.

NINETEEN

"What is it?" Eddie asked.

"Something that's been missing for a very long time," Nina replied in a reverential whisper. The US government had taken the same approach to preserving the fragile sheet of browned animal skin as the Brotherhood, pressing it between two pieces of glass. Despite this, the ancient document's condition was considerably worse than its matching half; it had passed through more hands over the centuries.

But it was still readable, the closely spaced Greek text clear. She gazed at the long-lost words of Kallikrates, starting to translate . . .

"So?" said Eddie impatiently. "What *is* it?"

"The Brotherhood had the other half," she explained, indicating the torn top of the page. "Their part described the mental effects of what happens when the three statues are brought together—the 'visions.' But this . . ." She rapidly skimmed through the rest of the writing. "This is about the *physical* effects. And it matches what happened in Tokyo—the statues becoming charged with earth energy, the levitation . . ."

"Levitation? What, you started floating around the room?"

"Not me, the statues. And they just kind of . . . hung there. But never mind that." She kept reading, hungry to learn more. "In the Brotherhood's text, Nantalas, the priestess, believed that the statues were the keys to god-like powers, which came from something she called the sky stone."

"A meteor?"

"Seems likely. The statues are meteoric rock, after all—they must have been cut from it. But this text actually says what that power *is*." She pointed at the top of the parchment. "It follows on directly from the part I read in Rome. When she put all three statues together and touched them to the sky stone, it 'rose from the floor, lifted by the power of the gods. Even though the chamber was not open to the sky, lightning flashed through the Temple of the Gods and the ground shook with thunder. After Nantalas lowered the stone, the king agreed that such power should be used against the enemies of Atlantis, but knew there would be those in the royal court who would be fearful of angering the gods by doing so. He said that he would bring the court to the Temple of the Gods so they could witness with their own eyes the power of the sky stone.' The royal court," she added thoughtfully. "If they were involved, it would have been recorded in the altar room . . ."

"How big was the stone?" Eddie asked.

"It doesn't say. But the inference seems to be that it was fairly large—bigger than the statues, certainly."

"So the whole thing's basically an earth energy weapon, then? Only a natural one?"

"It looks like it. And the Atlanteans had it, eleven thousand years ago."

"Then where is it now?"

"I think that's what a lot of people are trying to find out." She gave him a worried look. "And Eddie . . . I'm the key to finding it. When I had all three statues in

Japan, I felt . . . *drawn* to something. I didn't know what at the time, but it *has* to be this sky stone."

"Drawn to it?" he said doubtfully. "How?"

"It's hard to explain, but it was like—like a bird's homing instinct, perhaps. I just *knew* what direction it was in, and that it was a long way away. And Takashi was expecting it—one of the first things he asked me was if I had felt it. The mole in the Brotherhood gave this Group the first half of Kallikrates's texts, and they obviously had enough influence over the US government to get access to this." She tapped the glass protecting the parchment. "They must think that the meteorite is some Atlantean superweapon, and want to get their hands on it. And they need me to find it."

"That can't be good," said Eddie. "Maybe I should've smashed those fucking statues after all."

"I'm starting to think you're right. The question is, what are we going to do?"

He looked at the parchment. "Is there anything else on there that's useful?"

Nina quickly checked the remainder of the text. "Nothing that seems relevant."

"Great. In that case, stick it back in the box and let's get out of here."

Nina closed the leather case, placed it back in the envelope, then returned it and the folder to their container. She picked up the box and was about to send it down the chute back to the automated library when her phone rang, startling them both. "We've got reception all the way down here?" she said, puzzled, as she fumbled it from her pocket with one hand. The number was unfamiliar.

"They must have a booster," said Eddie, suddenly wary. "You expecting any calls?"

"Nope." She answered it. "Hello?"

"Hello, Dr. Wilde." *Dalton.*

Nina lowered her voice so Ogleby and the guard wouldn't overhear. "Hello, Mr. President," she said, making the title sound almost derogatory. Eddie instantly became more alert than ever, checking what was happening outside the cubicle. As yet, nothing—but he was certain that wouldn't last. "To what do I owe the extremely dubious honor?"

"What do you think of Silent Peak?"

"It's impressive, if you like colossal wastes of taxpayer dollars. But you didn't call me to get my opinion on that, did you?" Eddie leaned closer to listen to the other side of the conversation.

"No, I didn't." The ex-president was relishing every word. "I called to say . . . good-bye. The base commander is just being told about a major security breach. I'd imagine you've got less than a minute before they come for you. In force."

A sickening chill ran through Nina's body. "A breach that'll be traced back to you," she said with straw-grabbing defiance.

Dalton almost laughed. "No. It won't. For one thing, my people covered their tracks, and for another . . . you won't get the chance to tell anyone. So once again—good-bye, Dr. Wilde."

"Son of a bitch!" Nina hissed—but Eddie had taken the phone from her.

"President Victor Dalton, before you hang up," he said, receiving an odd look from Nina at his use of Dalton's full name, "I've got something to say."

"You're going to threaten me, I suppose, Chase?" came the reply. Eddie could almost see his smirk. "Use your little video of our discussion as leverage? It'll never get out, I assure you. My contacts will see to that. Forewarned is forearmed, as the saying goes."

"No, what I actually wanted to say is al-Qaeda bomb kill the president jihad terror!"

Silence, then: "You limey *bastard*!" The line went dead.

"What the hell was *that*?" Nina demanded.

He gave her a grim smile. "The NSA records every phone call made in the States. All those red-flag keywords'll make sure it's a priority for investigation.

Deal with spooks like Alderley for long enough, and you pick up tips. Maybe someone'll recognize Dalton's voice and realize he just admitted to getting us in here."

Another phone rang—one on the wall by the airman. "That's great," said Nina as he answered it, "but it's not going to help us much right now, is it?"

The guard's expression jumped from boredom to sudden concern as he listened. "Dr. Ogleby!" he yelled, dropping the receiver and drawing his sidearm. "We have a security breach!" He ran to Nina and Eddie's cubicle. "You two, freeze!"

Ogleby scurried up behind him. "What's going on?"

"Sir, these two are intruders! They're not authorized to be here!"

"What? But—but they were on the system!"

"I'm just going by what Colonel Kern told me, sir."

Eddie cautiously raised his hands. "Hey, ah don' know wart the prahblem hee-ah is, but there's ahhbviously been some mistarke."

Ogleby boggled. "Where exactly are you supposed to be from, Captain? Australia?"

The airman stepped into the cubicle. "I've got orders to take you both into custody. Miss, drop that box."

"No, don't drop it!" Ogleby snapped. He glared at the guard. "The contents are fragile, you idiot! Dr. Wilde, put it down very carefully."

"Like *this*?" Nina said, tossing it straight at the airman.

He reacted instinctively, pulling the trigger—

There was a loud clanging impact and a crack of glass. The flying box jolted, but carried on along its arc to hit the man's gun hand. Before he could bring his weapon back up, Eddie lunged at him and drove a crunching punch into his face. The airman fell, a heel to his groin making sure he wouldn't be getting up for a while.

Eddie shot a look of mixed anger and relief at his wife as he took the gun. "That was a fucking stupid thing to do."

"Jesus!" Nina gasped. The back of the box had a

prominent convex dent where the bullet's force had been just barely absorbed by the metal and glass of the folder. "He tried to shoot me!"

"What did you expect? That sign said deadly force is authorized."

"Yeah, but it didn't say it's *mandatory*!"

Ogleby stumbled backward, hands up in fear. "Don't kill me, don't kill me!"

Eddie followed him, the gun raised. "Just tell us how we get out of here."

Before he could reply, honking klaxons sounded in the hangar outside. Red lights started flashing. "You don't," said Ogleby, a spark of defiance returning. "That's a lockdown alarm."

The Englishman shoved him hard against a cubicle wall. "How many men in the base?"

"About forty," he gulped. "They'll be on their way down here already—if you want to stay alive, you should surrender while you have the chance."

"I don't think we'll be given the option," Nina said grimly. She went to the door and looked out toward the great vertical shaft. The elevator on which they had descended was no longer there, Kern having ridden it back to the surface—but as she watched, another platform in the opposite corner came into view, bearing a group of uniformed men carrying rifles. "Shit! Eddie, they're here already!"

Eddie's glance into the hangar warned him that shooting their way out was not an option—nine M4 assault rifles against a single Beretta M9 pistol was a fight that would only end one way. Instead, he pulled Nina back into the cubicle. "Come on!"

"Where?" she demanded, confused. "There's no way out!"

"Yes, there is." He dived onto the exit chute of the automated delivery system, the metal rollers squealing as he juddered down the incline. "Let's roll!"

He hit the flap with a bang and disappeared through it. She looked back through the door. The elevator was almost at the bottom of the shaft, the men preparing to leap out.

Nina threw herself onto the rollers.

She crashed through the flap—and immediately found herself in peril as a mechanical arm swung at her head. She yelped and twisted aside, a metal claw sweeping through her hair. The chute led to an oversized hopper where boxes being returned to the stacks were sorted . . . and the system apparently didn't like unexpected objects.

The flickering laser beam of a barcode scanner flashed in her face, momentarily dazzling her. A section of the hopper's side popped out like a pinball flipper and thumped painfully against her, forcing her toward what was presumably the destination for rejected items.

The rollers gave way to smooth metal. Nina slid helplessly down it—seeing machinery like a giant mangle descending to squash her at the bottom—

Hands grabbed her just before she reached it, dragging her to a stop. "Got you!" Eddie grunted as he pulled her over the chute's side. The giant rollers thumped together, then retracted, denied their meal.

"God!" she gasped. "What is this, Satan's amusement park?"

"Kern did say he was right below us. This way." He ducked under another chute, heading toward the stacks. "And watch what you step on. I think the tracks are electrified."

"As if we didn't have enough to worry about." Eddie hopped over the track; she waited for a shuttle to clatter past before following. "Where are we going? We're heading away from the elevators."

Staying clear of the rails, they hurried down an aisle. "Have to see if we can find those emergency stairs Kern mentioned," said Eddie.

"That's a hell of a climb!"

"You want to stay here reading ancient documents for the rest of your life? Wait, don't answer that. But if we can get off this floor, we've got a chance."

"We still have to get back to the surface—and even then, there's only one door that goes outside."

"Yeah, but it's a pretty big door!"

Shouts came from behind them: The troops were spreading out in pursuit. Eddie looked back, alarmed. "Christ, we'll be sitting ducks if they shoot at us down this aisle."

Nina had drawn ahead, passing an intersection. "If we turn at the next—whoa!" One of the towering shuttles rounded the corner directly behind her—and kept going, forcing her onward. It was carrying a large container, not leaving enough room for her to squeeze past. "Eddie, I can't get back to you!"

"Go on ahead!" he shouted. "Go left, I'll catch up!"

Nina ran ahead of the advancing machine. Eddie doubled back to the intersection, cutting across to the next aisle. He looked along it. The next junction was about eighty feet away; he could catch up with her there—

"Here! Over here!"

The yell was from behind him, one of the airmen at the start of the aisle.

Bringing up his rifle—

Eddie flattened himself against the end of the towering stack as bullets seared past. Even as the echoes of the gunshots faded he ran again, cutting across the endless rows of shelves. He had to draw the troops away from Nina, then find a way to double back past them.

Ranks of stacks flashed past. He kept his pace and footfalls as precise as those of a hurdler—if he tripped on the tracks, he would be an easy target.

Another aisle ahead—and a shuttle bearing several boxes rolled into view. If it turned toward him, he would be trapped—

It carried on past the intersection, heading for the cabins. Eddie swung around the corner and into the new aisle, running away from the retreating machine. It would give him temporary cover from the pursuing airmen, maybe even cause them to lose track of him.

More shouting, this time over a loudspeaker. "Don't

shoot, don't shoot!" Ogleby's amplified voice boomed. "You'll hit the files! Catch them and take them outside—and *then* shoot them!"

That restriction would help—if the guards took orders from a civilian. Not willing to gamble his life on that, Eddie kept running. If Nina had taken the route he'd suggested, she would be eight or nine aisles back to his right. But now that shots had been fired, she might have followed a different path.

He reached the next junction and ducked into the cover of the cross-aisle, stopping to look across the cavernous hall. No sign of Nina. Damn! Had she carried straight on, or gone into another aisle?

He glanced back around the corner. The shuttle had switched tracks to deliver its cargo to a collection point, leaving the way free for some of the airmen to run toward him. The others would be charging up the neighboring aisles to cut off their prey. Eddie took a deep breath and ran again, heading—he hoped—back toward Nina. He glimpsed two men as he crossed an aisle and a single shot cracked past behind him, plunking into one of the metal storage boxes, but he was already clear.

"I said *don't shoot*!" screeched Ogleby over the PA system. "Do! Not! Shoot! How hard is that for you to understand?"

The next aisle had nobody in it, nor the one beyond that. Eddie turned up it and raced deeper into the hangar. If he could reach the next intersection before any of his pursuers saw him . . .

Sparks lit the aisle as another shuttle rounded the corner ahead, coming in his direction—then stopped, its lifting arm rising up to pluck a large box from a shelf. He cursed. Squeezing past the machine would slow him, but he was too far down the aisle to turn back and find an alternative route.

Not that he could anyway. "Stop or I fire!" a man bellowed.

The guards had found him.

Eddie was more than ten feet from the stationary

shuttle as it lowered its cargo. He would be shot before he could get past the machine. He stopped, and turned. Two airmen had him in their sights. He held up his hands. "Nina!" he called out. "They've got me. Get out of here, don't let them catch you!"

"Shut up!" one airman shouted as he and his partner advanced. Another two men reached the junction behind them and followed. "Drop the gun!"

Eddie obeyed, then glanced back at the shuttle. If it set off again, he might be able to dive behind it as it passed. But it was still lowering the box.

He would have to risk it. It was clear that Dalton's plan was for them to simply "disappear." Better to try to run than meekly accept his fate.

The guards approached. The leading man took one hand off his rifle to take a set of flex-cuffs from his belt. The M4's muzzle swayed away from Eddie.

This was his chance.

He tensed, about to rush for the shuttle—

Metal crashed above. The startled airmen looked up—and were knocked to the floor by a cascade of storage boxes falling from a high shelf.

Nina popped her head through the gap where the containers had been. "Eddie, run!"

"I told *you* to run!" he complained. But he was relieved beyond belief to see her. She ducked back as he slithered sidelong past the shuttle. Fallen boxes clanged and thumped as the groaning guards tried to get up.

Eddie rounded the corner, emerging in the next aisle in time to see Nina jump to the floor. "Are you okay?" she asked, hurrying to him.

"Yeah, but there're more of 'em out there. Let's find the stairs." They headed for the nearer of the hangar's long side walls.

Ogleby's voice came over the loudspeakers. "You morons!" he shouted at the airmen. "They're getting away! They're in area seven. Stop them!"

"Shit, he can see us!" said Nina. There had to be security cameras somewhere above. If Ogleby could guide the troops after them, they had no hope of escaping.

Eddie looked ahead. They were coming up to another intersection, a set of points clacking to direct an approaching shuttle. He snatched a box file from a shelf. "What are you doing?" asked Nina.

"Putting things on the wrong track." He kicked at the points to force the switch open, then jammed the box into the gap. "Down here, get back."

They retreated into the cross-aisle as the shuttle rumbled into the intersection. With the points out of position, it tried to continue straight ahead where it should have turned—then hit the box. The metal container was crushed by the shuttle's weight, but it was enough to jolt the entire machine . . .

And send it off the tracks.

The thirty-foot crane tower made it very top-heavy. The shuttle wobbled before finally overbalancing and crashing against one of the stacks—which itself toppled, containers sliding off its shelves in a cacophonous chorus. It hit another stack, and that too fell, a giant domino reaction sweeping inexorably across the hangar.

But it wasn't only the stacks that were falling. The top of the shuttle's tower snagged the power grid as it tipped, tearing down a section. It slapped across the tracks—

There was a loud bang and a huge spray of sparks as the system short-circuited. The sudden overload blew out other parts of the Cold War–era electrical system—and the entire hangar abruptly fell into darkness. Ogleby's horrified cry at the sight of the destruction of his library was cut off with a squawk of feedback.

"Wow," said Eddie as the last echoing slam of a felled stack faded away. "That worked better than I thought."

"It doesn't really help us, though, does it?" Nina complained. "We can't see anything either!" But as her eyes adjusted, she realized they were not in total blackness. Amber emergency lights high overhead had come on, casting a dim fireside glow across the great chamber.

She could just about make out Eddie's grin. "We can

see enough. Come on." He took the lead as they ran into the gloom.

With the power off, they no longer had to worry about the repository's machines, and in short order they reached the side of the hangar. About fifty yards away, an illuminated box shone red above a recess in the wall: an EMERGENCY EXIT sign. They ran to it. Behind them, their hunters shouted across the stacks, but they were having enough trouble locating one another, never mind their prey.

Eddie barged through the door at the back of the opening. More sickly lights revealed a metal staircase switchbacking upward into a tall shaft. No sign of movement above, but he still paused. "Can you hear anyone?"

Nina strained to listen, picking out a distant clamor of feet pounding on steel. "Someone's there, but they're a long way up." Eddie nodded and started up the steps. "Whoa, wait! I know your hearing's not great, but didn't you hear what I just said? They're probably waiting for us at the top."

"Good job we're not going all the way up, then. Come on, give it some high knees!" He set off again, Nina following in confusion.

"What do you mean?" she panted. "How are we going to get out?"

"Not by running up three thousand bloody stairs, for a start." As they climbed, another sign came into sight: the next level. "That big lift was on this floor."

"I think it may be a little hard for them to miss us if we ride up on that!"

"Depends what we ride up *with*." They reached the landing; Eddie checked that nobody was lurking beyond the door before entering.

Lines of dark and silent armor lined up inside the vast space greeted them. The main lights were still on in this level, but the brightest illumination came from the portable rigs set up around the tank undergoing maintenance. Nina cautiously peered around one of the M60s to see the two mechanics standing by their charge, talking animatedly; they had heard the alert, but seemingly had no idea what was going on. "We'll have to go past those guys to reach the elevator."

"I'll take care of 'em," Eddie assured her.

"How? As soon as they see you they'll raise the alarm."

"Why?" He indicated his now rather untidy uniform. "I'm an officer, aren't I?"

"Yeah, but the second you open your mouth they'll know saahmthang's wraahng," she said, imitating his attempt at an American accent. "What are you going to do, use sign language?"

Eddie cracked his knuckles and gave her a devilish smile. "I think they'll get the message."

TWENTY

In the administration block, Colonel Kern listened to a crackling report over the intercom from Silent Peak's lowest level. "We still haven't been able to restore full power down here, sir. We need a maintenance crew to fix the breakers."

"We'll have to call a team in from Groom," said Kern, concerned. "What about the intruders?" From the moment the alert had come through directly from the Pentagon that their security clearances had been forged, his honored guests had been reduced in status to targets.

Ogleby came on the line. "They've wrecked the place!" he cried. "Kern, I hold you entirely responsible for this fiasco. How the hell did you allow them to just stroll in here?"

"I see from the system that you approved their clearances too," Kern replied irritatedly, checking a monitor. "But it looks like security's been breached at a very high level. There'll have to be an investigation—"

"Sir!" his lieutenant interrupted, pointing excitedly at a status board. "The main elevator—it's coming up!"

"I think we've found them," Kern told Ogleby before ending the call. He turned to his subordinate. "Assemble a group, everyone armed, then get to the elevator. But keep the guards at the main door in case it's a ruse and they're trying to escape some other way."

The lieutenant acknowledged and rushed out. "Keep monitoring things here," Kern ordered a corporal as he headed for his office.

He opened a desk drawer and took out his sidearm. Silent Peak's quiet obscurity and official status as a reserve facility meant that only its security personnel were routinely armed, but right now he wanted every man on the base to have a gun at the ready. Whatever Nina Wilde and her companion were doing here, it was going to be stopped. Flicking off the Beretta's safety, he hurried after the lieutenant.

In the control room, the corporal's eyes bugged as he saw on a CCTV screen what the enormous elevator was carrying. "Uh, sir?" he called, but his commander had already gone.

* * *

Kern met his men outside the cluster of cabins, where the lieutenant had rounded up twelve troops. Some were support staff armed only with pistols, but the majority were members of the base's security detail, carrying M4 rifles. "Okay, everyone with me," he ordered, starting to run. The men fell in alongside him. "We have two intruders who infiltrated the base using falsified credentials, and gained access to the repository. They're to be considered armed and dangerous." He hesitated before continuing, but the command from the Pentagon had been clear. "You have shoot-on-sight authorization."

The responses from the running men showed that few, if any, shared his misgivings.

They raced down the length of the hangar, passing the parked aircraft and vehicles. The great chasm of the shaft opened up ahead as they neared it. A deep mechanical grumbling grew ever louder—the massive elevator platform was approaching the top.

"Spread out," said Kern as the group reached the

shaft. "I want every part of the platform . . . covered . . ." His voice trailed off as the elevator's cargo rose into view.

The corporal's nervous voice sounded over the PA system. "Uh, Colonel Kern, sir! They've, ah . . . they've got a tank."

The M60's main gun was pointing directly at Kern. "Yeah, I noticed."

* * *

"Okay, we're at the top!" Nina announced, standing in the commander's position to peer through the narrow portholes in the armored cupola atop the turret. "And we've got a welcoming committee."

Eddie, in the driver's seat inside the cramped forward compartment, had also seen the troops through the three slot-like periscopes in front of him. "Doesn't look like they want to give us tea and biscuits," he said as weapons came up. He switched his foot from the brake to the oversized gas pedal and shoved it down. The twenty-nine-liter diesel engine roared, the tank jerking forward with a piercing squeal from its tracks. He saw Kern dive aside as the M60 cleared the platform and accelerated down the hangar.

Nina yelped and instinctively ducked as bullets clonked against the turret. "Whoa! That just made them mad."

Eddie wasn't worried—not about the gunfire, at least. Against the inches-thick steel armor, Kern's men might as well have been firing Ping-Pong balls.

His real concern was the line of parked military vehicles. He had checked the M60's fuel gauge during the ascent, and found it had only the bare minimum needed to power it for maintenance. It would soon run out— meaning that the troops could simply drive after them and wait for the engine to die.

He turned the steering yoke to the right. The brakes on that side shrilled, the tank making a juddering change of direction to head for the trucks.

Nina yelped again as the unexpected turn jarred her heavily against some of the cabin's many hard-edged protrusions. "What are you doing? You're going to crash into those trucks!"

"Not into 'em—*over* 'em! Get into the gunner's seat!"

"I thought there wasn't any ammo?"

"This thing's got a twenty-foot steel battering ram—it doesn't *need* ammo!"

Nina understood what he meant, but was still uncertain as she clambered awkwardly across the cabin into the gunner's position. The primary controls consisted of another aircraft-style yoke. "How does it work?"

"It's not rocket surgery! Just turn it and see what happens!"

There was a periscope lens above and to the right of the controls; she peered into it, seeing the view ahead. The M60 was thundering straight at the first truck. She hesitantly turned the yoke a little. With a skirl of hydraulics, the turret turned in response. A vertical twist of the handgrips and the main gun rose, the view through the periscope also tilting upward.

She swung the turret back to its original position—to find the truck looming in her sights. "Hold on!" Eddie shouted.

The M60 slammed into the truck's front quarter. It was shoved sideways until it hit its neighbor—and the tank then rode up over it, crushing it flat. The second truck suffered the same fate, glass exploding everywhere as steel tracks chewed through its cab.

Eddie turned the yoke back to the left. The M60 lurched around as if grinding the remains of the trucks beneath a treaded heel, then advanced on the first of the Humvees. There were two rows of the big four-by-fours, too widely spaced for the M60 to squash them all in one go; Nina braced herself, rotating the turret and lowering the main gun to hit the second line.

The Humvees were smaller than the trucks, but the ride over them was no less bumpy, throwing Eddie and Nina about in their seats. The back ends of the leading row were flattened into scrap. Those in the second line fared little better, the M60's gun barrel slicing into their engine compartments and tearing off wheels.

Eddie turned the tank again to demolish one last truck, then swung it back toward the giant hangar doors. There were other guards ahead, but they were already scurrying for safety. The way out was now clear. The M60 was at its full speed of thirty miles per hour. Hardly blistering performance, but with so much weight behind it the armored vehicle was almost unstoppable. He kept his foot down, glancing at the fuel gauge.

It was practically on empty. Whatever happened, the tank wouldn't take them much farther than the end of the valley outside—if it even got that far.

That would leave them on foot, in the desert . . . not far from Groom Lake, one of the most heavily patrolled and jealously protected military facilities in the United States, if not the world. They were still a long way from being safe.

Before they could worry about that, though, they still had to get out of Silent Peak itself. Nina looked through her periscope. "Can this thing break through that door?"

"It weighs over fifty tons—I don't think it'll be a problem. But hang on anyway. There'll be a bit of a bump."

"My husband, master of understatement," Nina said. Eddie grinned and psyched himself up for the looming impact. The M60 barreled straight at the towering doors, a metal wall filling his narrow field of vision—

The gun punched through the steel as if it were paper—but the rest of the tank had a tougher time as it ran into the frame supporting the enormous structure. Even braced, Eddie was still pitched out of his chair as the M60 was almost dragged to a halt, ensnared in the tangled gridwork. The diesel snarled, the tracks shrieking as they fought for purchase—then suddenly the behemoth ripped itself loose and slithered out onto the runway. Wreckage crashed down behind it.

Off to one side, he saw the Learjet. He briefly thought about crippling it, but remembered that Abbot and his copilot were aboard, and that a tank was not a precision weapon—he didn't want to add murder to the list of charges against himself and Nina. Instead he drove the M60 past it and headed down the valley.

"We made it!" Nina shouted. "We got out!"

"We're out of the *hangar*," he replied, "but it's about ten miles to the nearest road, and we've only got a teacup of diesel left." The fuel gauge was now on empty.

She clambered through the connecting passage into the driver's compartment. "How many miles per gallon does this thing get?"

"None. It's more like gallons per mile."

"So, not exactly a Prius, then." She looked through the periscopes. The dust-covered runway stretched away to the southern end of the valley. Even at the tank's top speed, it would be another couple of minutes before they reached open desert. "How far will we be able to get?"

As if in answer, the diesel's roar momentarily hiccuped. The engine was straining to draw the last dregs of fuel into its cylinders. "At a guess, maybe, er . . . fifty yards?"

He checked the valley walls. Off to the runway's left they were too steep to climb, almost cliffs, but those on the right were lower and more accessible, with potential for concealment. The downside was that going that way would take them deeper into the enormous military range, in the direction of Groom Lake and Area 51.

But there was no other choice. He angled the M60 across the runway toward the lower western side of the valley. The engine coughed again as its insatiable thirst drained the fuel tank dry. Their speed began to drop.

"Shit, we're not even going to reach the bottom of the hill," he realized. "Go back into the turret and open the top hatch. Soon as we stop, get out and run for that little gully there." He pointed at a narrow channel winding up into the brown rocks. "I'll be right behind you."

Nina retreated to the commander's position, pulling the lever to unlock the hatch above. She glanced back through a porthole at the gaping hole in the huge door—and saw tiny figures spilling through it. "Eddie! They're coming after us!"

"In jeeps or on foot?"

"On foot."

"Good—that gives us a few minutes' start, at least." The lack of fuel reaching the choking engine caused a literal death rattle to echo through the cabin. The M60 slowed sharply. "That's it, we're done. Get out now!"

Nina forced the heavy hatch open and climbed out onto the top of the turret. Behind her, the massive diesel finally cut out. The squeal of the tracks faded as the tank ground to a standstill. She lowered herself to the hull, then jumped off, running for the gully.

Eddie exited via the driver's hatch and quickly caught up. "Dunno how the fuck we're going to get out of this one."

"No, no, no," Nina admonished. "You're supposed to say something positive."

"I would, but unless somebody offers us a free helicopter ride we'll have a job." They reached the gully and started up it. The ascent was steeper than it had looked from the tank, wind-deposited sand making finding footholds a treacherous task. "Head over to your left, it looks a bit easier."

She hauled herself up to a flatter area of rock, looking back toward the base. The running figures were making worryingly rapid progress. "Oh God, they're catching up! How long before they can shoot at us?"

Eddie followed her up. "If any of 'em are good shots, they already can! But they're air force, so we're probably safe until they're within twenty feet . . ."

"Why do people in one branch of the forces hate everyone in the others more than the people they're supposed to be fighting?" Nina gasped as she ran up the slope. A clump of boulders ahead offered temporary cover from gunfire.

Beyond them, a hundred or so yards distant, rose a

ridge. "We need to get over that," said Eddie. "The rock on the right, go up behind it."

Nina changed direction. The slope became steeper, slowing her. Her throat began to burn with each breath. A look back: The men chasing them were blocked from view by the boulders. "At least they can't shoot at us now—"

A distant sound caught her attention. Eddie immediately picked up on her alarm. "What is it?"

"I can hear something! Sounds like—"

"A chopper," he finished for her. Even with his diminished hearing, he could make out the thump of rotor blades. Someone at Silent Peak had called for help, and with the other secretive military facilities in the region essentially on permanent alert, it hadn't taken long for the response to arrive.

No sign of the aircraft yet, though. They still had a chance to find cover. "Come on, go!" he shouted. "We've got to get over the ridge!"

"I'm going, I'm going!" Nina complained, panting.

Feet rasping over rock and sand, they pounded up the slope. The incline became steeper as they approached its top. Eddie had to use his hands for support to clear the final yards. "Almost there . . ."

The helicopter's rotor noise became a boom as it came into view. A Black Hawk; it was about half a mile away, but curving toward the base. "Down!" Eddie commanded, but more as an automatic response to an airborne threat than in any real hope of finding concealment—they would be plainly visible against the barren hillside.

He looked for cover. Nothing usable on this side of the ridge. On the other side was a shallow natural bowl, broken rocks strewn within.

Not great, but better than nothing. "Over this side, quick!" They scrabbled over the ridge and half-ran, half-slid down to the nearest large rock and crouched behind it. Nina cautiously peered around the boulder to find the Black Hawk.

It was changing course, turning sharply to head toward them. "Oh crap," she squeaked.

Eddie was already searching for better cover, but nothing presented itself. Wherever they went, the Black Hawk could simply hover overhead. "So much for 'em not being able to shoot at us."

"This is *not* my fault! Any ideas?"

"You don't have a white flag, do you?"

Even if she had, it became clear a moment later that they wouldn't get the chance to use it. A man leaning from the Black Hawk's cabin opened fire with a machine gun. Bullets cracked noisily off the rock above them. Nina shrieked and scrambled around the boulder in an attempt to keep it between her and the helicopter; Eddie followed, stone chips biting at his heels. Choking dust swirled around them as the aircraft descended.

The assault continued without pause. A chunk of stone the size of a human head splintered from the rock and smacked down between Eddie and Nina. "Jesus Christ!" she cried, flinching away—and in her peripheral vision catching movement at the top of the ridge.

The Security Forces had found them.

"Eddie!" She dropped flat as more gunfire struck from a different direction. More men were climbing over the hill.

Their orders were obviously to kill the intruders. Eddie gave Nina a last despairing look, grabbing her hand as the Black Hawk moved directly overhead—

The gunfire stopped.

The helicopter briefly hung above them, then veered away. Nina squinted through the billowing dust to see the troops also departing, one man with a hand to his head as if listening to a message through an earpiece—and unable to believe what he was hearing. He glared at the couple, then lowered his weapon and followed his companions out of sight.

Eddie wiped grit from his face. "What the hell? Why did they stop?" He risked raising his head to look for the Black Hawk. It was on a course back to its home base.

"You got a problem with that?" Nina asked. "Because I don't."

"Neither do I, but why are they just fucking off like that?" He double-checked the ridge, expecting to see the pursuing troops lurking in wait, but it appeared that they really had retreated. "Stay there and keep down—I'll see what's going on."

"Shouldn't we, y'know, run while we can?" Nina called after him, but he ignored her and quickly scaled the ridge, dropping to his stomach near the top and peering over it.

The troops had indeed retreated, but not far. One man was surveying the ridge; he did a double-take as he spotted Eddie, pointing him out to his fellows, but none of them took a shot at him, or even raised a weapon.

"What are they doing?" Nina asked as he returned.

"I dunno, but I don't like it. They don't want to kill us—but it doesn't look like they're going to let us leave either. They didn't look happy about it, though. Somebody's ordered them to stand down."

"Who?"

"I wish I knew. But I get the feeling they'll keep us here until we find out."

That turned out to be the case. After several minutes, they heard another approaching chopper: not the Black Hawk that had attacked them, but a much smaller OH-6 Cayuse scout helicopter. It passed over the bowl, then moved to land near the abandoned tank.

Another few minutes passed, then a man appeared at the crest of the rise. "Dr. Wilde! Mr. Chase!"

Eddie leaned out, regarding the new arrival cautiously. He was an air force colonel, carrying something in one hand: a satellite phone. "Yeah? What's up?"

"Can I come down to you?"

Nina and Eddie traded bewildered glances. "Sure, why not?" Nina called out.

The colonel picked his way down the slope, almost

slipping on some loose gravel at its foot, but managing to retain his footing and dignity as he reached them. It was clear from his disgusted expression that he didn't want to be dealing with them at all, but was obeying orders from above. He held out the phone. "I've been told to give you this."

Still confused, Nina accepted it. She held it to her ear, tilting it so Eddie could listen in. "Hello?"

"Dr. Wilde, hello," said an unfamiliar voice. The accent was American, a refined New England baritone.

"Who is this?"

"You don't know me—at least, not yet. But I think you're aware of the organization I represent. I'm the chairman of the Group."

Nina couldn't help but be suspicious. "So . . . what do you want?"

"I want to talk to you. Both of you, in person. Since I've just saved your lives, I hope you'll show your gratitude by agreeing to meet me."

TWENTY-ONE
Washington, DC

Under the angry eyes of the troops from Silent Peak, Nina and Eddie were led to the helicopter, which flew them to Nellis Air Force Base northeast of Las Vegas. A jet waited for them, larger than the Lear; a C-37A, the US military's version of the Gulfstream V business aircraft, luxuriously appointed as a VIP transport. They were accompanied by two air force officers, who like the colonel appeared displeased to have been assigned this particular escort duty. Once in flight, they sat at the cabin's far end, occasionally shooting dirty glances toward the couple.

Since there was nothing else that could be done, Eddie chose to stretch out in a reclining seat and doze through the eastward flight. Nina regarded him jealously. She was too concerned for her racing mind to allow her to rest. What she had heard about the Group was apparently true. If they had enough influence to intervene in the internal security of the US military—quickly enough to halt an ongoing search-and-destroy operation—then they must have direct access to the very highest levels of the American government.

And they had used that power to save her and Eddie's

lives. She was grateful for that . . . but what price would be asked in return?

By the time the plane landed, night had fallen over the eastern seaboard. The two officers took them down the steps to the runway, where a limousine waited. Eddie peered inside. A man in a dark suit gestured for him to enter. "Come on in, Mr. Chase," said the stranger. "Sit down. You too, Dr. Wilde. I won't bite."

"I might," Eddie muttered, climbing in to sit facing him. Nina hesitantly took a place beside her husband.

The man in the backseat was in his sixties, tall and broad-shouldered in a way that suggested he had been an athlete in his youth. Despite his age, he was obviously still strong and in excellent health. His gray hair was slicked back from his prominent forehead, a pair of rectangular spectacles giving him a stern, patrician air. He had a downturned mouth that didn't seem accustomed to smiling. "Welcome to Washington," he said. "I'm glad to see you both alive and well."

"I'd be gladder if I knew what the hell was going on," said Eddie.

"Well, that's what I'm going to tell you." He pushed a button to speak to the driver. "Let's go." The limo set off, the Gulfstream retreating beyond the darkened rear window.

"Okay," said Nina, "my first question is: Who are you?"

"My name is Travis Warden. You may have heard of me, or you may not. It depends how closely you read the financial pages."

"They're not really my thing," she admitted.

"That's true for most people. Which is why the histrionics aimed at the financial world over the past few years are ironic at best, and hypocritical at worst. Anyone taking the time and effort to analyze the data that was freely available would have seen that the boom before the economic crash was unsustainable. But"—he shrugged—"nobody wants to believe that the good times will ever stop rolling, so they fail to plan for the inevitable." He gave his passengers a meaningful look. "Well, almost nobody."

"You *did* make plans," said Eddie.

"We did. By *we*, I mean the Group. It's our business to plan for the future. Not just for the next year, or the next electoral cycle. We plan for *decades* ahead, generations."

"That seems a bit presumptuous," Nina said.

"Only those who prepare for the future deserve a hand in shaping it."

"So the Group is a collection of merchant bankers?" she asked. Eddie couldn't suppress a smirk. "What?"

"That's Cockney rhyming slang," he told her. "For wan— "

"Yes, *thank* you for that, honey."

A small tic under Warden's right eye betrayed his impatience. "Some of the Group's members are bankers, yes. But I'm more of . . . an investor, you could say. An investor in the future. I put capital where it's needed to ensure that the Group's long-term goals happen. Not just here in the United States, but all over the world. The Group is an international organization with one ultimate goal: global order."

"So you're like the Bilderberg Group?"

A dismissive snort. "The Bilderberg members just talk. We *act*." The limo paused at the airport's outer gate for the barrier to be raised, then turned onto a road and headed for the distant lights of Washington. "We want to end human conflict."

"That's kind of a grand plan," said Nina, deliberately challenging. "Everyone from Alexander the Great through Genghis Khan up to Hitler has had their own ideas on how to do it. And they've all failed. What makes yours any different?"

His answer shocked her. "You, Dr. Wilde. You make our plan different. You make it *possible*."

"This is all coming back to those bloody statues, isn't it?" Eddie rumbled.

Warden ignored him, fixing his stern blue eyes on Nina. "Competition over resources is the cause of most conflict in the world. Specifically, energy resources. Wars are fought, lives destroyed, tyrants propped up just so that we can literally burn a mineral sludge—and the system of global politics and economics has become so warped by this fact that it's now dependent on it. Governments can't imagine things being any other way . . . but just as the recent economic crash was bound to happen, a total collapse is inevitable if things continue as they are."

"I know we have booms and busts," said Nina, "but a complete collapse? Really?"

Warden's tone became more lecturing. "All the economic models that shape the world are based on the conceit that growth can be—*must* be—infinite. A child could point out the flaw in that idea, since we live in a finite world, but just as nobody wanted to believe that the debt bubble would burst while they were living the high life on the back of it, so no one wants to play the role of Cassandra now."

"Not even the Group? You seem to have a lot of influence, to put it mildly."

"We do, but not even we're powerful enough to overturn the system. Until now, the most we've been able to do is guide it."

"Until now," Nina echoed. "By which you mean, you've got me."

"You make it sound as though you're my prisoner," Warden said. The downturned corners of his mouth strained slightly upward, which seemed to be as close as he ever came to an actual smile. "If you want to get out of the limo, just say so."

"We want to get out of the limo," Eddie immediately responded.

The tic returned. "After you've heard what I have to say."

"Thought there'd be a catch."

The elderly man looked back at Nina. "The Group has been planning for this eventuality for a long time. But sometimes wild cards—*Wilde* cards, even, if you'll excuse the pun—mean that major changes can happen very quickly. Earth energy is one of those cards, and you, Dr. Wilde, are the one who holds it."

"How much do you know about earth energy?" she asked.

"As much as anyone. We have access to the IHA's files, everything that Jack Mitchell did at DARPA, Leonid Vaskovich's work, the repository at Silent Peak, and more besides. The most important things we know about it, though, are first that a very particular kind of superconducting material is needed to channel it. And second, that a living organism is also needed for the process to work."

"You mean a person."

He shook his head. "In theory, any kind of organism can generate the effect, as long as its DNA contains the specific genome sequence that makes its bioelectrical field compatible. In practice, though . . ."

"There's only me," Nina said grimly.

"You're the only *known* example. There must be thousands, even tens of thousands of people in the world who can also activate the earth energy effect. King Arthur and the Atlantean priestess Nantalas are two people from history who could, so it's likely that their ancestors—and descendants—also had the gene. But nobody knows who they are."

"And it's not exactly easy to test for 'em," said Eddie. "*Hey, would you mind holding these statues to see if they levitate and you have visions?* Might raise a few questions."

"Exactly. Which is why you, Dr. Wilde, are so important to the Group's plans—and why Harald Glas is determined to kill you to stop them."

The reminder that she was still a target placed a cold stone in Nina's stomach. "Why is Glas so opposed to you? Victor Dalton said he used to be a member of the Group."

Warden's permanent scowl somehow managed to deepen. "Dalton," he said distastefully. "I'm hoping to have some news about him soon. But yes, Harald was one of us—until a few months ago. Your discovery of all three statues meant that a plan we'd thought of as merely a contingency, a kind of best-case scenario, suddenly had the potential to become very real. He was opposed to it. Violently opposed."

"Why?" Nina demanded. "And what *is* this plan of yours?"

He leaned forward. "Unlimited power. If we can harness earth energy, then it ends at a stroke our reliance on fossil fuels, and thus the conflicts over control of them. Oil, coal, gas—they become unnecessary if you have limitless power generated by the planet itself."

"So that's why Glas has a problem with it," said Nina, making the connection. "It'd put him out of business."

The not-quite-smile returned. "Precisely. Harnessing earth energy would be a paradigm shift on a par with the invention of the automobile—and if your livelihood back then was making buggy whips, you'd very soon be out of business. But if an angry buggy whip maker had assassinated Henry Ford, some other car manufacturer would have taken his place. In your case, though . . . you're irreplaceable."

"Wait, so this guy wants me dead just to protect his *profits*?" Nina cried. "Oh that's great. Yay for capitalism!"

"We can provide you with full protection. You're very important to us." The old man sat back. "So that's the Group's plan, Dr. Wilde. As to how it can be accomplished, that depends entirely on your cooperation. And yours, Mr. Chase. You said that this was about the statues. That's true—they're a vital part of what we hope to achieve." He turned back to Nina. "If you were to help us, you would use the statues to locate what the Atlanteans called the sky stone—a meteorite, of course, but one composed of a naturally superconducting material that channels earth energy. Once we have it, we'll be able to build power stations around the world at confluence points. Not only that, but the potential of a diamagnetic material that can be made to levitate without needing a power source is incalculable. It would revolutionize air travel, for a start—aircraft could be made completely pollution-free."

"And what about the, ah, biological aspects?" asked Nina. "I can't exactly travel the world nonstop laying hands on your power plants to make them work. I kinda have plans of my own."

"You won't have to. If you give us a blood sample, we'll be able to sequence your DNA to isolate the specific gene that allows you to cause the effect. With your permission, of course," Warden added. "Once we have that, it can be implanted into some other organism. It doesn't even have to be an animal—a plant might work, even bacteria."

"Hear that, love?" said Eddie. "You can be replaced by a bucket of germs."

She gave him a sarcastic look. "If that's what turns you on . . ."

A low buzz came from Warden's jacket, and he took out a phone. "Yes?" he barked into it. "Where we discussed? Excellent. What channel?" He disconnected and touched a control on his armrest. Part of the polished wood hinged upward, a small television screen rising smoothly out of it. He turned it to face Nina and Eddie. "I think you'll enjoy this."

A news channel came on, showing the entrance to what looked like a restaurant. The crawl at the bottom of the screen read ARRESTED BY FBI. BREAKING NEWS: FORMER PRESID . . . As they watched, four suited men bustled another out of the door.

Even though their prisoner was trying to hide his face from the waiting TV camera, he was instantly recognizable. Victor Dalton.

A breathless female newscaster attempted to keep up with the story. "These pictures, taken just minutes ago, show FBI agents removing former US president Victor Dalton from a restaurant on K Street in Washington, DC. The details are still sketchy, but from what we understand, the disgraced president has been charged under the Espionage Act"—her voice conveyed near disbelief—"on suspicion of releasing classified information to unauthorized personnel." On the screen, Dalton was shoved into the rear seat of a black SUV. "As yet, we haven't received any statements from the Justice Department or the White House, but as soon as we do—"

Warden muted the sound. "Well?"

"Well . . . wow," said Nina, not sure how to react. "I take it that was your doing."

"It was. We knew Dalton had a grudge against the Group—he blamed us for not keeping him in office after his little videotaped indiscretion, even though it was obvious his position was untenable. We didn't realize he'd actively sided with Glas against us until it was too late, but we certainly weren't going to let it stand." There was a disquieting matter-of-fact ruthlessness to his voice.

"So what happens to us?" Eddie asked. "First thing he'll do will be try to drag us down with him. Seeing as we blackmailed him into getting us into Silent Peak."

"I wouldn't worry about that," said Warden, with another grim unsmile. "He'll have much larger concerns than personal vendettas. Some of the other skeletons in his closet will come to light." He retracted the screen, then glanced through a window. "Ah, we're almost there. We can continue this discussion in my home."

The limo slowed, turning through a set of automatic gates onto the lengthy drive of an especially large house. It pulled up outside, the driver quickly exiting to open the door for his passengers.

"Nice pad," said Eddie as he got out. "So this is how the top one percent live."

"More like the top one percent *of* the top one percent," Nina replied. Warden's home was an elegant three-story building that had been styled after a British Georgian mansion—or, for all she knew, genuinely was one that had been transported across the Atlantic brick by brick. Either way, its value would be well into the multimillion-dollar range . . . and she imagined it was not the investor's only property.

Warden led them inside, taking them down a long hall displaying artworks traditional and modern to a door at the far end. He paused at it. "Before we go inside, I'll first ask you both to remain calm. The Group sometimes has to make deals with people we would rather not work with. My other guest is one of those people. And I know that you've had bad experiences with him in the past."

With that, he opened the door . . . to reveal Alexander Stikes in the large room beyond.

"What the *fuck* is he doing here?" Eddie yelled, taking up position to shield Nina. "Get that bastard out of here, or I'll do it for you!"

Stikes was seated on a long couch, not in the least surprised to see the new arrivals. He moved his left arm to reveal a gun in a shoulder holster beneath his jacket. "Let's not have any unpleasantness, shall we, Chase? We're all guests here."

"Not for long," said Nina. She rounded on Warden. "If that murdering son of a bitch is working for you, I think any business we might have had is finished."

"If you'll let me explain," he said, quietly but firmly. "As I said, sometimes needs must. Mr. Stikes had obtained the statues—"

"Stolen," she cut in, with a hate-filled glare at the former SAS officer.

"Stolen, yes, but he had possession of them. That forced us to negotiate with him."

"And Sophia," Eddie growled. "Where does she fit in? Is she one of your fucking Group too?"

"Absolutely not," snapped Warden, with genuine loathing and anger at the accusation. "Sophia Blackwood was Harald Glas's responsibility. For God knows what reason, he took her in after your last encounter with her in Switzerland. When Mr. Stikes contacted us through Ankit Jindal, Glas sent her to act as our representative—without consulting the rest of us."

Eddie was becoming more furious by the moment. "Are you telling me," he said in a low, deeply threatening voice, "that Kit was working for *you*?"

Warden lowered his head. "Unfortunately, yes. And all I can do is apologize for what happened."

"*Apologize?*" Eddie exploded. "He *murdered* my friend to protect Stikes—to protect those fucking statues! Fuck this. Nina, we're going."

He turned to leave, but Stikes stood, reaching for his gun. "You're not going anywhere, Chase."

"Stikes!" Warden practically barked the name. "Sit down and shut up. And put the gun away. You don't do a damn thing unless I tell you to. Understand?" Stikes's face was a picture of thinly veiled anger as he returned to his seat.

"Jindal was working for us," said Warden, addressing Eddie and Nina again. "His position in Interpol meant he was perfectly placed to watch for any information on statues like Takashi's. After you found the first statue in Egypt, we were planning to have Takashi send the second one to you in the hope that you would use them to locate the third. Unfortunately, Pramesh and Vanita Khoil found out about it. Our computer security wasn't as good as we'd thought, apparently. They arranged to have Takashi's statue stolen in order to stop us."

"I take it they weren't on the Group's wavelength," said Nina.

"Hardly. We want to end global conflict; they were actively encouraging it to bring about their insane new world. But we were using Jindal to guide you down a particular path, so that you would find all the statues and bring them together. We had no idea what lengths he would go to in order to do that. It was . . . it was a mistake." The amount of effort it took for Warden to force the words out suggested it was not an admission he made frequently, if at all.

Eddie was far from impressed. "You should have chosen your people better." He stared pointedly at Stikes. "You still should."

"Again, the only thing I can do is apologize. The last thing we wanted to do was alienate you. We need you, Dr. Wilde—and we're willing to do whatever it takes to make things right."

"What do you mean?" Nina asked.

"Exactly what it sounds like. What do you want? The opportunity to conduct your archaeological research without being hindered by the political considerations and budget limits of the IHA, perhaps? You could have your own foundation—funded by the Group, with absolutely no restrictions. Would that be an appealing proposition?"

"Nah, we're not interested," said Eddie. No response from his wife. He nudged her. "Are we, love?"

"I don't know . . . ," she said. "You'd be willing to do that?"

Warden nodded. "We'd be willing to do whatever you like. You're in a position occupied by very few people through the entire course of history, Dr. Wilde. You can choose the direction taken by the whole of humanity: into a bold new future, or carrying on toward ruin as things are now. The decision is yours."

"Nina, you're not seriously thinking about saying yes, are you?" Eddie demanded.

"I'm thinking that . . . I need to think about it," she replied before turning back to Warden. "If I said yes, what would you need me to do?"

"Bring us the statues, so we can locate the meteorite," said Warden. "After that, at some point we'll need a blood sample from you, as I said, but that won't be necessary until the earth energy collection stations are nearing completion. As for whatever you might want in return, we would see to it right away. After the meteorite is found, of course."

"Of course," Nina echoed quietly. Another short silence, then: "I need time to decide. You've given me a lot to think about."

Warden nodded. "I understand."

"There's one thing you can do for me right away, though."

"Which is?"

She pointed at Stikes. "Get rid of him. You should never have hired him in the first place."

"I'll see to it."

"*What?*" snapped Stikes, standing sharply.

Warden waved him to silence. "Give me your number," said Nina. "I'll be in touch. And if we could get back to New York as soon as possible, I'd appreciate it."

"I'll have you flown there," the Group's chairman told her. "My driver will take you to the airport. But please, Dr. Wilde . . . don't take too long to reach a decision."

"You'll know as soon as I've made it. Come on, Eddie. Let's go."

Eddie said nothing, silently fuming as they left the room. Once they were gone, Stikes rounded on Warden. "You're not going to do what she wants, are you?"

"Why not?" he replied. "She's vital to us, and if indulging her obsession with archaeology is the price of her cooperation, it'll be well worth it."

"I meant about firing me!"

"Relax, Stikes." Warden took a seat. "You're useful. For now."

"Thank you," Stikes replied caustically. "In that case, I have some *useful* advice: Don't believe her. She won't go along with it—and Chase definitely won't, however much money you wave in front of them. I know them."

"We'll see."

"I'm sure we will. So we should have a contingency plan in place."

"Do you have something in mind?"

Stikes's cold gaze turned toward the door through which Nina and Eddie had exited. "As a matter of fact, I do."

* * *

It wasn't until they were back at their apartment in New York, away from anyone who might report what was said to Warden or his people, that Eddie finally felt free to unleash what had been bottled up inside him for the past hours. "Have you gone fucking *mad*?" he erupted at Nina the moment the door was closed. "What the hell are you doing, going along with them?"

"Eddie—"

"You know you can't trust 'em, especially not Stikes!"

"Eddie—"

"And it's because of them that Mac's dead! They hired Kit, he was working for them—and now Stikes is too!"

"*Eddie—*"

"This is what you call us sticking together, no matter what? I can't fucking believe that you'd even—"

"*Eddie!*" She grabbed his arms, getting right in his face. "Of course I don't trust him! I said all that because I needed to buy some extra time."

"Yeah?"

"Yeah!"

"Oh." His shoulders slumped. "I feel like a bit of an arse now."

She smiled and briefly kissed him. "I'll let you feel the whole of one when we go to bed. But no, I don't trust Warden or this Group of his any more than you do."

"So you wanted to buy more time, okay. But for what? Warden's going to want an answer pretty soon—and there's still Glas to worry about."

Nina paced across the room. "We need to find out the truth about the statues—and, more important, the meteorite. What it can really do, how it does it—and how dangerous it might be. Not secondhand, like the Kallikrates text, or whatever Warden says about it. I'm sure Glas would have his own opinion too. No, we need to go to the source."

"Where's that?" Eddie asked.

She stopped and faced him. "Atlantis."

TWENTY-TWO

The Gulf of Cadiz

The North Atlantic in November is an inhospitable place. Even though the weather on this day was not particularly bad, there was still enough of a swell to cause the research vessel *Gant* to pitch unsettlingly beneath the wet-slate sky. The helicopter's landing on the pad at the ship's stern was bumpy, to say the least.

"Welcome aboard!" called Matt Trulli, waving as Nina and Eddie hurried through the drizzle to meet him. "Great to see you both. Been up to anything exciting?"

"You could say that," Nina replied with a pained smile. "You know, the usual."

"Ah, right," Matt said knowingly. "So what got destroyed this time?"

Eddie started to count items on his fingers. "A skyscraper, a helicopter, a secret US base . . ."

"Jesus, mate, I was kidding!" He shook Eddie's hand firmly. "Seriously, though, I'm glad to see you again. I knew you were innocent."

"Thanks," said Eddie, smiling. "Would be nice if that were the end of it, but nope, we've still got problems."

"Which is why we're here," said Nina. "Can we go inside?"

"Sure." Matt brought them through a hatch into the ship's interior, then headed down a passage. "Should warn you, Hayter's about as happy as you'd expect that you were coming."

"How's progress been on the excavations?"

"Pretty good, I'd say. He can give you the details, but the biggest problem's been that there's a fairly huge piece of wreckage from the *Evenor* right on top of where you want to look. Too big to lift, even for *Sharkdozer;* we've had to cut it up. Most of it's been moved now, though."

"Good. I saw when we came in to land that the subs are on the ship—why aren't they working?"

The Australian grinned. "'Cause I knew you were coming! Figured you'd want to work the arses off them, so I brought them back up top to recharge."

"You know me so well," Nina replied with a grin of her own.

They went into a large compartment overlooking the foredeck, where the archaeological expedition's two submersibles were suspended from their cranes. Waiting for them was Lewis Hayter. As Matt had implied, his thin face was not exactly brimming with joy at his boss's arrival. "Oh, Nina," he said sullenly. "You're here."

She decided to try to make the best of the situation. "Hello, Lewis. I caught up with the daily reports on the flight over—it looks like you've made excellent progress. Thank you."

He nodded, a little off balance from the praise. "We're doing the best we can. It's cutting things fine, though—even if the weather holds, the *Gant* will still have to return to port in five days at the most. I don't think we'll be able to do any further work until the spring."

"Think of it as a positive," she said. "It means you definitely *will* be back in the spring! The entire excavation can be extended, and you'll still be in charge. If that's what you want, of course . . ."

It was a transparent attempt at manipulation, and they both knew it, but Hayter had little choice except to go along with it. "I think that would tie in with my plans," he said eventually.

"Great. So, what's the situation with the Temple of Poseidon?"

Hayter, with occasional interjections from Matt, gave a report on the state of the dig that Nina had ordered. With both submersibles, the heavy-duty underwater excavation machine *Sharkdozer II* and the more exploratory-purposed but still capable *Gypsy*, working to clear the rubble from the altar room, progress had been relatively swift—by archaeological standards. "If you just wanted the stones moved, we could have done it in half the time, but you lot get so shirty about breaking the stuff underneath them," said Matt jokingly, making Eddie laugh and temporarily uniting both archaeologists in humorless disapproval.

"What about any finds?" Nina asked Hayter.

"We uncovered more of the texts on the walls," he told her, bringing up a collection of images on a laptop. "Still nothing from the very end of the chronology, but we must be close now. The new translation software has given us a fairly good idea of what it all says; the team back at the IHA are working out the subtleties."

"Nothing new about the statues?"

"Not so far. Nantalas was mentioned once, but only in reference to what we'd already found—her so-called visions. She was trying to persuade the king to let her use the sky stone's powers for war again."

"She's a nice lass, this Nantalas," said Eddie.

"How close are we to the last section of text?" Nina asked. "Eddie, you saw it in person when we first discovered the place. Can you remember exactly where it was?"

"Show me that computer graphic thing," he told Hayter, who brought up a program on the laptop. The numerous photographs taken in the ruins had been mapped onto the walls of a 3-D model of the altar room, producing a patchwork wallpaper effect that could be viewed from any angle. "That's the shaft that we first came through?" He indicated a particular feature, and Hayter nodded. "Okay, I remember that there was a pillar about there"—he pointed at another part of the virtual chamber—"so the writing ended . . . somewhere 'round *here*."

The closest photograph was just a few feet from the spot. Matt compared the graphic with a wider shot taken inside the actual room. "We're pretty near. Once we shift that last piece of wreckage, we should be able to clear these stones in . . . I dunno, not long. A few hours."

"And how long to move the wreckage?" Nina asked.

"It'll be a bit of a long stint, but I reckon we could do it all in a single dive."

"How quickly can you have the sub ready?"

"It's already prepped—we still have to go through the safety checks and lower it into the water, but about an hour."

"Great! Let's get going, then."

"Might have known you'd be in a rush! No worries— we'll have pictures for you before the day's out."

"I don't just want pictures," she replied. "I want to see it for myself. I'm going with you."

Hayter looked startled at the suggestion, Matt less so. "You want to come along?" the archaeologist asked. "In the subs?"

"No, I thought I'd put on goggles and flippers and use a very long snorkel. *Yes,* in the subs."

"Sarcasm isn't really necessary," he said sourly. "It's just that *Gypsy* only has room for two people in addition to the pilot. As expedition leader I'll be one of them, and I'll need Lydia in support, as she knows the site firsthand."

"Not a problem," said Nina. "Eddie and I can go in Matt's sub."

"We can, can we?" Eddie grumbled.

"Oh, you knew it was going to happen. You got to go down to the Temple of Poseidon last time—there's no way I'm going to miss the chance now. Anyway, *Sharkdozer* has room for three people, doesn't it, Matt?"

"Four if you don't mind being up in each other's arm-pits," the Australian told her jovially.

"We'll keep it to three, then. The only person who should put up with Eddie's armpits is his wife. And even then . . ."

"Oi!" protested her husband.

Hayter was still displeased with the prospect. "Are you sure this is a good idea, Nina?"

"This won't be my first time underwater, Lewis. And if you're worried about having your boss looking over your shoulder, don't be. Until we uncover the last of the Atlantean text I'll only be there as an observer, and even then it's still your dig."

That mollified him, however slightly. "Well, I suppose that if Matt's happy to have you as passengers . . ."

Matt shrugged. "No problem for me."

"Excellent," said Nina. She got to her feet. "In that case, let's go and find out the fate of Atlantis."

* * *

It took more than the predicted hour, the safety proce-dures being slowed by the *Gant*'s wallowing, but even-tually both submersibles were descending toward the ruins of Atlantis.

Even though she knew there would be nothing to see until they reached the ocean floor eight hundred feet below, Nina nevertheless leaned around Matt in the cen-tral pilot's position to watch their descent through the large acrylic bubble window. The light from the surface faded surprisingly quickly, the cold blue of the ocean outside becoming darker and more ominous before ulti-mately turning to darkness.

Matt switched on the sub's spotlights. Nina experi-enced an oddly vertiginous feeling; the intense beams picked out particles in the water as the submersible dropped past them, the effect making it seem as though they were plunging like a falling elevator.

But she knew they were perfectly safe. Nothing might be visible through the viewport, but Matt's sub was equipped with a LIDAR laser scanning system that swept the ocean around them far beyond the range of the human eye. The engineer had used similar systems in his previous craft, but this went a step farther by covering a full 360 degrees. *Sharkdozer II* was an odd-looking vessel: Its main hull was a fairly standard cigar shape, but protruding from each side like the steroidal limbs of a bodybuilder were huge mechanical arms, almost comically out of proportion with the rest of the sub. Making them even stranger were the tool-equipped secondary arms sprouting from behind their wrists, designed for more delicate work than the brute-force claws of their parents. The whole submersible was mounted upon four helicopter-like skids, each of which could be independently adjusted hydraulically to give it as much lifting leverage as possible against the ocean floor. The LIDAR scanner, allied with the cameras on each of the four "hands," meant the arms could be operated even if they were out of direct sight of a viewport.

The only thing currently on the LIDAR display was the expedition's other sub. *Gypsy* was some thirty yards to their right, the spears of its own spotlights visible through a small secondary porthole. It was a much more conventional vessel, equipped with a single, far smaller manipulator arm and numerous camera mounts and sample racks. Hayter's voice crackled over the radio. "Passing three hundred feet, confirm."

"Confirm," Matt replied. Radio communications were possible underwater, but only at very limited ranges, and the message was already distorted.

Eddie examined the controls for the arms. Rather than being simple joysticks, they were also able to bend and twist. "How much can these things lift?"

"If the sub's properly braced on the seabed, up to three tons," Matt told him. "If I'm free-floating and holding it on the thrusters, about half that." He activated the autopilot to hold *Sharkdozer* on its descent and took one of the arm controls. "Here, check this out."

The submersible tipped slightly on its port side as he

moved the left stick to swing the corresponding arm outward. A turn and twist, and its claw came into view through the forward viewport, steel glinting in the spotlights. He worked a smaller videogame-like thumbstick. "Wave hello to Nina and Eddie!" The claw obediently waggled up and down.

"Cute," said Nina.

"Wait till you see this." A flick of a switch, and he worked the smaller control again. The secondary arm unfolded and reached out to tap gently on the thick bubble with a rubber-tipped "finger." A computer graphic superimposed over the LIDAR display showed exactly where both arms were positioned relative to the sub. "That's some real precision engineering there. I could sign my name at a thousand feet down with that."

"I think it'd ruin your pen, though," said Eddie. The Australian grinned and returned the arms to their original places.

"Typical guys," Nina scoffed. "We're on our way to one of the most important archaeological sites in the world, and all you care about are your big-boys' toys."

Matt laughed, then took back the main controls. Both submersibles continued their long fall into the cold, dark void.

After some time, an electronic chirp from the instruments told the trio that something had changed. "What is it?" Nina asked. "Are we there?"

"Nearly," said Matt. "Look at that."

He pointed at the LIDAR display. Something had appeared at the bottom of the screen, a tangled, twisted mass that at first glance resembled some sort of seaweed. But it was no plant. A grid overlaid on the image showed the scale: It was hundreds of feet across, and growing larger as the sub's descent brought more of it into LIDAR range. "What is it? It can't be the wreck of the *Evenor,* it's too big."

"No, but it is a wreck," Matt told her. "It's the SBX."

Nina felt a chill at the realization that she was looking at a mass grave. Before Atlantis's existence had been officially revealed to the world, the IHA had been secretly exploring the ruins under the cover of SBX-2, a giant American floating radar platform ostensibly deployed to monitor the threat of missiles being fired into Europe from North Africa. It had been sabotaged and sunk, with the loss of over seventy lives. The mangled state of the wreckage meant that some of the bodies had still not been recovered.

"Jesus, look at that," Eddie said quietly as more of the sunken station was revealed. SBX-2 had capsized, landing on the seafloor with its six great pontoon supports sticking up like the legs of a dead insect. The superstructure had been crushed beneath them by their weight, girders jabbing outward from the rusting ruins.

"We're about four hundred meters from the main dig site," Matt announced solemnly, making a course adjustment. The ghostly wreckage on the display slowly disappeared behind them. It was replaced by the contours of the seabed as *Sharkdozer* neared the end of its journey.

Other shapes appeared, not the smooth curves of current-swept silt but the angular outlines of human constructions, standing out where the sediment of millennia had been cleared from around them. Nina couldn't help but draw in an astounded breath.

Atlantis.

She had discovered its location, overseen its exploration by the IHA. But this was the first time she had ever visited the ruins in person. She leaned forward again, shoulder to shoulder with Matt. "How long before we can see it for real?" she asked, excited.

"A little room, please?" the Australian asked, nudging her with his elbow as he tweaked the controls. She reluctantly retreated—about three inches. "Give us thirty seconds, and the first thing we'll see will be the Temple of the Gods." He pointed it out on the LIDAR screen. "Then after that, we'll be at the Temple of Poseidon."

The wait was almost intolerable. Nina moved forward again, not even another nudge from Matt sufficient to move her back. She stared intently into the darkness outside. Then . . .

"There!" she cried. "There it is!"

Her first true sight of the ruins of Atlantis hazed into view through the murk. It didn't appear particularly impressive, just the collapsed remains of a building—but to her it was utterly breathtaking. A civilization lost for eleven thousand years, discovered through the work and dedication of first her parents and then herself . . . and now she was finally seeing it firsthand. "Oh my God. That is incredible . . ." She felt as though she was about to cry.

Eddie punctured her bubble. "Great. We've come to the bottom of the Atlantic to look at a building site."

"Shut. Up!"

They approached what was left of the Temple of the Gods. Compared with some of the other majestic structures the expedition had unearthed, it was not particularly big—an oval perhaps seventy feet across at its longest. Large sections of its walls had toppled outward, giving the impression that it had exploded from within.

"So that's where they kept this sky stone?" Eddie asked.

"That's right," said Nina. "It's quite an unusual place, actually. Atlantean temples are usually devoted to a single god, but this was dedicated to . . . well, dozens of them, as far as we can tell. Although now that we know about the sky stone from the rest of the Kallikrates text, there might be an explanation. Nantalas said that it contained the power of the gods—plural. So the Atlanteans made sure to honor them all."

"If they knew there was something special about the meteor, enough for 'em to build a temple to put it in, why didn't they use its power right away?"

Nina looked out at the broken building as they glided past. "There could be any number of reasons. They might have been afraid of it; the text said that some of the royal court were opposed to using its power. Or maybe they didn't originally have all three statues—or anyone who could use them. It was obviously a big thing for Nantalas to be able to channel earth energy, so it could have been as rare an ability then as it is now, even among Atlanteans."

"Maybe you're her great-great-great-great-et-cetera-granddaughter," Eddie suggested.

Nina treated the jokey comment with more seriousness. "Maybe. I'm descended from *someone* from Atlantis, so who knows?"

The collapsed temple disappeared from view. Beyond it, something far larger came into sight.

The Temple of Poseidon.

Even after the destruction wrought upon it by the impact of the sunken *Evenor,* it was still an imposing structure. The submersible was approaching its northern end, where Eddie had first entered the temple five years earlier. An enormous wall of dark stone rose out of the sediment, stepped in tiers like a ziggurat near its base before curving smoothly inward to form a great arched roof.

Nina noticed a sudden tension in her husband at the sight. "Hugo?" she asked quietly. Eddie gave her a silent nod; one of his closest friends had died here. Matt also became uncharacteristically somber for a moment. Eddie had not been the only one to suffer a loss at Atlantis.

The submersible drew closer. "That's the tunnel," said Eddie, pointing at a small hole in the wall. The shaft had been constructed by the Atlanteans as a secret passage leading directly to the altar room.

"You don't need to crawl through a little hole to get inside now," said Matt as he guided the *Sharkdozer* toward the roof. The wreck of the *Evenor* came into sight, a long white ax that had sliced the four-hundred-foot-long temple in two. Something bright flickered in the gloom atop the rubble. "There's the altar room."

He brought the sub into a hover near the object, a marker pole covered in reflective material that caught the spotlights. Not far from it was a twisted mass of metal—part of the *Evenor*'s superstructure. The excavated sections of the altar room were visible before it, orichalcum sheets glinting on the walls.

Gypsy moved ahead of them and came to a stop above the dig site. "*Sharkdozer* in position, confirm," said Matt over the radio.

"Read you, *Sharkdozer*," Hayter's crackly voice replied. "*Gypsy* also in position."

"Roger that." Matt turned to Nina and Eddie. "This is the boring part, I'm afraid."

"That's okay," said Nina. "I want to watch the whole thing. You never know what might turn up."

"I'll give it a miss," Eddie said. He took a creased paperback thriller from inside his leather jacket and thumbed it open. "Been meaning to finish this for ages. I got interrupted by the whole wanted-for-murder business. I'll just read it while you're telling Matt how to dig."

"I'm not going to do that," she assured Matt.

"Too bloody right you're not!" the Australian replied with mock offense as he took the manipulator controls. "Okay, *Gypsy*, I'm ready to start."

The other submersible moved closer, spotlights and cameras panning for a clearer view as Matt began the long and involved task of removing the debris covering the altar room. The first priority was the wreckage from the *Evenor;* even though most of it had already been cut away, it was still a hefty chunk of steel heavier than the *Sharkdozer* could lift using its thrusters alone. It wasn't until the sub touched down on top of the temple and used its skids to brace itself that the arms could apply enough leverage to start raising the broken section of superstructure.

It took the better part of an hour to get it safely clear. Once it had been dumped in the silt away from the building, work began in earnest. None of the fallen slabs was as heavy as the ship debris, but they were still fairly massive in their own right.

Time passed. Matt took a break to recharge with an energy drink and a sandwich, while Nina forced herself not to tap her fingers impatiently. Eddie smirked at her over the top of his novel, knowing how she was feeling. Then the work continued, the obstructing blocks gradually becoming fewer in number. Until—

"There!" said Nina as Matt hauled one of the remaining slabs out of the way. "There it is!"

A golden light reflected back at them from the sheet of precious metal covering the newly revealed wall. It had been damaged in several places, a great jagged rip through one entire section obliterating the text . . . but the crucial part was still more or less intact.

The last inscription. The final written words of the great empire of Atlantis.

"There, there there *there*!" Nina jabbed a finger excitedly. "Get the camera on it, quick!"

Eddie snapped his book shut. "Calm down, love! It's not going anywhere."

"I know, I know. But, well . . . I want to see it!"

"She was like this the first night I was back home," he told Matt. "Couldn't keep her hands off my pants."

"*Eddie!*"

"What you do in private isn't my business," Matt said, amused. "But give me a sec here, Nina—I still need to put this stone somewhere." He worked the controls, Nina fidgeting beside him. Finally, the block was released. "All right, let's have a dekko. *Gypsy,* you got your cameras switched on?"

"We never turned them off," said Hayter over the radio, sounding almost as enthusiastic as Nina. "Nina, we've got our translator hooked up to our high-definition camera. It's got better resolution than the ones on your sub, so we should get our pictures first—"

"Sorry, Lewis," Nina cut in as she opened the laptop containing her own copy of the translation software, "but I'm going to be selfish on this one. My primary interest here is the very last piece of text, so I want to work on that straightaway. Once we've got the pictures, you can record the rest of the inscriptions. Okay?"

"If you insist," came the sour reply.

Matt delicately brought the hulking submersible closer to the wall with careful blips of its thrusters. He stopped when the viewing bubble was about six feet away, the magnifying effect of the thick hemisphere almost making the text readable with the naked eye. But instead, he extended one of the secondary arms until its camera was less than a foot from the metal sheet. "You ready, Nina?"

"Recording," she answered. "Go ahead."

Matt slowly panned the arm back and forth over the final section of text. A window on the laptop's screen displayed the live feed; another, larger window showed the whole inscription building up section by section as the computer automatically matched them together like pieces of a jigsaw puzzle. It wasn't long before the image was complete, at which point another program began the more complex task of translating the ancient language into English.

"Okay, Lewis," Nina said into a headset, "I've got what I need. You can move in now."

The snideness behind Hayter's simple "Thank you" was clear even through the distortion. Matt backed the *Sharkdozer* away, and *Gypsy* took its place, cameras peering intently at the rest of the ancient record.

"So, what does it say?" Eddie asked, leaning across the confined cabin to examine the screen.

"Give it a chance," said Nina. "It's a lot faster than translating by hand, but it's not *Star Trek*." Words were already starting to appear, though: the image-recognition software was picking out familiar patterns. "Nantalas gets mentioned several times . . . and so does the sky stone."

More minutes passed, the gaps in the translation gradually filling in. Some parts remained blank; either the condition of the orichalcum sheet was too poor for the computer to pick out the letters, or the words were simply unknown, having never been found in any previously translated Atlantean texts. But even with gaps, Nina saw a clear narrative taking form.

"It's what I thought," she said softly. "This really is an account of the last days of Atlantis—the last hours, even. Someone was still keeping records right up until it fell into the ocean."

"What caused it?" asked Eddie.

"From the look of this . . . Nantalas herself. And the sky stone. Listen." She began to read the translation, attempting to smooth out the computer's awkward and over-literal phrasing. " 'The king and the royal court came to the Temple of the Gods to witness Nantalas bring together all three keys of power and touch them to the sky stone. There was much . . .' This is a bit jumbled—ah, something like 'awe and terror as the great stone rose from the ground, shining with a holy light.' "

"So it's definitely earth energy, then," Eddie mused. "I don't get it. It would have been like having nuclear power back in the Stone Age. How could it be forgotten about for eleven thousand years, apart from when Merlin and King Arthur fluked into using it with Excalibur?"

Nina was reading ahead. "I think I know. 'Nantalas commanded the stone to rise and fall, using no words but those in her thoughts. She then told the court that she would . . .' I guess in context it would have to be *demonstrate,* 'she would demonstrate the power that would crush the enemies of Atlantis. But . . .' "

"But?" said Matt after a moment. "Come on, Nina, don't leave us hanging!"

"It didn't exactly go as planned," she told the two men. "The computer couldn't translate some of the words, but there's enough to get the gist. Basically, the demonstration blew up in her face."

"Literally?" said Eddie.

"Pretty much. It says there was lightning, 'a storm unmatched in history as Zeus unleashed his fury upon those who had dared to claim the power of the gods as their own.' Huge earthquakes, buildings collapsing—

and great waves. Where we are now, the Temple of Poseidon, was right at the heart of the Atlantean capital—and it was directly connected to the Atlantic by canals, so it was essentially at sea level. The text describes huge waves sweeping inshore."

"Atlantis sinks beneath the waves," said Matt ruefully. "Just like the legends always said."

"There's something else, though." Nina read on. " 'The sky stone itself was snatched into the heavens on a thunderbolt, flying to the southeast faster than an arrow.' The southeast . . ." She trailed off.

"What are you thinking?" Eddie asked.

"When I was in Tokyo, the feeling that I somehow knew the direction something was in . . . it was off to the west. Two hundred and sixty degrees, Takashi said. I wonder . . ." She opened another application, bringing up a map of the world. "Here's Atlantis," she said, pointing at a spot between the coasts of Portugal and Morocco. "And here"—her finger moved across to Japan—"is Tokyo. Two hundred and sixty degrees west from there would intersect a line going southeast from Atlantis somewhere around . . . *here*."

"Eastern Africa," said Matt, looking at the map.

"That doesn't narrow things down much," Eddie commented. "You think the stone ended up there? How?"

"Some sort of earth energy reaction, perhaps. We already know it could levitate against the planet's own magnetic fields, so maybe whatever Nantalas did overcharged it, actually repelled it, and sent it flying off across half a continent." She scrolled down through the translation. "Nantalas tried to find it."

"How?"

"She still had the three statues. They gave her a . . . I don't really want to call it a *vision*, because of the supernatural overtones, but since I had one myself I don't really know how else to describe it. She told the king it had ended up in . . ." She read the translated words several times before coming up with a way to express them properly. "I think it's 'the Forge of Hephaestus.' Hephaestus was the god of blacksmiths and craftsmen," she continued, anticipating the question, "and also fire and volcanoes."

"So you think the stone ended up in a volcano?"

"Considering what else happened in Atlantis, I'd say it was a possibility. Listen to this: 'The mountains north of the city are spewing fire and ash. The island shakes as the gods of the land and the sky and the sea all turn their anger upon Atlantis.' Interesting—the text's now in the present tense. It's not a record for posterity anymore, more like a last journal entry . . . 'The witch Nantalas has begged the king for her life. She says she can find the sky stone. The king asks her why, when it has brought only destruction and the wrath of the gods upon the empire. She says a new Temple of the Gods must be built and the sky stone sealed in it for eternity, so that nobody may ever again repeat her blasphemy.' She managed to convince him to let her lead the search."

"Crikey, she must have been one hell of a good talker," said Matt. "I'm amazed he didn't give her the chop on the spot."

"I think she knew that even if she found it, she would still be killed for what she'd done. But I guess the king thought it was worth trying—if they could pacify the gods, maybe they could save Atlantis."

Eddie shook his head. "Well, we know how that turned out. But did she find it?"

"I don't even know if she managed to escape Atlantis before it sank. We're almost at the end of the text." Nina became more solemn as she read the last few lines. "'The people are fleeing, but there are not enough ships. One of the mountains has collapsed into the earth, leaving only a pillar of fire. Even the great temples are falling. Only the Temple of Poseidon is strong enough to hold, and I do not know for how long.' And then . . ." She brought the composite image back up on the laptop's screen, pointing out the final words. "The inscriptions are much cruder now—they were written in a hurry. 'The king and queen have fled. The dead lie in the streets. The ground does not stop shaking. The gods have cursed us. The sea . . .'"

"What?"

She gave Eddie a grim look. "It says, 'The sea is rising. Atlantis falls.' And that's where it ends."

"Christ. That's pretty bloody biblical."

"The end of an entire civilization," she said, almost sadly. "We know there was a diaspora that survived for a few centuries, but eventually the last Atlanteans were conquered, died, or were absorbed by other cultures. But it all ended right here—when Nantalas thought she could control earth energy."

"But she blew it. Literally."

"Right. It seems that she channeled so much energy through the meteorite that it caused an earthquake, volcanic eruptions, tsunamis . . ." She gestured at the main viewport, outside which the second submersible was still photographing the rest of the inscriptions. "She sank the entire *island*. I remember when we first found Atlantis, someone had the theory that the collapse of a subterranean volcanic caldera could account for how it ended up eight hundred feet below the surface. If that's right, then it was an uncontrolled release of earth energy that actually caused it."

"One person could do all that?" Matt asked in disbelief.

"One person can kill a million—if they happen to have their finger on the trigger of an atomic bomb. That's essentially what happened. They didn't know what they were dealing with . . . and their arrogance, their hubris, destroyed them. It's like you said, Eddie—it's as if they had nuclear power eleven thousand years ago. Only they didn't have the knowledge or the wisdom to use it properly."

"Do we now?" he replied, not entirely rhetorically.

The silence that followed was unexpectedly broken by

a chirp from the LIDAR system. "What was that?" Nina asked.

"I dunno," said Matt, turning back to the instruments. "That's the rangefinder—it means something new's just come into scanning distance. But there shouldn't—"

The sharp boom of an explosion shook the submersible—followed by an even louder *crump* of crushed metal as *Gypsy* imploded in front of them.

TWENTY-THREE

The *Sharkdozer* was knocked backward by the shock wave. "Jesus!" Eddie shouted. "What the fuck was that?"

Nina looked ahead. The view was obscured by a swirling mass of bubbles . . . then they cleared enough to reveal that the other submersible was a crumpled wreck. Something had exploded against its side, tearing a ragged hole—and the crew compartment had instantly collapsed, crushed like a soda can under the wheel of a truck. The inside of its viewing bubble was smeared with a pale red film.

The remains of Hayter and his crew.

Matt grabbed the controls, pulling his sub up and back from the wreckage. The LIDAR trilled again. "There's someone else down here!" he cried.

Now clear of the temple walls that had blocked its view, the sensor showed three new signals nearby—one large, two small. The larger intruder was ahead and off to the left, higher up, the others moving in from behind.

Eddie squeezed forward to look at the screen—and immediately saw a new threat. "Matt, watch out!"

Another blip had detached from the signal ahead,

heading straight for them. Very quickly. "Torpedo!" the
Australian yelled. He turned the *Sharkdozer* away, but
the big, heavy submersible was sluggish—

Another explosion, much closer. The sub rang like a
gong as it lurched sideways, smashing against the ruins.
Nina screamed as the impact threw her across the cabin.
The lights flickered before coming back on—noticeably
dimmed.

Alarms shrilled, numerous indicators on the instrument panels flashing a warning red. "Is the hull
breached?" Nina asked, frightened.

"If it was, we'd be dead," Matt replied. "We've lost
main power, though—we're on the reserves. And there's
a lot of other damage."

"We need to surface," said Eddie urgently.

"Too bloody right we do! Hold on, I'll dump the
emergency ballast." He reached up to a large, red-
painted lever on the ceiling and pulled it.

There was a deep *thump* from beneath them, the sub
shuddering . . . but nothing else happened. Matt pulled
the lever again. Still no result. "Aw, shit . . ."

"What?" Nina demanded. "What's wrong?"

"The ballast's not dropping, that's what's bloody
wrong! We should be flying up like a helium balloon
right now!"

"Is it broken?"

"There's nothing to break! It's a bloody big slab of pig
iron held on by an electromagnet—cut the power, it
falls, we float!"

"Forget floating," Eddie warned, watching the LIDAR
display, "just get us moving!" All three enemy blips
were closing on the center of the screen.

Matt opened the throttles, steering the *Sharkdozer*
clear of the temple. "She's slow," he warned. "Feels like
a damaged thruster."

Eddie reached past him to take one of the manipulator
controls. "What are you doing?" said Nina.

"Seeing what's wrong." A monitor screen showed the
view from the starboard arm's camera as it moved out

from the sub's side. He brought it around to look back along the hull.

Matt made a sound of dismay at the sight of one of the thruster pods, the casing of which had been torn away to expose the propeller blades within. "Eddie, move it down and look under us," he ordered.

Eddie did so. The camera revealed that both the portside skids had been bent underneath the *Sharkdozer* by the collision with the temple . . . and the buckled metal had trapped the ballast slab in place beneath its keel. "The thing's stuck under there! How long will it take to get back to the surface using the thrusters?"

"Too long!" Matt pointed outside as the vessel continued its turn. A set of spotlights was visible in the dark water.

Closing fast.

The approaching submersible took on form as the *Sharkdozer*'s own spotlights illuminated it. Unlike Matt's utilitarian craft, this was sleek and purposeful in design, its sharp prow resembling that of a powerboat. Instead of a hemispherical viewport, it had a pair of long windows set into its bow, giving the impression that it was watching them through slitted eyes.

The wreck of the *Evenor* came into view. "Matt, go down there," Eddie told him. "We can use it as cover."

"Yeah, and we might get snagged on it if we get too close!" But he tipped the *Sharkdozer* into a descent.

Nina stared at the LIDAR. All three enemies were changing course to intercept. "Can we outrun it?"

"The sub?" said Matt. "Not a chance, even if we had full power. It's a Mako; I know the bloke who designed it. It's a pleasure boat, a millionaire's toy—but it can still shift." He frowned. "No way it could have gotten out here on its own. Max range is only about a hundred kilometers . . ."

He turned his full attention back to piloting as the wreck loomed ahead. Torn metal stabbed outward from the crushed hull, the area around it strewn with debris. Nina watched the approaching jagged shards with growing nervousness before glancing back at the LIDAR. "Oh my God! One of them's right on us!"

A smaller blip had closed to within fifty feet of the *Sharkdozer*'s stern. Eddie hurriedly moved the arm to bring it into the camera's field of view. More lights shone in the darkness.

He recognized their pattern immediately. A deep suit, a halfway house between traditional scuba gear and full-body deep-diving systems; the torso and bubble helmet were rigid, allowing the user to breathe ordinary air without risking the dangers of the bends, while the limbs were enclosed in standard neoprene dry suits. Eddie had used deep suits himself on several occasions, and knew their capabilities—which included high-speed movement with the aid of their built-in thrusters.

He also knew what the diver's weapon could do.

Their opponent held an ASM-DT rifle, a Soviet-designed weapon for use both underwater and above. In air, it fired the same 5.45-millimeter ammunition as the Kalashnikov AK-74 rifle; beneath the surface, it used identical cartridges to propel not bullets, but six-inch-long hydrodynamic nail rounds.

And the gun was pointing at the *Sharkdozer.*

"Incoming!" was all he had time to shout—

The diver opened fire on full auto, blasting a stream of nails at them. Matt was already taking evasive action, but it was too late—the lumbering submarine was an unmissable target at such close range.

Piercing clangs rang through the pressure compartment as the nails struck the hull. There was a flat *thump,* followed by a fizzing sound—and the *Sharkdozer* jolted. An urgent warning siren hooted, more red lights flashing. "He hit an air tank!" Matt reported.

Nina pointed at the *Evenor.* "Matt, there!" A large hole was visible in the side of the survey vessel's hull, angling upward toward its main deck. "Can we fit through it?"

"It'll be tight, but if it stops us getting shot I'll have to try!" Matt replied, changing course.

Eddie shifted the arm to keep their attacker in view. The diver was fumbling with his gun, changing the large and awkward magazine. "He's reloading—we've got a few seconds."

"I dunno how much I can do in that time, mate!" Matt told him as he took the sub into the gap. Mangled metal clawed at them from all sides—and something larger hove into view across their path, a twisted steel beam. "Hang on!"

He jammed the controls hard over—and rolled the submersible onto its side.

Loose objects clattered across the cabin, Nina only holding herself in place by grabbing Matt's chair, while Eddie thumped painfully against the wall. The beam swept past, scraping along the *Sharkdozer*'s fiberglass upper bodywork. There was a sharp crack as something was torn away, the sub slewing sideways . . . then they were clear.

Matt rolled the vessel back upright. "What's that drongo behind us doing?"

Eddie found the diver again, who had now reloaded the gun and was following the sub through the passage. "Still gaining." He looked ahead. The *Sharkdozer* was coming to the end of the mangled tunnel. "Matt, as soon as you get to the top, go hard right."

"But that won't—"

"Just do it!" He worked the manipulator arm again, extending it farther out—and back.

"Turning now!" Matt warned, pushing the controls over to their limit. The *Sharkdozer*'s thrusters pivoted, throwing the craft into a tight turn.

Eddie opened the claw and swung the arm around as the sub emerged from the *Evenor*'s ruined deck. He searched for the pursuing diver's lights.

They reappeared on the monitor, much closer. He pushed and twisted the joystick as if trying to guide a giant robot's punch, closing the claw again—

It clamped around the deep suit's chest section.

Eddie thumbed the control harder and the claw tightened, the diver's limbs flailing as he struggled to break free. If he could crush him, or at least puncture his suit, it would make the fight slightly less one-sided . . .

The man brought up his gun—but didn't point it at the submarine. Instead, he aimed at the arm itself. Jets of gas burst from the muzzle as he fired more nail rounds, clanks echoing through the metal into the cabin—and a light on the console flashed urgently. "Matt, what'd he do?"

Matt checked the instruments. "He's shot out the claw's hydraulic line!"

"You mean it's jammed?" The camera now showed the trapped diver turning his gun around to bash at the arm with its stock. Without hydraulic pressure, the claw would soon be forced open.

And once he was free, the diver would resume his attack—from almost point-blank range.

Eddie considered using the arm to slam the man against the wreck, but the *Sharkdozer*'s momentum had carried it away from the angled deck. Instead, he flicked the switch to engage the secondary arm. The view on the monitor changed from the main manipulator to its smaller counterpart. He extended the arm. The paralyzed claw and the man clutched within it came into view.

The diver's face was now visible inside his helmet. He looked up in surprise—then his expression turned to shock. He turned the gun back around, but by the time it was pointing the right way the mechanical hand was right in his face . . .

Eddie didn't waste time trying to grab him. Instead he pushed a button marked DRILL.

A tool smoothly pivoted into place from the manipulator's wrist, the hand itself folding downward out of its way. The diamond tip of the eight-inch tungsten carbide bit scraped the diver's bubble helmet, scratching the tough material.

Before the man even had time to scream, Eddie started the drill.

It took under a second for the high-powered mechanism to chew through the polycarbonate helmet. *Now* the man screamed—and was abruptly silenced as water exploded into the deep suit with the force of an artillery shell. The transparent bubble filled with a churning pink froth.

The extra weight of the water inside the suit finally overcame the crippled claw's grip. The dead man broke free, falling away into the wreckage of the *Evenor.*

Eddie nodded in satisfaction. "That's what I call getting the bit between your teeth."

Nina gave him a look of distaste. "At least you didn't say *You're screwed!*" She looked back at the LIDAR screen. A large part of the scanner's field of view was now obstructed by the sunken ship, the second deep-suited diver hidden somewhere behind it.

But the Mako's blip was still visible, changing course to come after them.

"Eddie," Matt said urgently as he headed away from it, "use the other main arm and reach underneath us. If we can drop the ballast slab, we'll be on the surface in three minutes."

Eddie did so. The *Sharkdozer* rocked again as the port arm extended. Nina's gaze switched between the LIDAR and Eddie's monitor. "Can you see it?"

"Just a sec . . . there." The submersible's underside came into view as the claw twisted around. The iron slab was still wedged in place by the bent skids. He moved the arm closer—

It jerked to a stop. "What's wrong?" Nina asked.

"I dunno." He tried again, pushing the controls harder, but the arm still stopped short. "Matt, I can't reach it."

The Australian quickly checked the monitor. "That's as far as it goes—try the secondary arm, see if that'll reach."

"You don't know?" Eddie said, incredulous.

"It wasn't designed to scratch its own belly! Or dodge torpedoes, for that matter."

"Speaking of which," Nina said in alarm, "I think he's about to fire another one!"

A trill from the LIDAR confirmed her fears. A new blip appeared in front of the other submersible—drawing closer each time the display refreshed. Matt turned again, but the damaged *Sharkdozer* was even slower to respond than before. "Shit! It's going to hit us!"

Nina braced herself, but knew the effort was pointless. The Mako's first torpedo had destroyed Hayter's vessel and killed everyone aboard with a single direct impact, and there was no reason to think theirs was any stronger. She stared helplessly at the LIDAR display as the projectile raced at them—

Eddie abandoned his attempt to release the ballast—and instead swung the arm up at the torpedo.

The *Sharkdozer*'s occupants were thrown bodily against the cabin wall as the shock wave of another explosion pounded the sub like a strike from a colossal hammer. An air line burst, compressed gas shrieking into the crew compartment. Debris pounded the outer hull.

More alarms sounded, the instrument panel now a battery of flashing red lights. Matt clambered back into his seat and struggled to regain control of the tumbling submersible.

Nina pressed a hand to her forehead, feeling the warm dampness of blood against her palm. "What happened?" she asked Eddie.

"I caught the torpedo," he said. The manipulator arm was visible through the left viewport—or at least, what was left of it. The metal limb had been severed at the wrist, control cables and hydraulic lines hanging like torn tendons from the shattered stump.

Matt finally stabilized the *Sharkdozer* and rapidly turned a valve on the ceiling. The piercing squeal spluttered and died. "How much air did we lose?" Nina asked.

The engineer only needed to give her a worried look for her to know that their already perilous situation had become worse. The sub reeled queasily as he gunned the thrusters.

Another alert from the LIDAR. Eddie tensed, but it wasn't another torpedo. The third enemy—another deep-suited diver—had just reappeared from behind the *Evenor.* "They're both catching up."

"I know, I know!" Matt said. "We can't outrun them."

Eddie pointed over his shoulder at a dark shadow on the sea floor. "Down there! We can lose 'em in the ruins."

Nina shook her head. "They're not tall enough to hide us—but I know something that is," she continued, suddenly hopeful. "The SBX! It's big enough to give us cover."

"It's also messed up enough for us to get stuck in the wreckage, or worse," Matt warned.

"At least we'll have a chance."

Face full of trepidation, Matt swung the *Sharkdozer* around on a new course. The ocean floor rose on the LIDAR display: They were approaching the edge of the excavated area. Many more ruins lay ahead, the Atlantean capital extending far beyond the city's heart, but they were safely concealed beneath eleven millennia of silt deposits. "Where are they?"

Eddie studied the screen. The Mako and the diver were both following them—and gaining. "Behind us, and catching up. Matt, how badly are we damaged?"

"It'd be quicker to tell you what's *not* crook," the Australian answered, checking the warning lights. "Power's draining fast, the thrusters are damaged, and . . ." His face sank.

"And?"

"And we've got maybe ten minutes before we start running out of air. The recycling system's shot."

"You couldn't have *started* with that?"

"Wait, so even if we lose these guys chasing us, we're still not going to be able to get to the surface?" Nina said. "Well, that's marvelous!"

The first signs of the SBX's strewn wreckage came into

view at the edge of the LIDAR display. "Only way we can get up there before we croak is by dropping the ballast slab. We might be able to knock it loose on the rig debris," said Matt.

"Not with those arseholes shooting at us." Eddie thought for a moment, then made a decision. "We'll have to take them out."

"With what?" Nina protested. "They've got nail guns and torpedoes, and we've got a claw that doesn't work!"

"Better than nowt." He looked ahead. Broken metal poked out from the silt, the debris field becoming thicker. They were coming up on the remains of the SBX. Matt turned to avoid something resembling an enormous broken eggshell: part of the giant fiberglass dome that had covered the platform's main radar antenna.

Eddie looked at the LIDAR again. Their pursuers were still closing, the sub slightly ahead of the deep suit. "Have you explored any of this?"

"Nope," Matt told him. "It's a grave site—off-limits. The only people who've been allowed down to it are US navy divers."

"So you don't know what's in there?" The engineer shook his head. "Oh well, at least we'll all be in the same boat. One that's up shit creek!"

The *Sharkdozer* swerved to skirt a fallen girder standing out of the seabed like a flagpole. One of the SBX's six gigantic legs rose at an angle ahead. The concrete cylinder was surrounded by a nest of twisted metal. "Eddie, give me some hints here," Matt said urgently.

Eddie indicated a long beam protruding almost horizontally from the wreckage. "Can we fit under that?"

"Yeah—but there could be anything on the other side."

"You want to find out what?"

"Not especially."

Nina saw plumes of bubbles from the diver's rifle obscure his spotlights on the video monitor. "He's shooting again!"

"But I want a nail up my backside even less!" Matt

decided quickly, turning the *Sharkdozer* on a course that would take it beneath the overhanging girder. A couple of the six-inch steel spikes clipped the submersible's back end, but the rest shot harmlessly past. "What do you want me to do?"

"Just go through and make sure he has to go under that beam to come after us," Eddie said as he took the arm controls. On the monitor, the Mako's lights were now dazzling as it caught up. Another few seconds and it would be impossible for a torpedo to miss. He raised the remaining manipulator, turning it to look ahead. The long strut stood out clearly in the sub's floodlights. He brought the arm higher, the paralyzed claw now on a collision course with the beam. "Soon as you're clear, turn so he can't get a shot at us."

"There's nowhere *to* bloody turn!" The space beneath the leg was choked with mangled debris from the radar platform's underside.

They were through—

The raised arm hit the girder with a crash, the base of the claw catching its edge—and acting as a pivot. The *Sharkdozer* swung sharply upward, before the strain on the already damaged manipulator became too much and half the claw was wrenched away. Matt jammed the thrusters into reverse to stop his sub from plowing into the wall of curved concrete above.

Behind, the girder shuddered, a mournful groan of metal echoing through the freezing waters . . . then it broke free and dropped toward the seafloor.

It hit the Mako as it fell. The submersible was slammed to the seabed in a roiling cloud of silt. The impact flung the pilot against his control panel, knocking him unconscious.

Not that anybody aboard the *Sharkdozer* was in a position to celebrate. Even full reverse power was not enough to slow it in time to prevent the collision. Matt tried to swerve to turn a head-on impact into a glancing blow—

There was a hideous crunch as the tubular steel bumpers protecting the viewing bubble were flattened, the acrylic hemisphere itself grinding horribly against the concrete. Hairline cracks flicked out from the ragged line where the viewport had been abraded into opacity. Another, harder impact threw the sub's occupants around as the port-side arm was sheared from its mounting, taking an entire section of the outer hull with it and exposing the cylindrical pressure vessel of the crew compartment within. The LIDAR display went blank as the turret housing the scanning lasers was ripped away.

The *Sharkdozer* slewed round, only stopping when it thudded starboard-side-on against part of the SBX's crushed superstructure. Nina was first to recover. "Is everyone okay?"

Matt clutched his left hand, blood oozing from a deep gash. A red smear ran along a sharp edge of the instrument panel. "Got a bit of a wallop," he gasped as he attempted with little success to make light of the pain. "Eddie, you all right, mate?"

Eddie had ended up at the back of the compartment beneath the submersible's entrance hatch. Loose equipment lay all around him. "Took a laptop to the head, but apart from that, just fine," he said, giving the offending computer a nasty look. "Did we get him?"

Matt moved the *Sharkdozer* away from the wall. The submersible was slower to respond than ever. He managed to turn it about. "Yeah, yeah we did!" The Mako was pinned beneath the fallen girder.

"Great," said Nina, relieved, but still wary. "So where's the other—"

Six-inch spikes stabbed into the submersible's hull.

TWENTY-FOUR

The diver had followed the Mako into the arena and opened up with his ASM-DT. The underwater weapon spat its remaining nail rounds in a line along the *Sharkdozer*'s wounded port side. The cobalt-steel pressure hull was too strong for them to penetrate—though they still hit with enough force for their tips to punch into the metal, jutting like porcupine spines.

But the sub had a weaker point.

The last two rounds hit the viewing bubble. Even though it was thicker than the nails were long, they still tore into the transparent acrylic, stopping less than an inch from the inner surface. Gunshot snaps rang through the cabin as more cracks radiated outward from the points of impact.

"*Shit!*" It was the greatest expression of pure fear Nina or Eddie had ever heard from Matt as he flinched back from the damaged port.

Eddie scrambled forward. "How bad is it?"

"It could go at any time!" Even as they watched, one crack slowly lengthened with a rasping squeal.

The diver was changing his gun's magazine. "One more hit'll finish us," Eddie realized. They only had sec-

onds before the diver reloaded, and no way to stop
him—

Except one. The sub itself.

"Ram him!" Eddie barked.

"It could crack the port!" Matt protested.

"We're dead either way—do it!"

Matt unwillingly pushed the throttles forward. Occupied with reloading, the diver at first didn't realize the
danger—until the increasing brightness of the *Sharkdozer*'s lights made him look up. Startled, he froze for a
moment before grabbing the control stalk protruding
from his suit's chest and spinning up his own thrusters—

Too late. The submersible hit him, pushing him backward toward the sunken rig's leg. The damaged bubble
creaked alarmingly.

The deep suit was caught on the *Sharkdozer*'s mangled bumpers. The diver's thrusters surged, but he
couldn't break free. He hurriedly resumed his attempt to
reload the gun, finally seating the magazine. Pulling
back the charging handle, he pointed the rifle at the fractured dome—

The submersible drove him against the concrete. Even
at a speed of only a few knots, the *Sharkdozer*'s sheer
mass was enough to make it a crushing impact. The deep
suit's humped fiberglass back split open, an air hose tearing and releasing a surge of bubbles into the water.

But the diver himself was still alive, protected by the
suit's rigid shell. The collision shook him loose from the
bumper, leaving him floating as the sub slowly bounced
backward. He raised the gun again—

Eddie lunged over Matt's shoulder and slammed the
controls sideways with one hand—and shoved the
throttles to full with the other.

The thrusters pivoted in response, the *Sharkdozer* spinning on the spot. The vulnerable viewport swung away
from the diver—and the damaged starboard thruster pod
came at him. The exposed screw blades sliced through
the water in a vortex of froth—

The submersible juddered, the motor's whine replaced

by a meaty *thunk-thunk-thunk* before the thruster cut out, clogged. Another red light joined the many already on the instrument panel. Outside, the water also took on a distinctly crimson tint. The rifle slowly spun past, part of a gloved hand still clutching its grip.

"He's *definitely* screwed," said Eddie, breathing heavily.

Nina watched the gun land before focusing on something much closer: the damaged viewport. The crash had extended more of the cracks. "Matt, how long before this thing breaks?"

"No way to know," Matt admitted, backing the sub away from the expanding red haze. "It might last hours—or it could go in two seconds."

Eddie counted to two under his breath. "Well, we got past that, so let's hope it lasts for hours, eh?"

"We're still fucked even if it holds! We've only got one working thruster, so it'll take even longer to get to the surface, and in about five minutes the air's going to start going bad."

"How long can we last?" Nina asked.

"Three of us, in a compartment this size? Maybe ten minutes before we pass out, fifteen at most. Twenty minutes, tops, we'll be dead from carbon dioxide poisoning."

Eddie pursed his lips. "No way we can fix the air system?"

"Not from inside." Matt slumped in his seat. "I don't want to be the one who has to say this, but . . . we're dead."

"What about the other sub?" said Nina. The Mako's lights were still shining brightly. "Is there any way we can dock with it?"

The Australian pondered the question, then faint hope entered his voice. "It's got a standard docking connector, so yeah . . . but we'd have to get it out from under that girder first."

Eddie returned to the arm controls. "We got enough power to move it?"

"Have to chance it."

Matt was about to guide the *Sharkdozer* toward the pinned sub when Eddie told him to wait. "Just let me get something first . . ." He worked the remaining arm, extending the undamaged secondary manipulator. "Take us down, over there. I'm going to pick up the gun."

"What for?" asked his wife.

Eddie nodded at the other submersible. The pilot was visible through its windows, still unconscious. "Just in case we get aboard and he wakes up." He lowered the arm to the seabed. It took him several attempts, but the steel digits eventually gripped the weapon. "Okay, got it." He shook off the dead hand, then moved the manipulator above the *Sharkdozer* and dropped the ASM-DT onto its top hatch with a clank.

Matt brought his injured vessel about and headed for the Mako. For the first time, they got a proper look at their opponent. While designed as a pleasure craft, able to take passengers down to a thousand feet below the surface, this one had been modified for a more aggressive purpose. A rack had been crudely welded to its flank to hold torpedoes, one of which was still in place.

"Bit of a botch-job," said Matt, scrutinizing the weapon with his engineer's eye. The torpedo was the underwater equivalent of an improvised explosive device, a length of metal pipe propelled by compressed air. A package of explosives with a simple impact detonator was crammed inside.

"They work well enough," said Nina, remembering the fate of Hayter's sub.

"Yeah. Looks like it was put together in a hurry, though."

"To kill us," Eddie said. "Or Nina, specifically. It's this bloke Glas, it's got to be."

"But how did he know we were here?" asked Nina.

"Maybe you can ask him when you see him," said Matt.

"What do you mean?"

"I mean, he's probably around here somewhere. This

sub couldn't have gotten out here on its own—it doesn't have enough range. It's got to have a mother ship. So if the pilot's still alive, he might tell you how to find it—and Glas."

Eddie clenched his fists. "He'll tell us."

"We've got to get aboard it first," Nina reminded him.

Matt moved the sub closer to the trapped craft. "Eddie, let me do that," he said, taking the manipulator controls. "This might be a bit tricky . . ."

He nudged the girder with what was left of the main arm. Their sub swayed beneath them. "I was afraid of that—I don't know if we'll be able to get enough leverage with only one thruster. Okay, Eddie, you keep it pushed against that beam. I'll see if I can shift it."

A tense minute passed as he applied power, the *Sharkdozer* swinging back and forth as the arm rasped against the girder. The beam slowly ground along the Mako's hull. "Come on, a bit more," said Eddie. "We can do it!"

"I'm giving it all she's got!"

A shrill screech echoed through the water as the arm slipped, gouging a foot-long scratch out of the rusting metal. Eddie choked back an expletive, trying to hold the manipulator in place. The girder was still moving, inch by inch, but he didn't know if it was enough . . .

The thruster's whine fluctuated. "We're losing power!" Matt cried. "Eddie, push it!"

Last chance—

Eddie shoved the arm forward. The *Sharkdozer* lurched—then the girder came free, scraping noisily over the Mako before dropping off its stern to whump down on the silt and wreckage below.

The *Sharkdozer* drifted to a stop alongside the other sub. "Okay, but we're not done yet," said Matt. "We need to lift it up so we can dock with its bottom hatch."

"But there's another hatch on the top, right there," said Eddie.

"Yeah, but we've only got a topside hatch, and I don't think the '*dozer*'ll take kindly to being turned upside down in the state she's in! There's a crane hook on its top—if you can grab it, we should be able to lift it. It's neutrally buoyant, so it'll stay put once we've moved it. I hope."

Another precious minute passed as Eddie, craning to see through the viewport, tried to get hold of the hook. Finally, it seemed to be secured. Matt checked the status of the air supply, grimaced, and with a mutter of "Better get on with it, then," powered up the thruster again.

The arm creaked and strained, but held. In a swirl of sand, the conjoined vessels slowly rose . . .

A new alarm sounded, a mournful, pulsing honk. "Oh God, what now?" moaned Nina.

"We're on emergency power," said Matt. "If you hear that, it means if you're not on the surface in five minutes, you're not getting there at all!"

"You built this bloody thing," said Eddie. "Couldn't you have used a less annoying alarm noise?"

Matt huffed and switched it off. "Next one I build'll have songbirds and heavenly choirs, just for you. If I get the chance." He looked down through the viewport. They were now about twenty feet above the ground. "Okay, that'll have to do."

Eddie released the arm, and Matt took the sub back down, inching it sideways to move beneath the Mako as it hung motionless in the water. The spotlights picked out its ventral docking port. "Okay, here we go." He switched one of the monitors to show a view looking directly upward from their own hatch. "Just got to line it up properly . . ."

"Can we do anything to help?" asked Nina.

"Yeah—wait by the hatch, and when I tell you, pull the yellow lever down as far as it'll go. That'll lock the docking clamps. Soon as they're secure, I can drain the collar and we should be able to open the other sub's hatch."

There was an edge to his voice that suggested he was far more worried about the operation than he was letting on. "Matt, is something wrong?"

"There's a lot of things wrong!" On the screen, the Mako's hatch came in sight. He slowed to line up with it. "You just get ready on that lever."

Eddie and Nina exchanged concerned looks but moved to the hatch as requested. The *Sharkdozer* stopped beneath the other vessel. "Okay, it's lined up. Here we go . . ."

A brief blip of the throttle, and the *Sharkdozer* wobbled upward. A shrill of metal against metal was overpowered by a louder *thunk* that reverberated through the hull. More power, then: "Pull it!"

Eddie and Nina grabbed the lever and hauled on it with all their combined weight. It moved a few inches—then jammed. "Matt!" Nina shouted. "It's stuck!"

Matt didn't reply, eyes fixed on the monitor. He turned the sub a few degrees before sharply bringing it upward. The vessel shook with another impact. "Now!"

This time, the lever moved all the way. A dull clunk came from above the hatch as the clamps locked into place, holding both submersibles tightly together. Matt gasped. "Ah, Christ! I wasn't sure that was going to work."

"Now he tells us!" said Nina, releasing her own sigh of relief.

A loud hiss of compressed air as the water was forced out told them that the docking collar was clear. Matt double-checked a gauge to make sure the seal was holding, then cautiously unlocked the hatch and pushed it open. Nina jumped as seawater gushed over the edge of the opening, but it was merely the last undrained dregs. Matt raised the hatch higher. The ASM-DT clattered down into the crew compartment, Eddie catching the rifle before it hit the deck.

The Mako's belly hatch was visible at the top of the docking collar, cold drips falling from the white-painted steel. "Can we get in?" Nina asked. "Is it locked?"

Matt climbed the ladder and pulled the other hatch's release latch before turning the wheel to unseal it. "Submarine theft's not exactly an everyday problem, so no."

"Just because you saved our lives, that doesn't give you the right to be a smart-ass." But she managed to smile at him.

He opened the hatch. There was a rush of air as the two vessels equalized their internal pressures. Matt was about to ascend the second ladder when Eddie stopped him. "Better let me go first," he said, holding up the gun. "Just in case."

He clambered up, stopping below the top of the shaft and peering warily into the cabin. No movement. Gun ready, he climbed the rest of the way.

The only sound was the low hum of the ventilation system. The cabin was almost infinitely more luxuriously appointed than the *Sharkdozer*'s pure utilitarianism, leather loungers arranged to give each passenger a view through a personal porthole. But Eddie's eyes were fixed on one seat in particular: the pilot's.

Its back was to him, but he could see an arm hanging limply over one side. Fixing the gun on the chair, he advanced to find the pilot alive, but out cold, face bloodied.

One of the monitors, he noticed, showed what looked like a navigation chart. At its center was what he took to be the Mako's current position, a red line weaving away from it. A record of its course?

"Is it safe?" Nina called, head poking over the top of the hatchway like Kilroy.

"Yeah," Eddie answered. He jabbed the pilot with the rifle. The man moaned faintly. Nina ascended, followed by Matt. "Matt, what do you make of this?" He pointed at the map screen.

"It's an inertial navigation system."

"Is that line its route?"

The Australian took a closer look at the display. "Yeah, it came from . . ." He looked back at Eddie. "The start point's less than four kilometers from here! And it's not on the surface—there's a depth tracker as well. The mother ship's another submarine."

"A sub that keeps smaller subs inside it?" Nina asked,

skeptical. "Does anyone even *make* submarines like that? We're not in a Bond movie!"

"Yeah, they exist. If a mega-yacht's not showy enough for you, there are companies that build them—if you've got the money. There's the Phoenix 1000, and I know that a Russian firm had a couple on the stocks a few years ago."

"Glas would have the money," said Eddie.

"Maybe," said Nina. "But what do we do now?"

"We should get you back to the surface," said Matt. He headed down the cabin.

"Where are you going?" Eddie asked.

"Got to detach the *Sharkdozer*, mate! It's way too big and heavy for this thing to drag along." He dropped into the other submersible.

Again, Nina picked up on something in his voice—a forced lightness, cheer covering concern—and this time Eddie noticed it too. "Matt, what're you doing?" he called as metallic clunks came from below. He and his wife exchanged worried looks, then rushed for the docking port. "Matt!"

They reached it just in time to see the *Sharkdozer*'s hatch slam shut. The latches closed. "Christ, what's he up to?" Eddie said, jumping down. He tried to reopen the hatch; the handle moved fractionally before sticking. The Australian had wedged it with something. He thumped a fist on the steel. "Matt!"

Matt's voice crackled from the *Sharkdozer*'s underwater PA system. "Sorry, mate, but I've got to do this. The only way I can release the docking clamps is from in here—and the moment I do, the collar will flood. So you need to shut that hatch so you can get out of here."

"No!" said Nina in horror. "We can't leave you! There—there's got to be another way!"

"There isn't. Like I said, the Mako can't haul this thing with it."

"But you'll . . ." Her breath caught. "Matt, you'll *die*."

"Not necessarily. I got a load of fresh air in here when we docked, and since there's only one person aboard now, it might last long enough for me to reach the surface."

"Bullshit!" said Eddie. "You said it was about to run out of power!" He yanked at the handle again, but it still refused to move.

"For Christ's sake," Matt said, "will you two listen to me and do what I tell you for once? *Someone* has to release the clamps from in here. The *Sharkdozer*'s my sub, I designed it—and now I've found out that not having a remote release is kind of a serious design flaw! So, ah . . . it's my responsibility."

"No way." Eddie started to climb back into the Mako. "I'll wake up that twat in the driver's seat and make him do it."

"Yeah? How's that going to work? You going to threaten to shoot him through a thick steel hatch?" A resigned sigh came through the speaker. "Eddie, you're a great mate, but you're really not as smart as you think you are."

Eddie stopped. "Would you have ever said that to my face?"

"Why do you think I waited until there was a thick steel hatch between us?" Both men were trying to sound jocular, but their attempts fell very flat.

"Matt, please," begged Nina. "You can't do this."

"If I don't, *none* of us'll get out of this. So please, just . . . just shut the hatch." A tremble entered his voice. "I'm going to release the clamps in twenty seconds, so if you don't want to get very wet, that's how long you've got."

"You can't—"

"Nina, I have to. You never know, maybe the batteries will last, maybe the dome'll hold up. There's always a chance. Hey, I've survived everything else I've been through with you, right?" The last few words were almost choked by barely contained emotion.

Nina's feelings were more open, tears running down her face. "Oh God, Matt . . ." With deep reluctance, she put her hands against the hatch and began to push it shut.

Eddie joined her. "This is wrong," he muttered, face tight. "It's fucking wrong."

"Twenty," came the Australian's voice over the intercom. "Nineteen. Eighteen . . ."

The hatch closed with a hollow bang, muffling Matt's countdown. Eddie stonily closed the latch mechanism and turned the wheel to seal it. A red light on the cabin wall turned green.

Both hatches were secured.

They faintly heard Matt say "Ten," followed after a pause by "Well. No point dragging it out, eh? Good luck to you both."

Nina gripped Eddie's wrist with one hand, the other clenched into a fist over her mouth. "Good luck, Matt," she whispered.

Eddie's voice was barely louder. "Fight to the end, mate."

Metal scraped below—then the Mako shook as water slammed against the bottom of the hatch. The *Shark-dozer* had separated, the ocean surging back into the docking collar.

Trailing bubbles, the stricken submersible drifted away into the darkness.

TWENTY-FIVE

The Mako's pilot slowly woke to a throbbing pain across his face.

A mushy splat of blood on the control panel revealed the cause. What had happened? Memories groggily returned. He had been chasing the IHA sub, about to unleash the last torpedo—then it had unexpectedly angled upward, and . . .

The rest was a blur. Something had hit the Mako, throwing him forward in his seat . . . then nothing. He had been knocked out. But he thought he had heard voices. How was that possible?

He squinted through the windows. No sign of the other sub—or the diver who had been with him. But something wasn't right.

It took him a few seconds to work out what. There were reflections in the Plexiglas . . . of people behind him.

He spun his chair around in alarm—to find the menacing barrel of an ASM-DT pointing at him. It fired, the single shot earsplitting in the confined space. A nail round stabbed into the seat between his legs, the metal spike less than an inch from his groin.

The man holding the gun gave him a nasty look. "If you don't do exactly what I tell you, the next one turns your bollocks into a shish kebab."

* * *

The Mako powered through the blackness.

Eddie and Nina had debated—more accurately, argued—over their next action while waiting for the pilot to wake up. Eddie's first thought had been to try to help Matt. But the pleasure submarine lacked manipulator arms, so had no way to release the *Sharkdozer*'s ballast. And by the time the pilot recovered and was coerced at gunpoint into getting under way, the other submersible had disappeared. Whether Matt was making a genuine attempt to return to the surface or had merely moved off to deter them from going after him they had no way of knowing: The Mako had no sonar beyond a very basic depth finder.

So, extremely reluctantly, they had turned to other options. The most obvious was returning to the surface. But the track on the inertial navigation system ultimately swayed the argument in Nina's favor. Their attackers had come from a mother vessel, a submarine . . . and it seemed likely that Glas was aboard it. Wanted internationally for multiple crimes, and with the Group's agents hunting for him, where better for the errant billionaire to hide? It explained the intermittency of his communications with his "partner," Dalton: Something as simple as making a phone call was impossible hundreds of feet beneath the sea.

The architect of everything that had happened—the man responsible for all the lives that had been lost—was just over two miles away. As Nina pointed out, it seemed a waste not to pay him a visit while they had a chance . . . and a torpedo.

"So, is your boss on this sub?" Eddie demanded, poking the rifle against the pilot's side to encourage a truthful answer.

"Yes, yes," he replied, dry-mouthed. "Herr Glas is there."

"How many others?"

"About ten."

"*About* ten, or *exactly* ten?" The gun pushed harder against his ribs.

"Okay, okay! More than ten. Ah . . . twelve."

"Sure?"

"Yes, yes, twelve! You killed two others."

"I'll make it three if you piss me about again." Eddie gave him one final jab with the barrel, then moved back to join Nina. "You sure about this?" he asked her quietly.

She shook her head, but said, "It's the only chance we've got to end this. Otherwise Glas'll just keep sending people after us. After *me*. Even if I manage to stay alive, other people will still get killed in the crossfire. People like Matt, and Lewis, and the other people on that sub."

"So what are we going to do? Cruise up to his window, wave, then blow the fucker up?"

"I was thinking more of giving him the finger first," she said, with a faint attempt at a smile. "But we should talk to him before that. I didn't believe that Warden was telling us the whole story any more than you did, so we ought to find out Glas's side of it."

"*Then* blow the fucker up."

"If we have to." She looked back at the pilot. The dot representing the sub on the inertial navigator was approaching its origin point. "How much farther?" she asked him.

"About a quarter of a mile," the pilot replied nervously.

The couple moved forward for a better view as the Mako continued toward its destination. Nothing was visible yet, but a readout on the navigation screen ticked down the distance in meters. Four hundred and fifty, four hundred . . . "What if it's moved?" Nina wondered, still not seeing anything. "Maybe they figured out that something went wrong and took off."

"Then we go back to the surface, and Chuckles here takes a swim with the sharks," said Eddie.

The pilot gulped. "It will be there, it will be!"

Three hundred meters. Their prisoner looked from side to side for any sign of the mother ship. Two hundred, and the pilot's hands visibly trembled as he reduced speed. "I think they've buggered off," Eddie growled, hefting the ASM-DT.

"No, no, they will be here!" the pilot squealed. "They will be, they will—*there*!"

He pointed off to the left. A faint line of lights appeared through the murk.

As they closed, the line grew longer. And longer.

"Wow," said Nina, unable to conceal her amazement. "That's a *big*-ass submarine."

The craft bearing the lights gradually took on form. The mother ship was well over two hundred feet long, a sleek white shape resembling an ultramodern megayacht—but one with the ability to plunge beneath the waves on a whim. Large circular portholes ran along the length of its hull, a long wraparound window marking the bridge atop the elevated, streamlined superstructure. "Must have cost a few bob," said Eddie.

"Ninety million dollars," the pilot volunteered.

"Did I ask for a fucking brochure?" The man fell silent, cowed.

Nina spotted movement through a porthole. "Shit, they'll see us!" She hunched down, tugging at Eddie's sleeve for him to do the same. "Where do we dock?"

"Behind the bridge," the pilot hesitantly answered, "or on the keel."

"Go to the top one," Eddie told him, pushing the gun behind his ear. The man obediently guided the Mako upward.

"You sure?" Nina asked.

"Be a lot easier for us to get out by jumping down than climbing up. We'll need to move fast."

The larger submarine slid past the windows as its offspring moved into docking position. The area aft of the superstructure was revealed as a flat deck; on the surface, it could be used by passengers to enjoy the sunlight, but underwater it acted as a landing platform. Bright lights revealed a port set into it.

"Can you dock on your own?" Eddie asked the pilot.

"Yes, it's—it's automatic."

"Good. Where does the hatch open, and how many people will be there?"

"The docking port goes into the engine room. I don't know how many people will be inside—three or four, usually."

"But there might be more," Nina said. "Coming to congratulate you for killing us."

"They won't be celebrating for long," said Eddie grimly. "All right, dock this thing."

Sweating, the pilot maneuvered the Mako into position. A graphic of the docking port appeared on a monitor, crosshairs guiding him into the perfect position. A series of bleeps, and the crosshairs turned green; he pushed a button, and the computers took over to lower the sub into position. A couple of bumps and clanks from below, then the engines shut down as flashing text on the screen announced that the minisub had docked safely.

"That everything you need to do?" Eddie asked. The pilot nodded. "Cheers, then." He smashed the rifle's butt against the man's head, knocking him back into unconsciousness. "You're fucking lucky I didn't kill you."

"What next?" said Nina as they headed for the hatch. "I don't want to rush down there without knowing who's waiting."

"We don't have to," Eddie replied. "We'll let them come to us."

* * *

At the bottom of the docking connector, two of the submarine's crew watched as an engineer released the hatch, stepping back from the residual drips of water before looking up into it. The Mako's own hatch was already open at the top.

But nobody was coming down it.

Seconds passed. "Where is he?" asked one of the men, moving closer to see for himself. The submersible's cabin lights were off.

"I don't know," said the engineer. He called up through the hatch. "Moritz?" No answer. Giving his companions a look of concern, he tried again. "Moritz! What's the problem?"

"Yours," said Eddie, stepping out of the gloom and firing the rifle down the shaft.

The nail round hit the engineer in the face and went straight through his head, bursting out behind one ear in a bloody spray. The man standing beside him only had time to flinch in shock before a second sharpened spike plunged into the top of his chest and ripped open his heart. Both corpses crashed down on the deck.

The third man turned to flee. Behind him, Eddie dropped from the docking port with a bang. Another shot, and six inches of steel punched through the running man's upper back to clang off the bulkhead beyond.

There was only one exit from the chamber. Eddie stepped over the bodies and opened a hatch to find a flight of steep metal stairs leading down into the submarine's engine room. Two more crewmen were in the compartment, one staring up at him in stunned surprise, the other already sprinting toward a door. The Englishman tracked him and fired. The recoil from a nail round was different from that of a bullet, but when the first smacked noisily into a bank of batteries just behind his target he immediately adjusted—and the next shot hit home, tearing into the man's neck.

He snapped the gun back at the other engineer—who was diving for a control panel. Eddie fired, but the man had already slapped his hand down on an alarm button—his last act on earth before the nail pierced his skull. A siren sounded, red lights flashing.

Nina emerged from the docking chamber. "So much for the stealthy approach!"

"It's not really my thing anyway." Eddie switched the ASM-DT to conventional ammunition and ran down the stairs. "Okay, what's a good thing to break?"

As well as the batteries, the two-deck-high room housed a pair of diesel engines for use when the submarine was on the surface, plus electrical generators and hydraulic pumps. But what caught his eye were two identical sets of machinery, complex networks of pipes and valves connected to large metal cylinders. Both systems were hooked to overhead ducts that led through the forward bulkhead into other parts of the sub. Eddie was no engineer, but it seemed a safe bet that the machines were part of the submarine's air supply. "Nina!" he shouted as he hurried across the room. "Find an intercom and tell Glas we want to talk to him."

She descended the stairs, spotting a panel with a telephone-like handset near the door. "What if he refuses?"

"Then he'll have trouble breathing!" He reached the nearer of the two machines. A prominent warning sticker told him that the device was an oxygen generator, using chemical reactions both to create and to recycle the life-sustaining gas, and that the greatest potential danger from it was potassium chlorate burns. That was, in an odd way, reassuring: Since it didn't store compressed oxygen in pressurized tanks, there was far less risk of an explosion.

He still retreated to what he hoped was a safe distance before taking aim. "Okay, Nina, get down!" He waited for her to duck behind the batteries—then fired.

The bullets tore into the generator's pipework. A pump shattered, gas escaping with a shrill hiss. The rest of the machinery rattled furiously for several seconds before rasping to a stop. Warning lights flicked on.

Nina hesitantly raised her head. "What did you do?"

"Took out one of their oxygen generators. There's a backup, but I've got enough bullets left to fuck that up too. Get on the phone and let them know. Oh, and say that if they try to force their way in here, we've wired the place to blow."

"We have?"

"No, but they don't know that!"

He found a toolbox and took out a crowbar as Nina went to the intercom and picked up the handset. "Hello, hi," she said into it. "This is Nina Wilde calling for Harald Glas—I guess you know me, since you've been trying to kill me for the past week. I just wanted to tell you that we've destroyed one of your oxygen generators, and we'll take out the other one if we don't hear from you in, oh . . . thirty seconds?"

Eddie used the crowbar to jam the hatch's handle. "Bit casual, and I would've told him to surrender straight off, but not bad. You're getting the hang of this whole being-threatening lark."

"Everyone at the IHA thinks I've already got it." Eddie moved back to cover the hatch as Nina waited for a reply. The seconds ticked by. "Is he going to answer?"

Eddie grinned crookedly. "Maybe we caught him while he was taking a dump. Even billionaires have to crap."

"There's a delightful thought," she said with a disgusted sigh.

Still nothing but silence from the intercom. Eddie eyed the remaining oxygen generator. Now that the threat had been made, they might have to go through with it . . .

A click from the handset. "Dr. Wilde. This is Harald Glas."

Nina switched the intercom to speaker mode so Eddie could hear. "First things first. If you try to break in here, we'll destroy the other oxygen generator, and the engines and batteries too. You'll be trapped down here. You got that?"

"I hear you." The Dane's voice was sonorous, measured, calm even under threat. "What do you want from me?"

"I want you to stop trying to kill my wife, for start-
ers," said Eddie. "Then if we're still making deals,
maybe also an Aston Martin. And a pony."

"You're as irreverent as I've heard, Mr. Chase."

"You seem very well informed about us," Nina said.

Glas didn't offer a response to that, instead saying, "I
assume you wish to see me in person."

"Yeah, that's right," Eddie replied. "You get your arse
down here—alone."

A brief hesitation. "I'm afraid that's not possible.
But . . . I will send a representative to bring you to me.
A hostage, if you prefer." The background hiss from the
speaker briefly cut out as Glas closed the mike; Nina
guessed that the newly appointed "hostage" was un-
happy about the arrangement. "They will be with you
shortly. Alone, as you wished."

"And unarmed," said Nina.

Another muted pause. "Agreed."

"If we see anyone else on the way to you, I'll shoot
your friend and blow up the engines," Eddie told him.
"So get everyone to lock themselves in the galley or
wherever."

"It will be done," said Glas. The intercom fell silent.

"You trust him?" Nina asked Eddie before answering
her own question. "Of course not."

"Go upstairs and wait in the air lock. If anything happens, get back into the sub and take off."

"I don't know how to drive the thing," she told him as
she ascended. "I don't even know how to detach it from
this sub."

"Bash every button until something happens, that's
my usual trick."

"Yeah, that's why I don't let you use my laptop." She
pushed the hatch until it was slightly ajar and she could
see out through the narrow gap.

Before long, someone knocked on the door. Eddie
looked up at Nina. "Well, here we go," he said, freeing
the crowbar from the handle before returning to cover.
"Okay, open it. Slowly!"

He held his finger tightly on the trigger as the door eased open; if he saw a weapon, he was ready to fire instantly. But instead a pair of slender black-gloved hands came into view, fingers spread wide to show they were not carrying anything. "Well?" said a familiar aristocratic voice, filled with irritation. "May I come in?"

Eddie could hardly believe it. "Oh, for fuck's sake!"

"Charming as ever, Eddie." Sophia Blackwood leaned through the opening, taking in the rifle pointed at her. "You can put that down; I'm not armed."

"I'll check that for myself. Shut the door, then put your hands against it."

Sophia impatiently complied. Eddie pushed the ASM-DT's muzzle against her back and performed a one-handed pat-down. He knew his ex-wife well enough to be unsurprised to find she had lied. "Not armed, eh?" he said as he pulled a compact Glock 36 pistol from the waistband of her black leather trousers beneath her blouse. "I should just shoot you on fucking principle. Glas thought he could use you to kill us, did he?"

"Actually, Harald doesn't even know I have that gun," she said as he finished his search. She looked up at Nina, who had cautiously emerged from the docking chamber. "It's got quite an interesting story, actually."

"Really," said Eddie, not caring. "You should send it to a publisher—maybe it'll outsell Dan Brown."

"I'm sure Nina will want to hear it. Part of it takes place in Rome."

Eddie stepped back, keeping the rifle fixed on Sophia. "Nina, take this," he said, holding out the Glock.

His wife quickly descended the stairs. "What *about* Rome?" she demanded. "What the hell was going on there? Your buddy killed Agnelli, and was about to kill me when—"

"When I shot him. Yes, I do remember—I was there," Sophia snarked.

Nina took the gun from Eddie. Checking, she found that it was fully loaded with a round already chambered. "And why *were* you there?"

Sophia gave her a patronizing look. "It's all rather complicated."

"Well, gee, if only I were a PhD so I could understand. Wait, whaddya know!" She put the magazine back into the weapon, making sure Sophia heard the click as it seated. "You can explain on the way to Glas."

"Oh, very well. If Eddie will let me take my hands off this door."

"Go ahead," he told her. "By the way, what's with the gloves? The air in a submarine bad for your cuticles?"

Her expression became considerably more hostile. "Actually, I have you to thank for that. And this." She brought up her left hand to point with her index finger at the scar running down her face; her ring and little fingers remained strangely rigid beneath the expensive black leather. "When you threw me off that cliff in Switzerland—"

"When he tackled you over it to stop you from shooting me," Nina reminded her.

"Whatever. The point remains that my dear ex-husband used me to cushion himself on the way down." Acid on her tongue, Sophia opened the door. Eddie glanced through. The corridor was clear. "I came out of the experience rather worse off than he did."

"I broke a rib and punctured a lung!" Eddie objected.

"And I lost *half my fucking hand*!" With a genuine flare of anger, she tugged off her left glove—revealing that a chunk the size of a large bite was missing from the edge of her palm, replaced, along with the two fingers above it, by a waxy prosthesis attached with an elastic strap. "It got torn off on a rock, and before I even had time to realize what had happened I hit another one—face-first." She turned the injured side of her face to them. Even after surgery to repair it, the scar was still ragged and deep. Despite her loathing for Sophia, Nina couldn't help feeling a pang of sympathy.

But only a pang. The Englishwoman was a ruthless multiple murderer, killing without a qualm anyone who threatened to obstruct her goals. Both Nina and Eddie had been in her sights on more than one occasion. "Well, sorry to hear that," she said lamely. "Okay, let's go."

Eddie was tempted to make some tasteless hand-themed joke, but restrained himself. Like Nina he had found the sight shocking, though for different reasons. Sophia had been his wife, after all, and to see the face he had known so well ravaged by injury was unsettling.

Scar aside, though, it was not quite as he remembered. "Who arranged for the plastic surgery?" he asked as Sophia put the glove back on and went through the door. He followed, keeping the gun fixed on her back; Nina cautiously took up the rear with the Glock at the ready. "Glas, I'm assuming."

"Yes," said Sophia, hands raised as she led them down the passage. "I knew him before I met you again in New York."

"When you say you *knew* him . . . ," said Nina suspiciously.

Sophia blew out an exasperated breath. "I seem to have acquired a reputation as a woman who sleeps with every wealthy and powerful man she meets."

"Oh, I wonder why?" Eddie muttered.

"But yes, I did."

"I might have bloody known!"

"It was after my father died, and the jackals in the City stripped every last morsel of flesh from his company's bones to leave me with nothing. I still had my title, so—to be bluntly mercenary about it—I was looking for a man with resources I could use to get my revenge. Harald was one potential suitor, as it were."

Eddie made a disgusted sound. "Along with René Corvus, Richard Yuen, Victor Dalton . . ."

"He wasn't the best choice at the time, I'll be frank. But he was still infatuated with me."

"What man wouldn't be?" Nina said sarcastically. "I mean, on average there's only a fifty percent chance that you'll kill them."

"It's not even close to fifty percent," Sophia replied,

irked at the accusation. "I didn't kill Gabriel Ribbsley. Or Joe Komosa, or—"

"Enough, Jesus!" Eddie cut in. "I don't need to hear the fucking list. The *literal* fucking list."

She gave him a small cat-like smile, pleased to have needled him once more. "But anyway, I managed to drag myself out of the lake not far from the waterfall and broke into a nearby house. I didn't know whom to call at first, but then I remembered that Harald had a residence in Switzerland for tax reasons. I had no idea whether or not he would actually be there, but as it turned out, he was."

"So he came and rescued you," said Nina. "Even knowing what you'd done—that you tried to nuke New York?"

"The human heart is a very forgiving thing."

"Like you'd know," Eddie scoffed.

"Cynicism is *so* unattractive in a man, Eddie. Up here." They reached a flight of stairs to the next deck. Eddie checked the passage and nearby doorways, but so far it appeared that Glas had been true to his word and ordered the crew to stay out of their way. They ascended. "But he got me medical treatment, without telling the authorities that I was still alive, and then for a while I was his . . ." She hesitated, as if her mouth had suddenly gone dry. "His *guest*. But," she continued, brushing the odd pause aside, "you know me, I do dislike being out of the loop. So I persuaded Harald to let me get more involved in his work. Which is when I learned that he was a member of the Group."

"I gather they weren't happy when they found out Glas had been protecting you," said Nina, remembering their conversation with Travis Warden.

"They were not," Sophia replied, sounding amused by the fact. "At first, they wanted me dead. Fortunately, Harald has always been something of an iconoclast, so he stood up to the rest of the Group. Then, and now. He split from them over a matter of conscience."

"Some conscience," Eddie said scathingly. "Seeing as he wants Nina dead."

She gave them a saccharine smile. "Every cloud, as they say. But I'll let him explain his reasons himself."

They continued down another hallway along the upper deck, heading for the submarine's bow. "Glas rescued you and talked the rest of the Group out of killing you," mused Nina. "So after all that he did for you . . . why did you shoot his guy in the back in Rome?"

The smile returned, this time knowingly conspiratorial. "Let's just say that it would be best for everyone, myself included, if you kept that to yourself for now."

"Glas doesn't know?"

"Maybe we should turn you in," Eddie suggested.

"Maybe *I* should remind you that I saved Nina's life in Rome. I could have let Harald's man kill her—I could even have killed her myself. But I chose not to."

"Without wanting to sound ungrateful," said Nina, "why?"

"There's a lot more going on than you think. But here we are, so remember what I just said." A set of polished wooden double doors marked the end of the hallway. She raised a hand to open them.

"Careful now," warned Eddie, pushing the gun into her back once more.

"For God's sake, Eddie," she complained. "He agreed to talk to you, and believe it or not, that's what he'll do. He's very much a man of his word."

"You'll forgive us if we don't entirely trust him," said Nina. "Or you."

Sophia knocked. "Harald? Your *hostage* has brought your guests."

"Come in" came Glas's voice from the room beyond. Sophia opened the doors.

Eddie used her as a shield, quickly checking for potential threats in what was revealed as an observation lounge, large circular windows looking out into the ocean's depths. But visitors to the room were more likely to be wowed by the wonders within than outside.

Rarity was the theme of the small but incredibly valuable collection, Nina immediately saw. One stand contained coins arranged on red velvet, among them a gold 1933 Saint-Gaudens Double Eagle—one of the most sought-after and expensive pieces in the world, worth many millions more than its original twenty-dollar face value. Another stand held stamps, the Swedish Treskilling Yellow at its center also priced in the millions. Further treasures were arranged around the room: bottles of vintage wine, a first folio of Shakespeare's plays, a leaf of Mozart's *Sinfonia Concertante* with annotations by the composer himself, and more.

Another, less obvious theme, she realized, was that everything was relatively small and easily transportable. Their owner was on the run; he had brought with him probably only a fraction of the rare items he possessed.

The man in question was waiting for them at the room's center. Their enemy. Harald Glas.

TWENTY-SIX

He was in his early fifties, with slightly unkempt graying hair, strong jaw blue with stubble. His tall, lean body had the build of a runner—but the Dane would not be racing again. He was confined to a wheelchair. Nina was startled; she'd had no idea that he was disabled.

"I'm not armed, Mr. Chase," he said as Eddie pointed the rifle at him. "And thanks to the Group's assassins"—his eyes flicked down at his immobile legs—"I am no longer a physical threat."

The gun didn't lower as the Englishman approached. "I'll be the judge of that. Hands up. Nina, if Davros here tries anything, shoot him."

Nina aimed the Glock as Eddie searched Glas, then the wheelchair. Satisfied that he had told the truth, Eddie finally lifted his finger from the ASM-DT's trigger and rejoined Nina.

"Thank you," said Glas. "Now, I imagine you have questions for me."

"Or we could just kill you," Eddie told him.

Glas was uncowed by the threat. "Then you will never find out what is truly going on—and the threat faced by the world." His gaze moved to Nina. "A threat that you are part of, even though you don't realize it."

"Well, now's your chance to enlighten me," said Nina, watching Sophia warily as she moved to stand beside Glas. "You've been trying to kill me. Why?"

"Travis Warden has probably told you a tall tale about me, yes? That I am opposed to the Group's plan to save the planet because it will wipe out my profits? And that by killing you I can prevent the Group from finding the Atlantean meteorite they need to channel earth energy."

"Something like that."

Glas nodded. "What would you say if I told you that controlling such energy is only a minor part of the Group's true goals?"

"I actually wouldn't be too surprised," Nina told him with a humorless smile. "I didn't trust him any more than I trust you."

"Then you are perceptive, as well as a survivor. Warden is a leech and a liar—his only interests are power and money.".

"But you were happy to be part of his little Super Best Friends Club while it suited you."

Glas leaned forward. "The Group is . . . an exceptionally powerful organization. Its original members formed it from a collaboration of much older groups after the Second World War, with the aim of using global commerce to prevent such a conflict from ever happening again."

"It hasn't exactly done a great job," said a disapproving Eddie. "There've been wars pretty much the whole time since 1945."

"But not *massive* wars," Glas countered. "Not the kind that can smash entire industrialized countries and destroy the global economy. The Group's influence helped stop some of these flashpoints from starting larger fires. A word to the right person at the right time can cool even the hottest head. For example, the Cuban Missile Crisis was not stopped because both sides saw sense—it stopped because they were *made* to see sense."

"You're trying to tell me the Group is a force for *good*?" said Nina in disbelief.

He was unapologetic. "That was its original intent, yes. And for twenty or thirty years, it was successful. But over time, power began to corrupt. An old and inevitable story. The Group stopped *influencing* the decisions of governments, and instead began *controlling* them."

"Buying power. People like Dalton."

"Yes, but on a greater scale than you can imagine. The Group holds power over senior politicians in more than a hundred countries. If you have ever wondered why the so-called left and right seem increasingly similar wherever you go, it is because both sides have the same backers. The more alike people think, the less conflict there will be among them. That is the Group's motivation. To end the wastefulness of conflict."

Eddie pursed his lips. "And that's bad because . . . ?"

"There are different ways to do so," Glas said. "The Khmer Rouge ended conflict in Cambodia by murdering anyone it considered a potential opponent—over two million people."

"So that's why the Group wants control of earth energy?" Nina asked. "To use it as a weapon?"

To her surprise, he chuckled. "No, no. Nothing that crude." His smile rapidly faded. "Are you familiar with the theory of exogenesis?"

The sudden change of subject left her briefly bewildered. "Uh . . . the basics, I guess. It's the idea that the earth was seeded with the building blocks of life by comets and meteorites. Or, if you take things a step farther, there's the concept of panspermia—that life itself was actually brought to earth after developing somewhere else." Eddie tried to contain a smirk. "Oh, God," she said impatiently. "*What?*"

"Come on. Pan*sperm*ia?"

His past and current wives were briefly united in eye-rolling disapproval. "He never changes, does he?" Sophia sighed.

"I'm afraid not," Nina replied. Eddie just shrugged. She turned back to Glas. "The sky stone that ultimately caused Atlantis's destruction, the meteorite—you think it was carrying exogenesitic material?"

"Is that even a real word?" Eddie said.

"Shush!"

Glas nodded. "Life, we believe, was brought to this planet four billion years ago by a meteorite. One single, very specific meteorite. It contained not only the naturally superconducting metal needed to channel an earth energy reaction, but also the proto-DNA from which all life on the planet evolved. The unmutated, pure, original form."

The words gave Nina an uncomfortable feeling of déjà vu. "That . . . that sounds an awful lot like Kristian Frost's plan," she said. "To use a sample of pure Atlantean DNA to create a biological weapon."

"I know."

"You know, or the Group knows?"

"Both. The Group considered Kristian Frost for membership, but chose not to approach him—partly because we distrusted his motives, but also because we knew the Brotherhood of Selasphoros was working against him. If the Group had known his true intentions before you uncovered them, it would have eliminated the threat."

"Eliminated *him*, you mean. Like you tried to eliminate me."

"I'm afraid that was the most direct way of stopping the Group's plan. They are well protected, but you were the weak link in the chain. I would apologize, but I was doing what I believed necessary for the future of the world."

"You've got one idea for the world's future," Eddie said angrily, "and the Group's got another. So what are they?" He raised the gun again. "Give me a reason why yours is so great and theirs is so terrible."

"As you wish." Again, Glas seemed unconcerned by the threat facing him, suffused by a calm confidence: the air of a man who believed utterly in his views and expected others to fall into line with them. "It is about . . . *freedom.*"

"Freedom?" said Nina. "That's . . . kinda vague. What sort of freedom? Freedom of expression, of movement, of thought, Jonathan Franzen's book, what?"

"Every kind of freedom. That is how the Group seeks to eliminate conflict, Dr. Wilde. Its goal is nothing less than the elimination of free will. Total control of every human being on the planet, now and forever."

Eddie frowned. "How? Using earth energy as a doomsday weapon—*Do what we say or we'll kill you?*"

"As I said, they are not that crude. Earth energy is only of minor interest to them. It is the DNA in the meteorite that they want. It's the key to their plans—to everything." His voice, his entire attitude, took on a new intensity. "The Group's power does not come only from money. It comes from *knowledge*—from information. Some of that knowledge has come from people you have encountered. The creation of a genetically engineered virus by the Frosts. The earth energy technology built by Jack Mitchell. Khalid Osir's life-prolonging yeast from the Pyramid of Osiris. Even the mass of data accumulated by Pramesh and Vanita Khoil's computers passed through their hands. All of it has helped form their ultimate plan, a plan they are now ready to carry out . . . a plan that depends on *you.*"

Nina was unnerved by the list of enemies past—and the idea that even after their defeats, they were still dangerous in the present. "So they need me to find the meteorite before they can do whatever they mean to do. How about you tell us what that actually *is?*"

"The implementation will be very complex, but the idea is extremely simple." Glas rotated his chair to face the ocean beyond the windows. "Every single organism on the planet descends from the DNA brought to earth by the Atlantean meteorite—the sky stone, as they called it. The genetic structures of modern life, everything from fish"—he gestured toward a porthole as an example flitted past—"to humans, are far more complicated after billions of years of mutation and evolution, but locked inside them is still that original code. Just as Kristian Frost needed a sample of pure Atlantean DNA as a reference point from which to create his virus, so the Group needs to find the pure DNA of the planet's first life to create theirs."

"They're making a virus?" said Eddie in alarm.

Glas turned back to his audience. "Not in the same way as Frost. His was a lethal weapon; theirs will be more subtle. It won't kill people—at least, not intentionally. There will almost certainly be a percentage of people who will suffer lethal side effects from the infection, however."

"But—but even one percent of the world's population would still be tens of millions of people," Nina pointed out.

"Yes. And the Group considers that acceptable. But killing people is not the purpose of the virus. Instead, it will *change* them."

"Change them how?" she asked, feeling increasingly chilled.

"Certain behavioral traits are genetic. Yes," he said, raising a hand as if to forestall an objection, "I know that behavior is also influenced by environment, but at a fundamental level some aspects are set from the moment of conception. Such as intelligence, or"—his eyes briefly flicked from Nina to Eddie—"aggression."

"Did I just get insulted there?" said Eddie. "Not a smart thing to do to a man holding a gun."

"On the contrary, I think you just proved his point," Sophia told him.

"One key trait," continued Glas, ignoring the interruption, "is *obedience*. You see it in animals; can a dog be easily trained, or will it constantly rebel and fight? The same is true of people. There are natural leaders, and natural followers, but to different degrees. What the Group intends to do is use a manufactured retrovirus to infect and alter the living human genome and strengthen those genes responsible for passive, obedient behavior at the expense of others likely to encourage resistance. These traits will be passed down through successive generations, until the whole world will happily accept the control of a self-chosen ruling elite."

Silence followed the revelation. "That sounds . . . hard to believe," Eddie eventually managed.

"You think so?" Glas turned again, staring out into the darkness. "Anyone can kill another person. *Controlling* another person is harder. If they succeed, though, the Group will control everyone beneath them—and their subjects will willingly obey, because they have no choice. Obedience will be programmed into their genes, as inescapable as the color of their skin. To end conflict, the price will be freedom." He looked back at them. "Is that a price you are willing to pay?"

Nina didn't answer, stunned by the implications of Glas's words. If he was telling the truth, then from birth to death people would be trapped in a life of placid submission to an authority over which they had no control, in which they had no voice. And worse, they would meekly accept such a system as the norm—as the only way to live. It was authoritarianism to a monstrous degree, a horrific *Brave New World* with no hope, or even thought, of escape or rebellion.

The image of Lola, heavy with her impending child, sprang into her mind. If the Group achieved its goal, the baby would face a grim future where every path had been mapped out in advance by someone else. No choices, no opportunity to find its own way through life . . .

"Can they actually do it?" she demanded. "I mean, if they got hold of the meteorite, and assuming it really is possible, how long would it take them to carry out this plan? Years? Months?"

"Weeks," Glas told her.

"Yeah, I was afraid you'd say that."

"Could be worse, could've been days," Eddie offered.

"They've already done a lot of the preliminary work," Sophia said, stepping forward, "by farming it out to genetic research companies they control—in pieces, so no-body sees the full picture."

"Until it's too late," Glas added ominously. "They are doing the same thing as the Frosts, and Khalid Osir and his brother. The theoretical work has already been car-ried out. All they need is a sample of the DNA to put it into practice. As soon as they obtain the meteorite, the plan will begin."

"So how long would it take to infect everybody?" Eddie asked.

"The virus would spread like any other highly infec-tious pathogen, such as an influenza strain. It could reach every country in the world within a year, and po-tentially have infected the entire worldwide population in three."

"What about a cure?" said Nina.

"The Group won't develop a cure. That would defeat the purpose of the virus. But they will have an immuniz-ing agent, a vaccine. They want to be sure they can choose who will be part of the elite. And like the virus, the vaccine will also work at the genetic level, passing down through generations. It will be the ultimate he-reditary dynasty, monopolizing power over mankind—over the human *will*. They must be stopped. At any cost."

"You were part of the Group," Nina said accusingly. "Couldn't you have talked them out of it?"

"The Group is, believe it or not, a democracy," Glas replied, clearly disgusted by the irony. "I was the only member who opposed the plan. When I took my opposition farther than just words, they . . . retaliated." He looked down at his useless legs. "They sent their new attack dog after me—Stikes. My people got me to safety, but only after I had been shot. I was lucky to survive."

"They tried to kill you?"

"They tried to *destroy* me, in every way. My life, my reputation, my business were all attacked. I was turned into a criminal without trial."

"I know how that feels," said Eddie.

"And you know what it is like to be on the run, Mr. Chase."

"Yeah. I didn't have my own personal submarine to use as a hideout, though." He waved a disparaging hand at the vessel around them. "Only way you could be any more like a Bond villain is if you had a white cat."

"It was the only place I could hide from the Group. I'm a businessman, not a soldier—my survival skills are in very different fields from yours. But even from here, I have been able to continue working against the Group. One of my subsidiary companies operates a Spanish fishing fleet; we surface and take on supplies from its trawlers out at sea."

"And when you surface, you also give orders to your people, right?" said Nina in a cold voice. "Orders like *Kill Nina Wilde*."

Glas nodded. "But that order can now be rescinded. All you have to do is one thing."

"Destroy the statues."

"Yes. Without them, the Group will not be able to find the meteorite. And without the meteorite, they cannot carry out their plan. Humanity's freedom will be protected."

"It still leaves a bunch of powerful arseholes in control, though," Eddie observed.

"But at least it will be possible to resist them."

"So we destroy the statues," said Nina. "Then what? Warden and his buddies will be kinda mad at us."

"They will. But in the end, they are businessmen and -women. Greed holds no grudges. Their time is too important to be wasted on revenge. No, they will not be pleased, but they will soon move on to other plans."

"And what about you?" asked Eddie. "You just going to cruise around underwater admiring your stamp collection for the rest of your life?"

A momentary twinge of Sophia's expression, quickly hidden, suggested that the idea was not one she relished, but Glas's own intentions were clearer. "I intend to *re-*

sist, Mr. Chase. Whatever the Group is doing, I will do what I can to oppose it."

"How will you know what it's doing?" said Nina.

"Some of their sources are also my sources. I may be in a wheelchair, but I am not yet out of the game." He brought himself closer to the couple. "So, what will you do?"

"I think . . . destroying the statues looks like the only option," said Nina reluctantly. Eddie nodded in agreement.

"Good. In that case, I shall return you to the surface. I assume the statues are hidden in New York?"

"That's right," said Eddie.

"I will have one of my people there as a witness when you destroy them. After that, our business will be concluded. If you wish, I will compensate you for the trouble I have caused you."

"I don't want your money," Nina said angrily.

Eddie shrugged. "A *bit* might be nice . . ."

"But I'll tell you who does deserve it," she continued, remembering what had happened in the ruins of Atlantis. "The families of the people your men killed today. There were three people in the submarine they blew up, and another one in—Matt!" she cried, suddenly hopeful. "Does this sub have sonar?"

◦ ◦ ◦

The air in the *Sharkdozer*'s cabin had become foul, hanging hot and heavy in the confined space. Even the intake of cleaner atmosphere from the Mako had ultimately made little difference.

Matt was slumped in the pilot's seat, breathing slowly and shallowly. But he knew his efforts to prolong his life were pointless. The ballast slab was still entangled by the mangled skids, trapping him eight hundred feet down, the meager dregs of energy left in the batteries nowhere near enough to haul the heavy submersible back to the surface. *A design flaw,* he thought groggily, engineer to the last. *Next time I'll use iron shot, not a slab . . .*

But there wouldn't be a next time. One by one, even the red warning lights on the instrument panels were going out, insufficient voltage remaining to keep their accusing glows alive. This was it: death in the darkness of the ocean he had spent his life exploring. *Suppose it was inevitable it'd end this way . . .* He felt a tear swelling in the corner of one eye, but no longer even had the strength to raise a hand to wipe it away.

Two lights left. One. Then that too winked out. The cabin was black, silent apart from his own labored breathing and the occasional creaks from the damaged viewport. With the sub now stationary, the strain on the acrylic hemisphere appeared to have eased, but he knew that on a microscopic level the immense pressure of the water outside was still relentlessly attacking the cracks.

Crushed into oblivion in a heartbeat, or slipping into unconsciousness and suffocation: Either way, he wouldn't know about it. He was about to close his leaden eyes to await fate's decision . . . when he realized that the darkness was receding.

But that was impossible. There was no light down here—

Matt was suddenly dazzled as brilliant beams swept into the cabin. Was he hallucinating—or were the stories of seeing bright light at the moment of death true? Were angels coming for him? But then a sharp jolt told him that he was still alive and lucid. Another vessel had just made contact with his submersible.

A *big* vessel, he saw as the spotlights went out, replaced by softer illumination from the other craft's interior. The *Sharkdozer* had been scooped up by the larger sub—and the ticking of a backup mechanical depth gauge revealed it was still ascending. What should have been a simple calculation took several seconds in his befuddled state, but if it continued upward at the same rate, he would be on the surface in a matter of minutes.

Even if he passed out from carbon dioxide poisoning, he could still be saved.

But who were his saviors?

The answer came as his vision adjusted to the light. The *Sharkdozer* was on the foredeck of a luxury submarine, its steeply raked bridge directly ahead of him. Two blurry figures came into focus through its windows, one stocky and balding, the other slimmer and red-haired. They waved at him.

Somehow, he found the energy to return the gesture. "Guess I'm not dead," the Australian gasped, with a feeble smile. "No way are *they* angels . . ."

TWENTY-SEVEN

New York City

The case containing the three statuettes sat open on Nina's office desk. Eddie lifted one of the trio from the protective foam bed, dancing it between its companions as if playing with a toy soldier. "Hard to believe these crappy little things caused so much trouble."

"And cost so many lives," said Nina morosely. After Glas had returned them to the survey ship—its crew astonished by the sight of the huge submarine emerging from the depths alongside them—Matt had been flown to a hospital in Portugal, but it would be weeks before an attempt to retrieve the bodies of Hayter and the others aboard the destroyed submersible could be made . . . if there was even anything left to recover. "But they might cost a whole lot more."

"Right now, the lives I'm most bothered about are ours. I don't trust Glas—he still might decide that the easiest thing to do would be take out them and you in one go. I'm sure Sophia'll have suggested it." He surveyed the buildings on the western side of First Avenue with suspicion, half-expecting to see someone aiming a rocket launcher at them from a window.

"I don't trust Glas either. But I definitely don't trust

Warden. Evil billionaire with Sophia on one side, evil billionaire with Stikes on the other. It's like being caught between . . ."

"Two big piles of shit?"

"I was going to say Scylla and Charybdis, but yours works too. Even if it's kind of gross."

"Why can't we ever meet any *nice* billionaires?" Eddie tapped the figurine against one of its companions. "So, we're finally going to smash these little buggers, then?"

Nina took the statue from him, turning it over in her hands. Had the blinds been closed, she knew, her touch would have produced a brief and faint earth energy reaction, but New York was too far from any of the mysterious natural lines of power to produce an effect visible in daylight. "I wish we didn't have to," she said, sighing. "They're another link to Atlantis, maybe to something even older. For all we know, they might have been made by some earlier civilization. We know the Veteres were able to use earth energy."

"Yeah, and it almost killed us," Eddie complained. The race that had walked the earth before humans was long gone, but the ancient booby traps it left to protect its secrets had still been active. "Nothing good's ever come out of it. And it can only get worse if the Group gets its hands on that meteor."

"Meteorite," Nina corrected absently, still gazing at the little statue. "Meteors burn up before they hit the ground."

"Meteor, asteroid, hemorrhoid, whatever. The point is, if Glas was telling the truth then it's bad news all 'round."

"*If* he's telling the truth? You think he might be lying?"

He shrugged. "There's a chance, but . . . if he is, he's gone to some pretty fucking big extremes to cover it. No, he was probably about as on the level with us as someone like that ever gets."

"I suppose." She stared into the crudely carved sockets representing the figure's eyes for a moment, then returned it to the case. "I suppose the next question is: How do we destroy them?"

"Just find me a hammer," Eddie suggested. "Five minutes of bashing, then we chuck the gravel into the river. Sorted."

"That's one way, I guess. But we need to wait for Glas's representative before we do it. If he acts as a witness, at least we know that Glas'll call off his dogs."

"When's he coming?"

"Glas said he'd be here today."

Eddie sat back. "Let's hope sooner rather than later, eh? I want to get all this over with."

"Me too, honey. Me too."

The phone rang ten minutes later. "Nina?" said Lola. "Mr. Penrose is here."

"Dammit," Nina muttered. She had been fending off demands from the United Nations bureaucracy to know exactly what had happened at Atlantis practically from the moment she reboarded the *Gant,* but knew that sooner or later she would have to deal with the matter directly. "Okay, tell him to come in."

Penrose entered. "Nina, Eddie," he said, voice grave. "I'm glad you're both all right. And Mr. Trulli too."

"Thank you," Nina replied. "I just wish I could say the same about Lewis and the others. Look, Sebastian, I know the UN wants my full report as soon as possible, but there's, ah, a personal matter that Eddie and I have to deal with first. I'd really appreciate it if you could give us time to take care of it. There's someone we have to speak to."

"I know," Penrose replied. His manner became hesitant, even nervous. "It's, er . . . the person you're waiting for is . . . me."

"What?"

"Harald Glas sent me. I'm here as a witness, to watch you destroy the statues."

"You're *what*?" Eddie barked, advancing on him with his fists balled. "You're in this with Glas?"

"Let me explain, please!" Penrose said hurriedly. He

held up his hands. "I have, ah, a confession to make. I've been . . . I've been working for the Group."

This admission of a spy in their midst chilled Nina. "Sebastian, what do you mean?"

"I've been providing information to the Group for some time. About the UN, behind-the-scenes political arguments, that kind of thing. But I've also been telling them about the IHA's operations—specifically, over the past year and a half, about anything relating to the statues." He glanced at the case on Nina's desk. "It's how Jindal knew about the connection between the two statues in the IHA's possession and the one in South America so quickly. I told the Group; they told me to pass the information on to him immediately."

Nina remembered that Kit's interest in the discovery had been surprisingly quick. "But if you're working for the Group," she said stonily, "why are you here on behalf of Glas?"

"It was Harald who first involved me in all of this," said Penrose, not quite able to look her in the eye. "Many years ago. He, ah . . . he did a huge favor for my family. For my daughter, specifically; I don't want to go into the details. But I owed him for that. So I started to repay him by providing useful information, and before long I was involved with the whole of the Group. When he split from them, I was, well, torn. I was still working for them—but I also had an obligation to Harald."

"You were a mole," said Eddie in disgust. "A double agent."

"I didn't have a choice. These people—once you're in with them, there's no way out. Even if, like Jindal, you agree with their goals, they still have power over you. I had to keep helping the Group, but at the same time I was secretly helping Harald as much as I could."

"*You* told him I was in Rome!" Nina realized. She rounded her desk, jabbing a finger into his face. Penrose flinched. "And you told him that we were going down to Atlantis. You got Lewis and the others killed, Sebastian. It was your fault!"

Eddie hauled him across the room. "You're going out the fucking window!"

"No, Eddie!" said Nina, as Penrose gasped in fear. "Let him go!"

He angrily released the other man. The sweating Penrose straightened his glasses before stammering out a reply. "I—I know it was my fault, I know. I'm sorry. As I said, I had no choice."

"You're still responsible, though. There's no way I can let this pass. The UN's got to be told—it's more than just a breach of confidence, it's a breach of security that's gotten our people killed." She was trembling with a cold fury as she jabbed her finger at him again. "You'll go to jail for this."

Penrose took a long, deep breath. "I . . . will resign my position and turn myself in to the authorities as soon as we're finished here," he said, voice quavering. "I always thought this might happen, sooner or later. But you do know that the members of the Group will never allow their existence to be publicly exposed. They'll either make this go away before it can get close to coming to trial . . . or they'll make *me* go away."

"Unless you only tell them about Glas's side of things," Nina suggested. "I doubt he'll voluntarily come to court to defend his character."

He considered this. "It would all *technically* be true, I suppose . . . yes, you're right. But before any of that, there's something we have to do first."

She regarded the case. "Destroy the statues."

"About fucking time," said Eddie. "I'll get a hammer."

He started for the door, but before he was halfway there the phone rang. Nina was tempted to leave it, but there was an outside possibility that it might be Glas. She picked it up. "Yes?"

"Nina, Larry Chase's wife is on the line," said Lola.

"Tell her to call back."

"I . . . I think you should talk to her."

The worry in her voice changed Nina's mind. "Okay, put her through."

The click of a switching line, then: "Hello? Nina, hello?" Julie Chase—on the verge of panic.

"Julie, what is it?" Nina asked. She hurriedly put the phone on speaker. "Are you okay?"

"Yes, I'm okay, but—it's Larry!"

"What about him?" said Eddie, giving his wife a look of concern.

"I just got home, and—and somebody's broken into the house, it looks like there's been a fight. And there's a note, someone left a note. It said that I had to call you, Nina."

She was startled. "Me?"

"What's going on?" cried Julie, almost in tears. "Where's Larry, what's happened to him?"

"Julie," Eddie said, "this note—what does it say, exactly?"

"It—it says that if I want to see my husband again, I have to call Nina and give her . . ."

"Give her what? Julie!"

"There's a phone number," came the words between sobs. "It says I have to tell you to call it."

"Read it out to us," said Nina, getting a pen.

Julie recited it. "Swiss number," Eddie told Nina quietly, recognizing the first few digits. "Julie, listen—we think we know what's going on, but we're going to have to hang up so we can call this number."

"You know where Larry is?"

"No, but I think we know who's got him. We're going to ring the number to see if he's okay. All right?"

"What should I do?" she wailed. "Should I call the police?"

"I don't think they'll be much help," Nina said grimly. Like Eddie, she already had a very strong suspicion about who was responsible, and that Larry would by now be beyond the reach of conventional law enforcement. "Julie, we'll call you right back, okay?"

"Can—can you get him back home?"

"I hope so." She disconnected, then started to dial the number Julie had given her.

"What about the statues?" Penrose asked nervously. "We still need to destroy them . . ."

Nina waved him to silence as the call was answered by a clipped English voice. "Hello, Nina. And Chase, I assume you're there too."

"Stikes," Nina replied with distaste. "What do you want?"

"I'm sure you already know. Thank you for calling me so promptly, by the way. Mr. Warden was getting a little concerned that he hadn't heard back from you. So I decided to encourage you to reach a decision."

"Where's Larry?" she demanded.

"Safe. For now. He's a little bruised, perhaps, but then my men did warn him not to resist." A small chuckle. "I considered taking Chase's niece or sister, but then I decided I preferred the irony of using someone he can't stand—but won't be able to allow to come to harm either."

Eddie stepped up to the desk. "I'm going to fucking kill you for this, Stikes."

"I doubt that. But I'm sure your father will be absolutely delighted to know that you care enough to threaten murder for him. Anyway, enough of the pleasantries—we have business to discuss. I do hope for Larry's sake that you have the statues, and haven't done anything foolish such as damage them."

"And what if we have?"

"Then I have no further use for your father, and I never carry dead weight. Come on, Chase, stop being obtuse. Do you have the statues?"

"Yes," Nina admitted.

"Excellent. Now, since the Group needs you as well for them to be of any use, here's what's going to happen. I'll send you an email shortly, telling you where I want you to meet me tomorrow. Just you, Nina—Chase is very definitely not invited, and there will be, shall we say, unfortunate consequences for his father if I see him. Bring the statues with you, and Larry will be released."

"How do we know you'll let him go?" she asked.

"You don't, obviously. But you *do* know what will happen to him if you don't do what I say. I never make idle threats. As I'm sure you must be aware by now."

Nina looked helplessly at Eddie. Delivering the statues—and herself—to the Group was a course that could lead to disaster. But refusal would certainly mean Larry's death. Stikes had already proved himself utterly ruthless in the past, and now that he was working for the Group he undoubtedly considered himself to be un-touchable for his crimes. "What do we do?" she silently mouthed.

Face tight with frustration, Eddie whispered, "Go along with him for now."

"Are you sure?"

He nodded as Stikes spoke again. "Well? Do I at least get the courtesy of an answer?"

"I'll bring the statues to you," Nina said, to Penrose's dismay.

"I'm glad to hear it. I'll send you the details now. Oh, and Nina?" Smug amusement filled the former officer's voice. "Wrap up warmly."

TWENTY-EIGHT

Switzerland

In better weather, the little ski resort of Chandère would have been beautiful. Backed by majestic peaks, with long flowing slopes running down to the woods around the traditional houses of pale stone and dark timber, it was an almost postcard-perfect representation of the idealized Alpine village. Adding to its picturesque quality was the narrow-gauge steam railway that ran along the valley, connecting it to other equally attractive tourist destinations.

Conditions today, though, were far from their best. Low clouds blotted out the mountaintops, a stiff, freezing wind driving snowflakes along like tiny knives of ice. The lack of sunlight draped a dismal pall over everything, flattening the scene almost to two dimensions. Even the jolly, toy-like locomotive seemed affected by the gloom, wheezing and straining to pull its carriages into the station.

The train finally clanked to a stop, sooty smoke swirling around the handful of disembarking passengers. Nina was among them, wearing a winter coat and woolly hat to protect herself from the cold. She was carrying a case, but unlike those of the other tourists, hers did not contain the accoutrements of a skiing holiday.

Instead, it held the three statues.

Stikes was waiting for her at the station's exit, leaning casually against a wall. "Dr. Wilde! Glad you could make it."

"Cut the crap, Stikes," she snapped. "Where's Larry?"

"Where are the statues?" She held up the case. "Good. Although you won't mind if I check, will you?"

Nina opened the case to reveal the trio of purple figurines within. "Satisfied?"

"For the moment." He signaled to two large men standing nearby, who quickly marched to join him. "Follow me."

She expected to be taken to a car, but Stikes instead headed for a tall and boxy building down the street. A cable-car station, steel lines rising up into the murk above the village. "Where are we going?"

"I'm sure the Chandère tourist board will be very disappointed that you don't know," Stikes said amiably. "We're going to the Blauspeer hotel; it's apparently quite famous. Exclusive, too. It's one of the Group's regular haunts for meetings."

"Gee, with a recommendation like that, I'll book next year's vacation while I'm here."

They entered the building. There was a sign on the door; Nina didn't know sufficient German to translate the whole text, but picked out enough to gather that the hotel served by the aerial tramway was currently closed to the public. The Group had presumably booked the entire place, wanting privacy.

Stikes spoke briefly to a man inside a control booth, then led Nina and his two goons to the waiting gondola. She looked past it up the mountainside. Little was visible through the clouds and blowing snow. Her destination was effectively isolated from the rest of the world. She shivered.

The Englishman opened the cabin door for her. "Cold? Get in, it'll be warmer."

"You're the perfect gentleman," she said with a sneer as she entered. Stikes merely smirked and joined her, his men doing the same. A gesture to the booth from the former SAS officer, and the cable car lurched into motion.

Pointedly turning her back on Stikes, Nina went to the front window as the gondola began its ascent. A few buildings passed below, then the woods at the bottom of the hill. The best of the mountain's ski runs were apparently reserved for the hotel's residents, a low fence above the railroad separating the rising slopes from the village. The Blauspeer had other attractions than downhill skiing, however; a long luge track coiled down through the trees separating two of the ski runs. There were also what looked like target ranges for biathlon contestants.

"I should ask the obvious question while we have the time," said Stikes. "Where's your husband?"

"In New York."

"No, he's not. He's in Switzerland—he took a different flight from you, but I know he's here." His voice became flinty. "I warned you what would happen to his father if he tried to interfere."

"But he hasn't interfered, has he? The only reason he's here is to make sure we get out of the country safely." She glanced back at his two silent companions. "I'm assuming you've got more than just these two clowns watching the place. You'd know if he were in town."

"I know Chase," said Stikes. "He's not the kind to sit around and wait." He looked out into the gray blankness obscuring the mountains. "He's here, somewhere."

"If you think so, why don't you try to make me tell you?"

"Normally I would, as I'm sure you remember. But I have my orders, so my hands are tied . . . for the moment." A small, nasty smile.

Nina turned away again. The ride continued for a couple more minutes before a large, blocky shape finally loomed into view ahead. The Blauspeer hotel stood on relatively flat ground partway up the mountain, the upper cable-car station actually built into one wing near the start of the luge track. The building looked quite old, timber-framed beneath its high, steeply sloping roof, but Nina suspected its facilities would be ultramodern and luxurious. An ice-skating rink and an outdoor café overlooking the valley came into view as the cable car approached the end of its climb; considering the conditions, both were unsurprisingly deserted.

The gondola stopped. Stikes, feigning politeness, ushered Nina out. Even inside the station, the wind was stronger and colder than in the village, cutting through her coat. She hurried toward the glass doors leading to the hotel proper.

Warden waited in the expansive lobby beyond. "Dr. Wilde," he said. "Welcome. I'm so glad you agreed to come."

Her voice was as icy as the conditions outside. "I wasn't exactly given a lot of choice."

"What do you mean?"

"Don't pretend you don't know." She jabbed a thumb at Stikes. "Your errand boy kidnapped my father-in-law and threatened to kill him if I didn't bring you the statues."

"What?" He looked at Stikes in genuine surprise. "Is this true?"

"You told me to bring Dr. Wilde and the statues here," Stikes replied smoothly. "I chose the most expeditious way to make sure that happened."

Warden's mouth twisted angrily. "I wanted her to come here *willingly*!" he barked. "You idiot!" Ignoring Stikes's affronted expression, he turned back to Nina. "Dr. Wilde, I apologize for this—this outrage. I assure you, I had absolutely no idea that Stikes would exceed his authority like this."

"Maybe you should have done what I said and fired him," said Nina.

Still fuming, Warden glared at Stikes. "Where is he now?"

The Englishman composed himself. "He's in the hotel, and perfectly safe."

"Is he a guest or a prisoner?" asked Nina pointedly.

"Make sure it's the former," said Warden. "Now get out of my sight!"

Stikes stiffened, offering a terse "Yes, *sir*" as he and his two men headed for the nearby elevators.

Warden muttered something unflattering as he watched them leave, then addressed Nina. "Again, I apologize. You're an absolutely vital part of what the Group hopes to achieve, and I want you to be completely free in your decision to join us. I hope Stikes's stupidity hasn't affected that. I'll make sure your father-in-law is freed, and fully compensated for whatever inconvenience and distress he's been caused."

"I'm sure he'll appreciate that," said Nina. Warden didn't seem to detect her undercurrent of sarcasm—though she couldn't help noticing that he was so arrogant as to assume that she would agree to go along with the Group, no matter what. "As for what Stikes has done, I don't think that'll have much effect on my decision."

"I'm very happy to hear that." Again, the financier failed to pick up on her not-exactly-buried subtext. "In that case, if you'll come with me, I'll introduce you to the Group."

* * *

Eddie gazed through the binoculars, holding one gloved hand above the lenses to ward off the blowing snow. "So that's the hotel? Looks like it should have Jack Nicholson as the caretaker."

He and the group of eight men with him, in white camouflage gear and balaclava masks, were at the top of a ridge about three-quarters of a mile from the Blauspeer hotel and several hundred feet higher. At this distance through the obscuring conditions, the building was barely more than a silhouette against the clouded valley, its shape defined more by its lights than by detailed features.

But Eddie could still see enough to tell that it was heavily guarded. Figures patrolled the grounds, making sure that the hotel's reclusive VIP guests maintained their privacy.

They were about to be gate-crashed.

His companions were some of Glas's loyal employees, a retinue of European security personnel urgently assembled on the billionaire's orders while Eddie was on the flight to Switzerland. A helicopter had made a risky flight into the thickening clouds to drop them on the other side of the mountain, out of sight of the hotel, so they could traverse a pass and approach from a direction that would—in theory—be more lightly guarded. He didn't know how good the men were, but had been assured that all were ex-military, willing and able to accomplish their mission.

That assurance was about to be tested. He tilted the binoculars down to the mountainside below. It was one of the hotel's slopes—a black run, steep and potentially dangerous, even deadly, to anyone not an expert skier. The poles of a ski lift were visible off to one side, but it was not running. The only way down was to ski.

Eddie had done a considerable amount of that during his SAS training, but mostly cross-country rather than downhill, and it had been some years since he had been on a skiing holiday. Now that he thought about it, the last time had been during his marriage to Sophia, over seven years before. Christ, where had the time gone? He hoped he hadn't become too rusty.

He would find out soon enough. The already grim sky was steadily darkening as evening drew in. They would have to move quickly—not least because Nina would be inside by now.

He continued his sweep of the slope. Before setting out, he had surveyed the area using online aerial photos; as expected, he spotted a small building at the bottom of the ski lift. It was the perfect place for a guard to find respite from the wind . . .

"Thermal," he said. A man produced a device resembling a compact video camera and handed it to him. Eddie switched it on and peered through the eyepiece at the hut.

Someone was there, a humanoid shape in bright blues, yellows, and reds standing out against the cold gray blankness of the snow. He panned the thermal imager across the vista below. More figures popped out from their surroundings, some standing watch in the shelter of buildings and trees, others trudging through the open along well-trodden patrol routes. "How many guards?" asked one of the men.

"I count, let's see . . . four at the bottom of the slope, and another eight or nine nearer the hotel." Even through the thermal imager, it was impossible to miss that all the guards were armed with MP5 submachine guns. He gave the gadget back to its owner, who conducted his own scan while Eddie checked the sky. Conditions were steadily worsening, the wind-driven snow getting thicker as the landscape dropped deeper into shadow. "Okay, get ready."

The team members quickly began to don their skis as Eddie took back the thermal imager and checked the guards' locations again. According to Glas, with whom he had spoken via Penrose before leaving New York, the Group maintained its own private security force; the men protecting the hotel were professional mercenaries. Even in law-abiding Switzerland, they wouldn't hesitate to kill an intruder, relying on the power and influence of their employers to cover it up. Moreover, Stikes was now in charge of them, and Eddie knew firsthand just how merciless the former officer and his subordinates could be.

To reach the hotel, he knew that his team would have to be just as ruthless. If they were caught, they would be killed. Their only chance of success—the only way to rescue both Nina and his father, and put an end to the Group's plans—was to take out the mercenaries first.

He checked his weapon: a white-painted Heckler & Koch MP7 personal defense weapon—an extremely compact submachine gun—equipped with suppressor and red-dot sight. The other men were similarly equipped, with a single exception. One man also carried a skeletal Steyr SSG 08 sniper rifle, with a thermal scope and a hefty silencer.

"How good are you with that?" Eddie asked its owner, a German named Amsel.

"I have the Schützenschnur in gold," Amsel replied proudly.

"Yeah, that's pretty good." It was the German army's marksmanship award; Glas seemed to have picked his men well. "Okay, you set up here, and I'll spot."

Amsel was comfortable enough in his skills to not even bother removing his skis as he lay at the crest of the ridge and prepared his rifle. Eddie scanned the slope with the thermal imager once more. The four men on the outer perimeter were still in position, all but one stationary in whatever shelter they could find. The fourth was traipsing across the base of the ski run, heading for the lift. The Englishman frowned. They only had one gun capable of hitting a target from this distance—if Amsel took out one guard and the other saw his comrade fall, he might raise the alarm before the German could take his second shot . . .

"You've got to be fast," he said, watching intently as the glowing figure closed the gap to his companion. The two guards were only fifty yards apart, easily able to see each other even through the snow. "The guy walking across—get him first, then the one by the ski lift. Quick!"

Amsel nodded, adjusting his grip on the Steyr as he brought his eye to the scope and hunted for his first target. "Come on, come on . . . ," Eddie muttered. The guard was still closing on the man by the lift—who had turned to watch his approach, raising a hand in nonchalant greeting. Any closer and it would be instantly obvious that the walker had been shot—

A deep, flat *whoomph* came from the Steyr's suppressor as it muffled the sound of the shot, Amsel jerking backward with the recoil. The sniper was using subsonic ammunition to minimize noise, but the bullet's relatively low speed meant it would take over two seconds to reach its target. Eddie watched the shimmering shape in the thermal imager, hoping that Amsel was as good as he boasted . . .

The man suddenly staggered, what looked like a white halo flaring around his head—a spray of hot blood. Eddie immediately panned across to the ski lift. The man there was reacting with surprise, a puff of warm breath leaving his mouth as he called out to his companion. He had seen him fall, but through the blowing snow didn't yet know why.

He would soon realize that this was more than a simple stumble, though. Eddie heard Amsel shift position as he found his next target, but kept his electronically enhanced gaze fixed on the ski lift. The man called out again, the glow of his breath brighter, more forceful.

The rifle thumped a second time. Eddie kept watching, tension rising. The guard fumbled for something on his chest.

A radio.

He raised it to his mouth—

Another halo. The guard slumped into the snow, a hot white pool slowly forming around his head.

"Good shot," said Eddie. But he had no time to offer more than cursory praise, already moving his sight back across the slope to find the remaining sentries. "Next one's by the little clump of trees off to the right, then the last one's near that hut with the sign on top."

Amsel confirmed that he had spotted them. Two more silenced shots, and the perimeter was clear. Eddie stood and put on his own skis. "All right," he said, "let's piste off."

The nine men began their rapid descent toward the hotel.

* * *

Warden brought Nina to a set of wooden doors. A sign beside them read ALPIN GESELLSCHAFTSRAUM: the Alpine Lounge. "Here we are," he told her.

He pushed open the doors theatrically and stepped through. Nina followed him into what was surely the Blauspeer's centerpiece, a huge Gothic room with a high vaulted ceiling crisscrossed by thick beams of dark timber, tall windows looking out over the valley. The view was currently obscured by snow, but Nina's eyes were on the room's occupants rather than the scenery outside.

Bright spotlights on the lowest beams shone down to illuminate a large circular table at the room's center. Around it sat fourteen people, twelve of them men, all at least middle-aged and the oldest well into his eighties.

The Group. The secretive organization pulling the strings of governments all over the world. A meeting of nearly unimaginable power and wealth . . . yet unknown to almost everybody whose lives it affected.

There were two unoccupied seats. Warden went to one, gesturing at the other beside it. "We'd be honored if you'd join us for dinner, Dr. Wilde," he said. "Please, sit down."

"Thank you," she said, taking in the calculating gazes regarding her as she sat and put the case on the table. There were no place settings, but she saw several large cloth-draped catering trolleys near an open dumbwaiter; presumably the Group's members had business to discuss before they ate.

She was not just involved in that business. She *was* that business.

Nina tried to will away the knot in her stomach as Warden took his seat and made introductions. The oldest, Rudolf Meerkrieger, a German media magnate controlling newspapers and broadcasting stations in over thirty countries. Anisim Gorchakov, the oligarch with his hand on the taps of the vast Russian natural gas reserves that fed the homes and industries of Europe and beyond. Sheik Fawwaz al-Faisal, head of a Middle Eastern consortium that decided the region's supply—and hence the price—of oil on a daily basis. The rotund Bull brothers, Frederick and William, American identical twins distinguishable only by the colors of their ties, who had made their colossal joint fortune in hedge funds by speculating on commodities such as fuel and food, driving up prices and cashing in on shortages. Victoria Brannigan, Australian heiress to a mining and refining empire that produced the raw materials on which the world's manufacturers depended, and the Dutch Caspar Van der Zee, in charge of the shipping fleet that carried those materials to where they were needed and the finished products made from them back to consumers.

And the others, different but the same, the invisible hand controlling the market revealed in plain sight. The men and women whose word could appoint or topple leaders, turn famine into glut and back again, all in service of their hunger for profit—and urge to control.

"So, I finally get to meet you all," said Nina once the round of greetings was concluded. "Well, not all. Mr. Takashi couldn't make it, obviously."

"No, unfortunately," said Warden. "A shame—he was the one who convinced us of the potential value of earth energy. If it can be harnessed, of course—but with your help, that will now be possible." He indicated the case. "One of the reasons we chose this hotel for our meeting is that this mountain is a natural earth energy confluence point. When you put the statues together, it should produce the same effect as it did in Tokyo, and allow you to pinpoint the location of the meteorite."

Nina saw that not a single member of the Group showed any regret over Takashi's death. To them, it was a mere inconvenience—nothing to become emotional about. "Well, let's not get ahead of ourselves," she said dismissively.

That produced emotion: muted shock, constrained outrage at the minor yet unmistakable challenge. They had assumed she was there to become a willing part of their plan; resistance was evidently not on the agenda. "Is there a problem, Dr. Wilde?" asked Meerkrieger, his aged voice creaking like tree bark.

"I have a few questions I'd like answered first."

"Of course," said Warden smoothly. "We want you to be completely comfortable with your role. What would you like to know?"

"More about the meteorite, the Atlantean sky stone, first of all. You think it's composed of a naturally super-conducting material, yes?"

Warden nodded. "That's right. We don't know how big it is, but hopefully it'll allow the extraction of enough of the metal to supply multiple earth energy collection stations."

"But there's more to it, isn't there? The connection I felt to it when I put the three statues together in Japan suggests that the stone has some intimate link with life on earth, as if it's somehow integral to its creation."

No words were spoken by her audience, but Nina immediately sensed a change in attitude from the watching billionaires. Eyes fractionally narrowed, forehead furrows deepened almost imperceptibly. Caution, concern, even outright suspicion that she knew more than she was supposed to. "Don't you think?" she added, trying to prompt a response.

"That's our theory, yes," Warden eventually said. "The basic building blocks of life were seeded by comets soon after the planet's creation, but the sky stone brought something more . . . complex. We don't know where it came from—Mars, maybe Venus before it overheated, some other planet that doesn't even exist anymore. It doesn't matter. What does is the end result. Through whatever chain of events, life began on earth after that meteorite fell, perhaps even jump-started by earth energy. It's part of our world—and it's part of us."

"Mm-hmm." Nina nodded. "But your interest in that

side of things is purely scientific, right? Your primary goal is harnessing earth energy."

"That's right," said one of the Bull brothers. "What else could it be?"

"Are you suggesting we've got another interest?" the other asked in an accusatory tone.

"Maybe you can tell me. You see, I had a private chat with one of the Group's members before coming here." Her words immediately set the cat among the pigeons, paranoid glances shooting back and forth. She enjoyed their discomfort before clarifying, "A former member, I should say."

"Glas," Warden hissed.

"Yeah."

"Where did you talk to him?" Brannigan demanded sharply.

"On his submarine."

That produced mutterings around the circular table. Gorchakov banged a fist. "I knew it! It was the only way he could have disappeared completely. I told you to have the American navy find it!" he said to Warden.

The Group's chairman held up his hands in an attempt to restore order. "The oceans are rather large, Anisim," he said. "I couldn't exactly ask President Cole to divert half his carrier groups on your hunch, could I?" As the consternation settled, he turned back to Nina. "So, you spoke to Glas. What did he tell you?"

"Well, once we got past the initial awkwardness about the whole him-trying-to-kill-me issue, he was very talkative. He told me *why* he'd been trying to kill me."

"So that you couldn't help us," said Warden. "I told you, he was desperate to maintain the profits of his energy business."

"That's strange, because these two guys here"—she indicated Gorchakov and al-Faisal—"should be in the same boat, but they don't seem at all worried. No, what Glas told me was that there's more to your plan than just gaining a monopoly on earth energy. There's something else you want a monopoly on, isn't there?"

Warden's expression was slowly turning cold. "And what would that be, Dr. Wilde?"

"Power. Over everybody. Forever. If you find the meteorite, you'll have a genetic Rosetta stone that will let you create a virus to modify human DNA, to give you control over an obedient and pliant population. Am I getting warm?"

A lengthy silence. First to speak was al-Faisal. "Glas should have been eliminated the moment he opposed the plan," he growled.

"I'll take that as a big yes," said Nina. "So, y'know, I really don't think I want to be a part of this. I have an old-fashioned notion that people have the right to decide how they're going to live their own lives—and by people I mean everybody, not some self-appointed elite. Crazy, I know."

The masks of civility were rapidly falling away from the others at the table. "You'll do what you're damn well told," snarled William Bull.

"You think 'the people' have *ever* controlled their own lives?" his brother went on. "That's fairy-tale liberal claptrap! There have always been the rulers, and the ruled. That's the way it is."

"We just want to put an end to all the wasteful overconsumption and infighting," added Brannigan.

"An end to conflict," said Warden. "That wasn't a lie. We *will* bring order and peace to the world. Finally."

"Peace on your terms," Nina sneered.

"Peace is peace."

"Does that include *resting* in peace? How many people will be killed by your virus?"

"No more than three percent of the global populace, we estimate," said Frederick Bull, as calmly as if discussing how many people owned a particular brand of phone. "But population control is part of our long-term plans anyway."

She regarded him in disgust. "So the price of your peace is over two hundred million dead—and genetic slavery for everyone else? Wow, what a bargain." She shoved back her chair and stood, picking up the case. "It doesn't matter anyway, because you can't achieve anything without my cooperation. And I'm sure as hell not going to give it."

"Your cooperation," said Warden coldly, "doesn't have to be voluntary. If necessary, it will be forced."

"You mean like this?" Nina reached into her jacket and whipped out a gun—Sophia's Glock. She thrust it at Warden's face, making him recoil in shock. Gasps of fright came from the others.

"Stikes didn't *search* her?" said Meerkrieger in disbelief.

"I *said* you should have fired him," Nina told Warden, who was shaking with fury. "Okay, I want you to tell your security goons to withdraw. I'm going to take the statues, and I'm going to take Larry Chase, and we're going to leave—"

A slow hand clap echoed through the room. Nina spun to see Stikes standing nonchalantly at one of the side doors, giving her mocking applause. She snapped the gun around at the former soldier. "Oh, put it down, Dr. Wilde," he said, raising his open hands to show they were empty. "We both know you're not going to shoot an unarmed man."

"I'm willing to bet you're not unarmed," Nina said coldly, the Glock not wavering.

"Actually, I am. But he's not." Stikes nodded toward another door across the room.

"Yeah, like I'm going to fall for that—"

"Nina!" The voice was English, shocked—and frightened despite an attempt at bravado.

Larry Chase.

She had no choice but to look. Larry was shoved into the room by a large man holding his collar with one hand—and pressing a gun into his back with the other. "Larry! Are you okay?"

"Yeah, but—what the hell's going on?" He stared at the people around the table in confusion. "That's Caspar Van der Zee! What is this?"

"It's a meeting of the secret rulers of the world," said Stikes, with a tinge of derision. "Now, Dr. Wilde, put down the gun. I know we can't shoot you, but"—his lips curled sadistically—"I *will* have Daddy Chase over there shot, in such a way that it takes him several excruciating hours to die. You've got ten seconds."

"If you shoot him, I'll kill you!" Nina warned.

"You wouldn't have come here at all if you were willing to let him die. Three, two—"

With an anguished look at her father-in-law, she tossed the gun onto the table. "Good," said Stikes, smirking. "Now sit back down. I think it's time we all finally saw what happens when you put the statues together, don't you?"

Nina reluctantly returned to her seat as Larry was pushed to the table. She was filled with concern—for both of them—but another thought dominated her mind.

Where is Eddie?

TWENTY-NINE

Her husband was well aware that he was behind schedule. The plan had been for Nina to draw out the meeting with the Group for as long as possible, but they both knew that sooner or later she would have to admit she had no intention of leading them to the meteorite. At that point, things would turn nasty, and he would need to be there to help her.

However, the approach had taken longer than expected, the need for stealth while dealing with the remaining guards outside the building delaying the team. Now, though, they were finally at the hotel itself.

There was a door to Eddie's right, but his focus was on another entrance to the left, nearer the downhill slope. Steam swirled from extractor vents above a stairwell descending into the ground, which had several large wheeled bins lined up near its top. Access to the kitchens. Even though the only guests at the hotel were the Group and their employees, the establishment was still fully staffed, ready to provide the VIPs with anything they requested. Since Eddie was determined to avoid innocent casualties, the hotel workers needed to be removed from danger.

He signaled for Glas's men to follow as he went to the stairwell, checking nearby windows for signs of activity. All were empty. He paused by the first bin, making sure that no one was having a crafty smoke at the foot of the steps.

Nobody there. The way in was clear.

The others arrived behind him. "Okay," said Eddie, "remember there are civvies here. Round 'em up, then find a storeroom or something and lock 'em in until we're done. Everyone ready?" Nods of confirmation. "Right, here we go."

He led the way down the stairwell. The door at the bottom was ajar, wisps of steaming air rising from the gap. He opened it wider. A white-tiled room came into view, twenty or so aproned staff busy preparing the resplendent evening meal for their billionaire guests.

Eddie quietly entered, gun at the ready. At first none of the kitchen staff noticed the intruders, being too involved with their work—then a woman chopping vegetables looked around at the cold draft. Her irritation instantly turned to fright.

"If I can have your attention, please!" said Eddie loudly to forestall her scream as the other camouflage-clad men rushed in behind him. "Dinner's canceled. Nobody'll be hurt if you do what we say, so stop what you're doing and keep quiet." A flash of movement—a waiter lunging for a telephone mounted on the wall. "Oi!" Eddie shouted as he fired, the silenced shot shattering the phone just before the waiter reached it. "That means you, Manuel!" The large man froze.

Eddie quickly surveyed his surroundings. Through the circular windows in a set of swing doors he could see a lift and stairs leading upward, presumably to the dining area, as well as a dumbwaiter near the exit, but of more immediate interest was a single door, at the kitchen's rear, to a storage area full of catering-sized bags of dry goods. "Okay, everyone in there. Move!"

Glas's men spread out to corral the staff into the storeroom, quickly searching them to confiscate phones. Eddie examined the makeshift cell's door; it didn't appear to be lockable. "Someone'll have to keep an eye on them."

"I'll do it," volunteered Amsel. Eddie nodded, and the German took up a position to watch both the storeroom and the main entrance. The waiter who had tried to reach the phone glowered at him through the door's little window.

Eddie hurried for the exit, the remaining men following. He hoped the delays hadn't made the situation worse for Nina.

* * *

Gorchakov picked up Nina's gun. He turned it over in his hands, then glared at Stikes. "Why did you not search her?" he demanded.

The Englishman was unconcerned by the anger directed at him from around the table. "To give her a false sense of security. I knew that if she thought she had an ace up her sleeve, she'd reveal her true intentions sooner rather than later. Don't forget, I've dealt with her before. I know what kind of person she is—and she's not the type to start blasting away at unarmed civilians. She leaves the shooting to her husband."

Nina expected him to question her again regarding Eddie's whereabouts, but he left the comment hanging. Instead Warden spoke. "This is twice you've done something without telling us, Stikes—first kidnapping Chase's father"—he gave Larry a brief glance—"and now this. Don't make us question our decision to take you on board."

"You took me on because you know I get results," Stikes replied. "And I have. You've got Dr. Wilde, and you've got the statues. Everything you need is here."

"If Dr. Wilde cooperates."

"Oh, she will." Stikes gave her a lupine smile. "One way or another."

"Don't bet on it," said Nina.

He sighed. "Are we really going to go through this routine again? I make a demand, you refuse, I put a gun to someone you care about, you cave in." He slid the case across the table to Nina. "So why not just save everybody's time and put the statues together?"

"Nina, I don't know what the hell's going on here," said Larry with nervous bravado, "but, er, much as I'd like you to do what he says so we can all go home, I'm getting the distinct feeling it's not a good idea. So don't give this bastard what he wants, not on my account."

Stikes regarded him with an odd sense of approval. "I didn't think you had that much backbone, Larry. Maybe you and your son have more in common than either of you would like to admit. Oh, and Gerard," he added to the man holding Larry, "shoot him in the knee."

"*No!*" Nina screamed as Gerard unhesitatingly pointed the gun at Larry's leg. Stikes snapped up a hand, and the big mercenary stopped, his finger tight on the trigger.

"I told you," Stikes said to her. He gestured at the case. "Now. The statues."

Nina and Larry exchanged helpless looks. The gun was still fixed on his knee; at point-blank range the bullet would shatter the bones, almost certainly crippling him for life—if he survived the blood loss from the wound. Larry's face was ashen with fear, but he still summoned up some reserve of defiance. "Nina, you shouldn't . . ."

"It's your choice, *Nina,*" said Stikes. "Don't keep everyone waiting."

"You son of a bitch," she hissed. Until Eddie arrived, she had no choice but to obey. Slowly, her disgust and reluctance almost tangible, she opened the case and took out the first statue.

The effect of her touch upon the stone figurine was immediate, the strange glow bright even beneath the glaring spotlights on the roof beams. "And the others," prompted Warden, fascinated by the display. "Put them together."

Nina linked the second figure with the first. The glow intensified. Supporting the paired statues in one hand, she picked up the last member of the triptych, the bifurcated figurine now held crudely together with adhesive tape. It made no difference on the effect, the purple stone coming alive with the shimmering blue glow. Just as in Japan, she felt a weird electrical tingling through her hands.

Everyone watching held their breath, even Larry and his captor. The statues shone, the tingle intensifying as she brought the figures closer together. There was another feeling, too—as much as she wanted to prevent the Group from finding the meteorite, her innate curiosity was becoming ravenous, urging her to take the next step and discover the secret of the stone. She had felt the effect before, in Tokyo; there, she had been caught unawares and snapped back to reality by shock. But now she knew what to expect. She could re-create the experience, and this time be in control . . .

"Put them together!" Warden ordered—but before he could finish speaking she had already done so.

Even prepared for what would happen, Nina was almost overcome by the rush of sensation. Again, there was the feeling of acquiring a new sense that extended far beyond the limits of her body, inescapably linking her to life in all its myriad forms. If what Glas had said was true and all living things on earth originated from one single source, the sky stone, then she was now following the common thread joining them together through billions of years.

And she felt the stone itself.

A sixth—or seventh?—sense, a homing instinct; however she could think to describe it, all she knew was that the thread led her directly to it. There was no life around it now, but there had been, once. She had impressions of heat, light where there should have been darkness, being beneath the ground yet not buried. The feeling was so intense that she could almost *see* it, a visual echo from the people who had been there long ago.

It was far away, she could tell, but closer than it had been when she was in Takashi's skyscraper. She knew in what direction—

That thought made her open her eyes. She knew, but now so too did the Group. The joined statues floated just above her cradling palms, shining brightly. Some of the Group were looking at the wall toward which the light was strongest, as if hoping to see through it all the way to the meteorite's hiding place.

She felt an instinctive urge to follow the path back to its origin—

The statues suddenly moved, gliding silently away from her across the table. She was so startled that she didn't think to try to grab them until they were out of reach. Meerkrieger jerked aside as the linked figures spun past him.

The glow began to fade . . . and the statues arced toward the polished wooden floor. "Catch them, catch them!" Warden cried.

Stikes was already running around the table. He dived headlong, landing hard and skidding along the floorboards just in time for the figurines to drop into his hands. He breathed out heavily in relief. "Haven't made a catch like that since I played cricket for Eton."

Warden rounded on Nina. "What happened? How did you do that?"

"I don't know," she replied, truthfully. The statues had responded to her impulsive thought, as if she had been able to channel and direct the earth energy flowing through them by the power of her will alone. But even in her confusion, she still had enough forethought to keep this to herself. "It just sort of—*happened*. Like they were drawn toward something."

"The sky stone," said Warden. "They were being drawn to the meteorite."

"We can triangulate," said Frederick Bull excitedly. "We know the bearing from Tokyo, and now we know the bearing from here too!"

His brother was already tapping away on his smartphone. "The bearing from here was a hundred and forty degrees east, more or less," he said, bringing up a map app. "It was two hundred and sixty degrees west from Tokyo, so . . ." He swiped his fingers across the screen to find where the two lines intersected. "Africa! Somewhere in Ethiopia, by the look of it."

"How could it end up so far from Atlantis?" asked al-Faisal doubtfully.

"I don't think we've even started to comprehend the full power of earth energy," said Warden. "But now that Dr. Wilde is helping us, even if"—he smiled smugly at Nina—"less than willingly, we can explore its possibilities."

"Our first priority is finding the meteorite, though," said Brannigan firmly. "We've got to get the progenitor DNA."

"And we shall," Warden replied. "But first—"

Two doors on opposite sides of the room opened simultaneously, cylindrical metal objects flying through them to bounce noisily off the floor and skitter toward the table. Everyone looked around at the unexpected interruption.

Nina recognized the items. *Stun grenades!* The instructions Eddie had given her earlier sprang back into her mind, and she closed her eyes and clapped her hands to her ears.

Stikes also instantly knew what they were. He dropped, releasing the statues safely onto the floor before he too protected his senses—

Both grenades detonated, their flashes blinding anyone looking at them and the twin piercing bangs so powerful in the enclosed space that they had the same effect on the unprepared as a blow from a baseball bat. The assembled billionaires screamed, reeling in their seats as their senses were temporarily obliterated.

With one exception. Gorchakov had realized the danger just in time to raise an arm in front of his eyes. Even deafened and dizzied, he tried to stand, clutching the Glock and pointing it at one of the doors as men in white rushed into the room—

A burst of silenced bullets hit him in the back as more attackers crashed through the other door. Blood sprayed over the table as Gorchakov toppled to the floor, dead. The Glock clattered down beside him.

Eddie, leading the first team, had already spotted another threat—one of Stikes's mercenaries holding his father at gunpoint. Both men were stunned, but even blinded. all the guard had to do was pull the trigger to hit Larry in the back.

He didn't get the chance. Two shots from the MP7, and the merc spun away with blood gouting from a pair of holes over his heart.

Across the room, Stikes had recovered from the initial shock and sprung back to his feet—only to find the other intruders' guns pointing at him. He looked around as if contemplating a flying leap through the window, but then slowly raised his hands. "I was wondering when you were going to show up, Chase."

Eddie pulled off his balaclava and strode across the room to him. He regarded his former senior officer silently for a moment—then punched him hard in the face. Stikes fell, holding a hand to his bloodied mouth. "Give me one good reason why I shouldn't kill you right now, you piece of shit," Eddie growled, his MP7 fixed on the other Englishman.

Stikes somehow managed a pained smile. "Because you went to a lot of effort to prove you're not a cold-blooded murderer, and it would be a shame to waste it?"

Eddie was forced to admit that he had a point. "No, I'm not a murderer," he said, lowering the gun. Stikes's unpleasant smirk widened at the minor moral victory— then the Yorkshireman booted him in the head. "Doesn't mean I'm not a complete bastard, though."

"You're neither of those things," said Nina, crossing the room to him. En route, she noticed that the Glock had ended up almost within Warden's reach, and kicked it away. "Are you okay?"

"Yeah. Sorry we were a bit late."

"Better than never." She kissed him. Stikes made a disgusted sound.

Eddie returned the kiss, then regarded the Group, recovering from the effects of the stun grenade. "So these are the rulers of the world? A bunch of old farts in suits? Pretty disappointing—I was hoping for at least one supervillain in a cape." He turned to Larry, who was also emerging from his befuddlement. "Dad? Dad! You all right?"

His father squinted at him in confusion. "Edward? What . . . what happened?" He took in the two dead men. "Jesus Christ!"

"It's okay," Nina assured him. "We're getting out of here. You're safe."

"What about this lot?" Eddie asked of the Group. "We've just pissed off the world's most powerful people. That might cause one or two problems down the line."

"We'll have to worry about that later. The main thing is that we've got Larry, and the statues."

He gave the three figurines on the floor nearby a disapproving look. "In that case, we should smash the fucking things to bits right now." He raised his gun to shoot them—only to halt as one of the commandos took out a cell phone. "Hey! Who are you calling?"

"Mr. Glas," came the reply, as if it were self-evident. "Sir? Yes, it's Vinther. We are successful. We have the statues, and we have the Group." He listened to the response. "Yes, sir. The hotel will be secured for your arrival." He disconnected.

"What?" Eddie demanded, the statues forgotten as he went to face Vinther. "Glas is here in Switzerland?"

"Yes, he entered the country in secret. He is about to come up in the cable car."

"And why the fuck wasn't I told about this?"

"Mr. Glas decided that you didn't need to know."

"Oh, he did?" said Eddie, bristling, but Vinther was already issuing instructions to the other men. Several left the room, spreading out into the hotel to mop up any of Stikes's remaining mercenaries. "Well, that's fucking nice."

Nina joined him. "Look, I know it's kind of an asshole move on Glas's part, but it doesn't matter. We did what we came here to do."

"I suppose," he rumbled, before jerking a dismissive thumb at Stikes. "Keep an eye on that twat," he told one of the remaining commandos.

Stikes stared at the couple, behind the blood his expression angry . . . but also coldly calculating.

* * *

In the kitchen, Amsel snapped up his MP7 as the main doors opened, but relaxed when he saw it was one of his comrades entering. "What's the situation?" he asked.

"Everything's under control," his companion reported. "We've captured the Group, and the others are making sure there are no more guards in the hotel. Mr. Glas is on his way up." He glanced at the storeroom door, through which the waiter was still glaring. "Any trouble from them?"

Amsel shook his head. "How long before Mr. Glas gets here?"

"A few minutes."

"Good. Don't leave me behind when you go, okay?"

The other man grinned. "We'll come and get you. See you soon." He turned and exited.

Amsel looked back at the storeroom. The waiter's fixed look of stony anger was becoming unsettling, but as looks couldn't kill he ignored it, turning away to maintain his watch on the kitchen's other entrances.

Inside the cramped room, the waiter slowly brought one muscular arm around behind his back, raising the tails of his jacket to find something the commandos' cursory search had missed, pushed into his waistband.

A gun.

His hand closed on the grip, but he didn't draw it. Instead he stood statue still amid the frightened hotel staff, waiting for the right moment . . .

THIRTY

In the Alpine Lounge, Vinther's phone trilled. He listened to the brief message, then returned it to his pocket. "Mr. Glas is here."

"Great," said Eddie, unenthused. The commandos had returned one by one, having found no more members of Stikes's security force, and were now guarding their prisoners at the round table. Stikes himself had been moved to the empty seat beside Warden; having wiped the blood from his face, he now sat impassively, cold blue eyes slowly sweeping over the room's occupants.

Something about that was niggling Eddie. Stikes seemed *too* impassive. His earlier anger at being punched and kicked had faded, replaced not by the scathing defiance the Yorkshireman would have expected, but by an air of blank calm. A poker face? It was as if he expected the tables to be turned. But the hotel had now been secured, thermal scans of the surrounding grounds confirming that there were no more mercenaries outside. So why did he seem so . . . *confident*?

Eddie briefly considered beating an answer out of Stikes, but was distracted by his father's pacing back and forth in bewilderment. "So this guy Glas," Larry said to Nina, "he was trying to have you killed? But now you're working *with* him?"

"Yeah, I know," said Nina. "It's complicated." She sighed. "Just once, it would be nice to know exactly who the good guys and bad guys are right from the start . . ."

"Complicated! That's an understatement. Strange powers, levitating statues, a cabal of billionaires trying to take over the world . . . it all sounds like Indiana Jones meets James Bond."

"It's been said." She looked around as the door opened.

Glas entered, strong arms propelling his wheelchair. He was followed by Sophia, who was dressed entirely in black, including a matching fur coat and hat. "You brought *her*?" said Eddie in tired dismay.

"I wouldn't miss this for the world," Sophia replied. "Hello, everyone. So lovely to see you all again." She gave them a red-lipsticked smile.

"The feeling's not mutual," said Warden in disgust.

"Oh, come now. There's no need for unpleasantness." She noticed the abandoned Glock and picked it up. "Ah! I was wondering where this went." She pocketed the gun and continued after Glas.

The Dane stopped behind Warden. "So, Travis, did you really think I would give up and die for you? You don't know me at all. You never did."

The American turned to face him. "You know what we're doing is the only way humanity can survive the coming shortages, Harald. You *know* it! Someone has to take charge, and who better than us? We already have de facto control; the plan would just enshrine it. We can end conflict in the world, permanently."

"Conflict is what made us!" Glas replied. "Without conflict you have no competition, no growth. What you want to achieve is stagnation and slavery."

"Conflict is wasteful, it squanders lives, potential, and money—but we've had this argument before." Ignoring the guns tracking him, Warden stood, looking down at Glas. "So, what's *your* plan, Harald? Are you going to shoot us?"

"Yes," said Glas bluntly. A ripple of fear ran around the table. "What you want to do is an obscenity against God and nature, and now that you know the approximate location of the meteorite, you will just keep searching until you find it. I cannot allow that to happen."

"You're going to kill them?" said Nina uneasily.

"It has to be done, Dr. Wilde. You know what they are trying to do. Is their vision of the world one you want to help create?"

"No, but there's got to be a better way than flat-out murder."

"There is not." He looked at Warden. "You tried to kill me to protect your plan. I am trying to protect the freedom of the entire human race. I have no choice. Dr. Wilde, Mr. Chase—both Mr. Chases—you may wish to leave now."

"There's no may about it," said Nina, appalled. "This isn't why I agreed to help you."

"What about the statues?" Eddie asked. They were still on the floor where Stikes had left them.

"I will make sure they are destroyed," said Glas.

"You know, I think *we* should do that. Not saying I don't trust you, but, well, I don't trust you."

"In that case, yes, you should destroy them. As a sign that you *can* trust me."

Eddie gave him a dubious look as he crossed the room to pick up the figurines, half-expecting the guns to be turned on him. But Glas's men remained focused on their prisoners. The tape holding the third statue together had come off and the two pieces separated; he shouldered his own MP7 so he could gather up all the segments.

"I think we should destroy them away from here," said Nina, retrieving the case, "so nobody can find the remains. Hopefully no one else outside this room knows what the statues can be used for, but better safe than sorry."

"Let's hope," said Eddie. He dropped the figures into the case. "Okay, Dad, let's go."

"With pleasure," said Larry.

The trio started for the exit, but Sophia's "Oh, before you go . . ." stopped them. She leaned over the back of Glas's wheelchair and whispered into his ear.

Glas listened to her with growing puzzlement. "I don't understand."

"No," she said, her black-gloved right hand reaching into her furs. "You never did." A steely edge entered her voice. "Which was the problem."

She fired the Glock into his back.

An exit wound burst open in Glas's stomach, blood and fluids splattering the shocked Warden.

⋅ ⋅ ⋅

In the kitchen, Amsel looked around sharply at the sound of a gunshot. The hotel was supposed to be secure, and everyone on the team was using silenced weapons—something had gone wrong.

He glanced back at the storeroom to check the prisoners—

The waiter was aiming a gun at him.

The window shattered as he fired. The bullet struck Amsel's temple, blasting away a chunk of skin and bone and brain.

⋅ ⋅ ⋅

Glas's men broke through their stunned horror and whirled to shoot Sophia—

Gunfire filled the room—but not from the commandos' MP7s. Instead it came from beneath the thin cloths covering the catering trolleys by the dumbwaiter, and high in the shadows of the rafters. The men were cut down by a storm of bullets from all angles, mottled red starbursts exploding over the whites of their camouflage gear.

Eddie's training had kicked in automatically when Sophia fired. He shoved Nina and Larry down between two members of the Group, diving on top to shield them. The assault ceased. He lifted his head, feeling the weight of the MP7 against his side . . . but knew raising it would be suicide.

He now understood Stikes's confidence. The entire meeting had been a trap, intended to draw Glas out of hiding—with Sophia's collaboration both encouraging the Dane to take the bait and keeping the mercenary leader informed of his actions. The men guarding the hotel's exterior had been mere decoys, sacrificial bait; those concealed in the Alpine Lounge were the real defenders, keeping out of sight until they received a signal to act.

Stikes stood. "Excellent work, everyone," he told his forces as they emerged from hiding, climbing out from under the trolleys and descending on lines from the overhead beams. All dressed entirely in black, they also wore helmets with mirrored visors to protect them from the effects of the stun grenades. "Well done."

Face quivering with fright and fury, Warden rounded on him. "What did you do? What the *fuck* just happened?" A glob of spittle flew from his lips with the profanity, landing on Stikes's chest.

The Englishman looked down at it with mild distaste before wiping it away. "I just removed all the obstacles to the Group's plan."

"But, but . . ." He jabbed a finger at Gorchakov's corpse. "We could all have been killed! Why didn't you tell us? You risked all our lives!"

"If I had told you," said Stikes, as if explaining to a child, "you would all have been too confident, which would have given away the trap. Your fear had to be genuine to bring Glas here. You must admit, it worked."

"But Anisim is dead!" protested Brannigan.

"If he hadn't gone for the gun, he would have survived. It's regrettable, but I'm afraid it was his own fault. And besides," he said loudly, raising a hand to overcome the vocal objections from around the table, "you have emergency measures to ensure that if a member dies, their interests remain under the Group's control. I suggest you activate them as soon as possible."

"We should have you fired," growled Meerkrieger. "No, we should have you shot!"

"I'm surprised at your attitude," said Stikes smugly. He gestured to a pair of his men, who roughly pulled Eddie, Nina, and Larry to their feet, confiscating the MP7 and the case. "We have the statues, we have Dr. Wilde . . . and Glas has been eliminated as a threat."

"Not quite yet," said Sophia. Glas was writhing in his chair, both hands squeezed against his stomach wound in a futile attempt to stem the bleeding. He tried to speak, blood bubbling in his mouth. "I'm sorry, Harald, I didn't quite catch that. A little louder, please?"

"Why?" gasped Glas. "Why did you . . . do it? I saved you—I protected you!"

"You *used* me!" she snapped, striding around his wheelchair to stand before him. "You'd wanted me for years, and then you finally had me—as your *slave*. Your harem girl."

"No, that . . . wasn't—"

"Oh, you made it very clear what would happen if I didn't do exactly as I was told. I could either obey you or go back to prison—or worse."

Despite the pain, Glas managed to shake his head. "No, that's . . . not true. I—I loved you!"

"Love?" she said scathingly. "You loved me in exactly the same way that you loved those coins and stamps in your precious collection! I was just one item among all the rest to you, something to make other people jealous because they couldn't own it." She bared her perfect white teeth. "Well, nobody *owns* me, and nobody *uses* me. Good-bye, Harald!"

"No, Sophia—"

She fired six rapid shots into Glas's chest. The crippled billionaire flailed with each impact, then slumped over an armrest, twitching.

The shocked silence in the room was finally broken by Nina. "*That's* got to bump the list up to fifty percent."

Warden clenched his hands together to stop them from trembling. "Stikes, I . . . I assume this was something else you chose not to tell us?"

"Of course," Stikes replied. "The only reason Sophia went on the run with Glas was that she had no choice. But she contacted me in secret whenever she had the opportunity, and together we set all of this up."

"And you *trust* her?" There was disbelief in his voice.

"Completely. You see, Sophia and I weren't merely working together. We have a more . . . intimate relationship." He smirked at Sophia, who in return kissed him.

Eddie made a gagging noise. "For God's sake! The two people I hate most in the world, and they're *shagging* each other? That's fucking disgusting."

Nina was equally appalled by the revelation. "That's about as revolting a picture as Genghis Khan getting it on with . . . with Margaret Thatcher!"

"You've just seen a man murdered," said Larry, voice shaky, "and *this* is what makes you both want to throw up?"

Warden ignored them. "Just because you're . . . *involved,* that doesn't mean she's reliable," he told Stikes. "We all know her reputation. She acts solely for her own interests, not anyone else's."

"In this case, Sophia's interests and the Group's are perfectly aligned," Stikes responded. "She's actually a very firm believer in the plan."

"Absolutely," said Sophia, smiling. "There are those who deserve simply by their superior nature to rule, and then there are . . ." She turned her gaze to Eddie. "The little people."

"Oh, fuck off," he replied. "Just 'cause you think you're better than everybody else doesn't mean you actually are. You're a stuck-up, selfish bitch with a superiority complex. Who can't play the low notes on a piano anymore."

Oddly, it was the last silly insult that erased her smile.

She clenched her left hand into a partial fist, the two prosthetic fingers jutting stiffly from it. "You know, Eddie, so many of the bad things in my life are directly attributable to you. I think it's high time I paid you back for them."

"Being married to you was like punishment in advance, so we're square."

"Ha ha," she said, scathing enough to strip paint. She advanced on him, raising the gun. "I've been looking forward to this for a very long time."

"Just a moment, Sophia," said Stikes. "If you don't mind, *I'd* like to kill Chase." A malevolent smile. "For old times' sake."

She glowered at him. "Excuse me, Alexander? I think I have the greater right."

"I had to serve with him."

"I had to *sleep* with him."

"Anyone else want to join in?" Eddie asked of the room—using the opportunity to assess his chances of either fleeing or grabbing a weapon. Neither option seemed likely to succeed. None of Stikes's men was close enough for him to reach without being shot down, and the exits were even farther away.

The doors, at least. There might be another way out—if he could get to it . . .

"All right, I think that trumps mine," Stikes admitted. "Very well. Enjoy it."

"Oh, I absolutely will," Sophia said. She brought up the Glock again—

Nina moved to block her line of fire. "You'll have to go through me."

The smile returned. "Two for the price of one? Excellent."

"No!" Warden barked. "We need her! Are you insane?"

"You have to ask?" said Nina.

Stikes issued orders to his men. "Move her away—and him as well," he added, indicating Larry. "Careful, Chase. Don't try anything foolish. We may need your wife, but we don't need her conscious. Or even fully intact."

"Go on," said Eddie to Nina and Larry as the mercenaries approached. "Both of you."

Nina clutched his hands. "Eddie, I'm not going to let this crazy bitch shoot you!"

"I'll be okay. Go on."

The guards pulled her away. "Eddie!"

"I must admit, Eddie," said Sophia, striding toward her ex-husband with the clack of stiletto heels, "if there's one thing that I'm very slightly jealous of about your relationship with Nina—and there *is* only the one thing, and it is only very, *very* slightly—it's that no matter what annoying and petty personal issues you have, when the chips are down you always support each other. If you'd had that kind of commitment to our marriage, who knows where we'd be now?"

"*I'm* the one who didn't have commitment?" said Eddie. "You were the one who was off like a shot to open your legs for the first rich guy who came along!"

She narrowed her eyes. "That's hardly an accurate description."

"No? You lost interest in me the moment your dad cut you off from his money, and you started trying to fuck your way back into high society. Sex for cash? You know, there's a name for people like you."

Sophia pointed the gun at his face. "Don't you *dare* call me that."

"Or what, you'll shoot me? You're going to do that anyway, so I might as well clear the air while I can. You're fucking pathetic, Soph. Daddy's little girl doesn't get what she wants, so she takes it out on everyone else. Same old story, only now *everyone else* is *literally* everyone in the world!"

Eddie could tell from her increasingly angered expression that the mentions of her father had touched a raw nerve. He pushed on with a sarcastic sneer. "Yeah, His Lordship was a great example of the *superior* classes, wasn't he? Turns his back on his own daughter, and then loses everything he owns to people like this lot"—he waved a hand at the Group, all watching as if transfixed by a soap opera—"because he's a chinless fucking idiot who thought having a title made him immune to how the real world works. The only thing you *could* be with a role model like that was a whor—"

Lips tight with fury, she stepped closer and slapped him, hard. Eddie took the blow—

And grabbed her gun hand, twisting her arm with savage force to pull her against him. He clamped his other hand around her throat, pushing the Glock's muzzle up against her chin. She cried out in choked pain.

"Okay, everyone freeze!" he shouted, backing up as the mercenaries aimed their weapons and looked to Stikes for instructions. "Anyone tries anything, she'll get her fucking head blown off."

Warden recovered from his shock at the sudden turn-around of events, making a sound that could almost have been a relieved chuckle. "I doubt anyone here would have a problem with that." His companions nodded in agreement.

"I would," Stikes said darkly. "Chase, let her go or I'll have Nina shot."

"You'll do no such damn thing," Warden snapped.

"In that case I'll have your *father* shot." Some of his men's guns moved to cover Larry. "However great your daddy issues are, I'm sure you don't want them resolved with a bullet, do you?"

Eddie kept retreating, hauling Sophia with him. "You don't know what I think of my dad."

"Edward!" protested Larry.

"He doesn't mean it," Nina whispered to him. "I'm . . . pretty sure."

"Chase!" said Stikes, losing patience. "Let her go and give up. You can't get away, so just accept the inevitable."

"Which is what?" said Eddie, briefly checking behind. He was now only a matter of feet from the catering trolleys.

"That I was always going to win. I'll even make it quick for you."

"Like when you made it quick for those women you murdered in Afghanistan?"

"Enough! Last chance, Chase."

"Yeah, I know," said Eddie. He dropped the gun . . . then shoved Sophia forcefully away as he threw himself backward—

Into the dumbwaiter.

THIRTY-ONE

Sophia was still close enough to block the mercenaries' line of fire. Eddie used the brief moment of protection to pull his legs inside the little elevator, curling into a ball—as his weight far overloaded its maximum capacity and sent the car plunging down the shaft.

The impact of landing knocked the breath from his lungs. Dizzied, he kicked open the doors and scrambled out, dropping heavily to the tiled floor.

Amsel's corpse lay nearby, blood oozing from a gaping head wound. The storeroom was empty, its door open—as was the outside exit. Stikes must have planted one of his men in the kitchen staff. The hotel workers themselves had fled.

He staggered upright. Amsel's weapons—

They were gone. Stikes's man must have taken them.

Which left him completely unarmed against a team of mercenaries out for his blood.

* * *

"Get down to the kitchens!" Stikes bellowed to his men. "*Now!*" The black-clad mercs sprinted for the exit.

Larry was still staring in astonishment at the empty

hole in the wall. "He—he jumped down the dumb-waiter!"

"Yeah, he does things like that," said Nina, trying not to let her enemies detect her concern for her husband's safety.

Stikes pushed past them to Sophia. "Are you all right?"

"Yes," she replied, shaken—before turning to look at the hatch. Her shock became outrage. "You let him get away!"

"We could have shot him, but I thought you wouldn't appreciate having the bullets go through you first," he said testily, before returning to the table. "Ladies, gentlemen, for your own safety I'd recommend that we leave the hotel until I get confirmation that Chase is dead."

"You want us to run away?" rasped Meerkrieger. "It sounds as if you're scared of him."

"Hardly," the Englishman said, stiffening. "It's just that Chase has, shall we say, a talent for destruction. I wouldn't put it past him to set the hotel on fire or cause a gas explosion in an attempt to escape." His audience's expressions showed that they had very quickly come around to his way of thinking.

"He won't try to escape," said Sophia. She pointed at Nina and Larry. "He'll try to rescue them."

"Then we'd better make sure he can't reach them. Or these." He picked up the case containing the statues. "We'll take the cable car down to the village. I'll call ahead to have transport waiting for us."

The Group members stood. "Are you sure this is necessary?" Warden asked.

"As long as Chase is running loose, I wouldn't take any chances. This way, please."

"You heard him," said Sophia, jabbing Nina with the Glock.

Everyone hurried for the main exit, Nina and Larry exchanging worried glances.

*　*　*

Eddie ran across the kitchen. He needed to get back upstairs to find Nina and his father, but the closest flight of steps, just outside the swing doors, would at any moment have mercenaries pounding down it. If he could get past it before they arrived, though, he might be able to find an alternative way up . . .

He saw fast-moving shadows on the stairwell wall through the circular windows. "Arse!" he muttered as he changed direction for the exterior door.

The swing doors crashed open behind him. Bullets blazed across the kitchen—but he was already pounding up the snow-covered steps outside. Whirling snowflakes pricked his eyes as he reached the top. Wherever he ran, the mercs would be able to follow his trail in the snow and pick him off—he had to buy himself some time.

The bins—

The nearest wheeled container was a few feet away. He grabbed the handles on its side. It shifted slightly, but refused to move from its spot.

If it was chained to the others, he was screwed.

He pulled harder—and with a crackle of ice from around its wheels it jolted away from its fellows. Eddie ran around it and pushed. Boots scraping against the slippery ground, he shoved it toward the stairwell. It was over half full, and the snow piled up on its lid wasn't making it any lighter. "Come on, come on," he gasped. "Come *on*, you smelly bastard—"

A cry of "Here, he's here!" from below—and a submachine gun let rip on full auto, bullets tearing up through the bin's side and erupting out through the plastic lid amid geysers of snow. Eddie yelled and dropped down, pushing with his shoulder

The bin lurched sharply as the wheels went over the edge of the top step—and suddenly the whole thing raced away from him, bouncing and crashing down the stairs. The firing stopped, the mercenary trying to retreat into the kitchen—but he was too slow. The bin hit like a charging bull, slamming him backward into the base of the stairwell. The crack of bones was almost lost beneath the echoing boom and clatter of metal and trash.

Eddie was already running for the front of the hotel.

With the bin blocking the kitchen door, Stikes's men would have to find another exit.

He rounded the corner. The towering windows of the Alpine Lounge glowed above him. From his low angle he couldn't see much of the room itself, but enough was visible to reveal that it was empty. The Group had left—taking their prisoners with them.

But where?

Movement through the blowing snow gave him an answer. At the hotel's far end, beyond the skating rink, the cable car emerged from the upper station and began its descent. Its interior lights shone brightly, revealing that it was packed to the brim with passengers.

One of whom had very distinctive red hair.

"Buggeration and fuckery!" Stikes's doing, he knew; the former officer was making sure Eddie could no longer interfere in the game by taking away the most important pieces. The statues, Nina to make use of them . . . and Larry to force her to cooperate.

He ran through the snow after the cable car. In a few minutes it would reach the village, and the Group and their captives would be whisked away.

He had to catch up. But he had abandoned his skis after reaching the bottom of the slope, and it would take too long to retrieve them. He needed a faster alternative . . .

The luge run.

The long wooden shed at its top was almost directly beneath the cable lines. If he could get to a sled, it would be the quickest way down the mountain short of flying.

Movement in the hotel. Two mercenaries barged through a set of glass doors, readying their MP5s—

Eddie altered course, raising his arms to protect his head and diving through a window in the side of a small hut beside the ice rink. His thick coat protected him from the broken glass, but the rough landing still hurt. He jumped up, seeing that the hut's rear wall was lined with shelves full of ice skates.

He also saw that there was only one exit—a door facing the hotel.

Which would bring him straight into the gunmen's sights—

The mercenaries opened fire, spraying the hut with bullets. Splinters exploded from the wooden walls. One man was shooting at chest height, the other aiming lower as he swept his gun back and forth in case their target had thrown himself flat.

Their magazines ran dry almost simultaneously. They put in fresh ammunition as they tromped through the snow to the door. Lines of bullet holes ran across the hut's façade, the largest gap between them little more than six inches. Anyone inside would be Swiss cheese.

The pockmarked door was kicked open—

Apart from broken wood and scattered skates, the hut was empty.

The mercenaries looked at each other, puzzled. There was nowhere their quarry could have exited unseen. One man leaned cautiously through the door to check if he was skulking in a shadowed corner . . .

A long spike of gleaming steel whisked down from the ceiling and stabbed deep into his eye socket.

The mercenary screamed and fell backward against his companion as Eddie dropped from the rafters, having used the same concealment tactic as Stikes's men had in the Alpine Lounge—with equal effectiveness. He wore a skating boot on his right fist like a misshapen boxing glove, the tail of its blade coated in blood. The mortally wounded man collapsed, the other merc trying to bring his MP5 back up.

The blade slashed again, sweeping across the second man's neck and sending an arcing cascade of gore over the clean white snow. Gurgling, the mercenary clutched helplessly at his slit throat, then slumped on top of his comrade.

Eddie tossed the boot away and snatched up an MP5, then resumed his run for the luge track. He spotted the cable car again as he neared the top of the slope, now little more than a small box of light fading into the snowy darkness below. Was he too late to catch it?

Only one way to find out. He raced into the shed, the open-ended building a garage of sorts for sleds. Some were luges, designed to be ridden feetfirst; others were "skeletons," where the rider lay on his stomach to make a headfirst descent.

It only now occurred to him that he had no idea how to control either.

"It's a sledge, how hard can it be?" Not quite convinced, he slung the gun and pulled a luge into the open. It had a leather strap resembling reins attached to its front, but there was no apparent steering mechanism on the runners. The only way to guide it was presumably by shifting his weight.

He would have to figure it out on the way down. Hauling it to the top of the track, Eddie was about to take his seat when he heard shouts from the ice rink. The two corpses had been found—and their discoverers were already following him, weapons at the ready—

Eddie threw himself bodily onto the luge as the first shots whizzed past him. His momentum sent it slithering onto the track . . . where it picked up speed with alarming rapidity.

He was in completely the wrong position to control it, lying prone with his head at the front and legs dangling off the back. He frantically grabbed the strap and pulled it tight, then looked ahead. Snowflakes stabbed at his eyes, forcing him to squint. There was just enough residual twilight for him to make out the line of the track, its sides marked by raised walls of snow and ice—and he was veering straight for one of them.

"Shit!" He pulled hard on the reins, leaning as far as he dared in the opposite direction. The luge's runners rasped over the icy ground as it skidded, going almost side-on down the track before he shoved down the toe of one boot to act as an anchor and swing him back into line.

He was only doing about 30 miles per hour—but lying

just inches off the ground with his head out front like a bony bumper, it felt more like 130. The ride was horribly rough, not even the snow on the track smoothing his descent. Another curve ahead. He shifted his weight again, the sled this time turning in a slightly more controlled manner. The wall whipped past a handbreadth away.

The lights of the cable car swung back into view as he came out of the bend. He was already gaining. If he kept up this pace—and didn't kill himself first—he would overtake it well before it reached the village . . .

A new sound over the grind of metal on ice. An engine.

The harsh rasp was unmistakable. A snowmobile.

He didn't dare look back to find it. The luge was still gaining speed, the track twisting through a stand of trees. Another wall rushed at him; he slammed down a foot and rolled almost fully on his side to swerve away from it. Too fast, nearly out of control—but the snowmobile was closing, its engine snarling as it bounced over the terrain. He was trapped by the track's confines, but the other driver could take the quickest route to intercept him.

The luge plowed through a hump of snow, the explosion of powder briefly blinding him. Gasping, he put both feet down to slow the sledge, the ice scraping viciously against his toes.

Another curve, his sleeve brushing the wall as he strained to make the turn. The snowmobile's engine was briefly muffled as he passed behind a large snowbank. He had almost caught up with the cable car—

The snowmobile's muted roar suddenly became a terrifying howl as it burst over the top of the bank and swept down into the track directly behind him.

Its headlight pinned him in its glaring beam. Eddie now had a clear view of the track ahead, but a crash was no longer the greatest danger. He looked back. The snowmobile was less than ten feet behind, twin front skis slashing through the ice.

The engine revved. The gap closed. He brought the luge skittering around another bend. The snowmobile followed, its rider feathering the throttle to hold it in a controlled skid before applying full power again. The light grew brighter.

Eddie braced himself—

One of the skis bashed against his foot. The impact knocked the sled around, sending him at a wall. He desperately tried to counter it, but overcompensated. The luge wriggled like a fish beneath him, almost throwing him off. He was forced to jam both feet down against the track to keep control—and the snowmobile rammed him again, harder. Pain shot through his ankle as his foot was almost crushed under the skid.

The snowmobile dropped back slightly, then revved again, rushing forward to run him over . . .

Another curve—and the wall was partly covered by a snowdrift. Eddie flung the luge into a sharp turn. It hit the wall—but the drift was just thick enough for the runners to ride up over it.

Even so, the impact flipped him off the sled. He sailed helplessly through the air. Trees loomed ahead—

He missed a trunk by less than a foot, smacking down in deep snow beyond it. The luge thunked off the tree and spun away in pieces.

His pursuer turned hard to follow him. The machine slammed over the wall, going airborne—

And smashing straight into a tree.

The snowmobile exploded, a boiling orange fireball lighting up the little forest. Eddie shielded his head as burning debris rained down around him. He waited a few seconds, then cautiously sat up.

The snow had cushioned his landing, but he was still sore and woozy, ankle throbbing from its run-in with the skid. He shifted, putting experimental weight on it. The effort made him wince as pain spiked through the joint. He was still able to move, but running after the cable car would hurt . . .

The cable car! He looked up. It would pass almost

directly overhead in seconds. He was still some way from the village, and without the sled there was no way he could possibly catch up before it reached the lower station. The MP5 was also gone, lost in the snow. He stared helplessly at the gondola as it rumbled over the trees.

Someone stared back at him.

Stikes.

* * *

"I don't *believe* it," said Stikes, banging an exasperated hand on the glass as he saw movement in the firelit snow below. "It's Chase!"

Nina shoved past the mercenary guarding her and pressed her nose to the window. To her delight, she saw a figure among the flaming remains of a snowmobile. "He's still alive!" She gave Larry a triumphant look. The elder Chase beamed at the news.

"Not for long," said Sophia, pushing between Group members to see for herself. She batted the guard's arm. "You! You've got a gun—shoot him!"

The mercenary turned to Stikes for confirmation. "Do as she says," he ordered. "Everyone move away from the door."

The cabin was already crowded, and it became even more cramped as the other passengers pressed back so Stikes could slide open the door. A freezing, snow-laden wind blew in. The mercenary braced himself against the frame as he leaned out and aimed at the man below.

* * *

Eddie searched for cover. The nearest tree was the one the snowmobile had hit, flames licking up its trunk. But if he ran straight for it he would be presenting his back to the gunman above.

Instead he dived back into the piled snow as the MP5 fired. Bullets slapped into the drift and debris behind him. He rolled as he landed to offer the smallest possible target. The cable car was carrying his attacker inexorably away; every passing moment would make him harder to hit.

But right now he was still well within range. Another roll as more shots kicked up fountains of snow. Each impact got closer, the mercenary adjusting his aim to follow him—

* * *

Everyone in the cable car flinched away from the noise of the MP5 as the mercenary fired.

Except Nina. She lashed out, knocking Stikes back from the door—then hurled herself bodily at the mercenary—

Tackling him out of the cable car.

"Nina!" Larry cried, but she was gone.

Trees rushed up at her. She screamed, the mercenary beneath her doing likewise as they plunged into the snow-laden foliage. Branches broke, the cracks louder and deeper as the limbs thickened farther down the tree—then suddenly the man slammed to a stop. Nina bounced painfully off him and tumbled, winded, the rest of the way to the ground. Blinded by spraying snow and thrashing boughs, she hit the hillside with a thud.

* * *

Warden looked out of the cable car in horror. "My God! We've got to get her back—she could be hurt, or even dead!"

"Wouldn't that be a shame," Sophia said quietly.

Stikes took out his radio. "This is Stikes! Chase and Dr. Wilde are on the hotel grounds, about five hundred yards from the village. They're directly below the cable-car line near a burning tree. Dr. Wilde *must* be taken alive—she may need medical attention. My orders regarding Chase stand; I want him killed on sight." He checked the scene behind. A figure was lolloping away from the fire toward the site of Nina's touchdown. "He's *still* alive!" He slammed the door shut in barely contained rage.

"A sentiment I've felt all too many times," said Sophia.

Larry spoke up unexpectedly, all eyes turning to him. "What can I say? That's my boy." He smiled at the hostile gazes of the other passengers.

* * *

Eddie moved as quickly as he could down the hill, the steep slope and deep snow tough to negotiate even without an aching ankle. He reached the still-quivering tree, seeing no sign of his wife. "Nina! Can you hear me? Nina!"

"Ow . . ." came a muffled voice. He followed the sound, discovering a cartoonishly perfect Nina-shaped hole in a snowdrift. Its maker was spread-eagled at the bottom.

"Fuck me, I've found a snow angel," he said, clearing away the snow. "Are you okay? Can you move?"

"No, and I dunno, in that order. Agh, Jesus . . ." Nina struggled to sit up, hair festooned with bits of branches and needles. "God*damm*it! Feels like my head's coming off," she said, pressing a hand against one temple—then looking around in alarm. "Eddie! The guy I pushed out of the cable car—where is he?"

Eddie hurriedly surveyed their surroundings. "I can't see anyone . . . oh, hang on." There was a dark patch beneath the tree, standing out against the snow even in the dying light. "Okay, I've found him. Don't think he'll give us any problems."

Nina blearily followed his gaze to see the mercenary impaled on a branch thirty feet above like some grotesque Christmas ornament. Blood dribbled down the boughs below him. "He's gone out on a limb."

"Hey! Shit puns are my department." He lifted her out of the snowdrift. "Where's Dad?"

"In the cable car." The gondola was now out of sight behind the trees. "And they've still got the statues too."

Eddie looked in the other direction. Lights were descending the mountainside from the hotel. "They're coming. We've got to get to the village."

"But they'll be waiting for us," Nina objected.

"Better than us waiting for them. Come on." They set off through the snow.

The village soon came into view, the cable car's elevated lower station standing out above the houses. The gondola had already reached its destination, but it would take Eddie and Nina another couple of minutes to wade through the snow to the edge of the hotel's grounds, never mind the village proper. "Dammit!" said Nina. "They'll be long gone when we get there."

Eddie had other concerns. The main entrance to the grounds was marked by a large gate at the end of a bridge over the railway—and he had just spotted more lights spreading out from it. He looked uphill. The mercenaries from the hotel were now following their trail through the snow, torches bobbing as they yomped down the slope. "Shit! They're catching up. Go that way." He pointed to the right, beyond the village's edge.

"What's over there?"

"Not men with guns, and that'll do me for now!"

Nina heard something over the *crump* of snow and their own panting, a deep rhythmic huffing like the breath of some giant animal. "It's the train!" Past the bridge, glowing embers from the steam locomotive's funnel swirled in the air as it headed back down the valley. "Eddie, the track goes right along the bottom of the grounds—if we can make it stop, we can get aboard."

He was already judging distances and speeds: of the train, himself and Nina . . . and the two groups of mercenaries closing on them. "There won't be time for it to stop."

"Then how are we going to get on it?"

"Jump!"

"*Jump?*"

"What, you've never train-surfed before?"

"No, because it's insane!"

"You never want to try anything new. Come on, hoof it!" They reached the fence and climbed over it.

The men coming from the gate had obviously been in radio contact with their comrades higher up; the dots of torchlight were all now heading along the bottom of the grounds. The group following Nina and Eddie's trail were less than a hundred yards behind—and closing the gap.

The train was rapidly approaching, the clanking of the locomotive's running gear growing louder. Another jab of pain stabbed through Eddie's ankle, but he forced himself to run faster as the train came into view, traveling through a shallow cutting below. The carriage roofs were a couple of feet higher than the upper side. "There!" he shouted, pointing at a slight rise on the cutting's edge. "Get ready to jump!" He grabbed Nina's hand.

The locomotive surged past, belching steam and hot, sooty smoke. "Oh God!" Nina cried as they ran the last few yards. "We're gonna *diiiie*—"

They leapt, clearing the gap—and landing hard on a metal roof. Nina staggered, but kept her footing—just. It was Eddie who stumbled, one foot slipping out from under him. He skidded across the roof, legs flailing over the side . . .

Nina still had hold of his hand. She gripped it with all her strength and wedged a heel against a domed ventilator cover. The jolt as she caught his weight felt as though her arm was tearing from its socket, but she fought through the pain and held on. Eddie dangled before managing to catch the carriage's rain gutter with his boot's ice-shredded toe. He forced himself back onto the roof.

Nina dropped on her butt with a bang. "Jesus!" she gasped, releasing his hand. "I thought you were going over!"

"So did I," Eddie admitted, gasping for breath—and then coughing as a dirty cloud rolled over them. "Bloody hell! Let's get off here before we end up smoked like fucking hams."

He crawled along the roof, Nina behind him, and looked down. Like the locomotive, the carriages were vintage, with open platforms at each end. Eddie lowered Nina down, then thumped onto the platform himself.

A door led inside. They went through—to find the tourists taking the last train of the day staring at them in astonishment. Their touchdown on the roof had been far from quiet.

"What?" said Nina, deciding that nonchalance was as good a response as any. "I've got a ticket." She fished inside her clothing to produce it; it was indeed a return fare.

"I don't," Eddie complained.

She flopped down in a seat and smiled. "Well, if the conductor comes along, you'll just have to hide in the john."

* * *

"They did *what*?" Stikes barked into his phone.

"Let me guess," said Sophia with a resigned sigh. "They got away from your men."

He shot her an irritated look. "They jumped on the train." Leaning forward, he addressed the driver of the Range Rover in which he, Sophia, Warden, and Larry were traveling. "Can we get to the next station before them?"

"Not on this road, sir," came the apologetic reply. "The train goes through a tunnel, but the road goes the long way around."

Stikes sat back, fuming. "Oh, that's too bad," said Larry mockingly.

"We still have Chase's father," Warden said from the front seat, regarding the man in question with disapproval. "Chase and Dr. Wilde came here to rescue him— they'll do the same again."

"Only if we can contact them to issue an ultimatum, and I doubt they'll be going back to the IHA to wait for one," Sophia told him. "They'll try to find the meteorite."

"So they can destroy it," Stikes added.

"But we have the statues," said Warden. "She can't locate it without them."

"And we can't locate it without her," Stikes pointed out. "We only know it's somewhere in Ethiopia. And Wilde probably got a much better idea where from this . . . *vision*."

Warden nodded. "So what do we do?"

Stikes straightened in his seat. "The first thing I need," he said imperiously, "is total and unrestricted access to the Group's resources worldwide. Men, information, money—everything, from all the members."

The American eyed him suspiciously. "Why?"

"If we're going to beat Wilde and Chase to the meteorite, we can't afford to waste time discussing how to proceed. We have to act quickly and decisively. There's still a chance we can catch them before they leave Switzerland, or at least before they reach Africa, but unfortunately they're very resourceful—as you've just seen. If we can get people and equipment in place in Ethiopia as soon as possible, we still have a chance of beating them. We can either capture Wilde and force her to locate the stone for us . . ."

"Or let her lead us to it," finished Warden.

"Exactly."

The American nodded again. "All right. I'll give you complete access." He took out his phone—then fixed Stikes with a warning look, raising a finger. "Don't screw this up."

"I won't," Stikes replied firmly. "I'm not going to let them win."

THIRTY-TWO

Ethiopia

Peter Alderley dabbed sweat off his drooping mustache as he warily surveyed the street outside the ramshackle café. "I shouldn't even be here, you know," he said. "MI6 generally isn't too happy about its officers taking unscheduled trips to foreign countries. If anyone finds out—"

"Hey, everyone!" Eddie suddenly cried, pointing excitedly at him. "British secret agent, right here! It's Peter Alderley! Come on, quick, get his autograph and listen to him drone on about restoring his 1973 Ford Capri!" None of the passing residents of Dubti, some forty miles from the border with Djibouti in Ethiopia's northeastern corner, seemed remotely interested in the revelation, or even found anything particularly unusual about the presence of three Westerners in their town. While the country in general was hardly a tourist trap, the wildlife reserve and national park to the south meant that international visitors were not uncommon.

"Eddie," Nina chided. He laughed and sat back.

"Very funny," Alderley muttered. "And it's a 1971, actually."

"We do appreciate this, Peter, really," Nina assured him. It was two days since they had left Switzerland, having contacted Alderley and on his advice traveled first to Slovenia before flying on via Egypt to the eponymous capital of Djibouti, where the MI6 officer met them for the road trip into the neighboring country. Alderley's contacts in both African nations had allowed them to make the journey without any official hassles— for a modest fee.

"And we appreciate this little lot too," added Eddie, nudging a rucksack beneath their table.

Alderley winced. "Be careful with that!"

"Why? It's not going to blow up."

The MI6 man's expression didn't inspire confidence. "Is it?" Nina asked.

"The actual explosives should be stable. But they're . . . well, past their sell-by date, put it that way. I couldn't exactly requisition them from the quartermaster at Vauxhall Cross! They've been tucked away here for years by someone I know. So I wouldn't throw them around."

"What about the detonators?" said Eddie.

"Standard RC units—you'll have used them before in the SAS. They've all got new batteries, but there's still some risk of deterioration, and since they're one-use items there's no way to test them in the field—other than actually firing them, I suppose. As for the trigger"—he took a device the size of a chunky mobile phone from the rucksack—"it's as reliable as any other electronic device in sub-optimal conditions, so . . . caveat emptor." He gave Nina an apologetic smile.

Eddie took the trigger unit from him. "What's the setup?"

"Simple enough, even for you." The Yorkshireman made a sarcastic face. "Five channels, controlled by the dial." Alderley indicated the control, around which were marked the numbers one to five and the words FULL and SAFE. It was currently set to the latter. "The numbers are for individual detonators, obviously, and FULL blows everything simultaneously. Just switch it on and push the red button. Boom. The range is up to about a mile."

"What about the blast radius?"

"I'd say you want to be at least fifty yards clear—more if you're taking out something that might produce shrapnel."

"We'll definitely want to be more than fifty yards away, then," said Nina.

"I see." Alderley took a sip from his bottle of Coca-Cola. "You're really not going to give me any more than that? Even after everything I've done to get you here?"

She shook her head. "This will probably sound like a horrible spy cliché, but the less you know the better. The people we're trying to avoid are extremely powerful."

"How powerful?"

"Enough to have the ear of presidents."

"And bring down ex-presidents," Eddie added.

Alderley's eyebrows flicked up. "Dalton?" Nina nodded. "I was wondering what kicked that off. The Yanks usually let their former leaders get away with anything short of murder, so I thought something major had to be going on. You know, you two really do pick quite a high class of enemies."

"They seem to pick *us*." Nina sighed. "But I'd imagine they probably have prime ministers on their speed dials as well. Which is why we wanted to keep you out of the loop."

"Well, if anyone at MI6 asks why I used my holiday allowance to make a last-minute excursion to Africa," said Alderley unhappily, "I'll just have to come up with some convincing excuse. If one exists."

"Tell 'em you found a 1973 Capri head gasket on the Ethiopian eBay and had to collect it in person," suggested Eddie with a smirk.

"It's a '71" came the irritable reply before his face became more somber. "But . . . you found out who was behind Mac's death, so that's why I'm taking the risk. I owe you that much. You helped lay him to rest."

Eddie's mood became equally downbeat as he remembered his friend and mentor. "He's not properly laid to rest yet," he said. "Not until we stop these arseholes. And I take care of Stikes."

"This isn't about revenge," Nina gently reminded him. "It won't bring Mac back. And you were the one who always said that revenge isn't professional."

"Stikes stopped it being professional when he made it personal. When he made it about family. It's the same with soldiers, cops . . . probably spooks too," he said, with a look at Alderley, who nodded. "You fuck with someone's family, then you deserve anything you get."

"Speaking of family," said Alderley, "I really should get back to mine." He finished his Coke and stood. "So good luck with . . . whatever the hell you're doing."

Nina also stood and shook his hand, then kissed his cheek. "Thank you for everything, Peter."

"Helping your husband put me in rather an in-for-a-penny-in-for-a-pound situation, so I thought I might as well go all-out. Try not to let the world get destroyed, eh?"

"Not on my watch," said Eddie. "Thanks, Alderley." There was an awkward silence before the two men finally shared a brief handshake.

"No kiss?" said Alderley.

"Go on, fuck off," said Eddie, but with a smile. The MI6 officer grinned, then exited the café. "Thought he'd never leave."

"Oh, stop that. And we'd better leave ourselves." Through his contacts, Alderley had arranged supplies and transport in the form of a battered old Land Rover.

Eddie picked up the rucksack containing the explosives. "Where exactly are we going?"

Nina made an uncertain face. "That's a very good question."

* * *

The Afar Depression is appropriately named. Not only does the huge area contain the lowest point in Africa, more than five hundred feet below sea level, but it is also likely to bring misery to anyone entering it. One of the hottest places on earth, it is also one of the most desolate, a great expanse of desert where only the hardiest scrubby vegetation survives. Within its boundaries there are no roads and, beyond a few isolated villages and nomadic tribes, no people. Adding to its inhospitability is the very nature of the region, a widening geological rift producing a chain of active volcanoes and even one of the world's few lava lakes.

The Land Rover was three hours out of Dubti, heading north by northwest, and even that small town now seemed like a metropolis in hindsight. The baking desert stretched endlessly away to the rippling horizon in all directions. The four-by-four had a GPS receiver on its dashboard, but it couldn't provide Nina and Eddie with a countdown of the distance to their destination. The reason was simple: They didn't actually know where they were going.

Not on a map, at least. Nina was providing directions, but that didn't stop Eddie, driving, from giving her a dubious look as the Land Rover jolted across the stony plain. "You *sure* we're going the right way?"

It was not the first time he had asked the question. "No, I'm *not* sure, Eddie," she said tiredly, taking a mouthful of unpleasantly warm water from a plastic bottle. "I have a *feeling*, that's all."

"Trusting your feelings is fine for Jedi, but I'd be a lot happier with something a bit more definite."

"So would I, but it's all there is. So we'll have to make do."

"Can't you even explain it better?"

"No, Eddie, I can't!" She composed herself, taking another drink before replacing the cap. "Sorry. I didn't mean . . ."

"Yeah, I know." He was silent for a moment, then

with uncharacteristic hesitation said, "And . . . there's something I want to say sorry for."

"What?"

"When we were in Peru, and I found out about Nan . . . I blamed you for me not being able to see her again before she died. I shouldn't have done that. It wasn't your fault, and I'm sorry."

She put her hand on his shoulder. "That's okay. I know what you were feeling. I was the same when I learned that my parents had died."

"Even so, I shouldn't—"

"Eddie." She stroked his cheek. "It's okay. Really."

A small smile of gratitude. "Thanks."

They drove on, Eddie surveying the parched desert. It was as inhospitable and empty a place as they had ever visited. "So, this feeling of yours," he said. "Wish I could figure out how it works."

"Yeah, me too!" Nina regarded the desolation ahead. "I can't really describe it. I just *know* somehow that it's in this direction. If all life on the planet really did originate from the meteorite, then technically everybody is connected to it at a genetic level. The earth energy effect apparently lets me feel that more directly."

"I thought it only worked when you were holding the statues—and that you had to be somewhere where the energy lines connect."

"So did I. But this is more like an aftereffect, an echo. It's like . . ." She struggled to find the words. "The best I can manage is that I can . . . feel it tickling my subconscious, I guess. It's this way. Somewhere."

"An idea how far would be good."

"Afraid it's not as precise as GPS. Sorry."

They drove on. Another hour passed. Eddie squinted into the distance—then looked sharply around at something in his peripheral vision. "What?" Nina asked.

"There's a plane over there." Sunlight glinted off a tiny dot in the sky to the northeast.

Nina's fatigue was instantly replaced by concern. "The Group?"

He snorted. "How would I know? I don't have bionic eyes. It's a long way off, though."

"Where's it going?"

Eddie stopped the four-by-four and stared intently into the blue void. "Might be on its way to Djibouti."

"Or it might be searching for the meteorite."

"Or us."

Nina looked into the back of the Land Rover. The rucksack had been secured in the cargo bed, padded as best they could manage against the vehicle's jolts by other bags. "So long as we have time to blow up the stone before they find us, that's the most important thing."

"That, and us getting out alive—I think that's pretty important too." He set off again. "Something I've been thinking about, though."

"What?"

"Just how big is this meteorite? If it's, I dunno, the size of a couch, or a car, we've got enough explosives to blow it to bits. But if it's bigger, we might end up making the Group's job easier. If all we can do is split it apart, then they can get right at the DNA or whatever's inside it."

It was a possibility Nina had also considered. "The best we can do is . . . the best we can do," she was forced to concede. "We just try to make it as hard for them as we possibly can. If they realize they've lost any chance to carry out their plan, well, like Glas said, they're businesspeople. Hopefully we can persuade them to free Larry without being vindictive."

"The Group might do that," said Eddie, grim-faced. "Stikes and Sophia won't."

"Yeah, I was kinda hoping you wouldn't point out the flaw in my one optimistic thought."

The Land Rover continued across the empty expanse. Eddie lost sight of the aircraft, not knowing if it had changed course or was simply too far away. The terrain became harder, forcing him to slow down to navigate the rocky surface. Something appeared on the horizon ahead, a mirage rippling through the distorting heat-haze.

Nina peered at it. "Is that a hill?"

"Hills, I think," said Eddie, as more shimmering peaks slowly rose into view. He noticed a faint column of what looked like steam drifting up from the tallest of them. "Or volcanoes." Nina's lack of a reply made him suddenly very uneasy. "Oh, for fuck's sake. You're not telling me . . ."

"I think that's where it is," she told him. The light but insistent tugging on her soul felt somehow more intense.

"In a fucking *volcano*?"

"It ties in with Nantalas's vision. And it fits with what I felt when I put the statues together in Switzerland. If Nantalas experienced the same thing, she'd interpret it based on her beliefs. Remember what the text said in the Temple of Poseidon, about Hephaestus? He was the Greek—and Atlantean—god of volcanoes."

"So it *is* inside a volcano. Great. How are we supposed to get to it?"

"I have absolutely no idea. I don't suppose there's a fireproof suit in our gear?"

"It's funny, but I don't think Alderley thought of that."

The mirage took on a solidity as they got closer. The volcano was not particularly high, but it dominated the surroundings, a near-perfect cone looming over its foothills. After the better part of an hour they were on its flanks, the steepness of the rocky slope finally outmatching even the Land Rover's hill-climbing abilities. Eddie stopped the four-by-four on a small sloping plateau and got out, looking up at the steaming summit. "So what do we do?" he asked. "Go to the top and look down into the crater to see if we can see the meteor? Or a secret base with a monorail. That'd be cooler."

Nina smiled. "I doubt even Blofeld would be dumb enough to build a base inside an *active* volcano . . ." She stopped, frowning slightly.

"What?"

"I'm not sure. It's another feeling, that there's something . . ." She slowly turned, raising a hand to shield her eyes from the sun as she looked across the hillside at a higher spot.

"The rock?"

"I don't know. I just feel some kind of connection to this place . . ." Almost absently, she headed up the slope.

"Hey, hold on!" Eddie hurriedly extracted the rucksack from the Land Rover, along with another bag of basic survival equipment, and went after her. "Take some bloody water, at least." He gave her the bag.

"Sorry. But whatever it is, I don't think it's far away."

They angled up the volcano's side. Though it was still active, the clumps of vegetation in the dirt, along with geological features that would require centuries, if not millennia, to erode, showed that it hadn't erupted for a considerable time. "One less thing to worry about," said Eddie when Nina pointed this out. "I don't want to be hopping over streams of molten lava like Lara bloody Croft."

"You don't quite have her figure," Nina joked. "But I don't think we'll—"

She stopped as she cleared a rise—and saw something ahead.

"Well, Christ," Eddie said, amazed. "There *is* something here."

Part of the hillside had suffered a landslide, a swath of rock reduced to rubble. But among the debris were stones that very clearly had not been shaped by the random forces of nature. Straight edges and right angles stood out from the scattered scree. Nina broke into a jog toward the broken remains. "There must have been something built on the volcano!"

"Or in it," said Eddie as he followed, pointing uphill.

About a hundred feet higher up was a dark opening in the scar where an earthquake had shaken loose the surface. Nina hesitated, wanting to investigate the stonework first, but then headed for the exposed passage. This expedition was not about archaeology.

The smashed masonry had come from a structure marking the way into the volcano, but the almost circular tunnel behind it appeared natural. "It must be a lava tube," she said as they approached.

"So what's all this?" Eddie asked as they reached more debris on the ground. "Did someone build an entrance to it, like a gatehouse or something?"

"I'll make an archaeologist out of you yet," she said, smiling. "But I don't think it was an entrance. Look how the stones are spread out—it's an even distribution across the whole opening. This wasn't built to mark the way in. It was built to *block* it."

"Until the landslide opened it up."

"Looks like it." They reached the opening. Even though little of the barricade was still intact, what remained had a distinctively harsh aesthetic that immediately suggested an Atlantean influence to Nina.

Eddie peered down the tunnel. It was about twelve feet in diameter, curling away into darkness like the trail of a monstrous earthworm. He sniffed for any telltale hints of sulfurous gases, but smelled only the desert air.

A feeling that something wasn't as it should be made him move a few steps into the tunnel and sniff again. Still nothing—but now he realized why. "What is it?" Nina asked.

"This tunnel goes down into the volcano, right? And we know it's still active because of the steam blowing out of the top."

"Yeah?"

"So how come air's getting sucked *into* the tunnel?" He returned to the ruined wall and scraped up a handful of fine dust, then let the grains trickle out from his hand. They didn't fall straight down, but instead curved away, drawn toward the shadows.

Nina joined him. He was correct; there was a definite flow of air down the lava tube, and it was at odds with the prevailing wind outside. But she had no clue how to explain it. "At least we won't have to worry about being gassed if we go down there."

"*If?*" said Eddie with a knowing smile.

"Yeah, we're going down there. I just wanted to, y'know, preserve the illusion of choice."

His smile broadened. "That vanished the moment I married you."

"Hey!"

He winked, then became more serious. "There should be a couple of torches in that bag. Let's have a look."

Nina found the pair of flashlights and gave one to her husband as she switched on the other and shone it down the passage. The curving walls were slightly ridged, producing the unsettling impression of being inside the rib cage of a snake. The lava tube changed shape as it progressed, its cross section undulating from a teardrop to a squashed ovoid, but the volume of molten rock that had formed it seemed consistent; the ceiling was never lower than eight feet high. "Do you think it's safe?"

Eddie placed a fingertip to his forehead as if channeling psychic powers. "Lemme consult my massive knowledge of volcanoes and say . . . I don't have a fucking clue." She stuck out her tongue, making him grin again. "There isn't molten lava gushing up it, so that's a good start. And so long as the wind's blowing down into it, we should be able to breathe okay. If it changes, though . . . We should have brought a canary in a cage."

"Poor birdie." She aimed the light at where the tunnel coiled out of sight. "Should we get the rest of the gear?"

He shook his head. "You've got the basics, and I've got the bombs. If we need anything else, we can always go back for it."

"Let's hope we don't need anything else."

"You think we're going to find this meteorite just lying there?"

"It'd be a nice change, wouldn't it?" She started down the shaft.

Eddie walked alongside her. "So, let me get this straight. This priestess, Nantalas, basically sinks Atlantis when she cocks up how to use earth energy, and the meteorite shoots off like an ICBM. She convinces the king not to kill her, but instead uses the statues to find it."

"Right. So they could make sure nobody ever tried to use the power of the gods again."

"Well, we know they were here. But just blocking off the entrance doesn't seem like their usual way of doing things. The other Atlantean places we've found . . . they were big on booby traps, weren't they?"

Nina stopped suddenly. "Oh, you had to remind me, didn't you?"

"Better now than when there's a giant scythe swinging at your head."

More cautiously, using the torch to check the curved walls above as well as the floor, she set off again. The entrance disappeared around a bend, dropping them into darkness as they continued deeper into the mountain. "I don't know how much effort the Atlanteans who came here would have put into building their defenses, though. They would have had other things on their mind."

"Like getting back home to save their families before Atlantis went glug-glug-glug."

"Yeah. Still, they obviously put some work into scaling the entrance—they could have just filled the tunnel with rocks, but they went to the trouble of constructing a wall."

"If they thought the meteorite was sent by the gods, maybe they thought it'd piss them off even more if they didn't show respect by building a proper barricade," Eddie suggested.

"I really am rubbing off on you! That's exactly what I was thinking. So, when are you going to enroll for a degree course?"

"The twelfth of never." They continued their descent, Eddie licking a finger and holding it up to check that the breeze was still blowing from behind them. It was. "So, they built a wall—did they build anything else down here?"

They rounded another bend—and halted as their torch beams fell upon something ahead.

Nina's eyes widened in astonishment. "I'd say . . . *yes.*"

THIRTY-THREE

The twisting lava tube opened out into a chamber cut from the volcanic rock—by human hands, not molten magma. The space was circular, about thirty feet in diameter. Offset from the entrance on the chamber's far side was an imposing pair of tall stone doors. A metal plate was fixed upon one of them, glinting with the reddish gold tint of orichalcum.

The doors were not what stopped Nina and Eddie in their tracks, however. It was what hung above them.

A giant hammer.

Its head was a single huge block of stone more than fifteen feet across, one side matching the curvature of the wall. The handle was a thick beam crossing the entire chamber from a slot chiseled into the rock: a pivot. The entire massive object was designed to pound down and crush anything in front of the doors into a very thin paste.

"I guess they *did* have time to build a booby trap," Nina whispered, as if afraid that her voice alone would trigger it. She shone her torch around the rest of the chamber. The walls, the lower parts coated by a layer of plaster, were covered with inscriptions: Atlantean texts.

Near the entrance were several niches containing dusty objects.

Bodies.

She looked more closely. The corpses were tightly wrapped in cloth shrouds, heads left exposed. Empty-eyed skulls leered back at her.

"Who are this lot?" Eddie asked in distaste.

Nina knew the Atlantean language well enough to pick out a familiar name crudely marked in the stone above one particular nook. "It's Nantalas!"

He directed his light at the shriveled head. "Ha! Maybe you really *are* related." The beam picked out some surviving strands of distinctly red hair.

"Very funny." She didn't recognize the names over the other bodies, but understood the gist of an inscription nearby. "These must be her acolytes, I suppose. They died with her."

"How?"

"Poison. It says that once the new Temple of the Gods was completed, they took their own lives in atonement for Nantalas's blasphemy. Then I guess the other Atlanteans who came with them walled up the tunnel." She read more of the texts. "They took the statues with them—they were going to hide them in the empire's farthest outposts so they could never be brought together again."

"That worked out well," Eddie said sarcastically. "Why didn't they just smash the things?"

"The same reason they didn't destroy the meteorite. They thought it was sent by the gods, so smashing it would just have made Poseidon and Co. even madder. And speaking of gods . . ." She perused one particular section of text, then looked up at the suspended hammer. "I was right about them interpreting the volcano as being the forge of Hephaestus. They built this thing to honor him, by having his symbol protect the stone."

"So it's a trap, right?"

"Oh yeah. Only someone who deserves to enter the

Temple of the Gods can get through the doors. Anyone else . . . well, whoever wrote this was big on smiting."

"This isn't the temple?"

"No, just an antechamber. The actual place is through there." She indicated the doors . . . then, her curiosity fully aroused, started to cross the chamber to examine them.

"Whoa, whoa!" Eddie pulled her back. "Smiting, remember?"

"I wasn't going to touch anything," she said, annoyed. "Besides, if they just wanted to stop anyone from reaching the Temple of the Gods, they could have filled in the lava tube. There must be a way in, otherwise why even bother with the test?"

"What test?"

She pointed at the orichalcum plate. Visible on it was an indentation in the metal: a handprint. "I think that's how you find out if you deserve to go through. Nothing'll happen as long as nobody touches it." She started back toward the doors. "Probably." Eddie winced as she crossed under the hammer . . . but it remained still. Warily, he followed her.

Nina peered at the metal plate. The handprint, fingers splayed, was not large; a woman's. Nantalas? There was something set into the center of the indented palm. A piece of stone.

Purple stone. Part of the meteorite, the same substance from which the statues had been made.

She stared at it, thinking. Why place a material that could conduct earth energy on a door?

The answer was obvious. It was a lock, one that could only be opened with a biological key. Someone who could channel earth energy would be able to unlock it simply by pressing their hand against the panel.

Someone like Nantalas.

Or herself.

"I know what it is," she told Eddie. "This place must be an earth energy confluence—maybe it's why the meteorite ended up here, because it was following the lines of energy. So if I touch the stone, it'll charge up just like the statues, and release the lock."

Eddie did not share her confidence. "And if you're wrong, it's hammer time and I have to mop you off the floor."

"I don't think I'm wrong. But just in case, you should go back over to the entrance. Take this with you." She gave him the bag of supplies.

He didn't move. "We can blow the thing open."

"We don't know how thick the doors are. And what if doing that drops the hammer? It's huge—we'd never clear it without using all the other charges, and if we do that we won't be able to destroy the meteorite. Eddie, I know what I'm doing. It's the only way to get into the temple."

Reluctantly, he backed up. Nina gave him a look of reassurance, then turned to the metal plate. She raised her hand and let it hover over the indentation as she spread her fingers to match the print.

Slowly, she moved it closer, about to press her palm against the stone—

"Stop!" Eddie yelled. She froze. "Don't touch the fucking thing!" He ran to her and bodily hauled her away from the door.

"Jesus Christ, Eddie!" she cried. "What is it?"

"The hammer's not the trap. That's the trap!" He pointed at the plate.

"What do you mean?"

"The whole point of building this place was to make sure nobody could ever use the meteorite's power again, right?"

"Yes . . . ," she said hesitantly, unsure where he was leading.

"So why would they make a door that only opens for the exact people who can do that? It'd be like building a bank vault that can only be opened if you're wearing a stripy jumper and carrying a bag with swag written on it! The last person they'd want to let in would be someone who can actually channel earth energy. Someone like you!"

She was silent for a long moment. Then: "Eddie?"

"Yeah?"

"I'm an idiot."

He grinned. "I didn't want to say it myself, but . . ."

"No, seriously. I. Am. A. Moron! How the hell did I not figure that out? Oh my God!" She clapped both hands to her forehead. "I fell right for it. I'd be a quarter inch thick right now if it weren't for you."

"Well, you'd have been able to slide right under the door." That triggered a thought, and he looked back toward the lava tube before regarding the doors quizzically.

"You just saved my life, Eddie," Nina went on. "Again. Thank you. You know, I don't appreciate you enough. When we get home, you can do that thing that I don't normally . . ." He was still looking at the doors. "Hello, hi," she said, waving a hand in front of his face. "Wife, right here, offering free perversions."

"It's a kink, not a perversion," he said. "And yeah, I'll definitely take you up on it. But have a gander at this first." He went to the door and knelt to peer at the crack beneath it, then took out a penknife and opened its longest blade. "Shine your light in there."

Nina illuminated the narrow gap—and was startled to discover that it was not what it seemed. "It's a fake!"

Eddie probed it with the penknife. The blade only went an inch deep before its tip found solid stone. "I thought there was something weird about the room," he said. "It must have been part of the lava tube before the Atlanteans dug it out—but if they built these doors to block the tunnel, why don't they actually line up with it?"

It was true; the doorway was offset from the entrance opposite by quite an angle. "The lava tube twists about, though," Nina said.

"Not by that much." He returned to the entrance and faced into the chamber, pointing directly across it at a patch of plastered wall more than six feet from the doorway's edge. "Even if it were twisting, the tube should have come in somewhere over there."

"What are you saying—that there's another door?"

"No—they didn't want anyone to get in, so it's probably blocked off. But I bet the tunnel carries on behind that wall." He crossed the chamber again and stood before the inscriptions. "This is a closed room, but I can still feel a breeze blowing through. Where's it going?"

Nina directed her light higher up the wall. At the top of the plastered section were several holes, each a few inches in diameter. "Through those, maybe." She gathered a handful of dust and tossed it at the small openings. The motes swirled in the flashlight beams—then were sucked into a vortex and vanished through the vents. "There's definitely something back there. How are we going to get to it?" Eddie drew his gun. "Oh, I see. You're going to shoot it open."

"Not exactly." He turned the gun around in his hand—and bashed its grip against the wall, cracking the plaster.

"Aah!" Nina cried, appalled. She rushed to him as he chipped away at the ancient inscriptions, larger chunks breaking loose. "What are you *doing*?"

"Sorry, but if we want to get through here, this wall's going to have to come down."

"Well, yes," she said, flustered, "but at least let me photograph it first!" She hurriedly rummaged through the bag for her camera.

Eddie sighed, but moved back so she could take several pictures. "All right, you done?"

"Yes, okay." She hung the camera's strap around her neck and grimaced. "I really wish we didn't have to do this, but . . . go ahead."

He returned to the wall and continued his attack. After a few minutes, enough plaster had been smashed away to expose a section of what was hidden behind it. A wall. But not solid volcanic rock. This was built from stone blocks—another barricade, sealing the entrance to the Temple of the Gods.

Eddie used his penknife again to explore the cracks between the stones. Unlike his examination of the fake door, this time the blade went all the way in without obstruction. He also noticed something else. "It's warm."

Nina put her hand against the exposed wall. It was noticeably hotter than the chamber's ambient temperature. "Well, we *are* in a volcano . . ."

"Yeah, but if it's warm on this side, God knows what it'll be like on the other. We don't know how thick this wall is. Only one way to find out, though." He looked at the bag of explosives.

Nina's shoulders slumped in dejection. "Guess I'd better take photos of the rest of the room . . ."

* * *

"Ready?" Eddie asked.

Nina cringed, covering her ears. "Yeah. Do it."

He switched the channel selector to 1, flicked up the protective cover over the detonation control . . . and pushed the red button.

Even though they were back outside the lava tube, the explosion from the underground chamber was still as loud as a shotgun blast. A gush of dust and smoke rushed out of the tunnel, loose stones clattering down the slope.

Eddie turned the detonator control back to SAFE and closed the trigger cover. "Looks like Alderley's mate took good care of the explosives. That was a bigger bang than I expected." They waited for the dust to settle, then started back down the lava tube. "Feel that?" he asked, after a few steps.

"Yeah," said Nina. The breeze blowing down the shaft was now a gust, strong enough to ruffle their hair. The residual haze in the air was rapidly being cleared. "I think we definitely opened up the wall." They continued down the curving tunnel. Rubble littered the floor as they got closer to the chamber. The final bend, and they raised their flashlights to see what awaited them.

To Nina's relief, the enormous hammer hadn't fallen, but was still hanging ominously over the room. Below it, the floor was strewn with debris. The wall blocking the exit had been obliterated—as had almost everything else. The blast had stripped most of the plaster from the walls, wiping out forever the last tale of the expedition from Atlantis . . . and also the remains of its members. The bodies in the burial nooks had been pulverized, ancient bones shattered to splinters. She regarded the devastation sadly. Photographs were little compensation for the loss of such a find.

"Hey," said Eddie quietly, recognizing her mood. "This was just the outer room, remember?" He nodded toward the newly opened passage. "The Temple of the Gods is right through there."

"You're right," she said, composing herself. Eddie headed for the exit; she gave a silent apology to what little remained of Nantalas and her acolytes before following.

Even with the stiff wind at their backs, the temperature beyond the chamber rose rapidly. And as they moved down the short tunnel, the light from their torches was joined by another source from ahead. Eddie at first thought it was daylight, but the color was wrong: too orange.

Nina had noticed it too. "You know how we thought the meteorite was in a volcano? I think it's *literally* in a volcano."

The tunnel opened out . . . and revealed that she was right.

They emerged on a large bowl-like ledge jutting from the inside of the volcano's throat. High above was a circle of blue sky, but the orange light was coming from below. The volcano was still active, a lake of molten lava bubbling away deep underground.

For the moment, though, Nina's attention was on the ledge itself. A dozen statues surrounded the center of the bowl. All were mythological figures: gods. She recognized Zeus, Poseidon, Apollo, Athena, Hera, and more . . . the Olympians, the most powerful figures in the shared pantheon of the ancient Greeks and the Atlanteans. They faced outward to keep watch in all directions, their poses and expressions a stern warning against approaching the object they guarded.

The sky stone. The meteorite. The object that had brought life to earth, and now held the potential to change that life—not with the power of gods, but with the science of men.

Eddie made a face. "I don't think we brought enough explosives."

It was not the size of a couch, or a car, as he had hoped. It was the size of a *house*. In places threateningly jagged, in others smoothed off as if melted, the irregular hunk of rock was a good sixty feet along its longest axis, rising at its highest almost thirty feet above the floor. The whole thing was covered with a grimy layer of ash and sulfur, deposited over millennia by the fumes rising up from the bubbling lava below. The statues around it were similarly defiled.

Nina and Eddie moved closer. As they left the cover of the tunnel, the rush of wind from it lessened—and the stench and heat coming from the bottom of the volcanic conduit hit them for the first time. The enormous updraft of hot gases rising past the ledge was sucking clean air from outside down the lava tube, keeping the natural bowl at least partially clear of the worst of the toxic vapors. "Christ, that stinks," Eddie muttered, trying to hold in a cough. "So, this is what everyone's been looking for?"

"This is it," said Nina. She went up to the stone, about to touch it, but then drew back her hand.

"What's wrong?"

"Considering what happened when Nantalas last touched the meteorite, it's probably not a great idea for me to start messing with it."

"You've got a point." Eddie looked up at the statue of

Poseidon, the god of the oceans holding a metal trident as if poised to hurl it at any intruder. "And he's got three. This is the Temple of the Gods, then?"

Nina turned away from the meteorite—and froze in momentary shock as for the first time she took in the sheer wall that had been behind her. "No," she said. "*That* is."

A vast structure had been carved out of the cliff, extending almost the full width of the ledge and rising in tiers to more than a hundred feet above. The elaborate yet harsh architectural style was unmistakably Atlantean. The lava tube emerged from the wall at its base between a pair of large pillars; on either side were more statues. Each level of the grand temple above them was lined with more ancient figures.

"God!" exclaimed Eddie, awed. "Or gods, I mean. How many are there?"

"All of them, I think," Nina replied. The Olympians were the big guns of the lost civilization's mythology, but there were hundreds of lesser deities below them . . . and it seemed that every single one was in attendance. The rulers of Atlantis had apparently been unable to decide which of their gods they had angered by unleashing the power of the sky stone—so they'd tried to appease them all.

"That's pretty bloody impressive. How the hell did they build all that in here?"

"Nantalas's expedition must have been bigger than we thought. Atlantis was the greatest empire the world would see for another few thousand years, so if anyone had the resources, they did." She raised her camera again and started taking pictures of the temple. Through the telephoto lens, she saw stairs linking the tiers behind the rows of statues.

"There isn't time for that," said Eddie, setting down the rucksack and removing the explosives and detonators. "We've found the thing, so let's blow it up."

"It's the *only* time for it," she countered. "You saw what the first charge did to the outer chamber—there was nothing left. When we blow up the meteorite, it'll wreck the temple. Even if I can't save it, I can't let this place go unrecorded."

Eddie reluctantly conceded. "Get your snaps, then." He checked the remaining detonators, then circled the rock as Nina continued. When he returned, his expression was decidedly more downcast. "You know how I didn't think we'd brought enough explosives?"

"Yes?"

"We definitely didn't. Remember what that geologist, Bellfriar, told us about the statues before we went to South America? He said the meteorite they came from had a lot of metal in the rock—and that'll make it really, really tough. There's no way these charges'll be enough to destroy it. Best they'll do is split it into smaller bits, but they'll still be too big for us just to chuck 'em into the lava." He looked back at the entrance. "We need a Plan B."

"What kind of Plan B?"

"My usual kind—blowing something up."

"But that's Plan A as well!"

He smiled, then collected one of the explosive charges and a detonator and headed for the lava tube. "Get all your photos—soon as I come back, I'll set the bombs on the rock and then we'll get out of here."

"Where are you going?"

"To make sure nobody gets through that tunnel after we leave." He jogged away, leaving Nina alone with the Atlantean gods.

She photographed the whole of the temple, then turned her attention to the statues around the meteorite. Whatever Eddie was doing, it was taking a while; he still had not returned by the time she had captured all of the Olympians. She considered taking a closer look at the temple, but curiosity about a more natural wonder won out and she made her way up the slope to the lip of the ledge.

The heat grew more intense the closer she got. Away from the fresh air coming through the lava tube, she found it harder to breathe as well. Coughing, she nevertheless climbed the last few yards to the edge and looked down.

It was like peering directly into hell. The volcano's conduit dropped dizzyingly down for hundreds of feet, a searing red eye at its end glaring back up at her. The level of the lava below had at some point sunk, leaving a seething molten lake churning in the subterranean magma chamber. The temperature was so great that she could only bear it for a few seconds before withdrawing, but she had seen more than enough. Even at its lowest level of activity, a volcano was still terrifying close up; she tried to imagine what it would have been like when Nantalas unwittingly released the full fury of the earth beneath Atlantis. It was almost too frightening to think about.

What made it more worrying was that she might be able to unleash a similar disaster—or be forced to do so. The sooner the meteorite was destroyed, and with it any chance of the Group's using its destructive potential, the better.

The thought of the Group made her look back at the entrance, from which Eddie was finally reemerging. Still coughing, she hurried back down to the much cooler center of the bowl. "Are you done?"

He nodded. "I'll show you on the way out. You got all your pictures?"

"Yes, but I wouldn't mind getting some close-ups of the temple. Do you need me to help with the explosives?"

"I can manage. You go and get some more photos."

"It's a shame they'll probably be all that's left of this place," she said glumly. "How long?"

"I'll need to find weak spots, so . . . fifteen minutes, maybe."

"Okay." Camera at the ready, Nina went to the temple as Eddie prepared the last three charges.

* * *

From the air, the volcano stood out from dozens of miles away, the column of steam at its peak standing tall in the sky like a marker flag.

An aircraft was heading straight for the beacon. Powering over the desert was an AgustaWestland AW101 helicopter, a civilian version of the military Merlin transport. The hold of this particular example had been fitted out with seats, all of which were occupied.

Alexander Stikes, seated directly behind the pilot, would have much preferred the twenty-four places to be filled with mercenaries under his command, but the surviving members of the Group had decided they wanted to witness the discovery of the meteorite firsthand. They had arrived in the Ethiopian capital the previous day and waited in Addis Ababa's most luxurious hotel, such as it was, for the ongoing search to produce results. It was a harsh irony: one of the world's poorest countries being visited incognito by a small group of people whose personal net worth outstripped that of the entire nation.

He turned to speak to Warden. "We'll be there in a few minutes."

"Are you sure this is the place?" the Group's chairman demanded.

"Not one hundred percent, but considering the circumstances it seems highly likely. A volcano would fit nicely with the Atlantean priestess's reference to the forge of Hephaestus. Benefits of a classical education," he added at Meerkrieger's raised eyebrow. "And our aerial reconnaissance drone spotted a vehicle crossing the desert toward it some hours ago; it's still there."

"Wilde and Chase?" said Warden.

"Who else?" Sophia said from beside Stikes.

The former officer nodded. "Considering that there's absolutely nothing in this part of the desert that would be of value to man or beast, they're the only people I can think of who would have a reason for coming out here."

"But we don't know they're in the country," Brannigan said from behind Meerkrieger.

"And we don't know they're not. Chase has proved very adept at getting around the world unnoticed."

"Good for him," said Larry loudly. Eddie's father was seated toward the back of the cabin with the mercenaries, under guard. The man next to him had standing orders from Stikes if the prisoner made a nuisance of himself, and he carried them out by driving an elbow hard into Larry's stomach. The older man curled up in pain, gasping for breath.

"We know they left Switzerland," Stikes continued, dismissing the interruption, "and they didn't return to the States, so it's highly probable that they're here. Wilde apparently has some sort of in-built direction finder, after all. And they have a very strong incentive to find the meteorite before we do."

"You'd better hope they haven't," Warden said, with an undercurrent of threat.

Stikes concealed his look of derision until he had turned away to check the view ahead. The volcano was rapidly growing. His cold eyes scanned it, searching for anything standing out against the barren rock . . .

"There," he said. "There they are!" He pointed, indicating his find to the pilot, who turned the helicopter toward it.

Warden leaned forward to look. A small block of color was visible on the mountainside: a vehicle. "Land as close to it as you can," he ordered, then addressed Stikes. "Will you be able to find them?"

"Tracking is one of my specialties," the Englishman told him smugly.

The pilot brought the helicopter into a hover over the small plateau, its downwash whipping up a storm of dust and grit that buffeted the parked four-by-four. He brought the aircraft down with a bump. "Right," said Stikes, addressing the members of the Group, "I think it will be best if you all wait in the chopper until my men and I find Chase and Wilde and locate the meteorite. It should—"

"We're not going to sit here baking in this thing," said

Warden firmly. The pilot was in the process of shutting down the engines; once the cabin's air-conditioning was switched off, the temperature in the enclosed space would quickly become intolerable. "I want to be there to see the stone the moment it's found."

"So do we," said both the Bull brothers simultaneously. The others agreed, even the elderly Meerkrieger undeterred by the prospect of negotiating the rough terrain.

"As you wish," Stikes said. "In that case, if you'll follow me . . ." As Warden picked up the case holding the statues, the mercenary leader made his way down the narrow central aisle to his eight men at the rear. "Everyone arm up and move out. Remember that in no circumstances is Dr. Wilde to be killed. Anyone else who might be there is fair game—except Chase. He's mine." He reached past several parachutes on a rack to push a button, and the broad rear ramp lowered to the ground. "All right, let's go."

He strode down the ramp, the Group members—looking obviously out of place in the raw natural environment despite their newly bought expedition clothing—and Sophia following. The mercenaries pulled back tarps and collected their weapons and survival gear from behind the ranks of seats, then marched after their leader, two of them pushing Larry between them.

Gleaming Jericho drawn, Stikes checked that the Land Rover was empty, then surveyed the steep and barren landscape. There was nobody in sight.

But he spotted a small depression in the blanket of stones covering the ground. On its own it would have meant nothing, but near it was another, and another . . .

A trail of footfalls, leading away from the four-by-four up the volcano's side. Two trails, in fact, one lighter than the other.

Sophia recognized his curling smile of triumph. "You've found them?"

"I have," he replied. He called out to the others, "This way!"

They set off up the slope, Stikes leading the pack like a foxhound.

* * *

Eddie had eventually found two promising spots on the meteorite to plant his charges, and was now carefully traversing the top of the great rock, looking for a third. If the explosives shattered it along its natural fault lines, the combined blasts might have more chance of pulverizing the separate pieces.

It was a long shot, though. So Plan B would have to come into effect, and even that had a major flaw—one that he only had to look up to see. If worse came to worst, people could descend on lines from the top of the crater. Considering the Group's resources, if they found the place it wouldn't take long for them to realize that.

And he was increasingly thinking there was no *if* about it. They had already triangulated the meteorite's general position based on the bearings taken in Japan and Switzerland, and he couldn't shake the feeling that the plane he had seen was carrying out reconnaissance. Finding the Temple of the Gods was a matter of money, matériel, and manpower, and the Group had all three in abundance.

He dismissed the grim thought as he spotted a wide crack in the meteorite's surface, deep enough to swallow his entire arm. That should do the trick.

It would take a few minutes to rig the detonator and place the explosive. He glanced at the towering temple, seeing the flash of Nina's camera from the second tier. "Might have bloody known she'd wander off," he grumbled before raising his voice to a shout. "Oi! I'll only be a couple more minutes—come back down!"

On the temple, Nina heard him, and reluctantly waved to show her agreement. There was still so much more to see. As well as the statues, the walls were inscribed with more Atlantean texts: accounts of the builders' journey across Africa and how they had constructed the temple despite the extreme conditions.

But now nobody would ever know their story. The temple was well within the fifty-yard blast radius Alderley had mentioned, so blowing up the meteorite would bombard it with debris, smashing the statues and shattering the ancient records behind them. She would be the only person ever to see the hidden wonder of the lost civilization close up.

She knew the sacrifice had to be made, though. Taking one last picture of a statue, whom she took to be Eupraxia, the goddess of well-being, she headed back to the narrow flight of stairs.

By the time she returned to the ledge, Eddie was out of sight on top of the meteorite, lying down to push the primed explosive as deeply into the rock as possible. She aimed her camera upward, trying to get as much of the temple as she could into the frame with the mouth of the crater high above . . .

A sound caught her attention. A soft scuff, like someone stepping on gravel.

She moved across the temple's front to the tunnel entrance. Nothing but darkness was visible. She listened for several seconds, but the noise didn't recur. Dismissing it as just the breeze shifting grit on the floor, she turned away, lining up her photograph again—

Crunch.

The same noise, louder, closer.

She whirled—and saw Stikes emerge from the lava tube, his gun pointed at her. Behind him, other faces came out of the shadows, all equally unwelcome: Sophia, Warden, the other members of the Group. And Larry, held at gunpoint by an unsmiling mercenary in desert combat gear.

"Dr. Wilde!" said Stikes with malevolent brightness. "We can't go on meeting like this."

"Eddie!" Nina yelled. "They're here, they found us! Set off the—"

Sophia rushed past Stikes and slammed a gloved fist against Nina's jaw. The blow knocked the redhead to her knees. She spat out blood and whipped up one leg, trying to plow a retaliatory strike into the other woman's stomach, but Sophia neatly sidestepped the attack and drove a boot into her chest. Nina let out a choked gasp of pain.

"What's the *matter*, Nina?" Sophia snarled as she delivered another savage kick, this time to her abdomen. "Eddie not been *keeping*"—a third impact—"up with your *training*?" She stamped on Nina's stomach, leaving her writhing and struggling to breathe.

"That's enough!" ordered Warden. "We need her alive!"

With evident reluctance, Sophia withdrew. Ignoring Nina's moans, Stikes surveyed the ledge. "Chase!" he called, his voice echoing off the temple. "Show yourself or I'll kill your father!" The mercenary forced Larry forward, gun pressed hard into his back.

A head slowly rose into view over the top of the meteorite. "Let 'em go, Stikes!" Eddie shouted. "This thing's wired to blow—if you don't, I'll take us all out and this whole thing ends right here."

There was a flurry of consternation among the Group, some of them pushing back through the mercenaries into the tunnel, but Stikes was unbowed. "You're bluffing. You won't let your wife die, especially not at your hand. Or even your father."

"Well, Eddie?" asked Sophia. "What are you going to do?" She kicked Nina again, drawing another pained cry.

"Leave her alone!" Eddie demanded.

"Or what? You'll blow us all up? Hardly. I know you better than that."

"We're wasting time," said Warden irritatedly. "Mr. Chase, I *will* let Mr. Stikes carry out his threat if you don't surrender right now. If you do, then . . . I'll let you and your father live."

"What?" snapped Stikes.

"What can they do? We have the meteorite, and we have Dr. Wilde—as you say, he won't risk anything happening to her." He turned back to Eddie. "What do you say, Mr. Chase? This is your chance to end this without any more death or violence."

To Nina's shock, Eddie held up his hands, then climbed down the sulfur-covered rock, jumping the last ten feet and walking out of the circle of statues toward the entrance. "Eddie!" she gasped. "You can't let them—" Her words were cut short by another blow from Sophia's boot.

"She's right," said Larry, forcing the words through his fear as the mercenary jabbed the gun harder into his back. "Edward, you can't just give up!"

Eddie didn't reply, stopping ten feet short of Stikes and Warden. The American nodded. "Good. You're doing the right thing."

"Yeah, I know," Eddie replied. "That thing you said about ending this without more death and violence?"

"Yes?"

He grinned. "Not my style."

Before anyone could react, he pushed the trigger button.

THIRTY-FOUR

A deafening explosion rocked the ledge—but it didn't come from the meteorite.

The trigger's selector dial was set to detonate only a single bomb: the one Eddie had planted in the entrance chamber. The blast shattered the stone beam running across the room . . .

And the hammer fell.

The enormous stone block plunged to the floor—splattering those Group members who had retreated in fear and some straggling mercenaries to a bloody pulp.

But the carnage didn't end in the entrance chamber. The earthquake force of the impact collapsed the roof of the lava tube. Rubble flattened more people—

Then the temple itself began to crumble.

A section of the first tier above the entrance splintered away, statues spinning through the air as it dropped. The people closest to the lava tube could do nothing but scream as it obliterated them like ants beneath a boot. The entire ledge shuddered, a great wedge-shaped chunk breaking from its edge and tumbling down to the lava lake far below.

Those farther away were flung off their feet as the

ground bucked beneath them. Eddie landed hard on his side, bringing up his arms to protect his head from flying debris.

As the echoing rumble of stone died away, coughs from inside the dissipating dust cloud revealed the survivors. There were not many. Of the twenty-four passengers from the helicopter, only ten remained alive, the others all buried under tons of broken rock.

Stikes painfully picked himself up and wiped his eyes. Sophia was sprawled on top of Nina, while Larry and his guard were both crumpled nearby. Warden sat up, moaning, while a few feet from him Meerkrieger held a hand to his bleeding head. The only other Group member who remained alive was Brannigan; behind her, what was left of the Bull brothers lay partially visible beneath a smashed stone slab, united in death as in life. Three other mercenaries were also stirring. Everyone else was dead.

Except one.

The thought made Stikes whirl. *Chase*—

The bruised Eddie realized he had dropped the trigger. Where was it? There—about six feet away. He started to crawl toward it . . . until the ringing in his ears faded enough for him to hear movement.

Running footsteps—

He fumbled to draw his gun—but Stikes kicked it from his hand. Eddie yelled in pain. The mercenary leader followed up with another crunching blow to his chest. "I should have shot you in Afghanistan when I had the chance!" he snarled, lining up another strike at his head—

Eddie whipped up both arms, one taking the full force of the kick while the other clamped around Stikes's ankle. Despite the pain he still twisted and rolled, yanking his opponent off balance. Stikes stumbled, landing heavily on one knee. He cried out—only for his yell to become a breathless groan as Eddie drove an elbow into his stomach. "Fuck off, you southern ponce!"

The Yorkshireman swiveled and unleashed a kick of

his own that struck Stikes's head with a satisfying crack. He pulled back to attack again, about to drive the former officer's jawbone up into his skull—

A gunshot boomed across the ledge, a bullet smacking off the stone floor beside the two fighting men. Eddie froze, seeing Sophia striding toward him, the smoking Jericho in her hand. She sighed. "*Fuck off, you southern ponce*? Really, Eddie, the quality of your bons mots just keeps getting worse. Nina's education clearly isn't rubbing off on you."

Stikes looked angrily up at her. "Why didn't you just shoot him?"

A little mocking smile. "Because I didn't think you'd appreciate the bullets going through you first, darling. Get up, Eddie." She gestured with the gun for him to stand, then looked back toward the entrance. The lava tube was now completely lost to sight, tons of stone blocking the exit. "You should have blown up the meteorite after all. We still have it, and we still have Nina and your father. And you, for that matter."

"Yeah," said Eddie, "but there's not much you can do with it, is there? There's no way out, and it doesn't look like you brought a JCB with you to dig through the tunnel."

"There's always a way out for the resourceful." She looked up at the circle of sky high above.

Warden staggered over to them. "What have you done?" he yelled at Eddie. "You psycho! You've trapped us in here!"

"Fuck me, so I have," Eddie replied sarcastically. "Hope you brought a packed lunch."

Stikes stood, barking commands to his surviving men to secure Nina and Larry, then reclaimed his gun from Sophia. Seething, he regarded Eddie for a long moment as if considering pulling the trigger, then pointed at his other two prisoners. "Get over there."

Meerkrieger and Brannigan, both visibly shaken, joined Warden. "What are we going to do now?" asked the Australian. "Chase is right—we'll never clear all that rubble."

"We may not have to," said Stikes, following Sophia's gaze and staring up at the shaft above the temple. "It'll be a tough climb, but I think it might be possible to reach the top of the volcano."

Meerkrieger was far from pleased at the suggestion. "I'm eighty-one years old! How do you expect me to climb up there?"

"No need to worry yourself about getting out of here," Stikes replied, his smug self-confidence returning. "There are ropes in the helicopter."

"And how are you going to get up to the helicopter in the first place?" asked Nina. She indicated the temple. The collapsing tier had brought the first two flights of stairs down with it, making it impossible to ascend the structure. She turned to Warden. "Face it, you've lost. Most of the Group are dead, and while you might have your precious sky stone, there's nothing you can do with it."

"The Group will go on even without its individual members," Warden said angrily, then his expression suddenly became more calculating. He looked at the meteorite, then back at Nina. Chillingly, he was now smiling. "There may not be anything we can do with the meteorite—but there is something *you* can do with it."

"What do you mean?" Brannigan demanded.

Warden hurried back to the rubble scattered around the entrance, searching the debris until he found the case he had dropped. He returned to the survivors and opened it, revealing the three small statues. "Put them together," he ordered Nina.

She shook her head. "Go to hell."

"Stikes?"

Stikes pushed his gun against Eddie's head. "I think you know the drill by now, Nina."

"What exactly is this going to achieve?" she said scathingly. "You don't need the statues to tell you where the meteorite is anymore. I mean, it's right there."

"You're forgetting the statues' true purpose," Warden told her. "What did Nantalas call them? The keys of power? You can access that power—and move the meteorite over to the temple so we can climb up!"

Even with a gun pressed against his back, Larry couldn't hold in an incredulous exclamation. "It's the size of a bloody whale! How do you expect anyone to move that?"

"Those little statues levitating is one thing," Eddie added, "but *that*? Come on, she's not Yoda!"

Warden snorted in disdain. "You've just illustrated perfectly why the Group will ultimately win. If you decide something is impossible before even attempting it, then you've already failed."

"We see what's possible," said Brannigan. "Then we make it happen."

"And in this case, we *know* what's possible. The Atlantean texts describe Nantalas levitating the sky stone. If she can do it, so can you, Dr. Wilde." He thrust the case at her. "Take the statues."

"And be careful with them," said Stikes, grinding the Jericho's muzzle into Eddie's cheek. "You wouldn't want to drop one and startle me, would you? It could have very unfortunate consequences for your husband."

"Nina, don't do it," Eddie warned. "If they get out of here with that DNA . . ."

He stopped as his wife's eyes met his. Just a look—but he instantly knew she had something in mind other than mere surrender. He didn't know what, but there was also an unspoken warning that he should be prepared for something major.

Nobody except Eddie picked up on it. "I . . . I don't have a choice," she said, making a show of seeming conflicted. She took out the first statue.

It glowed in her hand, brighter than ever before. The volcano was evidently the site of an extremely powerful earth energy confluence point. The second statue joined the first, shoulder to shoulder. The eerie rippling blue light intensified, a brilliant line pointing directly at the remaining figurine.

Everyone watched the display intently as she cradled the two statuettes in one hand and reached with the other for the third. As in Takashi's skyscraper and the Blauspeer hotel, she again experienced the electrical tingling coursing through her body.

"Put them together," ordered Warden. "Do it!"

She gave Eddie a final glance . . . then completed the triptych.

The effect this time was more powerful yet, because she was fully prepared for it, less overwhelming. She now knew that this was truly the source of life on earth, the feeling of having somehow come *home* undeniable. All life had started with the meteorite, and even after billions of years it was still linked, through the planet's own mysterious energies. She could sense its myriad descendants even in the heart of the barren Ethiopian wilderness. There was not a corner of the planet that the offspring of the primordial DNA had not touched.

She kept her focus on the statues. If her desperate plan had any chance of working, she needed to learn how to control the power running through them.

And quickly. Through the maelstrom of unworldly sensation she heard Warden's voice: "Take them to the meteorite. Now!"

Nina opened her eyes. The statues were not levitating; her hands were tightly clasped around their bases, holding them together, but she could feel the bizarre pressure as they tried to lift away from her. She moved toward the meteorite, everyone following with expressions of awe or expectation.

With two exceptions. Sophia took the opportunity to pick up Eddie's gun . . . and Eddie himself kept a close watch on Nina, waiting for the cue to make his move.

Whatever that cue might be.

Nina reached the meteorite. The statues' glow was now almost dazzling—and there was a strange charge in the air, as if the giant rock were humming in anticipation of the return of its long-separated splinters. She looked back. The faces of the surviving Group members were filled with rapacious greed.

"Do it!" Warden ordered again, but she didn't need the prompt, already drawing a nervous breath . . . and touching the three statues to the sky stone.

For a moment, nothing happened.

Then the coating of sulfur and ash where the figurines met the meteorite sizzled as if dissolved by acid, centuries of grimy volcanic deposits flaking away. The purple rock beneath was revealed . . . and it too began to glow.

The entire ledge suddenly shook, everyone on it battling to remain standing. Nina shielded her eyes as a blizzard of dirty dust cascaded off the meteorite, repelled from its surface as the unearthly light grew brighter. The onlookers staggered back.

Slowly, impossibly, the stone began to rise.

It creaked and crackled as its weight shifted. Small pieces broke off, maintaining their glow for a few seconds before the earth energy they were charged with dissipated and they clattered to the stony floor.

Nina felt the power running through her body—and somehow *knew*, an instinctual certainty from deep within, that she could channel it, direct it. She willed the enormous rock to move . . . and it began to glide lazily away from the center of the circle of statues. Another mental urging, and it slowed with the ponderous weight of a freight train, hanging silently two feet above the ledge.

Warden stepped forward, feet crunching through the sloughed-off dirt, and raised a hand to the meteorite— but held his fingertips an inch short, as if afraid that his touch would let gravity reclaim its hold. "We have it," he said in awe. "We have it all. Earth energy, the progenitor DNA . . . we can do it. We can carry out the plan."

Both Brannigan and Meerkrieger were caught up in his growing excitement. "No more conflict," said the Australian woman, moving closer to examine the shimmering rock. "No more waste. We'll have control over every single person on the planet."

"*Total* control," added the media baron. He signaled for Nina to lower the meteorite; it responded to her mental direction, settling on the ledge with alarming groans and snaps of overstressed stone. She stepped back, breaking contact by separating one of the statues from the others, but the huge rock remained aglow. The larger the object, it seemed, the longer it could hold its earth energy charge. "This is incredible!"

Warden was already making plans. "Once we get out, we'll bring in more people, set up lines down into the volcano. We'll cut the rock open and extract the DNA samples. As soon as we've got those, we can complete the sequencing process and release the virus. This is it," he said to his two remaining colleagues, his patrician scowl for once overcome by genuine euphoria. "This is our moment. We can remake the world—remake *humanity*! Everything that happens from now on will be according to our design."

"Not your design," said Sophia unexpectedly from behind them. "Ours."

The Group members whirled—and were cut down as she opened fire with Eddie's gun. Meerkrieger took two bullets in the chest, convulsing in agony before slumping lifelessly to the floor. Brannigan fell as another pair of shots tore into her. Warden was hit in the shoulder and collapsed with an anguished screech.

He raised a shaking hand, signaling to the mercenaries standing impassively nearby. "What are you doing?" he gasped. "Kill her—kill her! Help me!"

Stikes joined Sophia, his self-satisfied smile oozing wider. "I'm afraid they're all loyal to me, not to you."

"But they are still loyal to the Group," Sophia added. "The *new* Group, that is." She took Stikes's hand.

"Thank you for giving me full access to all the Group's resources, by the way," Stikes added. "Don't worry— we'll put them to good use."

In his desperation, Warden looked to the prisoners for assistance. "Do something! Please!"

All Nina could do was shrug helplessly. "What can I say? I told you not to trust them."

Eddie nodded. "Saw that coming a mile off."

Sophia brought the gun back down at Warden. "No, please!" he begged. "I—"

A single shot hit him in the forehead, blowing out the back of his skull in a gruesome bloom across the stone. Nauseated, Nina looked away. Larry retched, struggling to hold in a mouthful of vomit.

"Well then," said Stikes amiably, "now that's all dealt with, there's only one thing left to do." He raised his gun and pointed it at Eddie.

"Just a minute, darling," said Sophia. "We agreed in Switzerland that *I* get to kill Eddie, remember? And second, business before pleasure—we still need Nina to move the meteorite so we can get out of here."

Stikes glowered at Eddie, but reluctantly lowered the Jericho. "All right." He turned to the mercenaries. "Watch Chase and his father. Dr. Wilde, if you'd be so kind?"

Nina returned to the meteorite. The huge stone began to hum once more as she brought the glowing statues closer, the very air around it tingling. She looked around at her audience: the guards mystified, Sophia and Stikes as avaricious as the late members of the Group had been, Larry still shocked by what he had just witnessed . . .

And her husband giving her an unspoken signal.

Ready.

An almost imperceptible nod, then she turned back to the hulking stone. Slowly, carefully, she brought all three statues together once more.

The expansion of her consciousness was this time almost familiar, even comforting. She *belonged* here; the power was a part of her. It always had been, simply waiting for the moment when it would be unlocked. She could feel the flow of the earth's energy around her, an unimaginable torrent constantly circulating beyond the limits of the five human senses.

But now she could experience it. And channel it.

Control was out of the question: It would take too much time and effort even to begin to direct the power according to her specific wishes. But right now, she didn't *need* control. If anything, she was trying to achieve the opposite. She allowed more energy to flood through the meteorite, willing it to take in more power.

And more. And *more*.

The great stone rocked and groaned again as the shimmering light ran over its surface. It slowly rose, more small fragments breaking loose and lazily spinning through the air until the charge they held faded and they dropped. "Good," said Sophia, wide-eyed. "Good! Now move it to the temple."

Nina obeyed, directing ever-more earth energy into the rock as she held the statues against it. Its glow brightened, shadows of ancient gods shifting across the wall as she brought it closer to the Atlantean structure. Sophia followed, Stikes gesturing for the mercenaries to bring their prisoners after her. The Englishwoman surveyed the damaged tiers. "To the left," she ordered, pointing at a particular section. "Put it down with the tip next to the edge of that ledge. We'll be able to reach the stairs from—"

She broke off, flinching as a lightning bolt flashed from the meteorite to strike the temple several stories above. A statue exploded, shattered fragments showering the people below. "What's happening?" Stikes demanded.

"I don't know!" Nina replied, only partly lying. She was still channeling more energy into the stone, but had no control over how it would manifest itself.

Sparks crackled from the floating rock, another, stronger bolt lancing up the volcanic shaft and out into the empty sky above. Eddie felt a static-like charge rising around him, the hairs on the backs of his hands standing on end. Larry gave his son a worried glance. "Hang on," Eddie muttered to him.

"What was that?" snapped Stikes. He looked between the two Chases, realization growing that some conspiracy was afoot. "Stop!" he shouted at Nina. "Put the thing down!"

"It's almost in place," Sophia objected. The meteorite was nearly close enough to the ledge to allow a person to jump across. More flashes bridged the gap, stonework splintering where they landed.

"No, leave it!" He pointed his gun straight at Eddie's heart. "Dr. Wilde, put it down and step away *now,* or I'll kill them both!"

Nina closed her eyes . . .

And *willed* the entire power of the earth to flow into the meteorite.

Another flash, brighter than any before—

She was abruptly thrown backward as if shoved by a giant hand, grit and dust peppering her skin as a shock wave of energy erupted from the glowing rock. The statuettes flew from her hands, tumbling weightlessly through the air.

An unimaginably deep rumble shook the ledge—shook the entire volcano. More statues toppled from the temple to smash on the rocky floor. Igneous shards rained down from the wall of the shaft as the tremor pummeled them loose.

The quake had knocked everyone down. Pre-warned, Eddie was first to recover. He spotted Nina near Sophia and was about to shout for her to get the other woman's gun when the sight of the meteorite froze him in momentary shock.

The massive rock was no longer simply hanging in the air. Glowing so brightly it almost hurt to watch, it was rising with increasing speed up the shaft. It was what had happened in Atlantis thousands of years before, he realized: The sky stone had been overloaded with earth energy, and when it blew it would be thrown skyward . . .

To land somewhere else. Where the next set of arse-holes with ideas for world domination could find it.

Unless—

He jumped up and ran—not toward Nina, but for the remote.

Stikes sat up—and found one of his prisoners gone. He whirled, seeing Eddie running across the ledge, and grabbed the Jericho from the ground beside him. Teeth bared in an expectant snarl, he brought the gun around.

Eddie saw the detonator among the scattered debris. He dived headlong at it as Stikes's first shot whipped past. Ignoring the pain of the landing, he twisted the dial to the FULL position.

Stikes rose, adjusting his aim. His prone target had nowhere left to go . . .

Eddie flicked up the protective cover—and jammed his thumb down on the red button beneath.

For a heartbeat, nothing happened—

Then the meteorite blew apart.

THIRTY-FIVE

The three explosive charges Eddie had placed in the sky stone shattered the great rock's heart, sending countless pieces flying in all directions. They were still aglow, held in the air by the earth's invisible lines of force . . . but the smallest fragments almost immediately lost their charge and fell like hail. Most dropped down the volcanic shaft, heading for immolation in the searing magma chamber below, but some hit the ledge—and the people on it.

Eddie yelped as a stone bounced off his head, and looked up to see where it had come from. "Oh, bollocks," he gasped.

A swirling cloud of glowing rocks hung above him, ranging in size from golf balls to trucks. More energy bolts spat from them, stabbing at the rocky walls of the shaft. But the unearthly lights were rapidly going out, darkness spreading as increasingly larger chunks of debris exhausted their residual energy—and were reclaimed by gravity.

A piece of meteorite the size of a tennis ball smacked down beside him. Another, slightly larger, landed nearby a moment later.

A hard rain was going to fall.

There was danger below as well as above. The ground trembled, a low thunder rising from the base of the shaft as something huge slowly stirred from its long slumber.

The lava lake was boiling with the sudden release of earth energy. The volcano was erupting. Just as Nantalas had triggered a natural disaster in Atlantis, so Nina had here.

"Nina! Dad!" he shouted as he stood. "Get into cover!" He started to run for the temple—

Stikes recovered from his shock, raising his gun.

Eddie dived behind the statue of Poseidon as he fired. "Get up!" Stikes yelled to his men as more rubble fell around them, some pieces as big as footballs.

Nina had heard Eddie's shout and struggled upright, briefly mesmerized by the sight of the asteroid field hanging overhead. She snapped out of it at a cry of pain from nearby. Larry lay on the ground, one hand to his head where a falling stone had struck him.

Another, much larger lump of rock was directly above him, the shimmering glow across its surface fading . . .

She raced forward and seized her father-in-law by his arms. "Larry, *move!*" she screamed, trying to drag him clear.

The strange light vanished. The rock plunged—

Nina pulled harder, soles scrabbling for grip—and the stone slammed down where Larry had been lying, missing him by barely an inch.

Sophia gasped as she realized the danger she was in. No thought of helping any of the mercenaries, or even Stikes, crossed her mind; she ran for the shelter of the temple.

Ever larger debris pounded down onto the ledge. One of the mercenaries started to scream before being abruptly silenced by a half-ton chunk of meteorite that splattered him like an insect on a windshield.

Eddie pressed himself against the statue as another boulder smashed to the ground just feet away, showering him with gritty shrapnel. He felt the shock of the impact through his feet—but the other tremors from far underground were rapidly growing stronger. A second panicked mercenary tried to scramble clear as an Olympian toppled. He failed, the falling figure smiting him as mercilessly as its namesake of myth.

Eddie risked a look around his cover. Stikes was taking what little shelter he could find beneath another statue.

But he was thinking of more than mere survival. The Jericho came up—

Eddie ducked sharply back as another round cracked off Poseidon. Even after the last of the floating stones fell, he would still be cut off from the temple. He glanced toward the towering structure, seeing Nina supporting his father as they reached it.

She hauled Larry into an alcove, barely containing a terrified shriek as a boulder the size of a small car slammed down less than ten feet behind them. The hammer-blow booms of rock against rock grew louder with each strike. But even they couldn't drown out the rising rumble from beneath the earth—the impending eruption she had caused.

Too late to worry if she had done the right thing. All she could do now was wait for the last pieces of the meteorite to drop, then hope there was a way to escape.

She helped Larry lean against the alcove's wall, then looked outside. Huge boulders plunged past the ledge toward the molten lake below. Only a few parts of the shattered sky stone now remained aloft.

The largest was above the circle of statues, a thirty-foot-long dagger.

Its glow flickered to nothing . . .

The giant shard fell.

It stabbed deeply into the heart of the ledge—which broke apart as if split by a hammer and chisel. Over half of it sheared away and plummeted toward the lava, taking one of the surviving mercenaries with it and leaving Eddie, Stikes, and the last of his men on a ragged stump jutting out over the shaft. The remaining Olympians fell, the figure of Poseidon breaking apart and sending the metal trident clanging toward the nearby edge. Sections of the temple's lower tiers collapsed, their own lesser gods flung to destruction.

With most of the natural bowl now gone, hot, fume-laden air from the magma chamber swept onto what was left of the ledge. Eddie coughed, cupping a hand over his mouth and nose. If he didn't move quickly, he would be either suffocated or roasted. Eyes stinging, he peered over the broken remnants of the statue. Stikes and the mercenary, the latter closer, were still between him and the temple.

The temple—

The newly fallen tiers had created a ramp of sorts, unstable and treacherous yet high enough to reach the remaining stairs. And that wasn't all—a rising column of steamy vapor was being pulled toward it, swirling into a vortex that disappeared into the shadows of a higher level.

Air was being drawn from the volcanic shaft through a second lava tube, newly opened by the tremors. There was another way out!

All they had to do was reach it.

He looked back at the two soldiers in his way. Both had been knocked down by the meteorite's impact—

Eddie hurdled the wreckage of Poseidon and snatched up the metal trident, then ran as hard as he could. The ground shuddered with every step, almost throwing him off balance as he readied the ancient bronze weapon.

The mercenary sat up, astounded simply to be alive as he took in the devastation all around him. He breathed a sigh of relief—

Three metal prongs burst out of his chest.

Eddie slammed a foot against the dying man's back to tear the trident free with a trio of bloody spurts. "Nina!" he yelled, jabbing a hand at the ramp. "Climb up, over there!" He hefted the trident and charged again. If he killed Stikes, that would only leave Sophia to worry about.

Stikes saw him coming. He twisted and raised the Jericho—

The trident slashed through his sleeve, one of its points gouging a deep rent in the muscle of his forearm. He screamed—but still managed to pull the trigger.

The bullet caught Eddie's right biceps, tearing out a chunk of flesh the width of a finger. The pain made him recoil reflexively, throwing off his aim as he thrust the weapon down at the other man. The trident skimmed the side of Stikes's body, ripping clothing but not skin, and hit the stone floor—and the entire three-pointed head broke off.

Stikes fired again, but Eddie jumped sideways and the bullet seared past him. He swung the trident's shaft, catching Stikes a blow to the hand that fractured one of his fingers and sent the Jericho whirling toward the temple.

Nina had seen the new exit and started to run for the makeshift ramp, Larry behind her, when she heard the gunshots. "Eddie!" she cried, turning—

Larry yanked her back as Sophia emerged from cover and opened fire with Eddie's gun. Exposed, they seemed doomed—but the quake threw off Sophia's aim. The aristocrat's expression grew more furious with each missed shot. She started after her targets as they ducked back toward the alcove . . . only for the automatic's slide to lock back as she exhausted its ammo.

The two women glared at each other—then Sophia fled for the ramp, throwing away the empty gun. Nina looked back at her husband as he smashed the metal shaft down like a baseball bat onto the prone Stikes with a clang that was audible even over the volcano's rumble.

Eddie appeared to have the upper hand; she made a snap decision and ran after Sophia. The Englishwoman was already halfway up the pile of shattered stones; once she reached the top, the second lava tube would be just a short distance away. Nina pounded after her, Larry following.

Eddie swung at Stikes again, the shaft cracking off the other man's elbow as he tried to shield his head. Stikes screamed. "Yeah, how's it feel to be the one getting hurt for a change?" Eddie yelled as he delivered another blow. "This is for everyone you killed in Afghanist—"

Another tremor made him lurch—and Stikes took advantage, sweeping his legs around to hook a foot behind Eddie's knee, making his leg buckle. The Yorkshireman stumbled, the metal spear jolting from his hands. "You talk too much, Chase!" Stikes shouted as he jumped up. "You always did!"

Eddie sprang to his feet as Stikes charged at him. The two men crashed together, clawing and punching and kicking. Stikes slammed a balled fist against his opponent's bullet wound, making him roar in agony—only to cry out himself as Eddie gouged his thumb deep into the ripped flesh of his forearm. They backed apart, sizing each other up once more.

Sophia reached the top of the slope and looked down to see Nina still in pursuit. She snatched up a lump of debris and hurled it at her. Nina yelped and ducked aside, the missile barely missing Larry. Sophia picked up another stone . . .

Part of the meteorite, a ragged purple chunk from the heart of the disintegrated rock. She stared at it for a moment, expression calculating—then shoved it into a pocket and ran along the tier.

Nina swore. If Sophia escaped with the meteorite fragment, there was a danger that the Group's plan could be still carried out—with the worst person imaginable now in charge.

She scrambled up to the top of the slope, about to follow her—

Another seismic shock made her reel as the broken stones shifted underfoot—then a section of the tier ahead fell away and crashed down onto the level below, cutting her off from the lava tube. On the far side, Sophia reached its entrance and looked back at her with a mocking smile, then disappeared into the darkness.

The gap was too large to jump across. "Son of a bitch!" Nina snarled.

"Over there," Larry gasped as he caught up, pointing in the other direction. "There are stairs at the far end—we can go up to the next level, then jump down by the tunnel."

It appeared that he was right. They would have to scale a tilting pillar to reach the undamaged stairway, but it seemed negotiable. "Okay, you go first." She turned to look for her husband as Larry began to climb the column—and saw that he was in trouble.

Stikes had backed Eddie perilously close to the edge of their lava-lit arena. The gases rising from below were painfully hot, and parts of the shuddering ledge looked on the verge of plummeting toward their source. Eddie knew he had to make a move, and quickly. The safest maneuver would be to try to break past Stikes for less dangerous ground, getting clear of the edge before resuming the battle.

Instead, Eddie charged straight at him to attack head-on. The best way to end the fight was by doing the unexpected—

Stikes twisted aside.

He had predicted the move, expected the unexpected—and now Eddie paid for it as the other man's elbow smashed against his temple. He staggered, senses sloshing glutinously inside his skull . . .

Stikes's arm locked around his neck, vise-tight.

The mercenary had grabbed him from behind in an unbreakable hold, crushing his windpipe. Eddie tried to claw at his face, but could only reach with his wounded arm, the pain sapping the strength from his strikes. He tried to bend forward to flip his opponent over his shoulders, but Stikes was too well braced.

Nina was about to run back down the pile of fallen stone to help him—when she saw a chunk of the ledge only yards from the two men split away and fall toward the lava.

The remainder of the rocky outcrop would follow at any moment.

"I always win, Chase," the former officer hissed. The pressure on Eddie's neck increased, blood pounding in his head. "I always win!"

The gloating words flooded Eddie with anger. He was *not* going to be beaten—not by Stikes! He shifted his feet. "Not . . . this . . . time!"

Stoked by fury, he straightened his entire body—and lifted Stikes on his back.

He only raised him by a couple of inches, but it was still enough to unbalance the mercenary. Eddie took full advantage of the moment and bent at the waist, pulling his enemy over with him—then threw himself backward with every remaining ounce of strength.

Stikes gasped, winded, as he thumped down on his back with Eddie on top of him. The Yorkshireman smacked a reverse headbutt into his face, then, drawing in choked breaths, managed to stand.

A few steps away was a piece of the meteorite, a jagged chunk about two feet across. He picked it up. Pain burned in his injured arm as he raised the heavy rock above his head, about to smash it down on Stikes's skull—

Another section of the edge dropped away into the liquid inferno below—and a crack lanced across the ground near the temple. He heard Nina's voice over the volcano's thunder. "Eddie! *The ledge is gonna collapse!*"

Survival outweighed justice. He threw the rock at Stikes then ran, scooping up the Jericho as he raced for the temple. Behind him, more chunks broke away from the ledge and tumbled down the shaft, luminous splashes exploding from the lava lake as they hit.

Stones rattled and slipped underfoot as he shoved the gun into his jacket and clambered up the makeshift ramp. Nina was at the top, waving him on. "Nina, come on!" Larry shouted. "We're running out of time!"

She reluctantly turned away from Eddie to climb the pillar. The constant quakes almost jolted her loose, but finally she was within reach of Larry's outstretched arm. He grabbed her hand and helped her up the final few feet.

Eddie reached the summit of the slope and started to climb after her. Nina reached down, giving him a look of encouragement—which turned to horror. "Eddie, look out!"

Something stabbed agonizingly into his thigh.

The pain made him lose his footing. He dropped back down to the tier—driving the spikes deeper into his flesh.

It was the head of the trident, hurled by Stikes—who had scrambled up the slope after him, swinging the broken shaft like a club to deliver a savage blow. Eddie cried out, trying to dodge as Stikes struck again, but the pain of his impalement was so intense that he couldn't move his leg.

Nina watched helplessly. Short of throwing herself off the pillar at Stikes, there was nothing she could do to intervene.

Except—

A broken piece of purple stone the size of a fist lay on the floor. She grabbed it; it glowed.

Stikes raised the bronze shaft high above his head, about to plunge its jagged point down into Eddie's chest—

Nina hurled the stone.

She could have sworn that it veered slightly, as if guided to its target by her sheer willpower. Whether it did, or if she was just imagining it, the result was the same. The lump of rock cracked viciously against Stikes's nose, blood spurting from both nostrils. He staggered, the spear still held high . . .

Eddie wrenched the trident's head out of his leg, fury overpowering the pain, and stabbed it deep into the other man's stomach.

Stikes let out a gurgling scream. He dropped the shaft, clutching both hands to the bronze fork buried in his gut

and staring at Eddie in utter disbelief. "You can't . . . ,"
he gasped. "You can't have!"

"Yeah, I can," Eddie rasped, struggling upright. "For
old times' sake!"

He drove his boot into Stikes's groin with the force of
a train. Convulsing in agony, the ex-officer reeled . . .
and fell from the tier to the ledge below, slamming down
on his back.

With a crack that shook the chamber, the entire outcrop sheared away from the wall of rock.

The huge wedge of stone plunged down the volcanic
shaft, the hellfire glow up its sheer sides growing brighter
with each moment. Paralyzed with agony, Stikes couldn't
even scream—

The severed ledge hit the churning lava lake, the viscid
magma absorbing some of the impact that would otherwise have instantly killed its unwilling passenger. Even
so, the shock of landing felt to Stikes as if someone had
dropped a car on him, ribs cracking and organs ruptur-
ing. Spitting blood, he lay sprawled and broken as the
rock beneath him slowly sank into the molten sea.

The heat set his clothes alight as a glowing orange
wave rose over the fractured edges of the stone raft. It
surrounded him, closing in like jackals around dying
prey. The pain became unimaginable as his blond hair
seared and caught fire, a burning halo blistering his
skull. *Now* he managed to scream as the molten circle
shrank around him, consuming his feet, then his hands,
incinerating his entire body inch by inch . . .

High above, Eddie watched with savage satisfaction
as the fallen ledge was finally swallowed up by liquid
fire. "Got you," he growled.

"Eddie!" He looked up to see Nina on the tier above.
"Are you okay?"

One hand pressed hard against the stab wounds in his
leg, he limped to the pillar. "I'll live."

"What happened to Stikes?"

"He's a lava, not a fighter."

Nina withheld comment, clambering back down to

assist him. Larry looked over the edge, relief filling his face. "Oh, thank God! I thought—I thought he was going to kill you."

"He bloody nearly did," Eddie admitted. He saw the wound on his father's head. "Are you all right?"

"Got hit by a rock, but never mind me. Come on." He lay down on his front, both hands reaching for Eddie as Nina supported him from below. The constant rumbling grew stronger. "We need to get out of here PDQ."

"Where's Sophia?"

"She went up the tunnel," said Nina as Larry hauled Eddie up. She climbed after him. "Part of the floor collapsed—we'll have to go across the level above and jump down." Rising steam and fumes continued to be drawn into the lava tube. It was still clear, then—but with the quakes growing stronger all the time, it might not remain so for long. "And Eddie . . . she's got a piece of the meteorite."

He set his jaw against the pain as they hurried past toppled statues toward the stairs. "Can she get the DNA from it?"

"I don't know, but we can't take the chance. We have to catch her."

"There's always fucking something, isn't there?"

The temple shuddered as they made their way up to the higher tier and crossed it. Nina glanced down, and regretted it; the lava was rising after them, no longer a lake but a maelstrom boiling over the top of the magma chamber. "I think Stikes gave it indigestion! We didn't bring the world's largest bottle of Pepto-Bismol, did we?"

"How the hell do you manage to make jokes at a time like this?" Larry asked in disbelief.

"A habit I picked up from your son. It's either that or scream and panic!" They passed over the entrance to the second lava tube. "Okay, I think we can get down here. I'll go first. Larry, you help lower Eddie so I can support him."

"Might be safer if you both lowered me," Eddie suggested.

"Don't worry," said Larry. "I won't drop you."

"That's what you said when I was six, and I've still got the dent in my head!"

"God, you have one butterfingers moment, and nobody ever lets you forget it . . ."

Nina had already settled the issue by dropping to the tier below. No sign of Sophia beyond the dark opening in the wall, not that she had expected her to hang around. "It's clear. Come on."

She reached up to hold Eddie's legs as his father eased him down as far as he could. "You got him?" Larry called.

"Yeah. Ready?" she asked Eddie. He nodded. "Okay, let him go!"

Larry released his hold. Even with Nina's support, it was still a heavy landing. Eddie gasped in pain as his wounded leg hit the ground. "Oh God, I'm sorry!" she cried.

"Not—your fault," Eddie said, grimacing. "Fucking Stikes! If I had an asbestos fishing rod I'd haul him back up just so I could kick him off again."

"You might not need the rod to reach him in a few minutes," Nina warned him as she took another look over the temple's side. Though it was still hundreds of feet below, the lava was visibly rising. "Larry, come on!"

The elder Chase dropped down with a grunt as Nina and Eddie entered the lava tube. It was smaller and steeper than the one through which they had entered, the air within as choking as a poisonous sauna. But it was their only hope of survival. Eddie recovered his flashlight from a pocket and shone it ahead. The tunnel wormed away into darkness. "Can't tell how long it is," he said.

"It goes up, that's the main thing," Nina replied. "How fast can you move?"

"Faster than that fucking lava, I hope." He set off in a limping half walk, half run, Nina supporting him by his uninjured arm. Larry caught up and they hurried along the passage, which shuddered around them. Ominous crunching sounds came from the walls and ceiling, dust and grit dropping from newly formed cracks.

"This whole place is going to come down!" said Larry between coughs. "We'll never make it."

"Oi!" snapped Eddie. "Less of that—we *will* bloody make it. Know why? 'Cause I'm not having my niece go to three funerals on the same day!"

Abashed, Larry picked up the pace. Nina looked ahead. "I can see daylight!"

"And I can see stuff falling in front of it," said Eddie in alarm. Larger pieces of rubble were dropping from the ceiling. "Both of you, run! Go on, get out!"

"We're not leaving you," said Nina—at the same moment as Larry. They exchanged looks, then carried Eddie between them toward the oval of light ahead.

A loud boom echoed up the tunnel as part of the ceiling caved in. There was a sharp crackling noise like the opening of a gigantic zipper—and suddenly they were inundated by dust as a gash split open along the length of the roof. "Oh, fuck!" yelled Eddie, the pain in his leg forgotten as he broke into a panicked run. "Go, go, *go*!"

Nina and Larry didn't need to be prompted. All three charged for the exit. More ground-shaking thumps like a pursuing giant's footfalls came from behind as the entire tunnel collapsed section by section, displaced air shrieking past. A rock hit Nina hard on one shoulder, but she kept running for the light.

They reached it—and found nothing under their feet as they burst from the tunnel.

It opened onto a steep slope near the volcano's summit, another landslide having torn away the barricade the Atlanteans had built to block it. Flailing and wailing, the trio arced through the air amid flying debris before hitting the ground. Larry immediately tripped, Eddie managing a few loping steps before he too stumbled. Nina lasted longest, but even she couldn't keep her balance on the treacherous surface. They rolled down

the hillside before finally slithering to a stop on a shal-
lower ledge.

Nina groaned as a dozen new bruises made themselves
known. She sat up and discovered that her camera had
caused at least one of them. Its lens had broken off,
black dust trickling out of the body. She looked around
at a moan from nearby. "Larry?"

He lay on his back, one hand over another cut on his
head. "I'm—I'm all right," he mumbled. "But I think I'll
just stay here for a while." The ground shook, loose
stones rattling. He hurriedly sat up. "Or maybe not."

"Where's Eddie?"

"Over here." She turned and saw her husband
sprawled against a large rock. He gave her a pained
grin. "Give us a hand, will you?" As she helped him up,
he looked toward the summit. The plume of steam that
had been rising from the crater when they arrived was
now much bigger—and darker.

"You were right," said Larry as he stood. "We made
it!"

Another tremor rocked the mountainside. "Yeah, but
we're still standing on a volcano that's about to go
Krakatoa," Eddie reminded him. "We can't be too far
from where we went in, so the Land Rover should be
that way." He pointed downhill.

"If your ex hasn't taken it," said Larry.

Nina started down the slope, Eddie following. "How
would she know where we left it?" he said.

"We landed right next to it," Larry replied.

"You came in a chopper?" Eddie asked. His father
nodded. "Did the pilot stay with it?"

"Yes."

"Good. Saves us a drive, then."

"Again, if Sophia hasn't taken it," Nina added. She
pocketed the memory card before abandoning the broken camera. At least pictures of the Temple of the Gods
would survive . . . if they could escape the eruption.

The ledge where they had left their vehicle came into
view below; as Larry had said, the AW101 that had fer-

ried the Group into the desert was waiting. The four-by-four itself, however, was not. "There!" said Nina, pointing. The Land Rover was heading downhill. It dropped out of sight as it picked up speed.

"Shit!" Eddie spat. "That bitch took our ride!"

"At least she left us the chopper . . ."

The helicopter's rotors began to turn.

"Dammit!" said Nina. "I have *got* to stop with the fate-tempting!"

"We can still make it!" Larry said, overtaking the couple. "It took ages to get up to takeoff speed when we flew here."

Eddie winced at the resurgent pain as he took his hand from his thigh to draw the gun. "I've got our boarding pass."

Nina still supporting Eddie, they hurried toward the helicopter. Its rotors picked up speed, the shrill whine of its three Rolls-Royce engines rising. The rear ramp was still open; the pilot had apparently decided that getting off the ground before the volcano erupted outweighed standard operating procedure. "Come on, quick!" cried Larry as he ran for the gaping entrance.

"Dad, watch out!" Eddie shouted. He was sure the pilot would be another of Stikes's mercenaries—and unwilling to accept stowaways. He pulled free of Nina and raised the gun.

Larry reached the metal ramp and hurried up it. The passenger seats were all empty, tarpaulins bundled over the expedition's supplies behind them.

The pilot was at the controls at the far end of the cabin. He looked back—

And drew a pistol.

Fear froze Larry's muscles as the gun came around . . .

Eddie dived at him, knocking him down—and unleashed four shots in midair. Two punched through the cockpit windows . . . but the others hit their target. The pilot slumped over the console, making the helicopter lurch as the cyclic control stick was pushed forward beneath him.

Nina reached the foot of the ramp, seeing from the splatter of blood and brain matter on the windows that the pilot was no longer a threat. She vaulted the two men and hurried up the aisle to pull the dead mercenary back upright. The AW101 jolted again as the stick returned to the neutral position. "Are you okay?" she called down the cabin.

Eddie pushed himself off his father. "Are you?" he asked.

"I . . . I think so," said Larry, breathing heavily. "My God! You . . ." He regarded his son, wide-eyed. "Eddie, you saved my life. Thank you."

Eddie feigned a casual shrug, but was unable to keep an appreciative smile off his face. "All part of the job. Come on." He stood, helping Larry up. The smile quickly faded as he regarded the red-tinged cockpit windows. "Buggeration and fuckery. Don't suppose you know how to fly a chopper, do you?"

"Well, er, funnily enough . . ."

"You *do*?" Now it was the turn of Eddie's eyes to widen. "Shit, come on! You've got to get us out of here!" He pushed his father down the aisle.

Larry was already having second thoughts. "Okay, I've been at the *controls* of a chopper. The real pilot did all the hard stuff. Like taking off. And landing. I've only had about two hours' experience total."

"That's two hours more than me and Nina. Do what you can." He guided his father to the empty copilot's seat.

"I don't really think—oh, Jesus." Larry recoiled from the dead man in the neighboring position.

"Just don't look at him."

"How can I not? He's right there! And some of him's all over the windscreen!"

"We'll move him," said Nina. "Just try to look *through* the window and not *at* it." She and Eddie started to haul the corpse from the seat.

Larry could still barely contain his nausea. "How can

you be so . . . so *nonchalant*? It's a bloody dead body! Literally!"

"Sad fact is, you kinda get used to them," Nina said, briefly reflecting on just how much she had changed over the past five years. But there were more pressing matters to think about. They pulled the dead man into the aisle, Eddie dragging him back toward the ramp as she dropped into the newly vacated space. "So, Larry—can you fly this thing?"

Still trying to keep the worst of the gore out of his eyeline, Larry surveyed the controls. "It's about five million times more complicated than anything else I've ever flown, but . . . cyclic, collective, that must be the throttle, rudder pedals. I recognize the basics. I have no idea if I can actually get it into the air, though."

A tremor rattled the aircraft, a thunderous rumble coming from the volcano's peak. "Take your best shot," said Nina urgently.

Larry licked his dry lips and gripped the two sticks, placing his feet on the pedals. "All right. Okay. How did they do it? The instructor talked me through it once. Let's see—hold the main rotor in a flat pitch"—he held the cyclic control in front of him in its centered position—"bring the throttle up to takeoff revolutions—I don't know how fast that is . . ."

"Volcano, about to go boom," Eddie reminded him loudly.

"Okay, okay!" He increased power, the airframe swaying in response. "Get it up to speed, and then increase the collective pitch . . ."

He cautiously pulled up the collective control lever beside his seat. The AW101 shuddered—then rose slightly, its landing gear creaking as the weight on it was reduced. "That's it, that's it!" said Nina. "Keep doing more of that!"

Larry gingerly lifted the collective higher. The helicopter bounced alarmingly on its wheels. He stifled a yell and jammed the throttle to full power, bringing up the lever—

The chopper lurched again—and left the ground.

Ten feet up, twenty, and rising with increasing speed. The mountainside spread out below as it ascended. Eddie returned to the cockpit, grabbing Nina's seat for support. "Okay, now get us out of here." The AW101 kept climbing—vertically. He looked back, seeing the volcano's summit coming into view through the open rear ramp. The smoke and ash belching from it were now almost completely black, globules of glowing lava spitting into the air. "Dad, we need to go *forward*!"

"Yes, I know!" Larry snapped. "Let's see if this works . . ."

He pushed the cyclic. The aircraft's nose tipped downward . . . and it started to move. More pressure, and the tilt increased, the helicopter picking up speed away from the mountain.

"That's it, keep going!" Nina cried. She looked down at the ground. The barren hillside swept past below—as did the Land Rover. As she watched, the four-by-four slewed out of control and flipped over, mangled debris flying from it as it tumbled down the slope. "Whoa! Sophia just wiped out!"

Eddie glanced at the wreck, but the growing thunder of the volcano was foremost on his mind. The earth energy that Nina had unleashed might make it explode at any moment—and the helicopter was still dangerously close. The shock wave alone could swat it out of the sky. "Dad! How fast are we going?"

"You find the speedo and tell me!" Larry shot back, concentrating on keeping the AW101 in the air.

Eddie scanned the console, finally spotting the dial of the airspeed indicator. Sixty knots and accelerating. Another look over his shoulder. The retreating volcano was framed in the open ramp, more lava spewing out of the crater. As he watched, part of the hillside suddenly flowed like liquid, the subterranean quakes triggering a landslide. One had exposed the entrance to the Temple of the Gods—and now a vastly larger one was erasing it from the face of the earth.

Ninety knots, and three thousand feet in altitude. They were well above the summit, but still only about two miles from where they had taken off. Nina twisted in her seat, gawping at the sight that greeted her. "My God!" Great sprays of molten rock burst from the crater, splattering down on the crumbling cone of rock below.

It struck her that *she* had been the cause. One person, channeling earth energy, was directly responsible for a volcanic eruption. Any lingering doubts about whether she had done the right thing instantly vanished. Nobody should have that power.

And now nobody ever would. The meteorite and the primordial DNA it contained were destroyed, consumed by the rising lava, and the piece Sophia had taken would end up buried beneath dozens of feet of ash. Even the Group itself had been eliminated. That threat had ceased to exist.

Another remained, however, growing more deadly with every passing second. The gouts of lava became stronger as pressure built up inside the confined shaft, even the noise of the helicopter overpowered by the basso roar of escaping gas. More landslides stripped the volcano's flanks. One whole side of the mountain began to bulge, visibly swelling as she watched.

Four thousand feet. One hundred and twenty knots. Three miles from their start point. Still climbing and accelerating, but it might not be enough . . .

The distended mountainside *pulsed,* rippling from within. For a moment, the jet of lava and ash choked as the enormous pressure rising from below was blocked, the mouth of the shaft too narrow for it all to escape at once . . .

Then it forced its way through.

The volcano erupted.

THIRTY-SIX

The mountain's entire upper half disintegrated in a single burst of unimaginable violence, a shock wave racing outward. Behind it followed a colossal cloud of scaring ash and superheated steam, pulverized rock and globs of red-hot lava churning within like a lethal blizzard. The explosion would be heard hundreds of miles away, and shake buildings in Dubti.

The helicopter was much closer.

There was a strange silence after Nina and Eddie witnessed the obliteration of the volcano's summit, light outpacing sound—then the blast wave caught up with them. It was as if the AW101 had been rammed from behind. Nina screamed, but couldn't even hear it over the earth's uncorked fury. The chopper swung around, loose items flying through the cabin. Eddie was thrown backward, grabbing the harness straps on a seat just in time to stop himself from following the dead pilot out of the open rear ramp.

Senses reeling, Larry struggled with the controls. The helicopter spiraled toward the desert plain. The altimeter needle whirled down toward zero with terrifying speed. He applied full throttle and pulled up the collective for maximum lift, but the AW101 was still spinning, still falling.

Eddie dragged himself upright. The landscape blurred past beyond the windows. "Dad! Stop the fucking thing!"

"I don't know how!" Larry yelled. Below four thousand feet, and dropping—

"Turn it!" Nina cried. "We're spinning counterclockwise—turn the other way!"

In the turmoil, Larry's feet had come off the rudder pedals. He found them again and jammed one foot down to apply full power to the tail rotor. The helicopter rocked sharply, throwing more unsecured objects around its interior. Nina shrieked as an emergency kit rebounded off the console in front of her and broke open, showering her with its contents.

Three thousand feet—but the spin was slowing. Teeth bared, Larry gradually eased his foot up as the aircraft came back under control. "Jesus!" he gasped. "I think I've got it."

The chopper straightened out, pointing almost directly back at the ruined mountain. Eddie caught his breath, then returned to the cockpit to look over his father's shoulder. "We don't want to be going this way, though." He pointed at the compass. "Go south-southeast, about one sixty degrees. That'll take us back to the town we came from." A pause, then: "Nice work, Dad."

"Glad I finally did something you approve of," said Larry with a shaky grin.

Nina stared at the volcano. "Look at that . . . ," she said breathlessly. Though the initial shock wave had passed, a second destructive front was still advancing as a heavy, corpse-gray cloud swept outward. A pyroclastic flow, hot gas and pulverized rock scouring and sterilizing the earth beneath it. "We need to get back into the sky before it reaches us."

"I think I can do that," said Larry. He brought the AW101 around to the bearing Eddie had given him, then increased power to climb and gain speed. The desert rolled past below.

Eddie looked back. Through the open ramp, the pursuing cloud was visible, but it fell away as the helicopter ascended. Even as it retreated, though, the volcano's roar still rattled the fuselage. "Christ! I know we've got away from some big bangs before, but that's got to be the biggest. A fucking erupting volcano! Don't know how we're going to top that one."

"I kinda hope we don't have to," said Nina earnestly. "We deserve a vacation." She looked away from the frightening sight to Eddie's leg. Though his jeans were covered with dark dust, the torn holes made by the trident's prongs were glistening; he was still bleeding. "Eddie, sit down so I can clean you up. Those wounds might get infected."

"In a minute—I'll close the ramp first." He limped down the aisle, using the seats for support.

"Don't fall out," she cautioned jokingly. The contents of the emergency case were strewn around the cockpit; she started to search for first-aid equipment.

"How far away is this town?" asked Larry.

Nina picked up various items from the foot well, putting a cylindrical flare down on the console between the two pilots' seats before examining a package of sterile dressings and a tube of antibiotic ointment. "About seventy miles, maybe?"

He checked the airspeed indicator. "It shouldn't take too long to get there, then. Although I'll remind you that I don't have a clue how to land this thing."

"You did okay with the takeoff. I think you'll manage the landing too."

"I'll try to keep it below terminal velocity."

Nina smiled, then looked around. Eddie still hadn't reached the rear of the cabin. "Hurry up, honey! There's a draft!"

"You try walking with holes in your leg," he called back.

"I have. It sucked!"

He grinned, then turned back to the ramp. Some of the equipment stowed behind the seats had been hurled out of the aircraft during its spin, one of the tarps flapping furiously in the wind. A couple of the parachutes had also gone, but there were still enough left to allow himself, Nina, and Larry to bail out if worse came to worst. Holding a ceiling strap, he peered at the ground. They were at about seven thousand feet, and still climbing. Nothing below but sand and rock.

He straightened, looking for the ramp controls. There was a control box mounted on one wall. He hobbled toward it—

Something smashed against the back of his head.

Eddie crashed to the deck, stars going supernova in his vision. An intense, sickening pain oozed through his body. He tried to get up, but his limbs refused to cooperate, as weak and limp as a baby's.

"Hello, Eddie," said Sophia with a triumphant snarl.

She had been hiding beneath the other tarpaulin. The Land Rover had been empty, set to roll away to deny anyone else its use for escape. She stood over her former husband, letting the large wrench she had used as a weapon clang to the floor as she pulled the Jericho out of his jacket. The tool slid down the ramp and spun away in the AW101's slipstream.

Nina jumped from her seat, then froze as Sophia aimed the gun at her. "Well, look at this!" the Englishwoman shouted over the wind. "A family reunion. How sweet."

"Let him go, Sophia!" Nina demanded, surreptitiously scanning the floor for the dead pilot's gun—but where it had ended up, she had no idea.

"Oh, I absolutely intend to. But without one of these." She revealed the pack of a parachute on her back. "I could just shoot him, but that seems like rather poor payback for everything he's done to me." She kicked the helpless man at her feet, producing a groan. "I'm going to shoot *you*, though. After you watch him die."

"You fucking *bitch*," Nina spat.

"Oh, come on, Nina. An educated woman like you can do better than that, surely?" Sophia braced herself against the seats and used a foot to shove Eddie closer to the ramp. "But then, as I've always said, one can't expect class from an American."

Larry whispered to Nina from the side of his mouth. "I could shake the controls, make her fall out."

"Eddie'd fall out too," she replied in kind, still desperately searching for a weapon. No gun. Was there anything else she could use?

Maybe—if she could reach it without being shot.

Twisting awkwardly to keep the gun trained on Nina, Sophia kept pushing Eddie nearer to the ramp. "I think it'll take about thirty seconds for him to hit the ground from this height," she said. "I'm going to watch, just to make sure. Eddie does have the annoying habit of popping up when he's supposed to be dead, but not this time. This is the end. For both of you." Eddie was now almost fully on the ramp. "As soon as I see that little Wile E. Coyote puff of dirt, it's your turn."

A final thrust of her leg—and Eddie slithered down the ramp.

"No!" Nina screamed, but there was nothing she could do—

Eddie's eyes opened—and he grabbed a cargo ring set into the metal surface just as his legs went over the edge.

Straining to hold on as the wind and rotor downwash tore at him, he looked up. The infuriated Sophia towered over him, stepping to the ramp's top and holding on to its frame with her left hand as she leaned out. "*Why,*" she shouted, trying to jab at his fingers with her outstretched boot heel, "can't you *just*"—another strike fell a fraction of an inch short—"*die?*"

The final blow caught his knuckles. Eddie yelled in pain—

And lost his grip.

The gale snatched him backward, whipping him over the edge of the ramp.

"*Yes!*" Sophia cried, the exclamation of victory bursting out of her almost orgasmically. She glanced around at Nina—

A dazzling light shot down the length of the cabin and struck her hard in the back.

Sophia reeled as the flare that Nina had fired spun past, spraying her clothing with sparks and fire. She clutched the frame for support . . . but the two stiff prosthetic fingers prevented her from getting a firm grip. Her gloved hand slipped from the metal—and she followed Eddie down the ramp with a horrified shriek, tumbling away into the empty sky.

Nina dropped the flare's tube and ran down the aisle. "Come and get us!" she yelled to the stunned Larry. Determination driving out doubts, she passed the last row of seats, snatching a parachute off the rack—

And threw herself out of the back of the helicopter.

The slipstream pummeled her as she sailed into open air, the desert spreading out eight thousand feet below. The noise of the chopper's engines faded, but the wind's roar in her ears only grew louder as she picked up speed in free fall.

Parallax revealed two dark shapes against the landscape. Sophia—and Eddie. She forced back her fear, fixing her gaze on him as she grappled with the parachute's harness. Working her arms through the flapping loops, she strained to fasten the buckle across her chest. It clicked shut—but only then did she realize that there was another set of straps through which she was meant to put her legs. When she pulled the ripcord, the sudden force of braking could tear the parachute right off her body.

But there was no time to remove it and try again. All or nothing . . .

* * *

Eddie had been slammed back to full awareness by a massive adrenaline surge—one driven by pure fear. His military training had taught him how to try to recover in the event of a parachute failure . . . but this time he *had* no parachute. And there was nothing below that might save him either—no bodies of water, no tall trees, just flat, hard desert in every direction.

Even so, he rolled facedown and spread his arms and legs. The increased drag would slow his fall—slightly. He would still hit the ground at over a hundred miles per hour.

He was going to die.

He turned his head, trying to find the helicopter in the hope that Larry had at least tipped his killer out the back . . . and was shocked to see *two* figures plunging through the sky after him. The nearer was Sophia.

The other could only be Nina.

An awful, nauseating realization of defeat rolled over him. Sophia had gotten what she wanted—she had killed them both. And as he watched, a parachute blossomed above his ex-wife. Not only had she killed them, but she would live to gloat about it.

* * *

Sophia gasped as the slam of deceleration yanked her harness straps tight. She took hold of the steering lines—then flinched as something shot past her.

Nina! The American had been at the far end of the cabin—which meant she hadn't fallen out, but deliberately jumped. She was trying to save Eddie.

Sophia almost laughed at the futility of the gesture. It couldn't possibly succeed. And now she would have a grandstand view of both her enemies smashing down on the desert floor . . .

Something was wrong.

She could feel heat on one side of her head, but it wasn't from sunlight. She looked around—

And screamed.

Her parachute's pack was aflame, ignited by the flare. The wind-fanned fire was rising rapidly up the nylon webbing risers connecting her harness and the cords of the chute itself. She desperately tried to swat out the flames, but they were too big, too hungry, greedily consuming fabric and line.

A *twang* as one of the cords snapped. The parachute's edge rippled and flapped. A second line gave way, then another, and another . . .

Sophia's cry of utter terror was lost in the wind as the chute collapsed and she plummeted toward the ground, trailing smoke as the blaze spread to her clothes and hair.

* * *

Body tilted down, arms held back at her sides, Nina was rapidly catching up with Eddie. Steering herself in free fall had proved to be an almost instinctual matter of twisting her body and limbs to direct the airflow; what she would do when she reached her husband was another matter entirely.

He rolled over onto his back, waving his arms. The signal was clear: *Leave me!* She ignored it, guiding herself at him like a missile and arching her back to lift her head and slow down. Her body began to seesaw; she almost panicked before managing to stabilize herself by bringing out her arms and raising her knees.

Eddie was right below her, still gesturing for her to abandon him.

Not a chance—

The collision was like a tackle. They both spun and tumbled before Eddie brought them under control. Nina clutched his jacket, screaming into the wind. "Grab on to me!"

He tried to push her away. "It'll kill us both!"

"No! *You and me! Always and forever!*"

Their eyes were locked for a precious moment before he relented. "You've put this on wrong!" he cried as he hooked his right arm into one of her chute's loose leg straps and wound it tight.

"I was kinda rushed!"

He forced his left arm through her shoulder harness and bent his elbow to trap it, then strained to bring his hands together. A momentary glance down; they were well below two thousand feet, only seconds left before they hit the ground. His fingers interlocked; he gripped as hard as he could. "This is gonna hurt, but—*pull it!*"

Nina yanked the ripcord.

The spring-loaded pilot chute popped out of the pack, snapping open in the airstream—and snatched the main chute out after it with a *whump* of billowing fabric.

The sudden drag as the parachute deployed wrenched the harness upward. Nina screamed as it cut deeply into her shoulders, almost slipping loose on one side. Eddie cried out too as the jolt almost ripped his arms from their sockets, but he clung on, holding the backpack in place by sheer force of muscle.

The wind dropped. He looked up. The chute was fully inflated, slowing their fall, but it was designed to carry the weight of only one person, not two. No matter what, they were going to have a painful landing.

A shadow crossed the thin nylon, something falling toward it—

A burning meteor streaked past, missing the parachute by less than a foot as it hurtled toward the ground in a trail of fire. "What the hell was *that*?" Nina yelled.

It wasn't part of the helicopter, so that only left—"Sophia!"

* * *

Despite the flames gnawing at her skin, Sophia was still alive, still conscious, still screaming as she fell.

Something whipped through her pain-racked vision—a parachute, two forms dangling from its lines.

Nina had caught Eddie. They were going to survive.

"You . . . *bastards!*" she managed to shriek—

The wet thump of her impact on the stony ground was mixed with the horrible crack of shattering bones.

* * *

The parachute's aerofoil design meant Eddie and Nina were now traversing the landscape rather than merely plunging straight at it, but they were still descending too quickly. A hundred feet remained, ninety—

Eddie unclasped his fingers. "What're you doing?" Nina demanded.

"Making you lighter," he said, painfully slipping his arms out of the harness straps to hang from them by his hands. "Just before you land, turn side-on and let it drag you—try to kind of crumple from your feet upward when you hit. And for Christ's sake, bend your legs or you'll break 'em both."

Fifty feet. "What about you?"

"I haven't turned forty yet—there might just be a little bit of bounce left in me!"

Thirty. "Are you out of your mind?"

"You're the one who jumped from a fucking chopper!"

Twenty—

Eddie let go. Even with his legs bent to absorb the impact, he hit hard, rolling uncontrollably before bouncing to a stop in a cloud of dust.

Nina whisked past overhead, wailing "Oh *shiiiiit*!" as she was carried helplessly down. At the last moment, she remembered what Eddie had said and twisted sideways. Her feet scraped through the sand—then she slammed down like a toppling tree. The parachute flopped on top of her like a shroud.

Groaning, Eddie slowly tried to get up, discovering numerous new sources of pain throughout his body. No bones seemed to be broken, to his relief, although his already injured leg now hurt worse than ever. Wobbling, he stood and dizzily surveyed his surroundings. The black plume from the volcano rose into the sky on the northwestern horizon; much closer was another, smaller column of smoke.

He knew what it marked, resolving to investigate, but completed his turn. The helicopter was about half a mile away to the west, slowly heading toward him. On the ground, the parachute wobbled in the wind like a beached jellyfish. He limped toward it. "Nina? Nina! Are you okay?"

"No, I'm dead," came the weak reply. He pulled the entangling sheet and cords aside to find Nina sprawled facedown in the sand. "I *must* be dead. We couldn't have survived that. Could we?"

"Well, I'm alive, more or less—and like you said, we stay together, so you must be too." He quickly checked her for obvious signs of injury, finding nothing beyond plentiful cuts and grazes.

She sat up and blew sand off her face, giving him a pained smile. "Wow. So we actually made it."

"Yeah, we did." He kissed her then they both re-coiled.

"Ow," said Nina, putting a hand to her face and finding it bruised and swollen. "My lips hurt."

"My *everything* hurts," Eddie complained. "Think you can stand?"

"I'll try." Grunting, he helped her up. Nina winced at a sharp pain in her ankles; her touchdown had been far from soft. "Oh crap."

"What?"

"I just realized, we're still sixty miles from town in the middle of a desert. And I'm *really* not up to walking all that way."

Eddie jerked a thumb toward the approaching helicopter. "We've still got a ride."

Nina regarded it in relief. "I guess Larry's okay, then—shit!" She looked around in alarm. "What about Sophia?"

He indicated the nearby smoke. "I know where she is. Let's take a gander." Supporting each other as best they could, they hobbled toward it.

A little impact crater came into view, the smoldering line rising from the charred remains of a parachute backpack atop a broken, huddled shape within. Jagged spikes of broken bone jutted out from ruptured flesh. Splashed across the surrounding sand was an oozing

starburst of dark red. "Well," said Nina after a long silence. "I guess she's finally dead."

Eddie had been through the experience of believing
his ex-wife to be deceased twice before; this time, he was
almost out of sympathy. Almost. He moved closer, pulling what remained of the parachute over the mangled
body. "Good-bye, Soph," he said, then paused for a moment before reaching down.

Nina cringed in revulsion as he picked something up
from among the viscera. "Eddie, what the *hell*?"

"Thought we should take care of this," he said, limping back to her. In his hand was the piece of meteorite
Sophia had taken from the Temple of the Gods. "What
do you want to do with it?"

Nina considered the question. The chunk of purple
stone contained within it the secrets of earth energy, the
untold history of all life on the planet, and potentially
more besides. But . . .

She still didn't believe that there were things man was
not meant to know. But there were things man was not
meant to *have*. This was one of them. "Get rid of it,"
she finally said.

"You sure?"

"Yeah." She watched as he turned and threw the stone
with all his remaining strength into the empty wilderness. It landed with a puff of dust among other nondescript rocks, half-buried already; in time, it would be
completely lost.

"So that's it?" Eddie asked.

She nodded. "Earth energy, the meteorite, the Group,
Stikes, Sophia . . . they're all gone. Finished."

"Thank fuck for that. Now we can take a break." He
gave her an exhausted smile and put his arms around
her.

The noise of the helicopter made them turn. Larry had
brought the AW101 into an unsteady hover a few hundred yards away, gradually descending into a cyclone of
sand. Eddie watched—then stiffened. "Shit, that's not
good!"

"What's wrong?"

"That wobble, something's wrong—Dad!" He released Nina and waved his arms, frantically signaling for his father to ascend again. "Dad, go back up, it's not gonna—"

Too late.

The tremendous downwash from the main rotor was bouncing back up off the desert floor as Larry lowered the helicopter, drastically affecting the aircraft's handling. With an inexperienced pilot at the controls, the results were inevitable. The AW101 rocked like a toy boat, veering sideways. Larry tried to level out, but overcompensated—and the chopper lurched back, losing height.

Its landing gear dug into the ground, tipping the fuselage over—

The rotor blades carved into the desert with great sprays of sand, shearing off from the hub and flinging broken pieces high into the air. Torque twisted the aircraft's body around, crunching its nose into the dirt before it fell back down on its belly with a shrilling crash of torn metal.

"Dad!" Eddie cried, breaking into a staggering run. Nina caught up, and they hurried toward the wreck. Its engines cut out, leaving an eerie silence punctured only by the thumps of debris returning to earth. By the time they reached it, the stubs of the rotor blades had come to a halt.

The front windows were broken. Through them, Eddie saw Larry slumped over the central console. "Dad! Shit, Dad, are you all right?" No answer. No movement. He opened the side hatch and climbed inside, going to the cockpit. "Dad!"

For a moment, he thought his father was dead—then Larry coughed and took in a shuddering breath. "Eddie?" he gasped.

"Yeah, I'm here, Dad." Eddie carefully lifted him off the console. A line of blood ran down his cheek where he had hit a sharp protrusion on the instrument panel. "How bad are you hurt?"

"Not too bad . . . I think." Larry opened his eyes, squinting in the sunlight as he tried to regain focus. "Tell you something, though."

"What?"

"I definitely need more flying lessons." A faint laugh.

Eddie joined in. "Yeah, one or two. You've just wrecked a twenty-million-dollar helicopter!"

"Like father, like son," said Nina with a grin as she recovered a first-aid kit.

They patched up their various wounds as best they could, then took stock of the situation. Some of the Group's supplies were still secured at the cabin's rear, giving them a supply of water, and while the helicopter itself was a complete write-off, the radio was still functioning. Eddie sent out a mayday. The eruption of the volcano had already roused official attention; while the Ethiopian authorities were surprised that anybody had been near the isolated mountain, they nevertheless assured him that help was on the way, though the lack of precise GPS coordinates meant it might take a while to arrive.

He climbed out of the chopper and joined Nina and Larry, sitting nearby. "So," said Larry, mopping the blood off his cheek, "this is what you do for a living, then?"

"It's not *all* like this," Nina told him. "Sometimes there's actual archaeology involved."

"All the same, I'm impressed. Still quivering with terror, but impressed. I can't believe the things I've seen today. Floating rocks, exploding volcanoes . . ." He shook his head. "My daughter-in-law throwing herself out of a helicopter at eight thousand feet . . ."

Eddie gave him a mock shrug. "Meh. You get used to this stuff after a while."

"Speak for yourself!" Nina cried. "You know, before I met you I'd never once had anyone shoot at me. Or been in a car chase. Or a plane crash, or jumped a Humvee over a canyon, or been attacked by tigers and hippos and crocodiles—"

"They were caimans, not crocs," Eddie corrected. "But if you hadn't met me, you wouldn't have found Atlantis either, would you? Or the Tomb of Hercules, or Excalibur, or the Garden of Eden . . ."

"The *what*?" said Larry. "Did you just say . . ."

Nina nodded. "Uh-huh. But . . . yeah, you're right, Eddie." She signaled for him to sit beside her. He did so, and she leaned against him. "I'm glad we met."

"So am I," Eddie replied. This time, bruises weren't enough to stop them from kissing.

Larry waited for them to finish before speaking again. "You know," he said, "I'd like to hear about some of these adventures of yours." He was addressing them both . . . but looking at his son with a smile that held more than just the hope of hearing a story.

Eddie smiled back. "Sure, Dad. We've got time."